Fasten your seatbelts as
Liz Fielding and Lucy Gordon
take you on a whirlwind tour of the globe!
First stop: a majestic desert kingdom.
Next stop: exotic, vibrant China.
Final destination: falling in love!

Buy our new 2-in-1 editions of stories
by your favourite authors—
for double the romance!

HER DESERT DREAM

BY
LIZ FIELDING

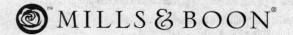

MILLS & BOON

All the characters in this book have no existence outside the imagination
of the author, and have no relation whatsoever to anyone bearing the
same name or names. They are not even distantly inspired by any
individual known or unknown to the author, and all the incidents are
pure invention.

First published in Great Britain 2009
Harlequin Mills & Boon Limited,
Eton House, 18-24 Paradise Road, Richmond, Surrey TW9 1SR

ISBN: 978 0 263 86962 0

Set in Times Roman 12¾ on 14 pt
02-1209-55908

Harlequin Mills & Boon policy is to use papers that are natural,
renewable and recyclable products and made from wood grown in
sustainable forests. The logging and manufacturing process conform
to the legal environmental regulations of the country of origin.

Printed and bound in Spain
by Litografia Rosés, S.A., Barcelona

Liz Fielding was born with itchy feet. She made it to Zambia before her twenty-first birthday and, gathering her own special hero and a couple of children on the way, lived in Botswana, Kenya and Bahrain—with pauses for sightseeing pretty much everywhere in between. She finally came to a full stop in a tiny Welsh village cradled by misty hills, and these days mostly leaves her pen to do the travelling. When she's not sorting out the lives and loves of her characters she potters in the garden, reads her favourite authors, and spends a lot of time wondering 'What if…?' For news of upcoming books— and to sign up for her occasional newsletter—visit Liz's website at www.lizfielding.com

CHAPTER ONE

LYDIA YOUNG was a fake from the tip of her shoes to the saucy froth of feathers on her hat but, as she held centre stage at a reception in a swanky London hotel, she had the satisfaction of knowing that she was the best there was.

Her suit, an interpretation of a designer original, had been run up at home by her mother, but her mother had once been a seamstress at a couturier house. And while her shoes, bag and wristwatch were knock-offs, they were the finest knock-offs that money could buy. The kind that only someone intimate with the real thing would clock without a very close look. But they were no more than the window dressing.

She'd once heard an actress describe how she built a character from the feet up and she had taken that lesson to heart.

Lydia had studied her character's walk, her gestures, a certain tilt of the head. She'd worked on the voice until it was her own and the world famous smile—a slightly toned down version of the mile-wide one that came as naturally as breathing—was, even if she said it herself, a work of art.

Her reward was that when she walked into a room full of people who knew that she was a lookalike, hired by the hour to lend glamour to the opening of a club or a restaurant or to appear at the launch of a new product, there was absolutely nothing in her appearance or manner to jar the fantasy and, as a result, she was treated with the same deference as the real thing.

She was smiling now as she mixed and mingled, posing for photographs with guests at a product launch being held at the kind of hotel that in her real life she would only glimpse from a passing bus.

Would the photographs be framed? she wondered. Placed on mantels, so that their neighbours, friends would believe that they'd actually met 'England's Sweetheart'?

Someone spoke to her and she offered her hand, the smile, asked all the right questions, chatting as naturally as if to the stately home born.

A dozen more handshakes, a few more photographs as the managing director of the company handed her a blush-pink rose that was as much a part of her character's image as the smile and then it was over. Time to go back to her real world. A hospital appointment for her mother, then an evening shift at the 24/7 supermarket where she might even be shelving the new brand of tea that was being launched today.

There was a certain irony in that, she thought as she approached the vast marble entrance lobby, heading for the cloakroom to transform herself back into plain Lydia Young for the bus ride home. Anticipating the head-turning ripple of awareness as she passed.

People had been turning to look, calling out 'Rose' to her in the street since she was a teen. The likeness had been striking, much more than the colour of her hair, the even features, vivid blue eyes that were eerily like those of the sixteen-year-old Lady Rose. And she had played up to it, copying her hairstyle, begging her mother to make her a copy of the little black velvet jacket Lady Rose had been wearing in the picture that had appeared on the front page of every newspaper the day after her sixteenth birthday. Copying her 'look', just as her mother's generation had slavishly followed another young princess.

Who wouldn't want to look like an icon?

A photograph taken by the local paper had brought her to the attention of the nation's biggest 'lookalike' agency and overnight being 'Lady Rose' had not only given her wheelchair-bound mother a new focus in life as she'd studied the clothes, hunted down fabrics to reproduce them, but had provided extra money to pay the bills, pay for her driving lessons. She'd even saved up enough to start looking for a car so that she could take her mum further than the local shops.

Lost in the joy of that thought, Lydia was halfway across the marble entrance before she realised that no one was looking at her. That someone else was the centre of attention.

Her stride faltered as that 'someone' turned and she came face to face with herself. Or, more accurately, the self she was pretending to be.

Lady Roseanne Napier.

England's Sweetheart.

In person.

From the tip of her mouth-wateringly elegant hat, to the toes of her matching to-die-for shoes.

And Lydia, whose heart had joined her legs in refusing to move, could do nothing but pray for the floor to open up and swallow her.

The angel in charge of rescuing fools from moments of supreme embarrassment clearly had something more pressing to attend to. The marble remained solid and it was Lady Rose, the corner of her mouth lifting in a wry little smile, who saved the day.

'I know the face,' she said, extending her hand, 'but I'm afraid the name escapes me.'

'Lydia, madam, Lydia Young' she stuttered as she grasped it, more for support than to shake hands.

Should she curtsy? Women frequently forgot themselves sufficiently to curtsy to her but she wasn't sure her knees, once down, would ever make it back up again and the situation was quite bad enough without turning it into a farce.

Then, realising that she was still clutching the slender hand much too tightly, she let go, stammered out an apology.

'I'm s-so sorry. I promise this wasn't planned. I had no idea you'd be here.'

'Please, it's not a problem,' Lady Rose replied sympathetically, kindness itself as she paused long enough to exchange a few words, ask her what she was doing at the hotel, put her at her ease. Then, on the point of rejoining the man waiting for her at the door—the one the newspapers were saying Lady Rose would marry—she looked back. 'As a matter of interest, Lydia, how much do you charge for being me? Just in case I ever decided to take a day off?'

'No charge for you, Lady Rose. Just give me a call. Any time.'

'I don't suppose you fancy three hours of Wagner this evening?' she asked, but before Lydia could reply, she shook her head. 'Just kidding. I wouldn't wish that on you.'

The smile was in place, the voice light with laughter, but for a moment her eyes betrayed her and Lydia saw beyond the fabulous clothes, the pearl choker at her throat. Lady Rose, she realised, was a woman in trouble and, taking a card from the small clutch bag she was holding, she offered it to her.

'I meant what I said. Call me,' Lydia urged. 'Any time.'

Three weeks later, when she answered her cellphone, a voice she knew as well as her own said, 'Did you mean it?'

Kalil al-Zaki stared down into the bare winter garden of his country's London Embassy, watching the Ambassador's chil-dren racing around in the care of their nanny.

He was only a couple of years younger than his cousin. By the time a man was in his thirties he should have a family, sons…

'I know how busy you are, but it's just for a week, Kal.'

'I don't understand the problem,' he said, clamping down on the bitterness, the anger that with every passing day came closer to spilling over, and turned from the children to their mother, his cousin's lovely wife, Princess Lucy al-Khatib. 'Nothing is going to happen to Lady Rose at Bab el Sama.'

As it was the personal holiday complex of the Ramal Hamrahn royal family, security would, he was certain, be state-of-the-art.

'Of course it isn't,' Lucy agreed, 'but her grandfather came to see me yesterday. Apparently there has been a threat against her.'

He frowned. 'A threat? What kind of threat?'

'He refused to go into specifics.'

'Well, that was helpful.' Then, 'So why did he come to you rather than Hanif?'

'I was the one who offered her the use of our Bab el Sama cottage whenever she needed to get away from it all.' She barely lifted her shoulders, but it was unmistakably a shrug. 'The Duke's line is that he doesn't want to alarm her.'

Line?

'He thought the simplest solution would be if I made some excuse and withdrew the invitation.'

The one thing that Kal could do was read women—with a mother, two stepmothers and more sisters than he could count, he'd had a lot of practise—and he recognised an *as if* shrug when he saw one.

'You believe he's making a fuss about nothing.'

'He lost his son and daughter-in-law in the most brutal manner and it's understandable that he's protective of his granddaughter. She wasn't even allowed to go to school…'

'Lucy!' he snapped. This all round the houses approach was unlike her. And why on earth she should think he'd want to babysit some spoiled celebrity 'princess', he couldn't imagine. But Lucy was not the enemy. On the contrary. 'I'm sorry.'

'I've no doubt there's been something,' she said, dismissing his apology with an elegant gesture.

'Everyone in the public eye gets their share of crank mail, but...' there it was, the *but* word '...I doubt it's more than some delusional creature getting hot under the collar over rumours that she's about to announce her engagement to Rupert Devenish.'

'You're suggesting that it's no more than a convenient excuse to apply pressure on you, keep her under the paternal eye?' He didn't believe it. The woman wasn't a child; she had to be in her mid-twenties.

'Maybe I'm being unjust.' She sighed. 'I might believe that the man is obsessively controlling, but I have no doubt that Rose is very precious to him.'

'And not just him.' He might suspect the public image of purity and goodness was no more than a well-managed PR exercise, but it was one the media were happy to buy into, at least until they had something more salacious to print on their front pages. 'You do realise that if anything were to happen to Lady Roseanne Napier while she's in Ramal Hamrah, the British press would be merciless?' And he would be the one held to blame.

'Meanwhile, they'll happily invade her privacy on a daily basis in the hope of getting intimate pictures of her for no better reason than to boost the circulation of their grubby little rags.'

'They can only take pictures of what she does,' he pointed out.

'So she does nothing.'

'Nothing?' He frowned. 'Really? She really is as pure, as angelic as the media would have us believe?'

'It's not something to be sneered at, Kalil.' Her turn to snap. 'She's been in the public eye since she was dubbed the "people's angel" on her sixteenth birthday. She hasn't been able to move a finger for the last ten years without someone taking a photograph of her.'

'Then she has my sympathy.'

'She doesn't need your sympathy, Kal. What she's desperate for is some privacy. Time on her own to sort out where she's going from here.'

'I thought you said she was getting married.'

'I said there were rumours to that effect, fuelled, I have no doubt, by the Duke,' she added, this time making no attempt to hide her disapproval. 'There comes a point at which a virginal image stops being charming, special and instead becomes the butt of cruel humour. Marriage, babies will keep the story moving forward and His Grace has lined up an Earl in waiting to fill this bill.'

'An arranged marriage?' It was his turn to shrug. 'Is that so bad?' In his experience, it beat the ramshackle alternative of love hands down. 'What does Hanif say?'

'In his opinion, if there had been a genuine threat the Duke would have made a formal approach through the Foreign Office instead of attempting to bully me into withdrawing my invitation.'

With considerably more success, Kal thought.

'Even so,' he replied, 'it might be wiser to do everyone a favour and tell Lady Rose that the roof has fallen in at your holiday cottage.'

'In other words, knuckle under, make life easy for ourselves? What about Rose? They give her no peace, Kal.'

'She's never appeared to want it,' he pointed out. Barely a week went by without her appearance on the front pages of the newspapers or some gossip magazine.

'Would it make any difference if she did?' She shook her head, not expecting an answer. 'Will you go with her, Kal? While I don't believe Rose is in any actual danger, I daren't risk leaving her without someone to watch her back and if I have to ask your uncle to detail an Emiri guard, she'll simply be exchanging one prison for another.'

'Prison?'

'What would you call it?' She reached out, took his hand. 'I'm desperately worried about her. On the surface she's so serene, but underneath there's a desperation…' She shook her head. 'Distract her, Kal. Amuse her, make her laugh.'

'Do you want me to protect her or make love to her?' he asked, with just the slightest edge to his voice. He'd done his best to live down the playboy image that clung to the al-Zaki name, but he would always be the grandson of an exiled playboy prince, the son of a man whose pursuit of beautiful women had kept the gossip writers happily in business for forty years.

Building an international company from the floor up, supporting Princess Lucy's charities, didn't make the kind of stories that sold newspapers.

'Consider this as a diplomatic mission, Kal,' Lucy replied enigmatically, 'and a diplomat is a man who manages to give everyone what they want while serving the needs of his own country. You do want to serve your country?' she asked.

They both knew that he had no country, but clearly Lucy saw this as a way to promote his cause. The restoration of his family to their rightful place. His marriage to the precious daughter of one of the great Ramal Hamrahn families. And, most important of all, to take his dying grandfather home. For that, he would play nursemaid to an entire truckload of aristocratic virgins.

'Princess,' he responded with the slightest bow, 'rest assured that I will do everything in my power to ensure that Lady Roseanne Napier enjoys her visit to Ramal Hamrah.'

'Thank you, Kal. I can now assure the Duke that, since the Emir's nephew is to take personal care of her security, he can have no worries about her safety.'

Kal shook his head, smiling despite himself. 'You won't, I imagine, be telling him which nephew?'

'Of course I'll tell him,' she replied. 'How else will he be able to thank your uncle for the service you have rendered him?'

'You think he'll be grateful?'

'Honestly? I think he'll be chewing rocks, but he's not about to insult the Emir of Ramal Hamrah by casting doubt on the character of one of his family. Even one whose grandfather tried to start a revolution.'

'And how do you suppose His Highness will react?'

'He will have no choice but to ask his wife to pay a courtesy visit on their distinguished visitor,' she replied. 'The opportunity to meet your aunt is the best I can do for you, Kal. The rest is up to you.'

'Lucy…' He was for a moment lost for words. 'How can I…'

She simply raised a finger to her lips, then said, 'Just take care of Rose for me.'

'How on earth did you swing a week off just before Christmas, Lydie?'

'Pure charm,' she replied, easing her shoulder as she handed over her checkout at the end of her shift. That and a cross-her-heart promise to the manager that she'd use the time to think seriously about the management course he'd been nagging her to take for what seemed like forever. He'd been totally supportive of her lookalike career, allowing her to be flexible in her shifts, but he wanted her to start thinking about the future, a real career.

'Well, remember us poor souls chained to the checkout listening to *Jingle Bells* for the umpteenth time, while you're lying in the sun, won't you?'

'You've got to be kidding,' she replied, with the grin of a woman with a week in the sun ahead of her.

And it was true; this was going to be an unbelievable experience. Rose had offered her the chance of a dream holiday in the desert. An entire week of undiluted luxury in which she was going to be wearing designer clothes—not copies run up by her mother—and treated like a real princess. Not some fake dressed up to look like one.

The euphoria lasted until she reached her car.

She'd told her colleagues at work that she'd been invited to spend a week at a friend's holiday apartment, which was near enough to the truth, but she hadn't told a soul where she was really going, not even her mother, and that had been hard.

Widowed in the same accident that had left her confined to a wheelchair, Lydia's 'Lady Rose' gigs were the highlight of her mother's life and normally they shared all the planning, all the fun, and her mother's friends all joined vicariously in the excitement.

But this was different. This wasn't a public gig.

The slightest hint of what she was doing would ruin everything for Rose. She knew that her mother wouldn't be able to resist sharing such an incredible secret with her best friend who'd be staying with her while she was away. She might as well have posted a bulletin on the wall of her Facebook page.

Instead, she'd casually mentioned a woman at work who was looking for a fourth person to share a last-minute apartment deal in Cyprus—which was true—and left it to her mother to urge her to grab it.

Which of course she had.

'Why don't you go, love?' she'd said, right on cue. 'All the hours you work, you deserve a break. Jennie will stop with me while you're away.'

That the two of them would have a great time together, gossiping non-stop, did nothing to make Lydia feel better about the deception.

Kal had been given less than twenty-four hours to make arrangements for his absence, pack and visit the clinic where his grandfather was clinging to life to renew the promise he'd made that he should die in the place he still called home.

Now, as he stood at the steps of the jet bearing the Emir's personal insignia, he wondered what His Highness's reaction had been when he'd learned who would be aboard it today.

It wasn't his first trip to the country that his great-grandfather had once ruled. Like his grandfather and his father, Kalil was forbidden from using his title, using the name Khatib, but, unlike the old man, he was not an exile.

He'd bought a waterfront apartment in the capital, Rumaillah. His aircraft flew a regular freight service into Ramal Hamrah, despite the fact that they remained stubbornly empty. No one would dare offend the Emir by using Kalzak Air Services and he made no effort to break the embargo. He did not advertise his services locally, or compete for business. He kept his rates equal to, but not better than his competitors. Took the loss.

This was not about profit but establishing his right to be there.

He'd been prepared to be patient, sit it out, however long it took, while he'd quietly worked on the restoration of his family home at Umm al Sama. But he'd continued to remain invisible to the ruling family, his family, a stranger in his own country, and patience was no longer an option. Time was running out for his grandfather and nothing mattered but bringing him home to die.

He'd do anything. Even babysit a wimp of a woman who wasn't, apparently, allowed to cross the road without someone holding her hand.

He identified himself to Security, then to the cabin crew, who were putting the final touches to the kind of luxury few airline passengers would ever encounter.

His welcome was reserved, but no one reeled back in horror.

A steward took his bag, introduced him to Atiya Bishara, who would be taking care of Lady Rose during the flight, then gave him a full tour of the aircraft so that he could check for himself that everything was in order.

He was treated no differently from any anonymous security officer who'd been asked to escort Lady Rose on a flight that, historically, should have been his grandfather's to command. Which said pretty much everything he needed to know about how the rest of the week was likely to pan out.

His aunt might pay a courtesy visit to Lady Rose, but even if she acknowledged his presence it would be as a servant.

Lydia rapidly exchanged clothes with Rose in the private room that had been set aside for her as guest of honour at the Pink Ribbon Lunch.

Lady Rose had walked into the room; ten minutes later Lydia, heart pounding, mouth dry, had walked out in her place.

She held her breath as a dark-suited security man fell in behind her.

Would he really be fooled? Rose had assured her

that he would be looking everywhere but at her, but even wearing Rose's crushed raspberry silk suit, a saucy matching hat with a wispy veil and the late Duchess of Oldfield's famous pearl choker, it seemed impossible that he wouldn't notice the difference.

But there was no challenge.

Smile, she reminded herself as she approached the hotel manager who was waiting to escort her to the door. It was just another job. And, holding that thought, she offered the man her hand, thanked him for doing such a good job for the Pink Ribbon Club, before stepping outside into the thin winter sunshine.

Rose had warned her what to expect but, since rumours of a wedding had started to circulate, media interest had spiralled out of control. Nothing could have prepared her for the noise, the flashes from dozens of cameras. And it wasn't just the paparazzi lined up on the footpath. There were dozens of ordinary people hoping for a glance of the 'people's angel', all of them taking pictures, video, with their cellphones. People who thought she was the real thing, deserved the real thing, and she had to remind herself not just to smile, but to breathe.

It was the photographers who saved her, calling out, 'Lady Rose! This way, Lady Rose! Love the hat, Lady Rose!'

The eye-catching little hat had been made specially for the occasion. Fashioned from a stiffened loop of the same material as the suit, it had a dark pink net veil scattered with tiny velvet ribbon loops that skimmed her face, breaking up the outline, blurring any slight differences that might be picked out by an eagle-eyed picture editor.

Breathe, smile…

'How was lunch, Lady Rose?' one of the photographers called out.

She swallowed down the nervous lump in her throat and said, 'It was a wonderful lunch for a great cause.' Then, when there was still no challenge, no one pointed a finger, shouted, *Fake!*, she added, 'The Pink Ribbon Club.' And, growing in confidence, she lifted her right hand so that the diamond and amethyst ring on her right hand flashed in the sunlight as she pointedly touched the little ribbon-shaped hat. 'Don't forget to mention it.'

'Are you looking forward to your holiday, Lady Rose?'

Growing in confidence—it was true, apparently, that people saw only what they expected to see—she picked out the photographer who'd asked the question and smiled directly at him.

'Very much,' she said.

'Will you be on your own?' he dared.

'Only if you all take the week off, too,' she replied, raising a laugh. Yes! She could do this! And, turning her back on the photographers, she walked down the steps and crossed to the real people, just as she had seen Lady Rose do a hundred times on news clips. Had done herself at promotional gigs.

She took the flowers they handed her, stopped to answer questions—she could have entered *Mastermind* with Lady Rose as her specialist subject—paused for photographs, overwhelmed by the genuine warmth with which people reached out to her. To Rose…

'Madam…' The security officer touched his watch, indicating that it was time to leave.

She gave the crowd a final wave and smile and turned back to the limousine, stepped inside. The door closed behind her and, within moments, she was gliding through London behind a liveried chauffeur.

At which point she bit back a giggle.

This wasn't like any other job. No way. At this point, if it had been an ordinary job, she'd be heading for the hotel cloakroom for a quick change before catching the bendy bus back to work. Instead, she was in a top-of-the-range Mercedes, heading for an airfield used by people for whom the private jet was the only way to travel. The final hurdle before she could relax and enjoy being Lady Rose without the risk of someone taking a second look and challenging her.

It was a thought to bring the giggle under

control. Not the fear of being challenged. The
thought of getting in a plane.

Kal paced the VIP lounge, certain that he was
wasting his time.

Lucy was wrong. Playing nanny to a woman
known to the world as 'England's Sweetheart', or
'angel' or even '*virgin*', for heaven's sake, wasn't
going to make him any friends in the Ramal
Hamrahn court. Unless there really was an attempt
on her life and he saved her. Maybe he should
arrange one…

He stopped fantasising and checked the time.

Another minute and she'd be late. No more than
he'd expected. She was probably still posing for
photographs, being feted by her fans.

He'd seen her on the news—she was impossible
to avoid—a pale, spun-sugar confection, all sweetness and light. He knew she was a friend of Lucy's
but, really, could anyone be that perfect?

He was about to pick up a newspaper, settle
down to wait, when a stir at the entrance alerted
him to her arrival. That she had arrived exactly on
schedule should have been a point in her favour. It
only served to irritate him further.

Lydia could not believe the ease with which she
moved through airport formalities but when you
were an A-list VIP, related to the Queen, even if it

was goodness knew how many times removed, it seemed that the ordinary rules did not apply. Forget the usual hassle with the luggage trolley. She hadn't even seen the bags that Rose had packed for this trip.

And no one was going to make her line up at a check-in desk. Clearly, people who flew in their own private jets did not expect to queue for *anything*.

She didn't have to take off her jacket and shoes, surrender the handbag and briefcase she was carrying to be X-rayed. Instead, she was nodded through the formalities and escorted to the departure lounge by Lady Rose's security officer.

Rose had explained that he would see her to the aircraft and after that she'd be on her own, free from all risk of discovery. And once she was in Ramal Hamrah, ensconced in the luxury of Princess Lucy's holiday cottage at Bab el Sama, all she had to do was put in the occasional appearance in the garden or on the beach to ensure that the paparazzi were able to snatch pictures of her while she lived like a princess for a week.

It was like some dream-come-true fairy tale. Checkout girl to princess. Pure Cinderella.

All she needed was a pair of glass slippers and a fairy godmother to provide her with someone tall, dark and handsome to play Prince Charming.

She wouldn't even have to flee when the clock struck twelve. She had a whole week before she turned back into Lydia Young, whose job as supermarket checkout girl was occasionally enlivened by a lookalike gig.

She automatically reached for the door to the VIP departure lounge, but it opened as she approached; a 'Lady' with a capital L did not open doors for herself. She was so intent on covering her mistake by adjusting the veil on her hat that she missed the fact that her escort had stopped at the door.

'Mr al-Zaki will take care of you from here, madam.'

Who?

She thought the word, but never voiced it.

All sound seemed to fade away as she looked up. She was tall, but the knee-meltingly gorgeous man waiting to 'take care' of her was half a head taller and as his eyes, dark and intense, locked with hers, she felt the jolt of it to her knees. And yes, no doubt about it, her knees melted as he lowered his head briefly, said, 'Kalil al-Zaki, Lady Rose,' introducing himself with the utmost formality. 'Princess Lucy has asked me to ensure that your holiday is all that you wish.'

Graceful, beautiful, contained power rippling beneath exquisite tailoring, he was, she thought crazily, the embodiment of Bagheera, the bold, reckless panther from her childhood favourite, *The Jungle Book*. She'd made her father read over and over the description of his coat like watered silk, his voice as soft as wild honey dripping from a tree.

Her own, as she struggled for a suitable response, was non-existent.

Kalil al-Zaki might favour well-cut British tailoring over a fancy Ruritanian uniform but he was as close to her own Prince Charming fantasy as she was ever likely to come and she had to resist the temptation to look around for the old lady with wings and a wand who'd been listening in on her thoughts.

CHAPTER TWO

'YOU'RE coming with me to Bab el Sama?' she managed finally, knowing that she should be horrified by this turn of events. The frisson of excitement rippling through her suggested that she was anything but.

'There and back,' he confirmed. 'My instructions are to keep you safe from harm. I have a letter of introduction from Princess Lucy, but the aircraft is waiting and the pilot will not wish to miss his slot. If you're ready to board?'

Lydia just about managed a nod and the noise flooded back like a shock wave as, his hand curling possessively around her elbow, he walked her to the door, across the tarmac towards the plane. Where she received shock number two.

When Rose had explained that she'd be flying in a private jet, Lydia had anticipated one of those small executive jobs. The reality was a full-sized passenger aircraft bearing the royal livery.

She'd fantasized about being treated like a princess, but this was the real deal; all that was missing was the red carpet and a guard of honour.

If they found out she was a fake they were not going to be amused and, as Kalil al-Zaki's touch sizzled through her sleeve, Lydia had to concentrate very hard on marshalling her knees and putting one foot in front of the other.

This was anything but a fairy tale and if she fell flat on her face there would be no fairy godmother to rescue her with the wave of a wand.

Concentrate, concentrate…

She'd already had an encounter with one of Rose's security guards. He hadn't looked at her the way that Kalil al-Zaki had looked and he certainly hadn't touched. The closest he'd been was when he'd opened the car door and his eyes had not been on her, but the crowd.

No matter what he said about 'keeping her safe', it was clear that this man was not your standard bodyguard, so who on earth was he?

Should she have recognised his name?

Think…

He'd mentioned Princess Lucy. So far, so clear. She was the friend who'd lent Rose her holiday 'cottage' for the week. The wife of the Emir's youngest son, who was the Ramal Hamrahn Ambassador to London.

Rose had filled her in on all the important background details, a little of their history, the names and ages of their children, so that she wouldn't make a mistake if any of the staff at Bab el Sama mentioned her or her children.

But that was it.

This was supposed to be no more than a walk-on role with only servants and the occasional telephoto lens for company.

A few minutes performing for a bunch of journalists, and getting away with it, had given her a terrific buzz, but playing the part convincingly under the eyes of someone like Kalil al-Zaki for an entire week was a whole different ball game.

Hopefully, the letter of introduction would fill in the details, she thought as his hand fell away at the top of the steps and she was greeted by the waiting stewardess.

'Welcome aboard the royal flight, Lady Rose. I am Atiya Bishara and I will be taking care of you today.' Then, looking at the flowers she was clutching like a lifeline, 'Shall I put those in water?'

Lydia, back on more or less familiar territory, began to breathe again. This was the basic looka-like stuff she'd been doing since she was fifteen years old and she managed to go through the standard 'How d'you do?' routine as she surrendered the flowers and the dark pink leather briefcase that exactly matched her hat. The one Rose had used to conceal the cash she'd needed for her week away and which now contained Lydia's own essentials, including her own passport in the event that anything went wrong.

'Your luggage has been taken to your suite, Lady Rose. I'll take you through as soon as we're in the air,' Atiya said as she led her to an armchair-sized seat.

A suite?

Not *that* familiar, she thought, taking out her cellphone and sending a one word message to Rose to let her know that she'd got through security without any hiccups. Apart from Kalil al-Zaki, that was, and Rose couldn't do anything about that.

That done, she turned off the phone and looked around.

From the outside, apart from the royal livery, the aircraft might look much like any other. On the inside, however, it bore no similarity to the crammed-tight budget airlines that were a necessary evil to be endured whenever she wanted a week or two in the sun.

'Would you like something to drink before we take off?' Atiya asked.

Uh-oh.

Take and *off*, used in tandem, were her two least favourite words in the English language. Until now her head had been too busy concentrating on the role she was playing, enjoying the luxury of a chauffeur-driven limousine, free-wheeling around the unexpected appearance of Kalil al-Zaki, to confront that particular problem.

'Juice? A glass of water?'

'Water, thank you,' she replied, forcing herself to concentrate, doing her best not to look at the man who'd taken the seat across the aisle.

And failing.

His suit lay across his broad shoulders as if moulded to him and his glossy black hair, brushed back off a high forehead curled over his collar, softening features that could have been chiselled from marble. Apart from his mouth.

Marble could never do justice to the sensuous droop of a lower lip that evoked such an immediate, such a disturbing response in parts of her anatomy that had been dormant for so long that she'd forgotten how it felt.

As if sensing her gaze, Kalil al-Zaki turned and she blushed at being caught staring.

Nothing in his face suggested he had noticed. Instead, as the plane began to taxi towards the runway, he took an envelope from the inside pocket of his jacket and offered it to her.

'My introduction from Princess Lucy, Lady Rose.'

She accepted the square cream envelope, warm from his body, and although she formed the words, *Thank you*, no sound emerged. Praying that the dark pink net of her veil would camouflage the heat that had flooded into her cheeks, she ducked her head. It was embarrassment, she told herself as she flipped open the envelope and took out the note it contained.

Dear Rose,
I didn't get a chance to call yesterday and explain that Han's cousin, Kalil al-Zaki, will be accompanying you to Bab el Sama.

I know that you are desperate to be on your own, but you will need someone to drive you, accompany you to the beach, be generally at your beck and call while you're in Bab el Sama and at least he won't report every move you make to your grandfather.

The alternative would be one of the Emir's guards, good men every one but, as you can imagine, not the most relaxing of companions.

Kal will not intrude if you decide to simply lie by the pool with a book, but you shouldn't miss out on a visit to the souk—it's an absolute treasure of gold, silks, spices—or a drive into the desert. The peace is indescribable.

Do give me a call if there is anything you need or you just need someone to talk to but, most of all rest, relax, recharge the batteries and don't, whatever you do, give Rupert a single thought.

All my love,
Lucy

Which crushed her last desperate hope that he was simply escorting her on the flight. 'There and back', apparently, in-cluded the seven days in between.

And things had been going so well up until now, she thought as the stewardess returned with her water and she gratefully gulped down a mouthful.

Too well.

Rose's grandfather had apparently accepted that taking her own security people with her would be seen as an insult to her hosts. The entire Ramal Hamrah ruling family had holiday 'cottages' at Bab el Sama and the Emir did not, she'd pointed out, take the safety of his family or their guests lightly.

The paparazzi were going to have to work really hard to get their photographs this week, although she'd do her best to make it easy for them.

There had been speculation that Rupert would join Rose on this pre-Christmas break and if she wasn't visible they might just get suspicious, think they'd been given the slip. Raise a hue and cry that would get everyone in a stew and blow her cover.

Her commission was to give them something to point their lenses at so that the Duke was reassured that she was safe and the world could see that she was where she was supposed to be.

Neither of them had bargained on her friend complicating matters.

Fortunately, Princess Lucy's note had made it

clear that Rose hadn't met Kalil al-Zaki, which simplified things a little. The only question left was, faced with an unexpected—and unwanted—companion, what would Rose do now?

Actually, not something to unduly tax the mind. Rose would do what she always did. She'd smile, be charming, no matter what spanner had been thrown into her carefully arranged works.

Until now, protected by the aura of untouchability that seemed to encompass the Lady Rose image, Lydia had never had a problem doing the same.

But then spanners didn't usually come blessed with smooth olive skin moulded over bone structure that had been a gift from the gene fairies.

It should have made it easier to respond to his smile—if only with an idiotic, puppy-like grin. The reality was that she had to concentrate very hard to keep the drool in check, her hand from visibly trembling, her brain from turning to jelly. Speaking at the same time was asking rather a lot, but it certainly helped take her mind off the fact that the aircraft was taxiing slowly to the runway in preparation for the nasty business of launching her into thin air. She normally took something to calm her nerves before holiday flights but hadn't dared risk it today.

Fortunately, ten years of 'being' Lady Rose came to her rescue. The moves were so ingrained that they had become automatic and instinct kicked in and overrode the urge to leap into his lap and lick his face.

'It would seem that you've drawn the short straw, Mr al-Zaki,' she said, kicking the 'puppy' into touch and belatedly extending her hand across the aisle.

'The short straw?' he asked, taking it in his own firm grip with just the smallest hint of a frown.

'I imagine you have a dozen better things to do than…' she raised the letter an inch or two '…show me the sights.'

'On the contrary, madam,' he replied formally, 'I can assure you that I had to fight off the competition.'

He was so serious that for a moment he had her fooled.

Unbelievable!

The man was flirting with her, or, rather, flirting with Lady Rose. What a nerve!

'It must have been a very gentlemanly affair,' she replied, matching his gravity, his formality.

One of his dark brows lifted the merest fraction and an entire squadron of butterflies took flight in her stomach. He was good. Really good. But any girl who'd worked for as long as she had on a supermarket checkout had not only heard it all, but had an arsenal of responses to put even the smoothest of operators in their place.

'No black eyes?' she prompted. 'No broken limbs?'

He wasn't quite quick enough to kill the surprise

at the swiftness of her comeback and for a moment she thought she'd gone too far. He was the Ambassador's cousin, after all. One of the ruling class in a society where women were supposed to be neither seen nor heard.

Like that was going to happen…

But then the creases deepened in his cheeks, his mouth widened in a smile and something happened to the darkest, most intense eyes she'd ever seen. Almost, she thought, as if someone had lit a fire in their depths.

'I was the winner, madam,' he reminded her.

'I'm delighted you think so,' she replied, hanging on to her cool by the merest thread, despite the conflagration that threatened to ignite somewhere below her midriff.

There had never been anyone remotely like this standing at her supermarket checkout. She was going to have to be very, very careful.

Kal just about managed to bite back a laugh.

Lucy—with Hanif's unspoken blessing, he had no doubt—was placing him in front of the Emir, forcing his uncle to take note of his existence, acknowledge that he was doing something for his country. Offering him a chance to show himself to be someone worthy of trust, a credit to the name he was forbidden from using. And already he was flirting with the woman who had been entrusted to his care.

But then she wasn't the least bit what he'd expected.

He had seen a hundred photographs of Lady Rose on magazine covers and nothing in those images had enticed him to use her friendship with Princess Lucy to attempt a closer acquaintance.

The iconic blue eyes set in an oval face, yards of palest blonde hair, the slender figure were, no doubt, perfect. If you liked that kind of look, colouring, but she'd lacked the dark fire, a suggestion of dangerous passion, of mystery that he looked for in a woman.

The reality, he discovered, was something else.

As she'd walked into the VIP lounge it had seemed to come to life; as if, on a dull day, the sun had emerged from behind a cloud.

What he'd thought of as pallor was, in fact, light. A golden glow.

She was a lot more than a colourless clothes horse.

The famous eyes, secreted behind the wisp of veil that covered the upper half of her face, sparkled with an excitement, a vitality that didn't come through in any photograph he'd seen. But it was the impact of her unexpectedly full and enticingly kissable mouth, dark, sweet and luscious as the heart of a ripe fig, that grabbed and held his complete attention and had every red blood cell in his body bounding forward to take a closer look.

For the briefest moment her poise had wavered

and she'd appeared as nonplussed as he was, but for a very different reason. It was obvious that Lucy hadn't managed to warn her that she was going to have company on this trip. She'd swiftly gathered herself, however, and he discovered that, along with all her other assets, she had a dry sense of humour.

Unexpected, it had slipped beneath his guard, and all his good intentions—to keep his distance, retain the necessary formality—had flown right out of the window.

And her cool response, 'I'm delighted you think so,' had been so ambiguous that he hadn't the least idea whether she was amused by his familiarity or annoyed.

His life had involved one long succession of his father's wives and mistresses, a galaxy of sisters who ranged from nearly his own age to little girls. Without exception they were all, by turn, tempestuous, sphinxlike, teasing. He'd seen them in all their moods and it had been a very long time since he hadn't known exactly what a woman was thinking.

Now, while the only thought in his own head should be *danger, out of bounds,* what he really wanted was for her to lift that seductive little veil and, with that lovely mouth, invite him to be really bad…

Realising that he was still holding her hand, he made a determined effort to get a grip. 'You are as astute as you are lovely, madam,' he replied, matching her own cool formality, as he released it. 'I will be more circumspect in future.'

Her smile was a private thing. Not a muscle moved, only something in her eyes altered so subtly that he could not have described what happened. He'd felt rather than seen a change and yet he knew, deep down, that she was amused.

'Rose,' she said.

'I beg your pardon, madam?'

'According to her letter, Lucy thought you would make a more relaxing companion than one of the Emiri guard.'

'You have my word that I won't leap to attention whenever you speak to me,' he assured her.

'That is a relief, Mr al-Zaki.'

Lydia had to work a lot harder than usual to maintain the necessary regal poise.

She had no way of knowing on what scale Princess Lucy measured 'relaxing' but she must lead a very exciting life if spending time with Kalil al-Zaki fell into that category.

With his hot eyes turning her bones to putty, heating her skin from the inside out, *relaxed* was the last word she'd use to describe the way she was feeling right now.

'However, I don't find the prospect of an entire week being "madamed" much fun either. My name is…' she began confidently enough, but suddenly faltered. It was one thing acting out a role, it was quite another to look this man in the eye, meet his dark gaze and utter the lie. She didn't want to lie to him, to pretend... 'I would rather you called me Rose.'

'Rose,' he repeated softly. Wild honey...

'Can you manage your seat belt, Lady Rose?' the stewardess asked as she retrieved the glass. 'We're about to take off.'

'Oh...' Those words again. 'Yes, of course.'

She finally managed to tear her gaze away from her companion—wild honey was a dangerous temptation that could not be tasted without getting stung—and cast about her for the straps.

'Can I assist you, Rose?' he asked as her shaking hands fumbled with the buckle.

'No!' She shook her head as she finally managed to clip it into place. 'Thank you, Mr...'

'Kal,' he prompted. 'Most people call me Kal.' The lines bracketing his mouth deepened into a slow, sexy smile. 'When they're being relaxed,' he added.

She just about managed to stifle a hysterical giggle. She hadn't hesitated because she'd forgotten his name. He'd made an indelible impression... No.

She'd been so busy worrying about whether he knew Rose personally, countering the effect of that seductive voice, that she'd overlooked the really important part of Princess Lucy's letter. The bit where she'd mentioned that Kalil al-Zaki was her husband's cousin. As she'd said the word 'Mr' it had suddenly occurred to her who he really was. Not just some minor diplomat who'd been given the task of ensuring a tricky visitor didn't get into trouble while she was at Bab el Sama.

Oh, dear me, no.

That wouldn't do for Lady Rose. Cousin of the Queen, patron of dozens of charities as well as figurehead of the one founded by her parents, she was an international figure and she was being given the full red-carpet treatment. Right down to her watchdog.

Kalil al-Zaki, the man who'd been roped in to guard their precious guest, was the cousin of the Ambassador, Sheikh Hanif al-Khatib. Which made him a nephew of the Emir himself.

'Kal,' she squeaked, slamming her eyes closed and gripping the arms of the chair as the plane rocketed down the runway and the acceleration forced her back into the chair, for once in her life grateful that she had her fear of take-off to distract her.

She was fine once she was in the air, flying straight and level above the clouds with no horizon to remind her that she was thirty thousand feet above the ground. Not that much different from travelling on a bus, apart from the fact that you didn't have to keep stopping so that people could get on and off.

Until now, what with one thing and another,

she'd been doing a better than average job of not thinking about this moment, but not even the sudden realisation that Kalil al-Zaki wasn't plain old *mister* anyone, but *Sheikh* Kalil al-Zaki, a genuine, bona fide prince, could override her terror.

She'd have plenty of time to worry about how 'charming' he'd prove to be if he discovered that she was a fake when they were safely airborne.

But just when she'd reached the point where she forgot how to breathe, long fingers closed reassuringly over hers and, surprised into sucking in air, she gasped and opened her eyes.

'I'm sorry,' Kal said as she turned to stare at him, 'but I've never liked that bit much.'

What?

His expression was so grave that, for just a moment, she wasn't sure whether or not he was serious. Then she swallowed.

Idiot.

Of course he wasn't serious. He was just being kind and, for once in her life, she wished she really was Lady Rose. Because then he'd be looking at her like that…

'You'll be all right now?' she managed, still breathless when, minutes later, the seat belt light pinged out. Doing her best to respond in kind, despite the fact that it was his steadying hand wrapped around hers. That she was the one who'd experienced a severe case of collywobbles. Wobbles that were still rippling through her, despite the fact that they had left the earth far beneath them.

'I believe so,' he replied gravely, but in no rush to break contact.

It was perhaps just as well that Atiya reappeared at that moment or they might have flown all the way to Ramal Hamrah with their hands intertwined.

Not that there would have been anything wrong with that…

'Shall I show you to your suite so that you can change before I serve afternoon tea, Lady Rose?'

'Thank you,' she said, using her traitorous hand to pull free the seat belt fastening so that she could follow Atiya. Straighten out her head.

Not easy when she discovered that the sumptuously fitted suite contained not only a bed, but its own bathroom with a shower that lent a whole new meaning to the words 'freshen up'.

'Would you like help changing?' Atiya offered, but Lydia assured her that she could manage and, once on her own, leaned back against the door, rubbing her palm over the hand Kal al-Zaki had held. Breathing slowly until her heart rate returned to normal. Or as near to normal as it was likely to be for the next week.

* * *

Kal watched Rose walk away from him.

His grandfather, a man who'd lost a throne, lost his country—but not the fortune that his father had hoped would compensate him for choosing his younger brother to succeed him—was a man without any purpose but to enjoy himself. He'd become part of the jetset, a connoisseur of all things beautiful, including women.

Kalil's father had, as soon as he was old enough, taken the same path and Kalil too had come dangerously close to following in their footsteps.

His boyhood winters had been spent on the ski slopes of Gstaad and Aspen, his summers shared between an Italian palazzo and a villa in the South of France. He'd gone to school in England, university in Paris and Oxford, postgrad in America.

He had been brought up in an atmosphere of wealth and privilege, where nothing had been denied him. The female body held no mystery for him and hers, by his exacting standards, was too thin for true beauty.

So why did he find her finely boned ankles so enticing? What was it about the gentle sway of her hips that made his hand itch to reach out and trace the elegant curve from waist to knee? To undress her, slowly expose each inch of that almost translucent peaches and cream skin and then possess it.

Possess her.

'Can I fetch you anything, sir?' the stewardess asked as she returned.

Iced water. A cold shower...

He left it at the water but she returned empty-handed. 'Captain Jacobs sends his compliments and asked if you'd like to visit the flight deck, sir. I'll serve your water there,' she added, taking his acceptance for granted.

It was the very last thing he wanted to do, but it was a courtesy he could not refuse. And common sense told him that putting a little distance between himself and Rose while he cooled off would be wise.

He'd reached out instinctively when he'd seen her stiffen in fear as the plane had accelerated down the runway. It had been a mistake. Sitting beside her had been a mistake. His brief was to ensure her security and, despite Lucy's appeal to amuse her, distract her, make her laugh, that was it.

Holding her hand to distract her when she was rigid with fear didn't count, he told himself, but sitting here, waiting to see if he'd imagined his gut-deep reaction to her was not a good idea.

Especially when he already knew the answer.

Then the name registered. 'Jacobs? Would that be Mike Jacobs?'

'You are in so much trouble, Lydia Young.'

She hadn't underestimated the enormity of

what she'd undertaken to do for Rose and they'd gone through every possible scenario, using a chat room to brainstorm any and all likely problems.

And every step of the way Rose had given her the opportunity to change her mind. Back out. Unfortunately, she was long past the *stop the plane, I want to get off* moment.

It had been too late from the moment she'd stepped out of that hotel room wearing Lady Rose's designer suit, her Jimmy Choos, the toes stuffed with tissue to stop them slipping.

Not that she would if she could, she realised.

She'd had ten years in which being 'Lady Rose' had provided all the little extras that helped make her mother's life easier. She *owed* Rose this. Was totally committed to seeing it through, but falling in lust at first sight with a man who had flirtation down to an art was, for sure, not going to make it any easier to ignore what Kalil al-Zaki's eyes, mouth, touch was doing to her.

'Come on, Lydie,' she said, giving herself a mental shake. 'You don't do this. You're immune, remember?'

Not since she'd got her fingers, and very nearly everything else, burnt by a stunningly good-looking actor who'd been paid to woo her into bed. She swallowed. She'd thought he was her Prince Charming, too.

It had been five years, but she still felt a cold shiver whenever she thought about it.

Pictures of the virginal 'Lady Rose' in bed with a man would have made millions for the people who'd set her up. Everyone would have run the pictures, whether they'd believed them or not. Covering themselves by the simple addition of a question mark to the 'Lady Rose in Sex Romp?' headline. The mere suggestion would have been enough to have people stampeding to the newsagents.

She, on the other hand, would have been ruined. No one would have believed she was an innocent dupe. If it had been anyone else, she wouldn't have believed it either.

She looked at the bed with longing, sorely tempted to just crawl beneath the covers and sleep away the next eight hours. No one would disturb her, expect anything from her.

But, since sleeping away the entire seven days was out of the question, she needed to snap out of it.

She'd been knocked off her feet by the heightened tension, that was all. Unsurprising under the circumstances. Anyone would be unsettled. Kal al-Zaki's presence had been unexpected, that was all. And she turned to the toilet case and overnight bag that had been placed on a stand.

The first was packed with everything a woman could ever need. The finest hairbrush that money could buy, the best skin care products, cosmetics, a selection of sumptuous scents; a perfect distraction for out of control hormones.

She opened one, sighed as she breathed in a subtle blend of sweet summer scents, then, as she sprayed it on her wrist, she caught an underlying note of something darker that tugged at forbidden desires. That echoed the heat in Kal al-Zaki's eyes.

Dropping it as if burned, she turned to the overnight bag. On the top, in suede drawstring bags, were the cases for the jewellery she was wearing, along with a selection of simpler pieces that Lady Rose wore while 'off duty'.

There was also a change of clothes for the long flight. A fine silk shirt the colour of champagne, wide-cut trousers in dark brown linen, a cashmere cardigan and a pair of butter-soft leather loafers in the right size. Supremely elegant but all wonderfully comfortable.

Rose had also packed a selection of the latest hardback best-sellers to while away the long flight. But then she hadn't expected that her stand-in would be provided with company.

Or not. According to Princess Lucy, it was up to her.

While she'd urged Rose to allow him to show her the sights, she'd made it clear that if she preferred to be alone then Kal would not intrude.

Not intrude?

What had the woman been *thinking*?

Hadn't she looked at him?

Anyone with half a brain could see that he wouldn't have to do a damn thing. One smile, one touch of his hand and he was already indelibly imprinted on her brain. In her head for ever more.

Intrusion squared.

In fact, if she didn't know better, she might be tempted to think that the Princess had planned a holiday romance as a little treat for her friend.

The idea was, of course, patently absurd.

Not that she didn't deserve a romance. A dark-eyed prince with a killer smile who'd sweep her off her feet.

No one deserved a little fun more than Rose, but anyone who knew her would understand just how impossible a casual, throwaway romance would be for her. And that was the essence of a holiday romance. Casual. Something out of time that had nothing to do with real life. That you left behind when you went home.

Anyone who truly cared for her would understand that.

Wouldn't they?

About to remove the pin that fastened the tiny hat to her chignon, she paused, sank onto the edge of the bed as a phrase in Lucy's letter came back to her.

Don't give Rupert a single thought…

She and Lucy were in total agreement on that one. Rose's grandfather, the newspapers, even the masses out there who thought they knew her, might be clamouring for an engagement, but she'd seen the two of them together. There was absolutely no chemistry, no connection.

Rose had made a joke about it, but Lydia hadn't been fooled for a second. She'd seen the desperation in her face and anyone who truly cared for her would want to save her from sleepwalking into such a marriage simply because it suited so many people.

Could Princess Lucy have hoped that if she put Rose and Kalil together the sparks would fly of their own accord without any need to stoke the fire? No doubt about it, a week being flirted with by Kal al-Zaki would have been just the thing to bring the colour back into Rose's cheeks.

Or was it all less complicated than that?

Was Lucy simply relying on the ever-attendant paparazzi, seeing two young people alone in a perfect setting, to put one and one together and make it into a front page story that would make them a fortune?

Who cared whether it was true?

Excellent plan, Lucy, she thought, warming to the woman despite the problems she'd caused.

There was only one thing wrong with it. Lady Rose had taken matters into her own hands and was, even now—in borrowed clothes, a borrowed car—embarking on an adventure of her own, safe in the knowledge that no one realised she'd escaped. That she could do what she liked while the world watched her lookalike.

Of course there was nothing to stop her from making it happen, she thought as she finally removed the hat and jewellery she was wearing. Kicked off her shoes and slipped out of the suit.

All it would take would be a look. A touch. He wasn't averse to touching.

She began to pull pins from her hair, absently divesting herself of the Lady Rose persona, just as she did at the end of every gig.

And she wouldn't be the victim this time. She would be the one in control, watching as the biter was, for once, bit.

Then, as her hair tumbled down, bringing her out of a reverie in which Kal touched her hand, then her face, her neck, his lips following a trail blazed by his fingers she let slip a word that Rose had probably never heard, let alone used.

It had taken an age to put her hair up like that and, unlike Rose, she didn't have a maid to help.

Just what she deserved for letting her fantasy run away with her. There was no way she was going to do anything that would embarrass Rose. Her part was written and she'd stick to it.

She began to gather the pins, but then realised that just because Rose never appeared in photographs other than with her hair up, it didn't mean that when she shut the door on the world at the end of the day—or embarked on an eight-hour flight—she'd wouldn't wear it loose.

She was, after all, supposed to be on holiday. And who, after all, knew what she did, said, wore, when she was behind closed doors?

Not Kalil al-Zaki, that was for sure.

And that was the answer to the 'keeping up appearances' problem, she realised.

Instead of trying to remember that she was Lady Rose for the next seven days, she would just be herself. She'd already made a pretty good start with the kind of lippy responses that regulars on her checkout at the supermarket would recognise.

And being herself would help with the 'lust' problem, too.

For as long as she could remember, she'd been fending off the advances of first boys, then men who, when they looked at her, had seen only the 'virgin' princess and wanted to either worship or ravish her.

It had taken her a little while to work that one out but, once she had, she'd had no trouble keeping them at arm's length, apart from the near miss with the actor, but then he'd been paid to be convincing. And patient. It was a pity he'd only, in the end, had an audience of one because he'd put in an Oscar-winning performance.

Kal, despite the way he looked, was just another man flirting with Lady Rose. That was all she had to remember, she told herself as she shook out her hair, brushed it, before she freshened up and put on the clothes Rose had chosen for her.

So which would he be? Worshipper or ravisher?

Good question, she thought as she added a simple gold chain and stud earrings before checking her reflection in a full length mirror.

It wasn't quite her—she tended to favour jeans and funky tops. It wasn't quite Lady Rose either, but it was close enough for someone who'd never met either of them, she decided as she chose a book, faced the door and took a slow, calming breath before returning to the main cabin.

In her absence the seats had been turned around, the cabin reconfigured so that it now resembled a comfortable sitting room.

An empty sitting room.

CHAPTER THREE

HAVING screwed herself up to be 'relaxed', the empty cabin was something of a let-down, but a table had been laid with a lace cloth and, no sooner than she'd settled herself and opened her book, Atiya arrived to serve afternoon tea.

Finger sandwiches, warm scones, clotted cream, tiny cakes and tea served from a heavy silver pot.

'Is all this just for me?' she asked when she poured only one cup and Kal had still not reappeared.

She hadn't wanted his company, but now he'd disappeared she felt affronted on Lady Rose's behalf. He was supposed to be here, keeping her safe from harm.

'Captain Jacobs invited Mr al-Zaki to visit the crew on the flight deck,' Atiya said. 'Apparently they did their basic training together.'

'Training?' It took her a moment. 'He's a *pilot*?'

Okay. She hadn't for a minute believed that he was bothered by the take-off, but she hadn't seen *that* coming. A suitable career for a nephew of an Emir wasn't a subject that had ever crossed her mind, but working as a commercial airline pilot wouldn't have been on her list even if she had. Maybe it had been military training.

A stint in one of the military academies favoured by royals would fit.

'Shall I ask him to rejoin you?' Atiya asked.

'No,' she said quickly. She had wanted him to keep his distance and her fairy godmother was, apparently, still on the case. 'I won't spoil his fun.'

Besides, if he returned she'd have to share this scrumptious spread.

Too nervous to eat lunch, and with the terrifying take-off well behind her, she was suddenly ravenous and the temptation to scoff the lot was almost overwhelming. Instead, since overindulgence would involve sweating it all off later, she managed to restrain herself, act like the lady she was supposed to be and simply tasted a little of everything to show her appreciation, concentrating on each stunning mouthful so that it felt as if she was eating far more, before settling down with her book.

Kal paused at the door to the saloon.

Rose, her hair a pale gold shimmer that she'd let down to hang over her shoulder, feet tucked up beneath her, absorbed in a book, was so far removed from her iconic image that she looked like a completely different woman.

Softer. The girl next door rather than a princess, because that was what she'd be if she'd been born into his culture.

Was the effect diminished?

Not one bit. It just came at him from a different direction. Now she looked not only luscious but available.

Double trouble.

As he settled in the chair opposite her she raised her eyes from her book, regarding him from beneath long lashes.

'Did you enjoy your visit to the cockpit?'

An almost imperceptible edge to her voice belied the softer look.

'It was most informative. Thank you,' he responded, equally cool. A little chill was just the thing to douse the heat generated by that mouth. Maybe.

'Did your old friend offer you the controls?' she added, as if reading his mind, and suddenly it all became clear. It wasn't the fact that he'd left her side without permission that bothered her.

The stewardess must have told her that he was a pilot and she thought he'd been laughing at her fear of flying.

'I hoped you wouldn't notice that little bump back there,' he said, offering her the chance to laugh right back at him.

There was a flicker of something deep in her eyes and the suspicion of an appreciative dimple appeared just above the left hand corner of her mouth.

'That was you? I thought it was turbulence.'

'Did you?' She was lying outrageously—the flight had been rock steady since they'd reached cruising altitude—but he was enjoying her teasing too much to be offended. 'It's been a while since I've flown anything this big. I'm a little rusty.'

She was struggling not to laugh now. 'It's not something you do seriously, then?'

'No one in my family does anything seriously.' It was the standard response, the one that journalists expected, and if it didn't apply to him, who actually cared? But, seeing a frown buckle the smooth, wide space between her eyes, the question that was forming, he cut her short with, 'My father bought himself a plane,' he said. 'I wanted to be able to fly it so I took lessons.'

'Oh.' The frown remained. 'But you said "this big",' she said, with a gesture that indicated the aircraft around them.

'You start small,' he confirmed. 'It's addictive, though. You keep wanting more.'

'But you've managed to break the habit.'

'Not entirely. Maybe you'd like a tour of the flight deck?' he asked. She clearly had no idea who he was and that suited him. If she discovered that he was the CEO of a major corporation she'd want to know what he was doing playing bodyguard. 'It sometimes helps ease the fear if you understand exactly what's happening. How things work.'

She shook her head. 'Thanks, but I'll pass.' Then, perhaps thinking she'd been less than gracious, she said, 'I do understand that my fear is totally irrational. If I didn't, I'd never get on one of these things.' Her smile was self-deprecating. 'But while, for the convenience of air travel, I can steel myself to suffer thirty seconds or so of blind panic, I also know that taking a pilot's eye view, seeing for myself exactly how much nothing there is out there, will only make things worse.'

'It's really just the take-off that bothers you?' he asked.

'So far,' she warned. 'But any attempt to analyse my fear is likely to give me ideas. And, before you say it, I know that flying is safer than crossing the road. That I've more chance of being hurt going to work—' She caught herself, for a fraction of second floundered. 'So I've heard,' she added quickly, as if he might dispute that what she did involved effort.

While opening the new wing of a hospital, attending charity lunches, appearing at the occasional gala might seem like a fairy tale existence to the outsider, he'd seen the effort Lucy put into her own charity and knew the appearance of effortless grace was all illusion.

But there was something about the way she'd stopped herself from saying more that suggested... He didn't know what it suggested.

'You've done your research.'

'No need. People will insist on telling you these things,' she said pointedly.

Signalling that the exchange was, as far as she was concerned, at an end, she returned to her book.

'There's just one more thing...'

She lifted her head, waited.

'I'm sure that Lucy explained that once we arrive in Ramal Hamrah we'll be travelling on to Bab el Sama by helicopter but—'

'Helicopter?'

The word came out as little more than a squeak.

'—but if it's going to be a problem, I could organise alternative transport,' he finished.

Lydia had been doing a pretty good job of keeping her cool, all things considered. She'd kept her head down, her nose firmly in her book even when Kal had settled himself opposite her. Stretched out those long, long legs. Crossed his ankles.

He'd removed his jacket, loosened his tie, undone the top button of his shirt.

What was it about a man's throat that was so enticing? she wondered. Invited touch...

She swallowed.

This was so not like her. She could flirt with the best, but that was no more than a verbal game that she could control. It was easy when only the brain was engaged…

Concentrate!

Stick to the plan. Speak when spoken to, keep the answers brief, don't let slip giveaways like 'going to work', for heaven's sake!

She'd managed to cover it but, unless she kept a firm rein on her tongue, sooner or later she'd say something that couldn't be explained away.

Lady Rose was charming but reserved, she reminded herself.

Reserved.

She made a mental note of the word, underlined it for emphasis.

It was too late to recall the 'helicopter' squeak, however, and she experienced a hollow feeling that had nothing to do with hunger as Kal, suddenly thoughtful, said, 'You've never flown in one?'

She had never been in a helicopter, but it was perfectly possible that Lady Rose hopped about all over the place in one in order to fulfil her many engagements. Quite possibly with her good friend Princess Lucy.

She hadn't thought to ask. Why would she?

After what seemed like an eternity, when she was sure Kal was going to ask her what she'd done with the real Lady Rose, he said, 'So?'

'So?' she repeated hoarsely.

'Which is it to be?'

'Oh.' He was simply waiting for her to choose between an air-conditioned ride in leather-upholstered comfort, or a flight in a noisy machine that didn't even have proper wings. Her well-honed instinct for self-preservation was demanding she go for the four-wheeled comfort option.

Her mouth, taking no notice, said, 'I can live with the helicopter.'

And was rewarded with another of those smiles that bracketed his mouth, fanned around his eyes, as if he knew just how much it had cost her.

'It's certainly simpler,' he said, 'but if I get scared you will hold my hand, won't you?'

Lydia, jolted out of her determined reserve by his charm, laughed out loud. Then, when he didn't join in, she had the weirdest feeling that their entire conversation had been leading up to that question and it was her breath that momentarily caught in her throat.

'I don't believe you're scared of anything,' she said.

'Everyone is scared of something, Rose,' he said enigmatically as he stood up. 'I'll leave you to enjoy your book. If you need me for anything I'll be in the office.'

Showers, bedrooms, now an office…

'Please, don't let me keep you from your work,' she said.

'Work?'

He said the word lightly, as if it was something he'd never thought of, but a shadow, so brief that she might have missed it had she not been so intent on reading his thoughts, crossed his face and she felt horribly guilty at her lack of gratitude. No matter how inconvenient, this man, purely as a favour, had given up his own time to ensure she had the perfect holiday.

Or was he recalling her earlier slip?

'For the next seven days you are my first concern,' he assured her. 'I'm simply going to check the weather report.'

Whew...

His first concern.

Wow...

But then he thought that she was the real thing. And when he turned those midnight-dark eyes on her she so wanted to be real. Not pretending. Just for a week, she thought, as she watched him stride away across the cabin on long, long legs.

No, no, no!

This was no time to lose it over a gorgeous face and a buff body and, determined to put him out of her mind, she turned back to her book. She had to read the same paragraph four times before it made sense, but she persevered, scarcely wavering in her concentration even when Kal returned to his chair, this time armed with a book of his own.

She turned a page, taking the opportunity to raise her lashes just enough to see that it was a heavyweight political treatise. Not at all what she'd expect from a man with playboy looks who'd told her that he did nothing 'seriously'.

But then looks, as she knew better than most, could be deceptive.

Atiya appeared after a while with the dinner menu and to offer them a drink. They both stayed with water. Wasted no time in choosing something simple to eat.

But for the continuous drone of the aircraft engines, the cabin was quiet. Once she lifted her head, stretched her neck. Maybe the movement caught his eye because he looked up too, lifting a brow in silent query. She shook her head, leaned back against the thickly padded seat and looked down at a carpet of clouds silvered by moonlight.

Kal, watching her, saw the exact moment when her eyes closed, her body slackened and he caught her book as it began to slide from her hand. It was the autobiography of a woman who'd founded her own business empire. She'd personally inscribed this copy to Rose.

He closed it, put it on the table. Asked Atiya for a light blanket, which he laid over her. Then, book forgotten, he sat and watched her sleep, wondering what dreams brought that tiny crease to her forehead.

'Sir,' Atiya said softly, 'I'll be serving dinner in ten minutes. Shall I wake Lady Rose?'

'I'll do it in a moment,' he said. Then, when she'd gone, he leaned forward. 'Rose,' he said softly. 'Rose...'

Lydia opened her eyes, for a moment not sure where she was. Then she saw Kal and it all came rushing back. It hadn't been a dream, then. She really was aboard a flying palace, one that wouldn't turn into a pumpkin at midnight. She had an entire week before she had to return to the checkout.

'What time is it?' she asked, sitting up, disentangling herself from the blanket that Atiya must have put over her.

'Seven minutes to eight in London, or to midnight in Ramal Hamrah if you want to set your watch to local time.'

She glanced at her wrist, touched the expensive watch, decided she'd rather do the maths than risk tampering with it.

'Atiya is ready to serve dinner.'

'Oh.' Her mouth was dry, a sure sign that she'd been sleeping with it open, which meant he'd been sitting there watching her drool.

Memo to self, she thought, wincing as she put her feet to the floor, searched with her toes for her shoes. Next time, use the bed.

'I apologise if I snored.'

His only response was a smile. She muffled a groan. She'd snored, drooled...

'Late night?' he asked, not helping.

'Very,' she admitted.

She'd had a late shift at the supermarket and, although her mother was determinedly independent, she always felt guilty about leaving her, even for a short time.

'I was double-checking to make sure that I hadn't left any loose ends trailing before taking off for a week,' she replied.

Everything clean and polished.

Fridge and freezer stocked so that Jennie wouldn't have to shop.

Enough of her mother's prescription meds to keep her going.

The list of contact numbers double-checked to make sure it was up to date.

While Rose wouldn't have been faced with that scenario, she'd doubtless had plenty of other stuff to keep her up late before she disappeared for a week.

And, like her, she would have been too wound up with nerves to sleep properly.

'I'd better go and freshen up,' she said but, before she could move, Kal was there to offer his hand, ease her effortlessly to her feet so that they were chest to chest, toe to toe, kissing close for a fraction of a second; long enough for her to breathe in the scent of freshly laundered linen, warm skin, some subtle scent that reminded her of a long ago walk in autumn woods. The crushed dry leaves and bracken underfoot.

Close enough to see the faint darkening of his chin and yearn to reach up, rub her hand over his jaw, feel the roughness against her palm.

She'd barely registered the thought before he released her hand, stepped back to let her move and she wasted no time putting some distance between them.

She looked a mess. Tousled, dishevelled, a red mark on her cheek where she'd slept with her head against the leather upholstery. She was going to have to duck her entire head under the cold tap to get it working properly, but she didn't have time for that. Instead, she splashed her face, repaired her lipstick, brushed the tangles out of her hair and then clasped it at the nape of her neck with a clip she found in the case that Rose had packed for her.

Then she ran through the pre-gig checklist in an attempt to jolt her brain back into the groove.

Smoothed a crease in the linen trousers.

Straightened the fine gold chain so that it lay in an orderly fashion about her neck.

Rehearsed her prompt list of appropriate questions so that there would never be a lull in the conversation.

Putting the situation in its proper context.

It was something she'd done hundreds of times, after all.

It was just another job!

Kal rose as she entered the main saloon and the *just another job* mantra went straight out of the window. Not that he *did* anything. Offer her his hand. Smile, even.

That was the problem. He didn't have to *do* anything, she thought as he stood aside so that she could lead the way to where Atiya was waiting beside a table that had been laid with white damask, heavy silver, crystal, then held a chair for her.

Like a force of nature, he just *was*.

Offered wine, she shook her head. Even if she'd been tempted, she needed to keep a clear head.

She took a fork, picked up a delicate morsel of fish and said, 'Lucy tells me that you're her husband's cousin. Are you a diplomat, too?'

Conventional, impersonal conversation. That was the ticket, she thought as she tasted the fish. Correction, ate the fish. She wasn't tasting a thing.

'No.' He shrugged. 'My branch of the family has been personae non gratae at the Ramal Hamrahn court for three generations.'

No, no, no!

That wasn't how it worked. She was supposed to ask a polite question. He was supposed to respond in kind. Like when you said, 'How are you?' and the only proper response was any variation on, 'Fine, thanks.'

'Personae non gratae at the Embassy, too,' he continued, 'until I became involved in one of Lucy's charitable missions.'

Better. Charity was Rose's life and, firmly quashing a desire to know more about the black sheep thing, what his family had done three generations ago that was so terrible—definitely off the polite questions list—Lydia concentrated on that.

'You help Lucy?'

'She hasn't mentioned what I do?' he countered.

'Maybe she thought I'd try and poach you.' Now that was *good*. 'What do you do for her?'

'Not much. She needed to ship aid to an earthquake zone. I offered her the use of an aircraft— we took it from there.'

Very impressively 'not much', she thought. She'd definitely mention him to Rose. Maybe they would hit it off.

She squashed down the little curl of something green that tried to escape her chest.

'That would be the one your father owns?' she asked. Again, she'd imagined a small executive jet. Clearly, where this family was concerned, she needed to start thinking bigger.

'Flying is like driving, Rose. When you get your

licence, you don't want to borrow your father's old crate. You want a shiny new one of your own.'

'You do?'

A lot bigger, she thought. He came from a two-plane family.

Something else occurred to her.

He'd said no one in his family did anything seriously, but that couldn't possibly be true. Not in his case, anyway. Obtaining a basic pilot's licence was not much different from getting a driving licence—apart from the cost—but stepping up to this level took more than money. It took brains, dedication, a great deal of hard work.

And, yes, a heck of a lot of money.

'You are such a fraud,' she said but, far from annoying her, it eased her qualms about her own pretence.

'Fraud?'

Kal paused with a fork halfway to his lips. It hadn't taken Lucy ten minutes to rumble him, demand to know what he expected from Hanif in return for his help, but she knew the family history and he hadn't expected his offer to be greeted with open arms.

He'd known the only response was to be absolutely honest with her. That had earned him first her sympathy and then, over the years, both her and Hanif's friendship.

Rose had acted as if she had never heard of him but, unless Lucy had told her, how did she—

'Not serious?' she prompted. 'Exactly how long did it take you to qualify to fly something like this?'

Oh, right. She was still talking about the flying. 'I do fun seriously,' he said.

'Fun?'

'Give me a chance and I'll show you,' he said. Teasing was, after all, a two-way street; the only difference between them was that she blushed. Then, realising how that might have sounded, he very nearly blushed himself. 'I didn't mean... Lucy suggested you might like to go fishing.'

'Fishing?' She pretended to consider. 'Let me see. Wet. Smelly. Maggots. That's your idea of fun?'

That was a challenge if ever he'd heard one. And one he was happy to accept. 'Wet, smelly and then you get to dry out, get warm while you barbecue the catch on the beach.'

'Wet, smelly, smoky and then we get sand in our food. Perfect,' she said, but a tiny twitch at the corner of her mouth suggested that she was hooked and, content, he let it lie.

Rose speared another forkful of fish.

'In her letter,' she said, 'Lucy suggested I'd enjoy a trip to the souk. Silk. Spices. Gold.'

'Heat, crowds, people with cellphones taking your photograph? I thought you wanted peace and privacy.'

'Even the paparazzi have children to feed and educate,' she said. 'And publicity oils the wheels of charity. The secret is not to give them something so sensational that they don't have to keep coming back for more.'

'That makes for a very dull life,' he replied gravely, playing along, despite the fact that it appeared to fly directly in the face of what Lucy had told him. 'But if you wore an *abbayah,* kept your eyes down, your hair covered, you might pass unnoticed.'

'A disguise?'

'More a cover-up. There's no reason to make it easy for them, although there's no hiding your height.'

'Don't worry about it.'

'It's what I'm here for.'

'Really?' And she was the one challenging him, as if she knew he had an agenda of his own. But she didn't wait for an answer. 'So what did you buy?' she asked.

He must have looked confused because she added, 'Car, not plane. I wouldn't know one plane from another. When you passed your test?' she prompted. 'A Ferrari? Porsche?'

'Far too obvious. I chose a Morgan.'

Her turn to look puzzled.

'It's a small sports car. A roadster,' he explained, surprised she didn't know that. 'The kind of thing that you see pilots driving in old World War Two movies? My father put my name on the waiting list on my twelfth birthday.'

'There's a waiting list?'

'A long one. They're hand-built,' he replied, smiling at her astonishment. 'I took delivery on my seventeenth birthday.'

'I'll add patient to serious,' she replied. 'What do you drive now?'

'I still have the Morgan.'

'The same one?'

'I'd have to wait a while for another one, so I've taken very good care of it.'

'I'm impressed.'

'Don't be. It stays in London while I'm constantly on the move, but for the record I drive a Renault in France, a Lancia in Italy and in New York…' he grinned '…I take a cab.'

'And in Ramal Hamrah?' she asked.

Suddenly the smile took real effort.

'There's an old Land Rover that does the job. What about you?' he asked, determined to shift the focus of their conversation to her. 'What do you drive for pleasure?'

She leaned forward, her lips parted on what he was sure would have been a protest that she wasn't finished with the question of Ramal Hamrah. Maybe something in his expression warned her that she was treading on dangerous ground and, after a moment, she sat back. Thought about it.

He assumed that was because her grandfather's garage offered so wide a choice. But then she said, 'It's...' she used her hands to describe a shape '...red.'

'Red?' Why was he surprised? 'Good choice.'

'I'm glad you approve.'

The exchange was, on the surface, perfectly serious and yet the air was suddenly bubbling with laughter.

'Do you really have homes in all those places?' she asked.

'Just a mews cottage in London. My mother, my father's first wife, was a French actress. She has a house in Nice and an apartment in Paris. His second wife, an English aristocrat, lives in Belgravia and Gloucestershire. His third was an American heiress. She has an apartment in the Dakota Building in New York and a house in the Hamptons.'

'An expensive hobby, getting married.' Then, when he made no comment, 'You stay with them? Even your ex-stepmothers?'

'Naturally. They're a big part of my life and I like to spend time with my brothers and sisters.'

'Oh, yes. I didn't think...' She seemed slightly flustered by his father's admittedly louche lifestyle. 'So where does Italy come in? The Lancia?' she prompted.

'My father bought a palazzo in Portofino when he was wooing a contessa. It didn't last—she quickly realised that he wasn't a man for the long haul—but he decided to keep the house. As he said, when a man has as many ex-wives and mistresses and children as he has, he needs a bolt-hole. Not true, of course. It's far too tempting a location. He's never alone.'

He expected her to laugh. Most people took what he said at face value, seeing only the glamour.

'From his history, I'd say he's never wanted to be,' Rose said, her smile touched with compassion. 'It must have been difficult. Growing up.'

'Life was never dull,' he admitted with rather more flippancy than he felt. Without a country, a purpose, his grandfather had become rudderless, a glamorous playboy to whom women flocked, a lifestyle that his father had embraced without question. His family were his world but after one relationship that had kept the gossip magazines on their toes for eighteen months as they'd followed every date, every break up, every make up, he'd realised that he had no wish to live like that for the rest of his life.

'You didn't mention Ramal Hamrah,' she said, ignoring the opportunity he'd given her to talk about her own grandfather. Her own life.

Rare in a woman.

Rare in anyone.

Most people would rather talk about themselves.

'Do you have a home there?'

'There is a place that was once home,' he told her because the apartment overlooking the old harbour, bought off plan from a developer who had never heard of Kalil al-Zaki, could never be described as the home of his heart, his soul. 'A faded photograph that hangs upon my grandfather's wall. A place of stories of the raids, battles, celebrations that are the history of my family.'

Stories that had grown with the telling until they had become the stuff of legend.

It was an image that the old man looked at with longing. Where he wanted to breathe his last. Where he wanted to lie for eternity, at one with the land he'd fought for.

And Kalil would do anything to make that possible. Not that sitting here, sharing a meal with Lady Rose Napier was as tedious as he'd imagined it would be.

'No one has lived there for a long time,' he said.

For a moment he thought she was going to ask him to tell her more, but all she said was, 'I'm sorry.'

She was quiet for a moment, as if she understood the emptiness, the sense of loss and he began to see why people, even those who had never met her, instinctively loved her.

She had an innate sensitivity. A face that invited confidences. Another second and he would have told her everything but, at exactly the right moment, she said, 'Tell me about your brothers and sisters.'

'How long have you got?' he asked, not sure whether he was relieved or disappointed. 'I have one sister, a year younger than me. I have five half-sisters, three half-brothers and six, no seven, steps of both sexes and half a dozen who aren't actually related by blood but are still family.'

She counted them on her long, slender fingers.

'Sixteen?' she asked, looking at him in amazement. 'You've got sixteen brothers and sisters? Plus six.'

'At the last count. Sarah, she's the English ex, and her husband are about to have another baby.'

Lydia sat back in her chair, stunned. As an only child she had dreamed of brothers and sisters, but this was beyond imagining.

'Can you remember all their names?' she asked.

'Of course. They are my family.' Then, seeing her doubt, he held up his hand and began to list them. 'My sister is Adele. She's married to a doctor, Michel, and they have two children, Albert and Nicole. My mother has two other daughters by her second husband...'

As they ate, Kal talked about his family in France, in England and America. Their partners and children. The three youngest girls whose mothers his father had never actually got around to marrying but were all part of a huge extended family. All undoubtedly adored.

His family, but nothing about himself, she realised. Nothing about his personal life and she didn't press him. How a man talked about his family said a lot about him. She didn't need anyone to tell her that he was a loyal and caring son. That he loved his family. It was there in his smile as he told stories about his mother in full drama queen mode, about his sister. His pride in all their achievements.

If he'd had a wife or partner, children of his own, he would certainly have talked about them, too. With love and pride.

'You're so lucky having a big family,' she told him as they laughed at a story about one of the boys causing mayhem at a party.

'That's not the half of it,' he assured her. 'My grandfather set the standard. Five wives, ten children. Do you want their names, too? Or shall I save that for a rainy day?'

'Please tell me that it doesn't rain in Ramal Hamrah.'

'Not often,' he admitted.

Neither of them said anything while Atiya cleared the table, placed a tray of sweet things, tiny cakes, nuts, fruit, before them.

'Can I bring you coffee or tea?' Atiya asked.

'Try some traditional mint tea,' Kal suggested

before she could reply. He spoke to Atiya in Arabic and, after a swift exchange, which apparently elicited the right answer, he said, 'Not made with a bag, it will be the real thing.'

'It sounds delicious.'

'It is.'

He indicated the tray, but she shook her head.

'It all looks wonderful but I can't eat another thing,' Lydia said. 'I hope there's a pool in Bab el Sama. If I keep eating like this I won't fit into any of my clothes when I get home.'

'I don't understand why women obsess about being thin,' he said.

'No? Have you never noticed the way celebrities who put on a few pounds are ridiculed? That would be women celebrities,' she added.

'I know. Adele went through a bad patch when she was a teenager.' He shook his head. Took a date, but made no attempt to push her to eat. Instead, he bestowed a lazy smile on her and said, 'Now you know my entire family. Your turn to tell me about yours.'

Lydia waited while Atiya served the mint tea.

Completely absorbed by his complex relationships, the little vignettes of each of his brothers and sisters that had made them all seem so real, she had totally forgotten the pretence and needed a moment to gather herself.

'Everyone knows my story, Kal.'

Kal wondered. While he'd been telling her about his family, she'd been by turns interested, astonished, amused. But the moment he'd mentioned hers, it was as if the lights had dimmed.

'I know what the press write about you,' he said. 'What Lucy has told me.'

That both her parents had been killed when she was six years old and she'd been raised by an obsessively controlling grandfather, the one who'd taken a newspaper headline literally and turned her into the 'people's angel'.

'What you see is what you get,' she replied, picking up the glass of tea.

Was it?

It was true that with her pale hair, porcelain skin and dazzling blue eyes she could have stepped out of a Renaissance painting.

But then there was that mouth. The full sultry lips that clung for a moment to the small glass as she tasted the tea.

A tiny piece of the crushed leaf clung to her lower lip and, as she gathered it in with the tip of her tongue, savouring the taste, he discovered that he couldn't breathe.

'It's sweet,' she said.

'Is that a problem?'

She shook her head. 'I don't usually put sugar in mint tea, but it's good.' She finished the tea, then caught at a yawn that, had she been anyone else, he would have sworn was fake. That she was simply making an excuse to get away. 'If you'll excuse me, Kal, it's been a long day and I'd like to try and get a couple of hours' sleep before we land.'

'Of course,' he said, easing her chair back so that she could stand up and walking with her to the door of her suite, unable to quite shake the feeling that she was bolting from the risk that he might expect the exposure of her own family in return for his un-accustomed openness.

Much as he adored them, he rarely talked about his family to outsiders. He'd learned very early how even the most innocent remark to a friend would be passed on to their parents and, in a very short time, would appear in print, twisted out of recognition by people who made a living out of ce-lebrity gossip.

Rose, though, had that rare gift for asking the right question, then listening to the answer in a way that made a man feel that it was the most impor-tant thing she'd ever heard.

But then, at the door, she confounded him, turning to face him and, for a moment, locked in that small, still bubble that enclosed two people who'd spent an evening together, all the more intimate because of their isolation as they flew high above the earth in their own small time capsule, neither of them moved and he knew that if she'd been any other woman, if he'd been any other man, he would have kissed her. That she would have kissed him back. Maybe done a lot more than kiss.

She was a warm, quick-witted, complex woman and there had, undoubtedly, been a connection between them, a spark that in another world might have been fanned into a flame.

But she was Lady Roseanne Napier, the 'people's angel'. And he had made a promise to his grandfather that nothing, no one, would divert him from keeping.

'Thank you for your company, Rose,' he said, taking her hand and lifting it to his lips, but his throat was unexpectedly constricted as he took a step back. He added, 'Sleep well.'

It was going to be a very long week.

CHAPTER FOUR

TIRED as she was, Lydia didn't sleep. Eyes closed, eyes open, it made no difference.

The hand Kal had kissed lay on the cover at her side and she had to press it down hard to keep it from flying to her mouth so that she could taste it.

Taste him.

His mouth had barely made contact and yet the back of her fingers throbbed as if burned, her body as fired up as if she'd had a faint electric shock.

In desperation she flung herself off the bed, tore off her clothes and threw herself beneath the shower, soaping herself with a gel that smelled faintly of lemons. Warm at first, then cooler until she was shivering. But still her skin burned and when Lydia lifted her hand to her face, breathed in, it was not the scent of lemons that filled her head.

It was nothing as simple as scent, but a distillation of every look, every word, the food they'd eaten, the mint tea they'd drunk. It had stirred the air as he'd bent over her hand, leaving her faint with the intensity of pure sensation that had rippled through her body. Familiar and yet utterly unknown. Fire and ice. Remembered pleasure and the certainty of pain.

Distraction.

She needed a distraction, she thought desperately as she wrapped herself in a fluffy gown, combed out her damp hair, applied a little of some unbelievably expensive moisturiser in an attempt to counteract the drying effects of pressured air.

She could usually lose herself in a book—she'd managed it earlier, even dozed off—but she'd left her book in the main cabin and nothing on earth would tempt her back out there until she had restored some semblance of calm order to her racketing hormones.

She chose another book from the selection Rose had packed for her and settled back against the pillows. All she had to do now was concentrate. It shouldn't be hard, the book was by a favourite author, but the words refused to stay still.

Instead they kept merging into the shape of Kal's mouth, the sensuous curve of his lower lip.

'Get a grip, Lydie!' she moaned, abandoning the book and sliding down to the floor where she sat cross-legged, hoping that yoga breathing would instil a modicum of calm, bring her down from what had to be some kind of high induced by an excess of pheromones leaking into the closed atmosphere of the aircraft.

Combined with the adrenalin charge of confronting the newsmen, tension at the prospect of facing airport security with Rose's passport, then the shock of Kalil al-Zaki arriving to mess up all their carefully laid plans, it was scarcely any wonder that the words wouldn't stay still.

That he was astoundingly attractive, took his duty of care to extraordinary lengths, had flirted outrageously with her hadn't helped.

When they'd sat down to their dinner party in the sky, she'd been determined to keep conversation on the impersonal level she employed at cocktail parties, launches.

Kal had blown that one right out of the water with his reply to her first question and she'd forgotten all about the 'plan' as he'd in turn amused, shocked, delighted her with tales of his family life.

And made her envious at the obvious warmth and affection they shared. His might be a somewhat chaotic and infinitely extendable family but, as an only child with scarcely any close relations, she'd been drawn in by the charm of having so many people who were connected to you. To care for and who cared back. Who would not want to be part of that?

And that was only half the story, she realised. Sheikh Hanif was his cousin and there must be a vast Ramal Hamrahn family that he hadn't even mentioned, other than to tell her that he and his family were personae non gratae at the Ramal Hamrahn court.

More, she suspected, than he told most people. But then Rose had that effect on people. Drew them out.

Instead, he had turned the spotlight on her, which was when she'd decided to play safe and retire.

There was a tap on the door. 'Madam? We'll be landing in fifteen minutes.'

'Thank you, Atiya.'

She reapplied a light coating of make-up. Rose might want her picture in the paper, but not looking as if she'd just rolled out of bed. Brushed out her hair. Dressed. Putting herself back together so that she was fit to be seen in public.

The seat belt sign pinged as she returned to the cabin and she shook her head as Kal half rose, waved him back to his seat and sat down, fastening her seat belt without incident before placing her hands out of reach in her lap. Not looking at him, but instead peering out at the skein of lights skirting the coast, shimmering in the water below them.

'Landing holds no terrors for you?' Kal asked and she turned to glance at him. A mistake. Groomed to perfection he was unforgettable, but after eight hours in the air, minus his tie, in need of a shave, he was everything a woman would hope to wake up to. Sexily rumpled, with eyes that weren't so much come to bed, as let's stay here for the rest of the day.

As if she'd know…

Quickly turning back to the window as they sank lower and the capital, Rumaillah, resolved from a mass of lights into individual streets, buildings, her attention was caught by a vast complex dominated by floodlit domes, protected by high walls, spread across the highest point of the city.

'What is that?' she asked.

Kal put a hand on the arm of her chair and leaned across so that he could see out of her window, but he must have dialled down the pheromone count, or maybe, like her, he was tired because, even this close, there was no whoosh of heat.

'It's the Emiri Palace,' he told her.

'But it's huge.'

'It's not like Buckingham Palace,' he said, 'with everything under one roof. The Emir's palace is not just one building. There are gardens, palaces for his wives, his children and their families. The Emiri offices are there too, and his Majlis where his people can go and see him, talk to him, ask for his help, or to intercede in disputes.'

'I like the sound of that. The man at the top being approachable.'

'I doubt it's quite as basic as it was in the old days,' he replied. There was an edge to his voice that made her forget about the exotic hilltop palace and look more closely at him. 'We've come a long way from a tent in the desert.'

We.

He might be excluded but he still thought of himself as one of them. She resisted the urge to ask him. If he wanted her to know he would tell her.

But, fascinated, she pressed, 'In theory, anyone can approach him?'

'In theory.'

There was something in his voice, a tension, anger, that stopped her from saying more.

'And you said "wives". How many has he got?'

'The Emir? Just one. The tradition of taking more than one wife began when a man would take the widows, children of brothers slain in battle into his family. Then it became a sign of wealth. It's rare these days.' Then, with a curl of his lip that could have been mistaken for a smile if you hadn't seen the real thing, 'My family are not typical.'

'And even they take only one at a time,' she replied, lifting her voice a little so that it was gently teasing.

'Legally,' he agreed. 'In practice there tends to be some overlap.'

'And you, Kal?'

'How many wives do I have?' And this time the

smile was a little less forced. 'None, but then I'm a late starter.'

That she doubted, but suddenly the runway lights were whizzing past and then they were down with barely a bump.

Before she left the aircraft she visited the cockpit—now that it was safely on the ground—to thank the crew for a wonderful flight and, by the time she stepped outside into the warm moist air of the Gulf, her luggage had already been transferred to the waiting helicopter.

'Ready?' Kal asked.

She swallowed, nodded.

She'd been bold enough when the reality of committing her safety to what seemed to be a very small, fragile thing beside the bulk of the jet had been a distant eight hours away.

Now she was afraid that if she opened her mouth her teeth would start chattering like a pair of castanets.

Apparently she wasn't fooling Kal because he said, 'That ready? It's not too late to change your mind.'

She refused to be so pathetic and, shaking her head once in a *let's get this over with* gesture, she took a determined step forward. His hand at her back helped keep her moving when she faltered. Got her through the door and into her seat.

He said something to the pilot as he followed

her—what, she couldn't hear above the noise of the engine.

He didn't bother to ask if she needed help with the straps, but took them from her and deftly fastened them as if it was something he'd been doing all his life. Maybe he had.

Then he gently lowered the earphones that would keep out the noise and allow the pilot to talk to them onto her head, settling them into place against her ears.

'Okay?' he said, not that she could hear, but she'd been sent on a lip-reading and signing course by the supermarket and had no problem understanding him.

She nodded and he swiftly dealt with his own straps and headset before turning in his seat so that he was facing her.

'Hands,' he said, and when she lifted them to look at them, not knowing what she was supposed to do with them, he took them in his and held them as the rotor speed built up.

She tried to smile but this was far worse than in a passenger aircraft. Everything—the tarmac, the controls, the reality of what was happening—was so close, so immediate, so in your face.

There was no possibility of pretence here.

No way you could tell yourself that you were on the number seven bus going to work and, as the helicopter lifted from the ground, leaving her stomach behind, she tightened her grip of his hands but, before the scream bubbling up in her throat could escape, Kal leaned forward and said, 'Trust me, Rose.'

And then he kissed her.

It wasn't a gentle kiss. It was powerful, strong, demanding her total attention and the soaring lift as they rose into the air, leaving the earth far behind them, was echoed by a rush of pure exhilaration that flooded through her.

This was flying. This was living. And, without a thought for what would follow, she kissed him back.

Kal had seen Rose's momentary loss of courage as she'd looked across the tarmac from the top of the aircraft steps to the waiting helicopter, followed by the lift of her chin, an unexpectedly stubborn look that no photographer had ever managed to capture, as she'd refused to back down, switch to the car.

It didn't quite go with the picture Lucy had painted of the gentle, biddable girl—woman— who'd lovingly bowed to the dictates of her grandfather. Who was desperate for some quiet time while she fathomed out her future.

That was a chin that took no prisoners and, certain that once she was airborne she'd be fine, he hadn't argued. Even so, her steps had faltered as they'd neared the helicopter and as they'd boarded he'd told the pilot to get a move on before she had time for second thoughts.

This was not a moment for the usual round of

'Lady Rose' politeness, handshakes, introductions. All that could wait until they arrived at Bab el Sama.

And he'd done his best to keep her distracted, busy, her eyes on him rather than the tarmac.

But as the engine note changed in the moment prior to take-off, her hands had gripped his so hard that her nails had dug into his palms and he thought that he'd completely misjudged the situation, that she was going to lose it.

Hysterics required more than a reassuring hand or smile, they needed direct action and there were just two options—a slap or a kiss.

No contest.

Apart from the fact that the idea of hitting anyone, let alone a frightened woman, was totally abhorrent to him, letting go of her hands wasn't an option.

His 'Trust me' had been a waste of breath—she couldn't hear him—but it had made him feel better as he went in for the kiss, hard and fast. This wasn't seduction, this was survival and he wanted her total attention, every emotion, fixed on him, even if that emotion was outrage.

He didn't get outrage.

For a moment there was nothing. Only a stunned stillness. Then something like an imperceptible sigh breathed against his mouth as her eyes closed, the tension left her body and her lips softened, yielded and clung to his for a moment, warm and sweet as a girl's first kiss. Then parted, hot as a fallen angel tempting him to sin.

At which point the only one in danger of losing anything was him.

How long was a kiss? A heartbeat, minutes, a lifetime?

It seemed like all three as his hands, no longer captive, moved to her waist, her back, drawing her closer. A heartbeat while he breathed in the clean, fresh scent of her skin; minutes as the kiss deepened and something darker, more compelling stirred his senses; a lifetime while his hormones stampeded to fling themselves into the unknown without as much as a thought for the consequences.

Exactly like his grandfather. Exactly like his father.

Men without a purpose, without a compass, who'd put their own selfish desires above everything.

That thought, like a pitcher of cold water, was enough to jar him back to reality, remind him why he was here, and he drew back.

Rose took a gasping, thready little breath as he broke the connection. Sat unmoving for long moments before her lids slowly rose, almost as if the long, silky lashes were too heavy to lift.

Her lips parted as if she was going to speak but she closed them again without saying a word, instead concentrating on her breathing, slowing it down using some technique that she'd probably learned long ago to manage nerves.

When she raised her lashes again, she was sufficiently in control to speak.

He couldn't hear what she was saying, but she mouthed the words so carefully that he could lip-read enough to get the gist, which was, as near as damn it, 'If you were that scared, Kal, you should have told me. We could have taken the car.'

It was the response of a woman who, with ten years of interaction with the public behind her, knew exactly how to rescue an awkward moment, who could put anyone at ease with a word.

It put a kiss that had spiralled out of hand into perspective, allowing them both to move on, forget it.

Well, what had he expected?

That she'd fall apart simply because he'd kissed her?

She might—or might not—be a virgin princess, but she'd already proved, with her dry and ready wit, that she was no shrinking violet.

He knew he should be grateful that his rescue mission had been recognised for what it was. Received with her legendary good humour, charm.

But he wasn't grateful. Didn't want to forget.

He wanted to pull her close, kiss her again until that classy English cool sizzled away to nothing, her 'charm' shattered in a pyrotechnic blaze that would light up the night sky and this tender Rose, nurtured under glass, broke out and ran wild.

It wasn't going to happen.

Even if had been an appropriate time or place, their destinies were written. Even if she rejected the Earl in waiting her grandfather had lined up to walk her down the aisle and chose someone for herself, it was never going to be the scion of a disgraced and dispossessed exile.

And when he took a bride, it would not be in response to carnal attraction, the sexual chemistry that masqueraded as love, stealing your senses, stealing your life. His marriage would be an affair of state that would cement an alliance with one of the great Ramal Hamrahn families—the Kassimi, the Attiyah or the Darwish. The surrender of one of their precious daughters an affirmation that he had restored his family to their rightful place.

Had brought his grandfather home.

But time was running out. He had been infinitely patient and he no longer had years. His grandfather was already on borrowed time, stubbornly refusing to accept the death sentence that had been passed on him until he saw his grandson married as a Khatib should be married. Could die in peace in the place where he'd been born.

An affair that would cause scandalised headlines worldwide would do nothing to help his cause. He had to keep himself focused on what was important, he reminded himself, even while he held Rose, could feel her corn silk hair tumbling over his hands, her soft breath upon his cheek.

Fight, as he'd always fought, the demanding, selfish little gene he'd inherited, the one telling him to go for it and hang the consequences. The knowledge that she wanted it as much as he did. The pretence that it would just be a holiday romance, wouldn't hurt anyone.

That wasn't true. You could not give that much and walk away without losing something of yourself, taking something of the other with you. Already, in the closeness of the hours they had spent together, he had given more than he should. Had taken more. He concentrated on the clean, vast infinity of the night sky—diamonds against black velvet—until it filled his head, obliterating everything else.

Lydia wanted to curl up and die with embarrassment. Not because Kal had kissed her. That had been no more than straightforward shock tactics, designed to prevent her from doing something stupid.

And it had worked.

She hadn't screamed, hadn't tried to grab the pilot and make him stop.

Why would she when the minute his lower lip had touched hers, she'd forgotten all about the fact that they were rising from the ground in a tiny glass bubble?

Forgotten her fear.

Forgotten everything as the warmth of his mouth

had first heated her lips, then curled through every part of her body, touching the frozen core that had remained walled up, out of reach for so long. As it felt the warmth, whimpered to be set free, he'd drawn her close and the kiss had ceased to be shock tactics and had become real, intense.

A lover's kiss, and as her arms had wrapped themselves around his neck she hadn't cared who he thought she was. He was kissing her as if he wanted her and that was all that mattered, because she wanted him right back.

She hadn't cared that he thought it was Rose who'd reacted so wantonly. Who'd wanted more. Who would still be kissing him as if the world was about to end if he hadn't backed off.

He was still holding her, still close enough that she could feel him breathing. Close enough that when she was finally brave enough to open her eyes she could see the *what-the-hell-happened-there?* look in his eyes. She wanted to explain that it was okay. That she wasn't Rose, just some dumb idiot girl who was having a very strange day.

That he could forget all about it. Forget about her.

But that was impossible.

She had to put things right, restore Rose's reputation. Instead, she closed her eyes again and concentrated on her breathing. Slowing it down. And, as her mind cleared, she realised that the answer was simple. Fear.

She could put it all down to her fear. Or his, she thought, remembering how he'd pretended to be the one who was scared as they'd lifted off.

If she could make him laugh it would be all right. They would be able to move on, pretend it had never happened.

But he hadn't laughed; there was no reaction at all and she realised that just because she could lip-read didn't mean that he could, too. He hadn't a clue what she was saying.

She took her hands from his shoulders, tried to concentrate on what he was saying as he looked up, beyond her. Shook her head to indicate that it hadn't got through.

He turned, looked straight at her as he repeated himself. 'And miss this?'

What?

She didn't want to take her eyes from him. While she was looking at him, while he was still holding her, she could forget that there was nothing but a thin wall of perspex between her and the sky.

But he lifted one of his dark brows a fraction of a millimetre, challenging her to be brave, and she finally tore her gaze from him, turned her head.

In the bubble of the helicopter they had an all round view of the sky which, away from the light pollution of the airport, the city, she could see as it was meant to be seen, with the constellations diamond-bright, the spangled shawl of the Milky Way spread across the heavens.

It was an awe-inspiring, terrifying sight. A reminder of how small they were. How vulnerable. And yet how spectacularly amazing and she didn't look away. But, although she wanted to reach back, share the moment with Kal, she remembered who she was supposed to be.

Not the woman on the checkout who anyone could—and did—flirt with. Not Lydia Young, who had a real problem with leaving the ground, but Lady Rose Napier, who could handle an unexpected kiss with the same natural charm as any other minor wobble in her day.

Instead, she concentrated on this unexpected gift he'd given her, searching for constellations that she recognised until she had to blink rather hard because her eyes were watering. At the beauty of the sky. That was all…

Kal must have said something. She didn't hear him, just felt his breath against her cheek, then, as he pointed down, she saw a scatter of lights below, the navigation lights of boats riding at anchor as they crossed a wide creek.

As they dropped lower, circling to land on the far bank, Lydia caught tantalising glimpses of the domes, arches of half a dozen or more exotic, beautiful beach houses. There was a private dock, boats, a long curve of white sand. And, behind it all, the dramatic, sharply rising background of jagged mountains, black against a sky fading to pre-dawn purple.

While she had not been fooled by the word 'cottage', had anticipated the kind of luxury that few people would ever experience, this was far beyond anything she could have imagined.

It reminded her of pictures she'd seen of the fantasy village of Portmeirion, more like a film set, or something out of a dream than anything real, and by the time the helicopter landed and she'd thanked the pilot, her heart was pounding with excitement, anticipation.

She'd been so determined to keep her reaction low-key, wanting to appear as if this was what she was used to, but that wasn't, in the end, a problem. As Kal took her hand and helped her down, she didn't have to fight to contain a *wow*. The reality was simply beyond words.

There was an open Jeep waiting for them, but she didn't rush to climb in. Instead, she walked to the edge of the landing pad so that she could look out over the creek. Eager to feel solid earth beneath her feet. To breathe in real air laden with the salty scent of the sea, wet sand, something else, sweet and heavy, that she did not recognise.

It was still quite dark, but all the way down to the beach lights threaded through huge old trees, shone in the water.

'I don't think I've ever seen anything so beautiful,' she said as Kal joined her. 'I expected sand, desert, not all this green.'

'The creek is in a valley and has a microclimate of its own,' he said. 'And Sheikh Jamal's father began an intensive tree planting programme when he took the throne fifty years ago.'

'Well, good for him.'

'Not everyone is happy. People complain that it rains more these days.'

'It rains more everywhere,' she replied, looking around for the source of the sweet, heady fragrance filling the air. 'What is that scent?' she asked.

'Jasmine.' He crossed to a shrub, broke off a piece and offered it to her with the slightest of bows. 'Welcome to Bab el Sama, Lady Rose,' he said.

CHAPTER FIVE

LYDIA, holding the spray of tiny white flowers, didn't miss the fact that he'd put the 'Lady' back in front of her name. That his voice had taken on a more formal tone.

That was good, she told herself. Perfect, in fact.

One kiss could be overlooked, especially when it was purely medicinal, but it wouldn't do to let him think that Lady Rose encouraged such liberties.

'The luggage is loaded.'

He might as well have been done with it and added *madam*.

'The pilot won't take off until we're clear of the pad. If you are ready?'

It was right there in his tone of voice. It was the one he'd used before he'd started flirting. Before she'd started encouraging him.

She turned to look at the Jeep, where a white-robed servant was waiting to drive them to the cottage. She'd been sitting for hours and, now she was on her feet, wasn't eager to sit again unless she had to.

'Is it far?' she asked. 'I'd like to stretch my legs.'

He spoke to the driver, who answered with a shake of his head, a wave of the hand to indicate a path through the trees.

Lydia watched the exchange, then frowned.

Kal wasn't telling the man that they'd walk, she realised, but asking the way. He'd seemed so familiar with everything that she'd assumed he had been here before, but clearly this was his first time, too.

She hadn't taken much notice when he'd said his family were personae non gratae at the Ramal Hamrahn court.

Court, for heaven's sake. Nobody talked like that any more. But now she wondered why, for three generations, his family had lived in Europe.

What past crime was so terrible that he and his siblings had never been invited to share this idyllic summer playground with their cousins? It wasn't as if they'd be cramped for space. Even if they all turned up at the same time.

'There's a path through the gardens,' he said. Then, 'Will you be warm enough?'

'You're kidding?'

Rose had warned her that it wouldn't be hot at this time of year and maybe it wasn't for this part of the world. Compared with London in December, however, the air felt soft and balmy.

Then, as a frown creased Kal's brows, she realised that her response had been pure Lydia. Not quite on a scale with Eliza Doolittle's blooper at the races, but near enough.

She was tired and forgetting to keep up the Lady Rose act. Or maybe it was her subconscious fighting it. Wanting to say to him *Look at me, see who I really am...*

'The temperature is quite perfect,' she added. And mentally groaned. She'd be doing the whole, *How kind of you to let me come* routine if she didn't get a grip.

Didn't put some distance between them.

In a determined attempt to start as she had meant to go on—before he'd taken her hand, made her laugh—she said, 'You don't have to come with me, Kal. Just point me in the right direction and I can find my own way.'

'No doubt. However, I'd rather not have to explain to Lucy why I had to send out a search party for you.'

'Why would she ever know?'

'You're kidding?'

She ignored the wobble somewhere beneath her midriff as he repeated her words back to her as if he was mocking her, almost as if he knew. 'Actually, I'm not,' she said, knowing that it was only her guilty conscience making her think that way.

'No? Then let me explain how it would happen.

At the first hint of trouble the alarm would be raised,' he explained. 'The Chief of Security would be alerted. The Emir's office would be informed, your Ambassador would be summoned—'

'Okay, okay,' she said, holding up her hands in surrender, laughing despite everything. 'I get it. If I go missing, you'll be hauled up before the Emir and asked to explain what the heck you were doing letting me wander around by myself.'

There was a momentary pause, as if he was considering the matter. Then he shrugged. 'Something like that, but all you need to worry about is the fact that Lucy would know what had happened within five minutes.'

Not something she would want to happen and, while she didn't think for one moment she'd get lost, she said, 'Point taken. Lead the way, Mr al-Zaki.'

The steps were illuminated by concealed lighting and perfectly safe, as was the path, but he took her arm, presumably in case she stumbled.

Rose wouldn't make a fuss, she told herself. No doubt someone had been holding her hand, taking her arm, keeping her safe all her life. It was what she'd wanted to escape. The constant surveillance. The cotton wool.

As he tucked her arm beneath his, she told herself that she could live with it for a week. And, as she leaned on him a little, that he would expect nothing else.

The path wound through trees and shrubs. Herbs had been planted along the edges, spilling over so that as they brushed past lavender, sage, marjoram and other, less familiar, scents filled the air.

Neither of them spoke. The only sound was the trickle of water running, the splash of something, a fish or a frog, in a dark pool. She caught glimpses of mysterious arches, an ornate summer house, hidden among the trees. And above them the domes and towers she'd seen from the air.

'It's magical,' she said at last as, entranced, she stored up the scents, sounds, images for some day, far in the future, when she would tell her children, grandchildren about this *Arabian Nights* adventure. Always assuming she ever got to the point where she could trust a man sufficiently to get beyond arm's length flirting.

Meet someone who would look at her and see Lydia Young instead of her famous alter ego.

The thought leached the pleasure from the moment.

She'd been featured in the local newspaper when she'd first appeared as Lady Rose, had even been invited to turn up as Rose and switch on the Christmas lights one year when the local council were on a cost cutting drive and couldn't afford a real celebrity.

Even at work, wearing an unflattering uniform and with her name badge clearly visible, the customers had taken to calling her 'Rose' and she couldn't deny that she'd loved it. It had made her feel special.

Here, now, standing in her heroine's shoes, she discovered that being someone else was not enough.

That, instead of looking at Lydia and seeing Rose, she wanted someone, or maybe just Kalil al-Zaki, to look at Rose and see Lydia.

Because that was who she'd been with him.

It was Lydia who'd been afraid of taking off, whose hand he had held. Lydia he'd kissed.

But he'd never know that. And she could never tell him.

He was silent too and once she risked a glance, but the floor level lighting only threw his features into dark, unreadable shadows.

Then, as they turned a corner, the view opened up to reveal that while behind them, above the darker bulk of the mountains, the stars still blazed, on the far side of the creek a pale edge of mauve was seeping into the pre-dawn purple.

'It's nearly dawn,' she said, surprised out of her momentary descent into self-pity. It still felt like the middle of the night, but she'd flown east, was four hours closer to the day than her mother, fast asleep in London.

She was on another continent at sunrise and, to witness it, all she had to do was stand here and wait.

Kal didn't even ask what she wanted to do. He knew.

'There's a summer house over there,' he said, urging her in the direction of another intricately decorated domed and colonnaded structure perfectly situated to enjoy the view. 'You can watch in comfort.'

'No…'

It was open at the front and there were huge cane chairs piled with cushions. Total luxury. A place to bring a book, be alone, forget everything. Maybe later. Not now.

'I don't want anything between me and the sky,' she said, walking closer to the edge of the paved terrace where the drop was guarded by a stone balustrade. 'I want to be outside where I can feel it.'

He let her go, didn't follow her and she tried not to mind.

Minding was a waste of time. Worse. It was a stupid contradiction. Distance was what she had wanted and the old lady with the wand was, it seemed, still on the job, granting wishes as if they were going out of fashion.

She should be pleased.

It wasn't as if she'd expected or needed to be diverted, amused. She had a pile of great books to amuse her, occupy her mind, and exploring the garden, wandering along the shore should be diversion enough for anyone. If the forbidden delights of Kal al-Zaki's diversionary tactics hadn't been such a potent reminder of everything she was missing. The life that she might have had if she hadn't looked like Lady Rose.

But then, as the mauve band at the edge of the sky widened, became suffused with pink, she heard a step behind her and, as she half turned, Kal settled something soft around her.

For a moment his hands lingered on her shoulders, tense and knotted from sitting for too long, and without thinking she leaned into his touch, seeking ease from his long fingers. For a moment she thought he was going to respond, but then he stepped back, putting clear air between them.

'You will get cold standing out here,' he said with a brusqueness that suggested he had, after all, been affected by their closeness. That he, too, was aware that it would be inappropriate to take it further.

'And you don't want to explain to Lucy how I caught a chill on your watch?' Light, cool, she told herself.

'That wouldn't bother me.' He joined her at the balustrade, but kept his eyes on the horizon. 'I'd simply explain that you stubbornly, wilfully insisted on standing outside in the chill of dawn, that short of carrying you inside there was nothing I could do about it. I have no doubt that she'd agree with me.'

'She would?' The idea of Rose being wilful or stubborn was so slanderous that she had to take a breath, remind herself that he was judging Rose on her behaviour, before she nodded and said, 'She would.' And vow to try a little harder—a lot harder—to be like the real thing.

'His Highness, the Emir, on the other hand,' Kal continued, 'would be certain to think that I'd personally arranged for you to go down with pneumonia in order to cause him maximum embarrassment.'

He spoke lightly enough, inviting amusement, but she didn't laugh, sensing the underlying darkness behind his words.

'Why on earth would he think that?' she asked, but more questions crowded into her head. Without waiting for him to answer, she added, 'And why do you always refer to him as His Highness or the Emir?' She made little quote marks with her fingers, something else she realised Rose would never do, and let her hands drop. 'Sheikh Jamal is your uncle, isn't he, Kal?' she prompted when he didn't answer.

'Yes,' he said shortly. Then, before she could say another word, 'Someone will bring tea in a moment.'

'This is your first visit here, too,' she said, ignoring the abrupt change of subject. 'Why is that?'

'Watch the sunrise, for heaven's sake,' he practically growled at her.

In other words, Lydia, mind your own business, she thought, unsure whether she was pleased or sorry that she'd managed to rattle him out of his good manners.

Here was a mystery. A secret.

That she wasn't the only one hiding something made her feel less guilty about the secret she was keeping for Rose, although no better about lying to him, and without another word she did as she was told.

Neither of them spoke or moved again while the darkness rolled back and the sun, still below the horizon, lit up bubbles of cloud in a blaze of colour that was reflected in the creek, the sea beyond, turning them first carmine, then pink, then liquid gold. As it grew light, the dark shapes against the water resolved themselves into traditional dhows moored amongst modern craft and beyond, sprawling over the steep bank on the far side of the creek, she could see a small town with a harbour and market which were already coming to life.

'Wow,' she said at last. 'Double wow.'

She caught a movement as Kal turned to look at her and she shrugged.

'Well, what other word is there?' she asked.

'Bab el Sama.' He said the words softly. 'The Gate of Heaven.'

She swallowed at the poetry of the name and said, 'You win.'

He shook his head and said, 'Are you done?'

'Yes. Thank you for being so patient.'

'I wouldn't have missed it,' he assured her as they turned and walked back towards the summer house—such an ordinary word for something that looked as if it had been conjured up by Aladdin's djinn—where a manservant was laying out the contents of a large tray.

The man bowed and, eyes down, said, '*Assalam alaykum, sitti. Marhaba.*'

She turned to Kal for a translation. 'He said, "Peace be upon you, Lady. Welcome."'

'What should I say in return?'

'*Shukran. Alaykum assalam,*' Kal said. 'Thank you. And upon you peace.'

The man smiled, bowed again, when she repeated it, savouring the words on her tongue, locking them away in her memory, along with Bab el Sama. He left them to enjoy their breakfast in private.

As she chose a high-backed cane chair and sank into the vivid silk cushions, Kal unwrapped a napkin nestled in a basket to reveal warm pastries.

'Hungry?'

'I seem to have done nothing but eat since I left London,' she said. 'I'll have to swim the creek once a day if I'm going to keep indulging myself this way.'

Maybe it was the thought of all that effort, but right now all she wanted to do was close her eyes and go to sleep. Tea would help, she told herself, just about managing to control a yawn.

'Is that a yes or a no?' he asked, offering her the basket.

'Breakfast *is* the most important meal of the

day,' she said, succumbing to the enticing buttery smell. 'I suppose it is breakfast time?'

'It's whatever time you care to make it,' he assured her as he poured tea into two unbelievably thin china cups. 'Milk, lemon?'

'Just a touch of milk,' she said. Then, 'Should you be doing this?' He glanced at her. 'Waiting on me?'

Kal frowned, unable, for a moment, to imagine what she meant.

'Won't it ruin your image?'

'Image?'

He hadn't been brought up like his grandfather, his father, to believe he was a prince, above the mundane realities of the world. Nor, despite his Mediterranean childhood, was he one of those men who expected to live at home, waited on by a doting mother until he transferred that honour to a wife. Even if he had been so inclined, his mother had far more interesting things to do.

As had he.

His image was not about macho posturing. He had never needed to work, never would, but once he'd fallen in love with flying he had worked hard. He'd wanted to own aircraft but there was no fun in having them sit on the tarmac. He'd started Kalzak Air Services as a courier service. Now he flew freight worldwide. And he employed men and women—hundreds of them—on their qualifications and personal qualities first, last and everything in between.

'Hanif nursed his first wife, nursed Lucy, too, when she was injured,' he said.

'He did?'

'Lucy has not told you?'

'Only that he loved her.'

'He loved his first wife, too.' The girl who had been chosen for him. A traditional arranged marriage. 'He has been twice blessed.'

'Maybe he is a man who knows how to love,' she said.

Was that the answer?

It was not a concept he was comfortable with and, remembering what Lucy had said about Rose not being able to lift a finger without someone taking a photograph of her, he carried his own cup towards the edge of the promontory and leaned against the parapet. A man enjoying the view. It was what any-one would do in such a place.

The sun was in the wrong direction to reflect off a lens that would betray a paparazzo lying in wait to snatch a photograph. Not that he imagined they would ever be that careless. The only obvious activity was on the dhows as their crews prepared to head out to sea for a day's fishing.

As he scanned the wider panorama, the distant shore, he saw only a peaceful, contented community waking to a new day, going about its business.

He let the scene sink into his bones the way parched earth sucked up rain.

As a boy, his grandfather would have stood in this same spot, looking at the creek, the town, the desert beyond it, certain in the knowledge that every drop of water, every grain of sand would, *insh'Allah,* one day be his.

Except that Allah had not willed it. His grandfather had followed his heart instead of his head and, as a result, had been judged unworthy. A lesson he had learned well.

He drained his cup, took one last look, then returned to the summer house.

Sparrows, pecking at a piece of pastry, flew up at his approach and a single look was enough to tell him that Rose had fallen asleep, tea untouched, croissant untasted.

And, now that the sun had risen high enough to banish the shadows from the summer house and illuminate her clear, fair skin, he could see the faint violet smudges beneath her eyes.

Clearly sleep had eluded her aboard the plane and a long day, a long flight, had finally caught up with her. This was no light doze and he did not attempt to wake her, but as he bent and caught her beneath the knees she sighed.

'Shh,' he said, easing her arm over his shoulder, around his neck. 'Hold on.'

On some level of consciousness she must have

heard him because, as he lifted her out of the chair, she curled her hand around his neck and tucked her head into the hollow of his shoulder.

She wasn't anywhere near as light, as ethereal as she looked, he discovered as he carried her along the path to Lucy and Han's seaside retreat. Not an angel, but a real, solid woman and he was glad that the huge doors stood wide to welcome her.

He walked straight in, picking up a little group of women who, clucking anxiously, rushed ahead to open doors, circled round them tutting with disapproval and finally stood in his way when he reached her bedroom.

'Move,' he said, 'or I'll drop her.'

They scattered with little squeals of outrage, then, as he laid her on the bed, clicked his fingers for a cover in a manner that would have made his grandfather proud—and he would have protested was utterly alien to him—they rushed to do his bidding.

He removed her shoes but, about to reach for the button at her waist to make her more comfortable, he became aware of a silence, a collectively held breath.

He turned to look at the women clustered behind him, their shocked faces. And, remembering himself, took a step back.

That he could have undressed her in a completely detached manner had the occasion demanded it was not in question. But this was not

London, or New York, or Paris. This was a world where a man did not undress a woman unless he was married to her. He should not even be in her room.

'Make her comfortable,' he said with a gesture that would have done his grandfather proud. Maybe it was the place calling to his genes, he thought as he closed the door behind him, leaving the women to their task.

Then, to an old woman who'd settled herself, cross-legged, in front of the door like a palace guard, 'When she wakes she should have a massage.'

'It will be done, sidi.'

Lord…

'Don't call me that,' he said, straightening, easing his own aching limbs.

'You don't want to be given your title, Sheikh?' she asked, clearly not in the slightest bit in awe of him. 'Your grandfather wanted to be the Emir.'

About to walk away, he stopped, turned slowly back to face her.

'You knew him?'

'When he was a boy. A young man. Before he was foolish.'

She was the first person he'd met in Ramal Hamrah who was prepared to admit that. He sat before her, crossing his legs so that the soles of his feet were tucked out of sight.

'Here? You knew him here?'

'Here. In Rumaillah. At Umm al Sama. He was the wild one. Headstrong.' She shook her head. 'And he was stubborn, like his father. Once he'd said a thing, that was it.' She brushed her palms together in a gesture he'd seen many times. It signalled an end to discussion. That the subject was closed. 'They were two rocks.' She tilted her head in a birdlike gesture, examining him closely. 'You look like him,' she said after a while. 'Apart from the beard. A man should have a beard.'

He rubbed his hand self-consciously over his bare chin. He had grown a beard, aware that to be clean-shaven was the western way; it would be something else the Emir could hold against him.

'My grandfather doesn't have a beard these days,' he told her. The chemo baldness hadn't bothered him nearly as much as the loss of this symbol of his manhood and Kal had taken a razor to his own beard in an act of solidarity. It had felt odd for a while, but he'd got used to it.

'They say that he is dying,' she said. He did not ask who had said. Gossip flowed through the harem like water down the Nile.

'But still stubborn,' he replied. 'He refuses to die anywhere but in the place he still calls home.'

She nodded, 'You are stubborn, too,' she said, reaching up to pat his hand. 'You will bring him home, *insh'Allah*. It is your destiny.'

'Who are you?' he asked, with a sudden sinking feeling, the certainty that he had just made a complete fool of himself.

'I am Dena. I was found, out there,' she said with the wave of an elegant hand, the rattle of gold on her skinny wrists. 'Your great-grandmother took me into her house. Made me her daughter.'

Oh, terrific. This woman was the adopted child of the Khatib and he'd spoken to her as if she were a servant. But from the way she'd settled herself in front of Rose's bedroom door…

He'd been brought up on his grandfather's stories, had studied his family, this country, clung to a language that his father had all but forgotten, but he still had so much to learn.

He uncurled himself, got to his feet. 'My apologies, *sitti,*' he said with a formal bow.

'You have his charm, too,' she said. 'When you speak to him tell him that his sister Dena remembers him with fondness.' Then, 'Go.' She waved him away. 'Go. I will watch over your lady while you sleep.'

His lady…

Dena's words echoed in his mind as he stood beneath the shower, igniting again the memory of Rose's lips, warm, vital as they'd softened beneath him, parted for him. His mouth burned but as he sucked his lower lip into his mouth, ran a tongue over it, he tasted Rose and, instead of cooling it down, the heat surged like a contagion through his body.

Do you want me to protect her or make love to her…?

Lucy had not answered his question, but it would have made no difference either way. He was not free. He flipped the shower to cold and, lifting his face to the water, stood beneath it until he was chilled to the bone.

And still he burned.

CHAPTER SIX

LYDIA woke in slow gentle ripples of consciousness. Blissful comfort was the first stage. The pleasure of smooth, sweet-smelling sheets, the perfect pillow and, unwilling to surrender the pleasure, she turned over and fell back into its embrace.

The jewelled light filtering through ornate wooden shutters, colours dancing on white walls, seeping through her eyelids, came next.

She opened her eyes and saw an ornate band of tiny blue and green tiles shimmering like the early morning creek. She turned onto her back, looked up at a high raftered cedar wood ceiling.

It was true then. Not a dream.

'Bab el Sama.' She said the name out loud, savouring the feel of it in her mouth. The Gate of Heaven. '*Marhaba…*' Welcome. 'Kalil al-Zaki…' Trouble.

'You are awake, *sitti?*'

What?

She sat up abruptly. There was a woman, her head, body swathed in an enfolding black garment, sitting cross-legged in front of a pair of tall carved doors, as if guarding the entrance.

She rose with extraordinary grace and bowed her head. 'I am Dena, *sitti*. Princess Lucy called me, asked me to take care of you.'

'She seems to have called everyone,' Lydia said.

So much for being alone!

She threw off the covers, then immediately grabbed them back, clutching them to her chest, as she realised that she was naked.

Realised that she had no memory of getting that way. Only of the sunrise with Kal, soft cushions, the scent of buttery pastry. Of closing her eyes.

'Bin Zaki carried you here, *sitti*. We made you comfortable.'

Lydia swallowed, not quite sure how she felt about that. Whether it was worse that an unknown 'we' had undressed her sleeping body or Kal.

The woman, Dena, picked up a robe, held it out so that she could turn and slip her arms through the sleeves, wrap it around her, preserve a little of her modesty before sliding out of the bed.

It clung to her, soft and light as the touch of a butterfly wing, leaving her feeling almost as exposed as if she was wearing nothing at all. The kind of thing a pampered concubine might have worn. With a sudden quickening of something almost like fear, laced through with excitement, she said, 'Where is Kal?'

'He went to the stables.' The woman's eyes, as she handed her the glass of juice she'd poured from a flask, saw the flush that heated her skin and smiled knowingly. 'He took a horse,' she said. Then, 'I will bathe you and then you will have a massage.'

What?

'That won't be necessary,' she said.

'Bin Zaki ordered it so. Princess Lucy always needs a massage when she comes home.'

'Really?'

But the woman had opened a door that led into a bathroom that was out of a fantasy. A deep sunken tub. A huge shower with side jets. A seat big enough for two.

'Which?' Dena asked.

'The shower,' Lydia said, dismissing the disturbing image of sinking into the huge tub, sharing it with Kal.

She really, really needed something to clear her head, wake her up.

Dena turned it on, adjusted the temperature, apparently oblivious of the fact that her floor length black dress was getting wet. Apparently waiting for her to shed the robe and step into the shower so that she could wash her.

No, no, no...

Lydia swallowed, said, 'I can manage. Really.'

She nodded. 'Come into the next room when you are ready and I will ease the ache in your shoulder.'

Lydia stared after her. Raised her left hand to her right shoulder, the one that ached when it was cold or damp. After a long shift on the checkout. The legacy of years of lifting other people's groceries across a scanner.

How did she know? What had given her away?

She shook her head.

Nothing. Dena couldn't know that she was a fake. If she did, the whole house of cards would be tumbling around her ears by now, she told herself as she slipped out of the wrap, stepped under the warm water.

If she was a trained masseuse she would be observant, that was all, would notice the slightest imbalance. It didn't mean anything.

She might have slept awkwardly on the plane or strained it in a hundred ways.

She turned up the heat and let the water pound her body, easing an ache which, until that moment, she'd been scarcely aware of herself.

Lathered herself in rich soap.

Washed her hair.

Putting off, for as long as possible, the moment when, wrapped in a towel that covered her from breast to ankle, her hair wrapped in a smaller one, she would have to submit herself to the ministrations of the slightly scary Dena.

But as she lay down and Dena's hands found the knots in her muscles, soothed away the tension of the last twenty-four hours, all the stress floated away and she surrendered to total pampering.

Wrapped tenderly in a robe, seated in a chair that tilted back, her hair was released and unseen hands massaged her scalp, gently combed out her hair, while a young girl did miraculous things to her feet, her hands.

Painted her nails, drew patterns with henna.

By the time they were finished, she was so utterly relaxed that when one of the girls held out a pair of exquisite French knickers she stepped into them without a flicker of embarrassment.

Slipped into a matching lace bra and left it for someone else to fasten.

Held up her arms as Dena slipped a loose silk kaftan over her head that had certainly not been part of the wardrobe packed by Rose.

It floated over her, a mist of blue, then settled over her shoulders, her arms, falling to the floor before nimble fingers fastened the dozen or more silk-covered buttons that held it together at her breast.

Then she stepped into a pair of soft thong sandals that were placed in front of her.

A week of this and she'd be ruined for real life, she thought, pulling her lips back against her teeth so that she wouldn't grin out loud.

Wow! Wow! Wow!

Thank you, Rose! I hope you're enjoying every second of your freedom. Having the most wonderful time.

And, with that thought, reality rushed back as she looked around for the clutch bag she'd been carrying.

A word and it was in her hand and she took out her mobile phone to send the agreed 'arrived safely' message, followed by another more detailed message to her mother. Not just to let her know that she'd got to her destination without mishap, but that the apartment was great and she was having a great time.

So far, so true. Unless... Did kissing Kal count as a mishap?

She looked at the message doubtfully, then, with a rueful smile, hit 'send', grateful that her mother had insisted that overseas mobile calls were too expensive, that the occasional text was all she expected. She would never be able to bluff her way through an entire week of this, not with her mother. With Kal...

She looked up and realised that everyone was waiting to hear what she wanted to do next.

She slipped the phone into a pocket in the seam of the kaftan and said, 'May I look around?'

Dena led the way, down a series of steps to a lower level entrance lobby with a two-storey domed ceiling richly decorated in floral designs with tiny ceramic tiles, her helpers following, all anxious to see her reaction. Clearly wanting her to love this place they called home.

They waited patiently while she stopped, turned slowly, looking up in awe at the workmanship.

'This is a holiday cottage?' she asked in amazement. 'It's so beautiful!'

Dena was unreadable, but the two younger women were clearly delighted.

The tour took in a formal dining room where ornate carved doors had been folded back to reveal a terrace and, below it, set in a private walled garden, a swimming pool.

More steps and then Dena said, 'This is the room the family use when they are here.'

Furnished with richly coloured sofas and jewel-bright oriental rugs that softened the polished wooden floor, Lydia might have been totally overwhelmed by its sheer size, but then she spotted a fluffy yellow toy duck half hidden amongst the cushions.

It was a reminder that this was someone's holiday home, a place where children ran and played. She picked it up and held it for a moment and when she looked up she saw that Dena was smiling.

'It is Jamal's,' she said. 'He left it there to keep his place while he was away.'

'Bless,' she said, carefully tucking it back where she'd found it and, looking around, saw the touches that made this unbelievably grand room a home.

The box filled with toys. A pile of books that suggested Lucy's favourite holiday activity was reading. A child's drawing of the creek, framed as lovingly as an old master. Children's books in English and Arabic.

'You like children?' Dena asked as she picked up an alphabet colouring book similar to one she'd had as a child. Except that the alphabet was Arabic.

She nodded. 'Even the little monsters…'

Even the little monsters who whined and nagged their stressed mothers for sweets at the checkout. Their soft little mouths, big eyes that could be coaxed so quickly from tears to a smile with a little attention.

She was so relaxed that she'd completely forgotten to guard her tongue but, while Dena regarded her thoughtfully, the younger women giggled, repeating 'little monsters' as if they knew only too well what she meant.

She managed a shrug and Dena, making no comment, folded back doors similar to the ones in the dining room, opening up one side of the room to the garden so that Lydia could step out onto a wide terrace that overlooked the creek.

'All children love Bab el Sama,' she said. 'You will bring your children here.'

It sounded more like a statement than a question and Lydia swallowed.

She had two careers and no time for romance

even if she could ever trust a man again sufficiently to let him get that close.

Maybe Kal was the answer. He, at least, wouldn't be pretending...

She, on the other hand, would be.

Since the one thing she demanded of a man was total honesty, to kiss with a lie on her lips was not something she could live with, no matter how alluring the temptation.

'I'm sure they have a wonderful time,' she said, responding to her first comment, ignoring the second as she walked quickly to the edge of the terrace as if to take a closer look at the beach.

They were much lower here than on the bluff where she'd watched the sunrise, not more than twenty feet above the beach. And, looking around, she thought that the adults must love it too.

There were pots overflowing with geraniums, still flowering in December, the rustle and clack of palm fronds in the light breeze, a snatch of unfamiliar music carrying across the glittering water.

It was peaceful, beautiful, with a delicious warmth that seeped into the bones and invited her to lift her face to the sun and smile as if she were a sunflower.

Even as she did that, a movement caught her eye and below, on the beach, she saw a horseman galloping along the edge of the surf, robes streaming out behind him.

The horse, its hooves a blur in the spray, seemed to be almost flying, elemental, a force of nature. Lydia's breath caught in her throat and she took a step closer, her hand lifting towards him as if reaching to catch hold, be lifted up to fly with him.

'It is Bin Zaki,' Dena said, but Lydia knew that.

He might have shed his designer suit, donned a robe, hidden his dark curls beneath a *keffiyeh,* but his chiselled face, the fierce hawkish nose were imprinted on her memory and, as he flashed by in a swirl of cloth, hooves, spray, the profile was unmistakable.

'He is chasing his demons. So like his grandfather.'

For a moment she didn't respond, scarcely registered what the woman had said, but Kal had gone, lost from sight as the beach curved around massive rocks, the final fling of the mountain range behind them. And already the sea was smoothing away the hoof prints, rubbing out all trace of his passing.

She turned to discover that Dena was watching her and, suddenly coming back to reality, she dropped her hand self-consciously.

'Demons? What demons?'

'He will tell you in his own good time. Do you need anything, *sitti?*'

Only to be held, enfolded, caressed, but not by some anonymous, faceless figure. All the longings and desires that haunted her had become focused on one man and she turned back to the empty beach as if his spirit was still there for her to reach out and touch.

'I think I'll take a walk,' she said, suddenly self-conscious, certain that Dena knew exactly what she was thinking. 'Explore a little. Is there anywhere I shouldn't go?'

'Bab el Sama is yours, *sitti*.'

Dena left her alone to explore and she skirted the terrace, noticing how cleverly it was shielded from the creek by the trees so that no one from below would be able to see the royal family at play.

Taking a path, she found steps that led invitingly downwards in the direction of the beach but, conscious of the silk kaftan flowing around her ankles, she turned instead along a path that led upward through the garden.

After the crash that had killed her father and left her mother in a wheelchair, she and her mother had moved from their small house with a garden into a ground floor flat that had been adapted for a wheelchair user.

She'd missed the garden but, ten years old, she'd understood the necessity and knew better than to say anything that would hurt her mother. It was the hand that life had dealt but even then she'd used her pocket money to buy flowering pot plants from the market. Had grown herbs on the windowsill.

This garden was like a dream. Little streams ran down through the trees, fell over rocks to feed pools where carp rose at her appearance.

There were exquisite summer houses tucked away. Some were for children, with garden toys. Some, with comfortable chairs, were placed to catch a stunning view.

One, with a copper roof turned green with verdigris, was laid with rich carpets on which cushions had been piled, and looked like a lovers' hideaway. She could imagine lying there with Kal, his lips pressed against her throat as he unfastened the buttons...

She lifted her hand to her breast, shook her head, trying to rid herself of an image that was so powerful that she could feel his hands, his mouth on her body.

As she backed away there was a scuffle near her feet as a lizard disappeared in a flurry of emerald tail. For a moment she stared at the spot, not sure whether she'd imagined it. Then she looked up and saw Kal standing just a few feet away.

The *keffiyeh* had fallen from his head and lay gathered about his neck. His robes were made of some loosely woven cream material and the hem was heavy with sea water and sand. As they stood there, silent, still, a trickle of sweat ran from his temple into the dust on his cheek.

After what seemed like an age he finally moved, lifting his elbow to wipe his face on his sleeve.

'I've been riding,' he said wearily.

'I saw you. You looked as if you were flying,' she said.

'That's me,' he said, the corner of his mouth lifting in a self-mocking smile. 'Addicted to the air.' He took a step forward but Lydia, almost dizzy with the scent of leather, of the sea clinging to his clothes, of tangy fresh sweat that her body was responding to like an aphrodisiac, didn't move.

Hot, sweaty he exuded a raw sexual potency and she wanted to touch his face. Kiss the space between his thumb and palm, taste the leather; lean into him and bury her face in his robes, breathe him in. Wanted to feel those long, powerful hands that had so easily controlled half a ton of muscle and bone in full flight, on her own body.

She cooled her burning lip with the tip of her tongue, then, realising how that must look, said, 'Maybe my problem with flying is that I didn't start in the right place.'

He frowned. 'You don't ride?'

'No.' Having studied every aspect of her alter ego's life, she knew that while most little girls of her class would have been confidently astride her first pony by the time she was three, Rose was not one of them. 'But, if I had to choose, I think I'd prefer it to fishing.'

His smile was a lazy thing that began in the depths of his eyes, barely noticeable if you weren't locked in to every tiny response. No more than a tiny spark that might so easily have been mistaken for a shaft of sunlight finding a space between the leaves to warm the darkness. Then the creases that fanned out around them deepened a little, the skin over his cheekbones tightened and lifted. Only then did his mouth join in with a slightly lopsided *gotcha* grin.

'Here's the deal,' he said. 'You let me take you fishing and I'll teach you to ride.'

His voice, his words seemed to caress her so that it sounded more like a sexual proposition than a simple choice between this or that outdoor activity. Standing there in the dappled sunlight, every nerve-ending at attention, sensitized by desire, she knew that if he reached out, touched her, she would buckle, dissolve and if he carried her into the summer house and laid her amongst the cushions, nothing could save her.

That she wouldn't want to be saved.

This powerful, instant attraction had nothing to do with who they were. Or weren't. It was pure chemistry. Names, titles meant nothing.

She lowered her lids, scarcely able to breathe. 'Is that your final offer?'

His voice soft, dangerously seductive, he said, 'How about if I offered to bait your hook for you?'

Baited, hooked, landed…

She swallowed, cooled her burning lower lip with her tongue. 'How could I resist such an inducement?'

A step brought him alongside her and he took her chin in his hand, ran the pad of his thumb over her mouth in an exploratory sweep as if to test its heat.

'It is a date, Rose.'

He was so close that she could see the grains of sand thrown up by the flying hooves which clung to his face and, as she closed her eyes to breathe in the pure essence of the man, his mouth touched hers, his tongue lightly tracing her lower lip, imitating the route her own had taken seconds before, as if tasting her.

Before she could react, clutch at him to stop herself from collapsing at his feet, it was over.

'You will fish with me this afternoon. I will ride with you at dawn.'

'Perfect,' she managed through a throat that felt as if it was stuffed with cotton wool. Through lips that felt twice their normal size.

Then, as she opened her eyes, he stepped back and said, 'You might want to wear something a little less…distracting.'

Before she could respond, he strode away in a swirl of robes and she did not move until she was quite alone.

Only when the path was quite empty, the only sound—apart from the pounding of her heart—was the rattle of palm fronds high above her, did she finally look down, see for herself how the light breeze was moulding the thin blue silk to her body so that it outlined every contour. Her thighs, the gentle curve of her belly. The hard, betraying, touch-me peaks of her breasts.

CHAPTER SEVEN

KAL stood beneath the pounding icy shower. He did not need hot water; the heat coming off him was turning the water to steam.

He closed his eyes but it didn't help. Without visual distraction, the image of Rose Napier, silk clinging to every curve, filled his head, obliterating everything from his mind but her.

If he had ever doubted her innocence, he was now utterly convinced of it. No woman who had a scintilla of experience would have let a man see such naked desire shining out of her eyes, been so unconscious of the *come-and-take-me* signals her body was semaphoring in response to his nearness. Given him such power over her.

But maybe they were both out of their depth.

Preoccupied with his own concerns and apparently immune to this pale beauty that the entire world appeared to be in love with, his guard had been down.

Knocked sideways from his first sight of her

and, knowing that he wouldn't sleep, he'd gone to the stables, determined to blow away the demands of his body in hard physical activity.

But as hard as he'd ridden he could not shake loose the image of those blue eyes. One moment *keep-your-distance* cool, the next sparkling with life, excitement. A touch of mischief.

Almost, he thought, as if she were two women.

The adored, empathetic public figure—as flawless and beautiful as a Bernini marble, as out of reach as the stars.

And this private, flesh and blood woman whose eyes appealed for his touch, for him to take her, bring her to life.

Living with those eyes, those seductive lips that drew him to her, would not make for a comfortable week. And he'd just made it a thousand times worse.

He'd ridden off the sexual energy that had built over their long flight. Had been totally in control, with the self-discipline to keep his hands off her.

All he'd had to do was keep his distance, leave it to her to initiate any outings. He had his own agenda and it certainly didn't include getting involved with a woman, especially one who was a national icon.

Until he'd taken a turn in the path and saw her standing before him, her hair hanging like silk around her shoulders. Wearing an embroidered silk kaftan that exactly matched eyes shining like a woman on her wedding night.

And he'd been the one insisting that the two of them should spend time alone together on a boat.

Offering to teach her to ride.

Unable to resist touching her lip with his thumb, his tongue, wanting to test the heat, knowing that it was for him.

It had taken every ounce of self-discipline to stop himself from carrying her into the pavilion hidden in the trees behind her. Making her his.

To force himself to step back, walk away.

He flipped off the water, stepped from the shower, grabbed a towel and wrapped it round him.

His clothes had been pressed and hung up but someone, Dena, probably, had added an array of casual and formal robes for his use while he was at Bab el Sama.

The kind of clothes that Hanif would wear. A sheikh, relaxing in the privacy of his own home, with his children around him.

It was Dena, undoubtedly, who'd dressed Rose in that silk dress, had painted her hands with henna. He frowned, wondering what she thought she was doing.

He shook his head. Rose was on holiday in an exotic location and no doubt Lucy had ordered that her friend be totally pampered.

She certainly looked a great deal more rested. Unlike him. He lifted his shoulders, easing them, then reached for his cellphone and called his grandfather at the clinic.

After he'd asked how he was, as if he didn't know—in desperate pain but stubbornly refusing palliative care until he was permitted to return home to die—and getting the same answer, he said, 'I met someone today who knew you.'

'And is prepared to admit it?'

'She said that you were stubborn, *Jaddi*. But charming—'

There was a short harsh laugh, then, 'She?'

'She said, "Tell him that his sister Dena remembers him with fondness."'

'Dena?' There was a rare catch in the old man's voice. 'She is well?'

'She is well,' he confirmed. 'She said it was time you were home.'

'Tell her… Tell her I will be there, *insh'Allah*. Tell her that I will not die until I have kissed her.'

'It will be so, *Jaddi'l habeeb*,' Kal said softly. 'I swear it.'

He put down the phone, spent a moment reminding himself why he was here, gathering himself.

Then he pulled out the jeans he'd brought with him, chose a loose long-sleeved white shirt from the wardrobe and pulled it over his head and stepped into thong sandals that seemed more suitable than any of the shoes he'd brought with him.

As he picked up the phone to stow it in his pocket, it rang. Caller ID warned him that it was Lucy and he said, 'Checking up on me, Princess?'

She laughed. 'Why? What are you up to?' Then, not waiting for an answer, 'I just wanted to be sure that Rose arrived safely.'

'So why not call her?'

'She wants to cut herself off from everyone while she's away. She wants to think about the future without anyone else offering their opinions, clouding the picture.'

'Instead, she got me,' he said. 'Tell me, was there a single word of truth in what you told me?'

'Absolutely. Cross my heart,' she swore. 'Why do you think her grandfather was so desperate to stop her? He doesn't want her doing anything as dangerous as thinking for herself, not without someone on hand to guide her thoughts in the right direction.'

'And that would be in the direction of the marriage he's arranged?' he asked casually enough, despite the fact that the thought of another man touching her sent a shaft of possessive heat driving deep into his groin.

'She's longing for a family, children of her own, Kal, and I think she's very nearly desperate enough to marry Rupert Devenish to get them.'

'What other reason is there for a woman to marry?' he asked.

Or a man, for that matter.

Far better to have people who had known you all your life, who understood your strengths and weaknesses, to seek a bride whose temperament, expectations matched your own, than rely on unbridled passion that, no matter how intense the heat, would soon become ashes. He'd seen it happen. His grandfather, his father...

'Oh, pish-posh,' Lucy said with the impatience of a woman who'd found a rare love and thought he should be making an effort to do the same. 'How is she?'

'Rose? She slept for a while, but now she's exploring the garden.'

'On her own?'

'I have no doubt that your Dena has someone within call.' Someone who would have seen him kissing her? 'She's safe enough,' he said abruptly. 'And we're about to have lunch.'

'Maybe when you've eaten you'll be in a better mood. Perhaps I should call you then?'

'No. Really. I've just spoken to my grandfather. And, as for your Rose, well, she isn't quite what I expected. I imagined unruffled serenity.'

'Oh? In what way is she not serene?'

In the quick blush that warmed her pale skin, in her eyes, a mouth, a body that gave away too much.

'Well,' he said, pushing away the disturbing images, 'I would have welcomed a warning that she's a nervous flyer.'

'Rose? I never knew that. How did she cope with the helicopter?' Her concern was genuine enough, Kal decided, giving her the benefit of the doubt.

'I managed to keep her distracted.' Before she could ask him how, he added, 'I was surprised to discover that she doesn't ride.'

'I think a pony bolted with her when she was little.' He could see the tiny frown as she tried to remember. 'Something like that.'

'Well, she appears to be willing to give it another go.'

'You're going to take her riding?'

'Amuse and entertain her, that was the brief.'

'Absolutely. I'm glad you're taking it so seriously. But the reason for my call is to give you advance warning that Rose should be getting a courtesy visit from Princess Sabirah later in the week. The household will be warned of her arrival, but I thought you might welcome a little extra time to prepare yourself.'

'Thank you, Lucy. If I haven't sufficiently expressed my grat—'

'It's little enough in return for everything you've done for my charity, Kal. Just do me one favour. Don't tell Rose that I was checking up on her.'

'I won't. Lucy…'

He hesitated. He knew his doubts were foolish. Lady Rose Napier had been hand delivered to him by her security guard…

'Yes?' she prompted.

'Nothing. Take care.'

He disconnected, pushed the phone into his back pocket and, bearing in mind that it was his duty to keep her safe, he went to find Rose.

Lydia resisted the urge to fling herself into the nearest pool to cool herself down. Instead, she walked the winding paths, swiftly at first, outrunning feelings she could not control, until her breath was coming in short gasps and she almost collapsed into a seat that seemed to have been placed precisely for that purpose.

She sat there for an age while her breathing returned to normal and the heat gradually faded from her skin, attempting to make sense of what had happened.

She might as well try to catch mist in her hand.

There *was* no sense in it. Love—or just plain lust—as she knew to her cost, made fools of everyone.

'Get a grip, Lydie,' she said intently, startling a bird from the tree above her. 'Rose is depending on you. This madness will go away.' Then, after a long time, 'It will go away.'

By the time she returned to the terrace her flush might easily have been put down to nothing more than a brisk walk on a sunny day.

Just as well, because one of the girls who'd taken care of her was sitting cross-legged in the shade, embroidering a piece of silk.

'You will eat, *sitti?*' she asked, rising gracefully to her feet.

Food was the last thing on her mind, but it had been a long time since the croissant that she'd barely tasted and eating was a proven distraction for heartache.

'Thank you… I'm sorry, I don't know your name.'

'It is Yatimah, *sitti.*'

'Yatimah,' she repeated, rolling the word around her mouth, tasting the strangeness of it. 'Thank you, Yatimah. Your English is very good.'

'Princess Lucy has taught me. She speaks Arabic as if she was born here, but her mother comes sometimes. From New Zealand. And her friends from England.'

'And they do not,' Lydia said.

'A few words,' she said with a smile.

'Will you teach me?'

'*Nam,*' she said. And giggled. 'That means yes.'

'*Nam,*' she repeated. Then, remembering the word Kal had taught her, she said, '*Shukran.* Thank you.' And received a delighted clap. Encouraged, she asked, 'What is "good morning"?'

'Good morning is *sabah alkhair* and the reply is *sabah alnur.*'

Lydia tried it and got the response from Yatimah who, an eager teacher, then said, 'Good afternoon is *masa alkhair* and the reply *masa alnur.* And goodnight is—'

'Leila sa'eeda.'

Startled by Kal's voice from the doorway, Yatimah scuttled away, leaving Lydia alone with him.

The last time he'd kissed her, she'd managed to dismiss it as if it was nothing. They both knew that wasn't going to happen this time and for a moment neither of them moved, spoke.

'Lucy called,' he said at last, stepping onto the terrace.

He'd showered and changed into a loose white collarless shirt that hung to his hips. Soft faded jeans. Strong, bare feet pushed into thong sandals. The clothes were unremarkable but with that thin high-bridged nose, polished olive skin, dark hair curling onto his neck, he looked very different from the man in the suit who'd met her at the airport. More like some desert lord surveying his world.

'She wanted to be sure you'd arrived safely.'

'Then why didn't she call me?' Lydia asked, brave in the knowledge that if she'd rung Rose, by the magic of the cellphone, she'd have got Rose, wherever she was. Except, of course, that Rose didn't know anything about Kal. She'd need to send a message, she thought, her hand going to the phone in her pocket, warn her…

'My own reaction,' he replied, 'but she seemed to be under the impression that you'd rather not talk to anyone from home. That you did not want to be disturbed.'

...or maybe not.

He turned to her in expectation of polite denial.

Being a lookalike was an acting role, stepping into the shoes of another person, copying the moves, the gestures, the facial expressions. Practising the voice until it became her own. But nothing that Rose had ever done had prepared her for this.

In a situation like this, all she had to fall back on was the supermarket checkout girl with the fast mouth.

And that girl wouldn't let him off with a polite anything. That girl would look him in the eye, lift an eyebrow and say, 'She should have thought about that before she invited you to my party.'

Just like that.

If she'd hoped to raise a smile, she would have been sadly disappointed.

Apart from the slightest contraction of a muscle at the corner of his mouth—as if she needed any encouragement to look at it—his expression didn't alter for so long that, but for that tiny giveaway, she might have wondered if he'd actually heard her.

Then, with the merest movement of his head, he acknowledged the hit and said, 'No doubt that's why she asked me not to tell you she'd called.'

'So why did you?' she demanded, refusing to back down, play the lady. She might not know what Rose would do under these circumstances, but she jolly well knew what she should do after that very close encounter in the garden.

That had gone far beyond simple flirting. Far beyond what had happened in the helicopter, where his kiss had been simple enough. It had been her own reaction that had turned into something much more complex; fear, strangeness, the need to cling to something safe would do that and it was easy enough to dismiss as an aberration.

But what had happened in the garden was different.

He'd touched her mouth as if marking her as his, taken her lower lip into his mouth as intimately as a lover, certain of his welcome.

And she had welcomed him.

That moment had been an acknowledgement of the intense attraction that had been bubbling beneath the surface from the moment she had walked into the airport and found him waiting for her.

It was a dance where they circled one another, getting closer and closer. Touching briefly. Moving apart as they fought it but, like two moths being drawn closer and closer to a candle, totally unable to resist the fatal attraction, even though they both knew they would go down in flames.

Except that she had no choice. She had to withstand the temptation or tell him the truth, because she knew how it felt to be made love to by someone who was acting. Knew how betrayed she'd felt.

And she couldn't tell him the truth. Couldn't betray Rose for her own selfish desires. Not that he'd want her if she did. He was not a man to accept a fake. A copy. If he knew the truth he'd lose interest, turn away.

And if he didn't…

'Kal…'

'You are hungry?'

Her life seemed to be happening in slow motion, Lydia thought. Neither of them moved or made a move to answer Dena's query for what seemed like forever.

It did not matter. Apparently oblivious to the tension between them, she bustled across the terrace to a table set beneath the trees, issuing orders to the staff that trailed after her.

A cloth was laid, food was set out.

'Come, eat,' she said, waving them towards the table.

Kal moved first, held out a chair for her, and she managed to unstick her feet from the flagstones and join him at the table.

'This looks wonderful, Dena,' she said, trying very hard to ignore his hands grasping the back of her chair, the beautiful bones of his wrists, the dark hair exposed where he'd folded back the sleeves of his shirt, the woody scent of soap and shampoo as she sat down and he bent over her to ease the chair forward.

It was like living inside a kaleidoscope of the senses. Everything was heightened. The food glowed, gleamed with colour, enticed with spices. The arm of her chair, worn smooth by many hands. The starchy smell, the feel of the damask cloth against her legs. A silence so intense that she could almost feel it.

Then a bird fluttered down, anticipating crumbs, and gradually everything began to move again and she realised that Dena was speaking. That both she and Kal were looking at her.

'What?' she asked.

Dena excused herself, leaving Kal to pass on the message, but he shook his head as if it was nothing important and instead took her on a culinary tour of the table.

Rice cooked with saffron and studded with pine nuts and sultanas. Locally caught fish. Chicken. Jewelled salads. Small cheeses made from goats' milk.

'It's a feast,' she said with every appearance of pleasure, even though alarm bells were going off in her head, certain that she'd missed something. That somehow they knew... 'I just hope Dena does not expect me to eat it all. I usually have a sandwich for lunch.'

'And here I was thinking that you spent every day at a lavish lunch, raising money for charity.'

His words were accompanied by a wry smile and the bells quietened a little, the tension seeping away beneath the honeyed warmth of his voice, his eyes.

'Not more than once a week,' she assured him. Then, managing a smile of her own, 'Maybe twice. But I only taste the food.'

'A taste will satisfy Dena. None of the food will be wasted.' He took her plate. 'Rice?'

'A spoonful,' she replied, repeating the same word each time he offered her a new dish. He put no more than a morsel of each on her plate but, by the time he had finished, it was still an awful lot of food to eat in the middle of the day and she regarded it doubtfully.

'It will be a long time until dinner, Rose. We eat late. And you're going to need plenty of energy before then.' She looked up. 'We're going fishing, remember?'

'Is it hard work? I thought you just sat with a rod and waited for the fish to bite.' She picked up a fork. 'Was that what you were arranging with Dena?'

He hesitated for a moment, as if he had some unpleasant news to impart, and the bells began jangling again.

'Kal?'

He shook his head. 'It was nothing to do with

this afternoon. She's had a message from Rumaillah. It seems that the Emir's wife has decided to pay you a courtesy call.'

The fork in Lydia's hand shook and the waiting sparrows dived on the scattered grains of rice.

'The Emir's wife?'

'I know that you hoped to be totally private here, Rose, but I'm sure you understand that Princess Sabirah could not ignore your presence in her country.'

Lydia felt the colour drain from her face.

When Rose had asked her to do this it had all seemed so simple. Once she was out of the country there would be nothing to do but indulge herself in one of those perfectly selfish holidays that everyone dreamed about occasionally. The kind where you could read all day and all night if you wanted to. Swim. Take a walk on the beach. Do what you wanted without having to think about another person.

And, like Rose, do some serious thinking about the future.

She'd had ten good years as Rose's lookalike and had no doubt that she could go on for ten more, but now she'd met Kal and the only person she wanted to be was herself.

No pretence.

No lies.

Not that she was kidding herself. She knew that

if, in the unlikely event that he'd ever met her as 'herself', he wouldn't have even noticed her.

Everything about him was the real deal, from his designer suit to the Rolex on his wrist—no knock-offs for this man. Including women.

The pain of that was a wake-up call far louder, the argument for reality more cogent than any that her boss at the supermarket could make, even using the in-store announcement system.

She had been coasting through her own life, putting all her energies into someone else's, and she would never move on, meet someone who wanted her, the real Lydia Young, unless she started building a life of her own.

'When?' she asked, ungluing her tongue. 'What time?'

Maybe she could throw a sickie, she thought a touch desperately, but instantly rejected the idea as she realised what kind of fuss *that* would cause. This wasn't some anonymous hotel where you could take to your bed and no one would give a damn. And she wasn't some anonymous tourist.

If Lady Rose took to her bed, panic would ensue, doctors would be summoned—probably by helicopter from the capital. And Kal or Dena, probably both, would call Lucy, the Duke of Oldfield and then the game would be up.

No, no, no...

She could do this. She had to do it.

'Relax. She won't be here for a day or two and she won't stay long,' Kal said, not looking at her, but concentrating on serving himself. 'Just for coffee, cake. Dena will arrange everything,' he added, that tiny muscle in his jaw tightening again.

What was that? Tension?

What was his problem?

'Does she speak English? What will we talk about?'

'I believe her English is excellent and I imagine she'll want to talk about your work.'

'Really?' Lydia had a flash image of herself politely explaining the finer points of the checkout scanner to Her Highness over a cup of coffee and had to fight down a hysterical giggle as the world began to unravel around her.

'Play nice,' he said, 'and you'll get a generous donation for one of your good causes.'

Kal's flippancy brought her crashing back to reality. This was not in the least bit funny and her expression must have warned him that she was no more amused by his remark than Rose, whose parents had been killed on a charity mission, would have been.

'I'm sorry, Rose,' he said immediately. 'That was unforgivable.' He shook his head and she realised that for some reason he was as on edge as she was. 'I'm sure she'll just want to talk about Lucy and her grandchildren. It's a while since she's seen them.'

As if that was better!

She'd assumed that being at Bab el Sama would be like staying in a hotel. Great service but everything at a distance. She hadn't anticipated having to live with the pretence of being Rose in this way. This minute by minute deception.

She'd come dangerously, selfishly close to confessing everything to Kal before Dena had interrupted her but she could not, no matter how desperately she wanted to, break Rose's confidence.

She had made this offer with a free heart and couldn't, wouldn't let her down just because that heart wanted to jump ship and fling itself at someone else.

'I appear to have spoiled your appetite,' Kal said, and she took a little heart from the fact that he didn't seem particularly comfortable to hear of their unexpected visitor either.

'I'm good,' she said, picking up her fork and spearing a piece of chicken so succulent that, despite her dry mouth, she had no trouble swallowing it. 'So tell me what, exactly, is your prob-lem, Kal?'

CHAPTER EIGHT

EXACTLY? Kal took a piece of bread, tore it in two.

'Why would you think I have a problem?' he asked, playing for time in the face of Rose's unexpected challenge.

'There's a muscle just by the corner of your mouth that you'd probably be wise to cover when you play poker,' she replied.

She reached out and touched a spot just below the right hand corner of his mouth.

'Just there.'

As their eyes locked, he kept perfectly still, knowing that if he moved an inch he would be tasting those long, slender fingers, sliding his tongue along the length of each one, and food would be the furthest thing from his mind. That the only thing he'd be eating would be her.

As if sensing the danger, she curled them back into her palm, let her hand drop.

'Should I ever be tempted to gamble, I'll bear

that in mind,' he said. Took a mouthful of bread before he blurted out the real reason he had been foisted on her by Lucy and she sent him packing.

Rose made no move to eat, but continued to regard him. 'Well?' she prompted, refusing to let the matter drop. 'I recall that you mentioned your family were personae non gratae at court and presumably, as a royal residence, Bab el Sama is an extension of that. Will Princess Sabirah's visit be awkward for you?'

The breath stopped in his throat. Not suspicion, concern. She was anxious for him...

'This was originally the site of the Khatib tribe's summer camp,' he told her, not sure where exactly he was going with this, but wanting her to understand who, what he was. 'The mountains provided not only water, grazing for the animals, but a fortress at their back in troubled times.' He looked up at the barren peaks towering above them. 'They are impassable.'

'So is that a yes or a no?' she asked, refusing to be diverted by history.

'Good question.'

And the answer was that, far from awkward, Lucy was using court etiquette for his benefit, putting him in a place where his aunt could not, without causing offence to an honoured guest, ignore him.

In London, in her elegant drawing room, it had

all seemed so simple. Before he'd met Rose. Now nothing was simple and if this had been for him alone he would have stepped back, taken himself out of the picture for the morning. But this was for his grandfather.

'Maybe you'd better tell me what happened, Kal,' she said when he didn't offer an answer. 'Just enough to stop me from putting my foot in it.'

'Your foot?'

'I'm sorry. You speak such perfect English that I forget that it isn't your first language.' She frowned. 'I'm not even sure what your first language is. Arabic, French…?'

'Take your pick,' he said. 'I grew up speaking both. And quickly added English when my father married for the second time. I know what "putting your foot in it" means. But, to answer your question, the court is wherever the Emir happens to be, so I'm safe enough unless he decides to accompany his wife.'

'And if he does?'

He couldn't get that lucky. Could he? Or was the Emir, like everyone else, fascinated by this English 'Rose' who'd been orphaned so tragically as a little girl. Who, from the age of sixteen, had taken up her parents' cause, devoted her whole life to the charity they'd founded, adding dozens of other good causes over the years.

'I'm wherever you happen to be, Rose. And you

are an honoured guest in his country. Who knows,' he said with a wry smile, 'he might be sufficiently charmed by you to acknowledge my existence.'

'Whoa, whoa…' She put down her fork, sat back. 'Back up, buster. I need to know what I'm getting into here.'

'"Back up, buster"?' he repeated, startled out of his own concerns. 'Where on earth did Lady Rose Napier pick up an expression like that?'

She blinked, appeared to gather herself, physically put the cool façade back in place. 'I meet all kinds of people in my work,' she said. Even her voice had changed slightly, had taken on a hint of steel, as if she was drawing back from him, and he recalled his earlier feeling that she was two separate people. The formal, untouchable, unreadable 'Lady'. And this other woman whose voice was huskier, whose lush mouth was softer, whose eyes seemed to shine a brighter blue. Who used unexpectedly colloquial expressions.

The one he couldn't seem to keep his hands off.

The selfish gene, the one he'd been fighting all his life, urged him to reach out, grasp her hand, stop that Rose from slipping away.

Instead, like her, he took a moment to gather himself, take a step back before, control restored, he said, 'What happened is no secret. Google my family and you'll find enough gossip to fill a book.'

'I'd rather save that for when I've run out of

fiction,' she replied crisply. 'The edited high-lights will do.'

'I wish it was fiction,' he said. 'My grandfather was hardly a credit to his family.'

He reached for a pitcher of water, offered it to her and, when she nodded, he filled both their glasses.

'Kalil al-Khatib, my grandfather, was the oldest son of the Emir and, although a ruler is free to name his successor, no one ever doubted that it would be him.'

'You have the same name as your grandfather?' she asked.

'It is the tradition. My first son will be named Zaki for my father.' If he achieved recognition, a traditional marriage, a place in the society that had rejected his family.

'That must become rather confusing.'

'Why?'

'Well, if a man has two or three sons, won't all their firstborn sons have the same name?' Then, 'Oh, wait. That's why Dena calls you "bin Zaki". That's "son of", isn't it?'

He couldn't stop the smile that betrayed his pleasure. She was so quick, so intelligent, eager to learn.

The curl of desire as, equally pleased with herself for 'getting it', she smiled back.

Then her forehead puckered in a frown as she

quickly picked up on what else he'd told her. 'But I don't understand. Why do you call yourself al-Zaki and not al-Khatib?'

'It's a long story,' he said, forcing himself to concentrate on that, rather than the curve of her cheek, the line of her neck. The hollows in her throat that were made for a man's tongue.

'I have all afternoon.'

He sought for a beginning, something that would make sense of tribal history, the harshness of the life, the need for a strong leader.

'My grandfather was his father's favourite. They both loved to ride, hunt in the desert with their falcons. They were, people said, more like twins than father and son. They were both utterly fearless, both much respected. Loved.'

He thought of Dena. She'd called herself his sister, but she was not related to him by blood. Had she loved him, too?

Then, realising that Rose was waiting, 'He was everything that was required of a ruler in those simpler times.'

'Everything?'

'Strong enough to hold off his enemies, to protect the summer grazing, the oases. Keep his people and their stock safe.'

'That would be before the oil?'

He nodded. 'They were still the qualities admired, necessary even in a charismatic leader, but it is true that once the oil started flowing and money began to pour into the country, the role needed a greater vision. Something beyond the warrior, the great hunter, the trusted arbitrator. A man to take the international stage.'

'And your grandfather couldn't adapt?'

'Oh, he adapted,' Kal said wryly. 'Just not in the right way. He was a big man with big appetites and wealth gave him the entire world in which to indulge them. He spent a fortune on a string of racehorses, enjoyed the gaming tables, never lacked some beauty to decorate his arm and, as the heir apparent to one of the new oil rich states, his excesses inevitably attracted media attention. None of it favourable.'

'I bet that went down well at home,' she said with a wry look and he caught again a glimpse of the inner Rose. The one she tried so hard to keep suppressed.

'Like a lead balloon?' he offered.

She laughed, then clapped her hand to her mouth.

'That is the correct expression?' he asked.

'You know it is, Kal.' She shook her head. 'I'm sorry. It's not funny.'

'It all happened a long time ago. My grandfather has long since accepted that he has no one but himself to blame for what happened.'

'So what did happen?' she asked, concentrating

on her food rather than looking at him, as if she understood how difficult this was for him. He, on the other hand, watched as she successfully negotiated a second forkful of rice and knew that he could sit here and watch her eat all day.

Instead, he followed her example, picking up a piece of fish, forcing himself to concentrate on the story.

'In an attempt to remind Kalil of his duty,' he went on, 'encourage him to return home and settle down, his family arranged his marriage to the daughter of one of the most powerful tribal elders.'

'Arranged?' He caught the slightly disparaging lift of her eyebrows, the sideways glance.

'It is how it is done, Rose. To be accepted as the husband of a precious daughter is to be honoured. And an alliance, ties of kinship between families, adds strength in times of trouble.'

'Very useful when it comes to hanging on to land, I imagine. Especially when it lies over a vast oilfield. Does the girl get a say at all?'

'Of course,' he said.

'But who would refuse the man who was going to be Emir?'

'Marriage binds tribal societies together, Rose. I'm not saying that ours is an infallible system, but everyone has a stake in the partnership succeeding. No one wants to match two young people who will be unhappy.'

'Yours?'

She sounded sceptical. He could see why she might be. He was the second generation to be born and live his entire life in Europe. But at heart…

'There's no place for love?'

'That would be the happy-ever-after fairy tale perpetrated by Hollywood?' he responded irritably.

He'd hoped that she would understand. Then, remembering Lucy's concern that she was being guided towards marriage not of her own choice, he realised that she probably did understand rather more than most. And found himself wondering just how much choice a girl really had in a society where being married to a powerful man was the ideal. When her family's fortune might rise or fall on her decision.

'Hollywood came rather late in the story, Kal. Ever heard of Shakespeare? "Love is not love, Which alters when it alteration finds, Or bends with the remover to remove: Oh, no! it is an ever-fixéd mark, That looks on tempests and is never shaken; It is the star to every wandering bark…"'

She said the words with such passion, such belief, that a stab of longing pierced him and for a moment he couldn't breathe. Wanted to believe that out of an entire world it was possible for two people to find one another. Reach out and with the touch of a hand make a commitment that would last a lifetime.

Knowing it for nonsense, that anyone who believed in it was going to get hurt, he shook his head.

'It's the same story for the same gullible audience,' he replied. That kind of attraction is no more than sexual chemistry. Powerful, undoubtedly, but short-lived. 'I've lived with the aftermath of "love" all my life, Rose. The hurt, the disillusion. The confused children.'

She reached out, laid her hand over his. 'I'm sorry.' Then, as swiftly she removed it. 'I didn't think.'

He shrugged. 'I admit that my family is an extreme case,' he said, but how could he ever put his trust in such here today, gone tomorrow feelings? He'd much rather leave the matter to wiser heads. 'Not that it was a problem in my grandfather's case. His response to the summons home for the formal betrothal was a front page appearance on every newspaper with his new bride, a glamorous British starlet who was, he swore, the love of his life.'

'Ouch!' she said. Then, her face softening, 'But how romantic.'

'The romance was, without doubt, intense…'
'Like a rocket', was the way his grandfather had described it. Hot, fast, spectacular and gone as quickly as the coloured stars faded from the sky. 'But the reason for the swift marriage was rather more prosaic. She was pregnant.'

'Oh.'

'He knew his father would be angry, his chosen bride's family outraged, but, universally popular and always a favourite, he was confident that the birth of a son would bring him forgiveness.'

'I take it he was mistaken.'

'When a favoured son falls from grace it's a very long drop, Rose.'

'So his father disinherited him.'

'Not immediately. He was told his new bride was not welcome in Ramal Hamrah, but that when he was prepared to settle down he could come home. My grandfather wasn't a man to abandon his bride and return like a dog with his tail between his legs.'

'I like him for that.'

'Everyone likes him, Rose. That was part of the problem.'

'And you,' she said gently. 'You love him.'

'He is my *jaddi'l habeeb,*' he told her. 'My beloved grandfather. While my own father was following in his father's footsteps, *Jaddi* taught me to speak Arabic, the stories of my people. Their history.'

'And he gave it all up for love.'

'While his studious, dutiful younger brother soothed outraged sensibilities and rescued his father's tattered pride by marrying the girl chosen for the heir. Within a year he had a son with blood that could be traced back a thousand years and was visibly putting all this new found wealth to work for his father's people.'

'A new man for a new age.'

'Smarter than my grandfather, certainly. When his father had a stroke *Jaddi* raced home, but he was too late. The Emir had slipped into a coma and was beyond extending the hand of forgiveness. There was to be no feast for the prodigal.'

'Poor man.'

He glanced at her, uncertain who she was referring to.

'I wonder if there was a moment when he knew it was too late. The Emir. Wished he had acted differently? You think that you have all the time in world to say the words. When my father was killed I wanted to tell him...'

She broke off, unable to continue, and it was his turn to reach out for her hand, curl his fingers around it, hold tight as she remembered the family that had been torn from her.

After a moment she shook her head. 'I'm fine, Kal.'

Was she? He'd never lost anyone close to him. Rose had only her grandfather and he wished he could share his many grandparents, parents, siblings with her.

'What did you want to tell him, Rose?' he pressed, wanting to know about her. How she felt. What her life had been like.

'That I loved him,' she said. And for a moment her eyes were noticeably brighter. 'He used to take me for walks in the wood on Sunday mornings. Show me things. The names of trees, flowers, birds.'

'Your mother didn't go with you?'

She shook her head. 'She stayed at home and cooked lunch but we'd always look for something special to take home for her. A big shiny conker or a bird's feather or a pretty stone.'

The Marchioness slaving over a hot stove? An unlikely image, but Rose's mother hadn't been born to the purple. She'd qualified as a doctor despite the odds, had met her polo playing Marquess in A&E when he'd taken a tumble from his horse.

Such ordinary domesticity must evoke a genuine yearning in the breast of a young woman who'd been brought up by a starchy old aristocrat who probably didn't even know where the kitchen was.

'I should have told him every day how much I loved him. That's all there is in the end, Kal. Love. Nothing else matters.'

'It's tragic that you had so little time to get to know him. Be with him. With both of them,' he said. 'To lose a mother so young… What do you remember about her?'

She started, as if brought back from some distant place, then said, 'Her bravery, determination. How much she loved my father.'

She looked at her hand, clasped in his, reclaimed it.

'Go on with your story, Kal,' she urged.

He didn't want to talk about his family. He wanted to know more about her. His six-year-old memories of his mother were of stories, treats, hugs. Were Rose's most abiding memories really of her mother's bravery? Or was that the result of years of media brainwashing?

'What happened after your great-grandfather died?' she pressed.

There was definitely something wrong here, he could sense it, but Rose Napier was no more than a means to an end, he reminded himself. She was not his concern.

'When *Jaddi* learned that his father had named his younger brother as Emir his heart broke, not just with grief,' he told her, refocusing himself on what was important, 'but with guilt, too. For a while he was crazy.'

He stared at the plate in front of him. Somehow, he'd managed to clear it, although he hadn't tasted a thing.

'What happened?' she pressed. 'What did he do?'

'He refused to swear allegiance to his younger brother, raised disaffected tribes in the north, attacked the citadel. He thought that the people would rise to him, but he'd been away for a long time. While they'd once adored the dashing young sheikh, in his absence they had grown to admire and respect his brother.'

'Was anyone hurt?'

He shook his head. 'When it was obvious that he lacked popular support, his allies were quick to make their peace with the man holding the purse strings.'

'It's like something out of a Shakespearean tragedy,' she said.

'I suppose it is. But it was of his own making. Even then, if he'd been prepared to acknowledge his brother as ruler, publicly bow the knee, he would have been allowed to stay. Play his part. When he refused to humiliate himself in that way, his brother exiled him from the tribe, stripped him of his name, title, banished him. All he was left with was the financial settlement that his father had hoped would compensate him for being supplanted by his younger brother.'

'And your father? Was he included in this punishment?'

'Banishment was for *Jaddi* alone, but the rest followed. If a father does not bear the name of his tribe, the title owed to him by birth…'

'So you are al-Zaki.'

'A name without history,' he said. Without honour. 'My father and I are free to come and go, as is my sister. I have an office, an apartment in Rumaillah but, without a family, I remain invisible.' His letters returned unanswered. Barred from his place in the *majlis*. Forbidden any way of appealing for mercy for a dying man. Reduced to using this woman.

'What do you think will happen when Princess Sabirah comes here? Will she "see" you?' she asked.

'Don't worry about it,' he said, angry with himself, angry with the Emir, angry with her for making him feel guilty. 'Her Highness won't do anything to embarrass her distinguished guest.'

That was what Lucy was relying on, anyway. If she acknowledged him, he would beg her to intercede with the Emir for his grandfather. That was all that was left, he thought bitterly. A chance to plead with the woman who shared the Emir's pillow to show pity on a dying man.

Lydia felt the emptiness in Kal's words, the loss, an underlying anger too, but to say that she was sorry would be meaningless and so she said nothing—she'd already said far too much, come close to blowing the whole deal.

The silence drifted back, broken only by the clink of dishes when Yatimah appeared to clear the table, loading everything on to the tray.

Having come—in a moment of high emotion—perilously close to letting slip the truth about her own father's death, she took the chance to gather herself before turning to Yatimah to thank her for the meal.

'*La shokr ala wageb, sitti*. No thanks are due for duty.'

'Will you say that again?' Lydia begged, grabbing the chance to move away from dangerous territory. Listening carefully and repeating it after her self-appointed teacher.

'I will bring coffee?'

'*Nam. Shukran.*'

When she'd gone, Kal said, 'You listen well, Rose.'

'I try to pick up a few words of the local language when I'm on holiday. Even if it's only hello and thank you.' The truth, and how good that felt, but before he could ask where she usually went on holiday, 'So, what time are we going fishing?'

'Maybe we should give that a miss today,' he said. 'Wait until you're really bored.'

She tried not to look too happy about that.

'You might have a long wait. I've got the most beautiful garden to explore, a swimming pool to lie beside and a stack of good books to read. In fact, as soon as we've had coffee I'll decide which to do first.'

'*Qahwa*. The Arabic for coffee is *qahwa*. You make the q sound in the back of your throat.'

'*Ga howa?*'

'Perfect.' Then, with one of those slow smiles that sent a dangerous finger of heat funnelling through her, 'Maybe we should add Arabic lessons to the schedule.'

Doing her best to ignore it, she said, 'You do know that I had planned to simply lie in the sun for a week?'

'You can listen, speak lying down, can't you?'

Lydia tried to block out the image of Kal, stretched out on a lounger beside her at the pool she'd glimpsed from the dining room, his skin glistening in the sun while he attempted to teach her the rudiments of a language he clearly loved.

Did he really believe that she would be able to concentrate?

'Lying in the sun resting,' she elaborated swiftly, all the emphasis on *resting*. 'You seem determined to keep me permanently occupied. Rushing around, doing stuff.'

'It won't be hard work, I promise you.'

His low honeyed voice promised her all kinds of things, none of them arduous, and as he picked up her hand the heat intensified.

'We can begin with something simple.' And, never taking his eyes from her face, he touched his lips to the tip of her little finger. '*Wahid.*'

'*Wahid?*'

'One.'

'*Ithnan.*' His lips moved on to her ring finger, lingered while she attempted to hold her wits together and repeat the word.

'*Ithnan.* Two.'

'*Thalatha.*'

Something inside her was melting and it took her so long to respond that he began to nibble on the tip of her middle finger.

'*Thalatha!*'

'*Arba'a.*' And he drove home the message with four tiny kisses on the tip, the first joint, the second joint, the knuckle of her forefinger.

'*Arba'a.*' It was her bones that were the problem, she decided. Her bones were melting. That was why she couldn't move. Pull free. 'Four.'

'*Khamsa.*' He looked for a moment at her thumb, then took the length of it in his mouth before slowly pulling back to the tip. 'Five.'

He was right. This was a language lesson she was never going to forget. She mindlessly held out her other hand so that he could teach her the numbers six to ten, already anticipating the continuation of a lesson involving every part of her body.

He did not take it and, catching her breath as she came back to earth, she used it to sweep her hair behind her ear, managing a very creditable. '*Shukran,* Kal.'

Yatimah placed a tray containing a small brass coffee pot and tiny cups on the table beside her.

Feeling ridiculously light-headed as she realised that he must have seen her coming, that he had not rejected her but chosen discretion, she said, 'Truly that was a huge improvement on Mrs Latimer's Year Six French class.'

'Mrs Latimer?' Lucy had been saying something about Rose not being allowed to go to school when he'd interrupted her. He wished now he'd been less impatient...

For a moment Lydia's mind froze.

'A t-tutor,' she stuttered as Kal continued to look at her, a frown creasing that wide forehead.

She longed to tell him everything. Tell him about her brave mother who'd lost her husband and her mobility in one tragic moment on an icy road. Tell him about school, how she'd left when she was sixteen because what was the point of staying on when she would never have left her mother to go away to university? Tell him everything...

She was rescued from his obvious suspicion by the beep of a text arriving on her mobile phone.

'Excuse me,' she said, retrieving it from her pocket. 'It might be...' She swallowed, unable to say the word *grandfather,* turned away to check it, assuming that it was simply a 'have fun' response from her mother to her own text.

But it wasn't from her mother. It was from Rose.

Vtl you b on frnt pge am!

Vital you be on the front page tomorrow morning...

Lydia swallowed. Had she been recognised?

Clearly she had to convince someone that she really was in Bab el Sama.

She quickly keyed in *OK* and hit 'send', returning the phone to her pocket. Realised that Kal was watching her intently.

'Is there a problem?' he asked as Yatimah offered them each a cup, then filled them with a thin straw-coloured aromatic liquid that was nothing like any coffee she'd ever seen.

'Good heavens, no!' she said with a nervous laugh which, even to her own ears, rang about as true as a cracked bell.

Only him.

Only her guilt that she was lying to a man who made her feel things that needed total honesty. And she couldn't be honest: The text was a timely reminder just how deeply she was embedded in this pretence. She was doing this for Rose and right now only she mattered…

They were four hours ahead of London, plenty of time to make the morning papers, but to accomplish that she had to get into the open in daylight. On her own. Wearing as little as possible.

She and Rose both knew that what the paparazzi were really hoping for was a picture of her in a private 'love nest' scenario with Rupert Devenish.

That was never going to happen, so in order to keep them focused, they'd planned a slow striptease to keep those lenses on her for the entire week.

First up would be a walk along the beach in shorts with a shirt open over a bathing suit.

After that she was going to discard the shirt to reveal a bathing suit top beneath it. Rare enough to excite interest, but nothing particularly sensational—it was a very demure bathing suit. Finally she'd strip down to the swimsuit. That should be enough to keep the photographers on their toes, but there was a bikini in reserve in case of unforeseen emergencies.

Rose's text suggested they were in the 'unforeseen emergency' category. What she didn't, couldn't know was that her good friend Lucy al-Khatib had provided her with a 'protector'. Kal was relaxed about letting her wander, unseen by the outside world, in the shelter of the gardens, but she very much doubted that he'd sit back and let her take a walk along the beach without her minder.

While it was true that his presence would absolutely guarantee a front page spot, she also recognised that the presence of some unknown man in close attendance would cause more problems than it solved.

She was going to have to evade her watchdog and get down to the beach and she had less than an hour in which to manage it.

Kal watched Rose sip gingerly at the scalding coffee. Clearly, whatever had been in the text had not been good news. The colour had drained from her face and a man didn't have to be fluent in body language to see that she was positively twitching to get away.

Which begged the question, why didn't she just say, *Great lunch, see you later…* and walk away? Or tell him that something had come up that she had to deal with?

Why was she sitting there like a cat on hot bricks, doing her best to pretend that nothing was wrong?

A gentleman would make it easy for her. Make an excuse himself and leave her to get on with whatever it was she wanted to do.

A man who'd been charged with her safety, in the face of some unspecified threat, would be rather less obliging. Lucy might have disparaged the Duke's concerns, but she hadn't dismissed them entirely.

She hadn't elaborated on them, either. Could it be that she was more worried about what Rose might do than what some imaginary assailant had in mind?

Maybe he should give her a call right now. Except that would leave Rose on her own, which didn't seem like a great idea.

'This is desert coffee,' he said conversationally. 'The beans are not ground but boiled whole with cardamom seeds. For the digestion.'

'Really? It's different. Very good,' she said, although he doubted she had even tasted it.

As she put the cup down, clearly eager to be away, he said, 'Traditionally, politeness requires that you drink two cups.'

'Two?'

She scarcely managed to hide her dismay and his concern deepened. What on earth had been in that text?

'They're very small. If you hold out the cup, like this,' he said, holding out his own cup, 'Yatimah will refill it for you.'

Obediently she held out the cup. Drank it as quickly as she could without scalding her mouth, handed the cup back to the girl.

And it was refilled a third time.

'She'll refill it as often as you hold it out like that,' he explained. 'When you've had enough you have to shake the cup from side to side to indicate that you have had enough.'

'Oh. Right.' She swallowed it down, shook the cup the way he told her, thanked Yatimah who, at a look from him, quickly disappeared. Rose, looking as if she wanted to bolt after her, said, 'If you'll excuse me, Kal, I'll go and get my book. Find somewhere quiet to read. You don't have to stand guard over me while I do that, do you?'

'Not if you stay within the garden,' he said, rising to his feet, easing back her chair.

'What about the beach?' she asked, so casually that he knew that was where she would be heading the minute he took his eyes off her. 'That's private, isn't it?'

'It's private in that no one will come ashore and have a picnic. Local people respect the privacy of the Emir and his guests, but the creek is busy.' He glanced across the water. 'There are plenty of boats where a photographer hoping to catch a candid shot of you could hide out.' He turned back to her. 'Lucy said you found the intrusion stressful but if you want to risk a walk along the shore, I'll be happy to accompany you.'

'Lady Rose Napier plus unknown man on a beach? Now, that really would make their day.' Her laughter lacked any real suggestion of amusement. 'I'll stick to the garden, thanks.' Then, 'Why don't you take yourself off on that fishing trip you're so keen on? Give me a break from the maggots.'

Give her a break? Where on earth had the secluded Lady Rose picked up these expressions?

'The maggots will be disappointed,' he said, coming up with a smile. 'I'll see you at dinner?'

'Of course.'

Her relief was palpable at the prospect of an entire afternoon free of him. He would have been offended but, from the way she'd responded to his kisses, he knew it wasn't personal.

'Although I'd better put in a few laps at the pool, too, or at this rate none of the clothes I brought with me will fit.'

'There's an upside to everything,' he replied.

His reward was a hot blush before she lifted her hand in a small, oddly awkward, see-you-later gesture and walked quickly towards the cottage.

Kal, getting the message loud and clear, didn't move until she was out of sight.

CHAPTER NINE

LYDIA'S luggage had been unpacked and put away and she quickly hunted through drawers, doing her best not to linger and drool over silk, cashmere, finest linen, as she searched for a swimsuit.

She had refused to accept a penny from Rose for this assignment. This was a labour of love, gratitude, respect and she'd insisted on taking a week of her paid holiday entitlement. But Rose had found a way to reward her anyway. She'd raided her wardrobe for more clothes than she could possibly wear in a week at the beach. Clothes she had never worn. Insisting that Lydia keep them.

The half a dozen swimsuits that she'd packed, each bearing the name of a world famous designer, were uniformly gorgeous. Each, inevitably, had the 'pink rose' theme and Lydia chose a striking black one-piece costume with a single long-stemmed rose embroidered across the front from the right hip, with stem and leaves curling diagonally across the stomach, so that the bud bloomed above her heart.

It was clearly a one-off that had been made especially for her and, with luck, the delighted designer would call the gossip pages and claim whatever PR was going. Which would help to establish that it could be no one but Rose on the Bab el Sama beach.

It fitted her like a glove, holding, lifting in all the right places. She didn't waste any time admiring her reflection, however, but threw the kaftan over it, ran a brush through her hair, freshened her lipstick and grabbed a book.

All she had to do now was find her way down to the beach unobserved and, avoiding the exit through the garden room to the terrace where Kal might still be lingering, she slipped out through the dining room.

Kal stood in the dark shadows at the top of a rocky outcrop, sweeping the water with a pair of powerful glasses, hoping to pick up anything out of place. Anyone who didn't have business on the water.

It was as peaceful a scene as a bodyguard could hope for. Fishermen, traders, local people pottering on their boats.

He glanced at his watch, wondering how much longer Rose would be. Because she'd come. He'd put money on it. But why?

He took out his BlackBerry and put Rose's name into the search engine. There was a picture of her leaving the lunch yesterday, '…radiant…' as she left for a week in Bab el Sama. Raising the question of whether she'd be alone.

There were other photographs. One of her with Rupert Devenish a couple of weeks earlier. Not looking radiant.

Maybe she had just been tired. Or perhaps the hollows in her cheeks, around her eyes were the result of a cold or a headache. Perhaps the camera angle was unflattering. Whatever it was, she had none of the glow that had reached out, grabbed him by the throat and refused to let go.

In fact she looked like a pale imitation of his Rose. He continued his search for answers until the soft slap of leather thongs against the stone steps warned him that she was on her way. He could have told her that to be silent she would need to remove her shoes. But then she hadn't expected him to be there.

She paused in a deep patch of shade at the bottom of the steps that led from the garden, a book in one hand, presumably an alibi in case he hadn't done as she'd suggested and conveniently removed himself from the scene, but instead taken his promise to Lucy seriously enough to stick around and keep an eye on her.

He kept very still as she looked around,

checking that the beach was empty. Even if she had looked up, he was well hidden from the casual glance, but she was only concerned that the beach was empty and, having made certain the coast was clear, she put the book on the step. Then she took the mobile phone from her pocket and placed it on top.

No...

The word stilled on his lips as she reached back and pulled the kaftan over her head to reveal a simple one-piece black swimsuit that displayed every curve, every line of her body to perfection. A slender neck, circled with a fine gold chain on which hung a rosebud pendant. Wide, elegant shoulders, an inviting cleavage that hadn't appeared on the photograph of her in the evening gown. A proper waist, gently flared hips and then those endless legs, perfect ankles, long slender feet.

For a moment she stood there, as if summoning up the courage to carry on.

Don't...

The thought of his Rose appearing on the front page of tomorrow's papers in a swimsuit, her body being leered at by millions of men, was utterly abhorrent to him and he knew that the rush of protectiveness he felt had nothing whatever to do with the charge that Lucy had laid on him.

He'd spent much of his life on beaches, around

swimming pools with women who would have raised their sophisticated eyebrows at such a puritan reaction and he knew his response was the very worst kind of double standard.

By modern standards, the costume she was wearing was modest.

Before he could move, do anything, she draped the kaftan over a low branch and she stepped into the sun. Shoulders back, head high, she walked towards the water, where she paused to scan the creek.

The light breeze caught her hair, lifting tiny strands that caught the light, lending her an ethereal quality.

Dear God, she was beautiful.

As cool and mysterious as a princess in some *Arabian Nights* story, escaped from some desperate danger and washed up on an unknown shore, waiting for Sinbad to rescue her, restore her to her prince.

'That's enough,' he whispered. 'Turn back now. Come back to me.'

She glanced round, looking up, as if she'd heard him, but it was a bird quartering the air that had caught her attention and, having watched it for a moment, she turned, then took a step…

'No!'

…bent to pick up something from the sand. It was a piece of sand-polished glass and, as she held it up to the light, he caught an echo of the flash out on the creek.

He lifted the glasses, scanned the water and this time found the telltale glint as the sunlight dancing on the water was reflected off a lens hidden beneath a tarpaulin on an anonymous-looking motor launch. It was anchored amongst half a dozen or so boats on the far side of the creek, its name obscured, deliberately, he had no doubt, and he had to fight the urge to race after Rose, drag her back.

But the one thing they were in complete agreement about was that she must not be photographed with him.

It would provoke a feeding frenzy among the press and it wouldn't take them five minutes to uncover his identity. His entire history would be rehashed in the press, along with the playboy lifestyle of both his grandfather and father, to fuel innuendo-laden speculation about why he was in Bab el Sama with Rose.

And no one was going to believe that the millionaire CEO of an international air freight business had accompanied Lady Rose Napier to Bab el Sama as her bodyguard. The millionaire grandson of an exiled sheikh, son of an international playboy, he hadn't been exactly short of media coverage himself before he'd stopped the drift. Found a purpose in life.

The fallout from that would cause a lot more embarrassment than even the most revealing photograph.

Worse, her grandfather, the Duke, would be apoplectic and blame Lucy for embroiling her in such a mess. Not to mention the fact that the Emir would be so angry that Kalil could kiss goodbye forever to any chance of *Jaddi*'s banishment being lifted so that he could die in peace at Umm al Sama.

His sole remit was to protect Lady Rose from danger. Shooting her with a camera didn't count, especially when she was going out of her way to make it easy for whoever was laid up in that boat.

He watched her as, apparently oblivious to scrutiny from both sea and shore, she wandered along the shoreline, stopping now and then to pick up a shell or a pebble. Lifting a hand to push back her hair. It was a classic image, one he knew that picture editors around the world would lap up, putting their own spin on it in a dozen headlines, most of them including the word *alone*.

So who had sent the message that had her scurrying to expose herself to the world's press?

He looked down at the shady step where she'd left her phone.

Lydia stood for a moment at the edge of the water, lifting her face to the sun, the gorgeous feeling of wet sand seeping between her toes taking her back to childhood holidays when her father had been alive, memories of her mother laughing as the waves caught her.

She remembered one holiday when she'd collected a whole bucket full of shells. By the end of their stay, they had smelled so bad that her father had refused to put them in the car. To stop her tears at the loss of her treasures, her mother had washed the most special one, given her a heart-shaped box to keep it in.

She still had her memory box. It contained a picture of her father, laughing as she splashed him with a hosepipe. Her mother with the world famous couturier she'd worked for before the accident. The newspaper picture of her in the very first 'Lady Rose' outfit her mother had made when she was fifteen.

There had been a rush of additions in that brief spell when she'd thought she was in love. All but one of those had been tossed away with many more tears than the shells when she'd realised the truth. She'd kept just one thing, a theatre programme, because all memories were important. Even the bad ones. If you didn't remember, you didn't learn…

After that the memories had nearly all involved her lookalike gigs. Her life as someone else.

Looking around, she saw the edge of an oyster shell sticking out of sand washed clean by the receding tide.

She bent to ease it out, rinsed it off in the water, turned it over to reveal the pink and blue irides-

cence of mother-of-pearl. A keepsake to remind
her of this moment, this beach, Kal al-Zaki kissing
her fingers as he taught her Arabic numbers. A
memory to bring out when she was old and all this
would seem like a dream that had happened to
someone else.

The last one she'd ever put in that old box, she
vowed. She was never going to do this again, be
Rose. It was time to start living her own life
making her own memories. No more pretence.

She stood for a moment, holding the shell, uncertain which way to go. Then, choosing to have
the wind in her face, she turned right, towards
the sea, wishing that Kal was walking with her
to point out the landmarks, tell her the story
behind a crumbling tower on the highest point or
the far bank. To hold her hand as she turned
through the curve that had taken Kal out of sight
that morning.

Until now Kal had been able to dismiss the turmoil
induced by his charge as nothing more than the
natural response of a healthy male for a woman
who had hit all the right buttons.

He was thirty-three, had been surrounded by
beautiful women all his life and was familiar with
desire in all its guises, but as he'd got older,
become more certain what he wanted, he'd found
it easy to stay uninvolved.

That he'd been knocked so unexpectedly sideways by Lady Rose Napier was, he'd been convinced, no more than the heightened allure of the unobtainable.

All that went out of the window in the moment she stepped out of his sight.

Lydia continued for as long as she dared, scanning the creek, hoping for some sign that there was someone out there.

Then, because she doubted it would be long before someone realised that she wasn't where she was meant to be and start looking for her, she turned back, relieved to be picking her way across the soft sand to the shade, the anonymity of the giant rock formation near the foot of the steps.

She'd half expected to find Yatimah standing guard over her book, her phone, her expression disapproving, but her escapade had gone unobserved. Relieved, she pushed her feet into the leather thong sandals, then turned to carefully lift the kaftan from the branch.

It wasn't there and she looked down to see if it had fallen.

Took a step into the shadows behind the rocks, assuming that it had been caught by a gust of wind and blown there.

And another.

Without warning, she was seized from behind

around the waist, lifted clear of the sand, her body held tight against the hard frame of a man.

As she struggled to get free, she pounded at the arm holding her, using the edge of the shell as a weapon, opened her mouth to scream.

A hand cut off the sound.

'Looking for something, Lady Rose?'

She stilled. Kal…

She'd known it even before he'd spoken. Knew that woody scent. Would always know it…

As soon as she stopped struggling he dropped his hand and, knowing he was going to be mad at her, she got in first with, 'I thought you were going fishing.'

'And I thought you were going to curl up by the pool with a good book.'

He set her down and, with the utmost reluctance, she turned to face him.

'I am.' Head up. And Lady Rose, the Duke's granddaughter at her most aristocratic, she added, 'I decided to take a detour.'

'And give one of your paparazzi army tomorrow's front page picture?'

She instinctively glanced at the phone lying defenceless on top of her book. 'Have you been reading my messages?' she demanded.

'No need. You've just told me everything I need to know.'

'No…'

'What is it, Rose?' he asked. 'Are you a publicity junkie? Can't you bear to see an entire week go by without your picture on the front page?'

She opened her mouth to protest. Closed it again.

His anger was suppressed, but there was no doubting how he felt at being deceived, made a fool of, and who could blame him? Except, of course, he hadn't. He'd been ahead of her every step of the way. Instead, she shook her head, held up her hands.

'You've got me, Kal. Bang to rights.' She took a step back. 'Can I have my dress back now?'

As he reached up, lifted the kaftan down from the place he'd hidden it, she saw the blood oozing from his arm where she'd slashed at him with the shell she was still clutching.

She dropped it as if it burned, reached out to him, drew back without touching him. She'd lied to him and he knew it.

'I hurt you,' she said helplessly.

He glanced at the wound she'd made, shrugged. 'Nothing that I didn't ask for.'

'Maybe, but it still needs cleaning.' Ignoring the dress he was holding out to her, she began to run up the steps. 'Sea shells have all kinds of horrible things in them,' she said. 'You can get septicae-mia.'

'Is that right?'

Realising that he hadn't followed her, she stopped, looked back. 'Truly.' Then, realising that perhaps that wasn't the best choice of word, 'I've been on a first aid course.' She offered her hand but, when he didn't take it, said, 'Please, Kal.'

Relenting, he slung the dress over his shoulder, stooped to pick up the book and phone she'd abandoned in her rush to heal, adding the number of his mobile phone to her contact list. Adding hers to his as he followed her up to the house, the bedroom where he'd left her sleeping a few hours earlier, into the huge, luxurious bathroom beyond.

'I've put my number in your phone,' he said, putting them on a table. 'In case you should ever need it.'

She rolled her eyes. 'Sit there!'

He obediently settled himself on a wide upholstered bench while she took a small first aid box from a large cupboard that was filled with the cosmetics and toiletries she'd brought with her and searched through it for sachets containing antiseptic wipes.

'Why did you do it?' He addressed the top of her head as she bent over him, cleaning up the scratches she'd made.

'This is nothing,' she said. 'I did a self-defence course and you're really lucky I wasn't wearing high heels.'

'I wasn't referring to your attempt to chop my arm off. Why did you strip off for that photographer?'

'I didn't strip off!' she declared, so flustered by the accusation that for a moment she forgot what she was doing. Then, getting a grip, 'I took a walk on the beach in a swimsuit. A very modest swimsuit.'

Modest by today's standards, maybe, but this close, clinging like a second skin, revealing perhaps more than she realised, as she bent over him—suggesting more—the effect was far more enticing than an entire beach filled with topless lovelies.

She looked up. 'Did you say "photographer"?'

'I did.'

She straightened abruptly as she saw exactly where his eyes were focused.

'You saw him?'

'He was in a launch out on the creek and well camouflaged from above. He forgot about the sun reflecting off the water.'

The tension went out of her shoulders, her neck. Relief, he thought. That was sheer relief.

'So why did you do it?' he persisted.

'I thought we'd established that,' she said, concentrating once more on his arm.

The speed with which she'd grabbed at the insulting explanation he'd offered suggested desperation to hide the real reason for her exhibitionism.

While he had his own suspicions, he was beginning to wish he'd overcome his squeamishness about plundering her phone for the answer.

'Maybe you'd better run it by me again.'

Apparently satisfied with the clean up job on his arm, or maybe just wanting to put a little distance between them, she gathered up the used wipes, dropped them in a bin.

'It's a game, Kal,' she said, busying herself, filling a marble basin with warm water. Looking anywhere but at him. 'We need each other. Celebrities need headlines, the media have an insatiable appetite for stories. The trick is to give them what they want and then hope they'll leave you alone.'

She plunged her hands in the water, then looked around for soap.

He took a piece from a crystal bowl but did not hand it to her. Instead, he put his arms around her, trapping her as he leaned into her back, his chin against her hair as he dipped his hands into the water and began to soap her fingers.

'Kal!' she protested, but feebly. They both knew she wasn't going anywhere until she'd told him what was going on.

'What, exactly, do they want from you?' he asked.

'Right now?' The words came out as a squeak and he waited while she took a breath. 'Right now,' she repeated, 'they'd give their eye teeth for a picture of me here, in flagrante with Rupert Devenish.' She tried a laugh, attempting to ignore the way his thumb was circling her palm. The way she was relaxing against him. 'He's—'

'I read the newspapers,' he said, not wanting to hear the words on her lips. Or that it was Lucy who'd filled him in on the marriage mania in the gossip columns. 'But that isn't going to happen, is it?'

Unless he'd got it totally wrong and the text had been from Devenish announcing his imminent arrival, urging Rose to convince the paparazzi that she was alone before he joined her.

In which case her eager response to him, the way she had softened in the circle of his arms, surrendered her hands for him to do with what he would, was going to take a little—make that a lot of—explaining.

'It's not going to happen,' she confirmed. 'I'm afraid they're going to have to make do with the clichéd Lady Rose, alone on a beach, how sad, picture.'

And it was his turn to feel the tension slide away from his shoulders.

But only halfway.

According to Lucy, Rose was falling apart because of the constant intrusion into her life. Ten years without being able to lift a finger unobserved, she'd said.

He wasn't getting that impression from Rose.

Far from it. She seemed totally relaxed about what could only be construed as a unwarranted intrusion into her private life.

'And if they aren't?' he asked.

A tiny tremor rippled through her and he knew that there was a lot more to this than she was telling him.

'Trust me, Rose,' he said. 'The picture will be a sensation.' He reached for a towel, taking her hands, drying them one finger at a time. Then, because he was still angry with her, 'And if I'm wrong you can always go for the topless option tomorrow.'

'Tomorrow will be too late…'

She caught herself, no doubt realising that she should have objected to the 'topless', not the 'tomorrow'. But he had the answer to at least one of his questions.

For some reason she wanted a picture of herself on the front page and for some reason it had to be tomorrow. And he went straight back to that mysterious threat.

Was this what it was all about? Give me a photograph or… Or what?

What on earth could anyone have over the universally loved and admired 'people's angel'?

Except, of course, that the woman in his arms was not Rose Napier.

On some subconscious level he'd known that from the moment she'd walked into the VIP lounge at the airport. Right from the beginning, he'd sensed the split personality, the separation between the woman playing a role—and occasionally slipping—and the woman who shone through the disguise, lighting him up not just like a rocket, but the whole damn fourth of July scenario. Whoosh, bang, the sky filled with coloured stars.

He didn't trust it, knew it was a temporary aberration, nothing but chemistry, but he finally understood why his grandfather had lost his head, lost his country over a woman.

He was here on a one-off last-chance mission and from the moment she'd appeared on the scene this woman had attacked all his systems like a virus taking over a computer memory, supplanting herself in place of everything that was vital, important, real.

Lucy had obviously told him a pack of lies—he was only here to inveigle his way into a meeting with Princess Sabirah, so why would he be bothered with something as important as the truth?

Presumably the real Rose was holed up in some private love nest with Rupert while this woman, this lovely woman who was superficially so like her, was nothing but a plant to keep the press focused on Bab el Sama.

So what had gone wrong? Had someone found out? Threatened to expose the switch? Directing his own personal photo shoot by text?

In which case he had no doubt that the topless

scenario would be the next demand. Because, even if she was a fake, that picture would be worth millions to the photographer who delivered it to a picture agency.

'You've got nothing to worry about,' he said, tossing the towel aside, not sure who he was most angry with, Lucy or this woman, whoever she was, for putting at risk his own mission.

No, that was wrong. Lucy had used the situation to give him a chance. This woman had lit him up, responding to his kisses as if he was the last man on earth. Lies, lies, lies…

'I guarantee you that there won't be a picture editor in London who won't grab that picture of you for their front page tomorrow.'

Her all too obvious relief flipped something in his brain and he stroked the pad of his thumb over the exquisite rose that curved invitingly across her breast in an insultingly intimate gesture, opened his mouth over her all too obvious response as the bud beneath the costume leapt to his touch.

Her throat moved as she swallowed, doing her best to ignore the intimacy of his touch, but the tiny shiver that rippled through her betrayed pleasure, desire, need and her response was not to pull away but buckle against him.

Too late, he discovered that he was the one caught in a lie, because it didn't matter who she was, he desired her as he had never desired any other woman. Not just with his body, but with his heart, his soul and simply holding her was not enough.

Nothing could disguise from her how very much it wasn't enough but, as the wildfire of desire swept through him, he was not alone. Her seeking lips found his neck, trailed moist kisses across his chin, touched his lips, her need as desperate as his.

'Whoever you are,' he murmured, looking down at her, 'you can trust me on that...'

For a moment she looked at him, her mouth soft, her lids heavy with desire and the slow-burning fuse, lit in the moment their eyes had first met, of that unfinished kiss, lay between them.

The air was heavy with the desire of two people for whom the need to touch, to explore, to be one, blotted out memory, bypassed hard-learned lessons, destroyed reason.

Lydia heard him, understood what he was saying, but wrapped in the powerful arms of a man she desired beyond sense, this was not a time for questions, answers. Time was suspended. There was no past, no future. This was for now. Only the senses survived—scent, taste, touch—and she reached out and with her fingertips traced the perfection of Kal's profile.

His wide forehead, the high-bridged nose, lingering to trace the outline of those beautifully carved lips.

The thin clothing pressed between them did

nothing to disguise the urgent response of his body and she was seized by a surge of power, of certainty that this was her moment and, leaning into him so that her lips touched his, she whispered, 'Please…'

As her fingers, her lips touched his, took possession of his mouth, Kalil al-Zaki, a man known for his ice-cold self-control, consigned his reputation to oblivion.

His arms were already about her and for a moment he allowed himself to be swept away. To feel instead of think.

Drink deep of the honeyed sweetness of a woman who was clever, funny, heartbreakingly lovely. Everything a man could ever want or desire.

Forget, just for a while, who he was. Why he was here.

Her mouth was like silk, her body eager, desperate even, but it wasn't enough and, lost to all sense as he breathed in the scent of her skin, the hollows of her neck, her shoulders, he slowly peeled away the swimsuit to taste the true rosebuds it concealed.

Her response was eager, as urgent as his own, and yet, even as she offered him everything, he could not let go, forget the lies…

How she'd played the virgin, acted the seductress. Was this just another lie to buy his silence?

She whimpered into his mouth as he broke free,

determined to regain control of his senses, yet unable to let go as she melted against him.

'Who are you?' he demanded helplessly. 'Why are you here?' When she didn't answer he leaned back, needing to look her in the face, wanting her to see his. But her eyes were closed, as if by not seeing, she would be deaf to his words. 'What do you want from me?'

'Nothing!' Then, more gently, 'I'm sorry.' And, without looking at him, she slowly disentangled herself and, shivering, clutched her costume to her and said, 'You can g-go fishing now, Kal. I promise I'll g-go and sit by the pool like the well behaved young woman I'm supposed to be.'

Torn between wanting her to behave and wanting her to be very, very bad indeed, he reassembled the shattered pieces of his cast-iron self-control, picked up his shirt and, taking her hands, fed them into the sleeves, buttoning it around her as if she were a child.

'I'm going nowhere until you tell me the truth,' he said. Then, with a muttered oath, 'You're shivering.' She couldn't be cold… 'What can I get you?'

'A proper cup of tea?' She sniffed and he lifted her chin, wiped a tear from beneath her eye.

Shivering, tears… He wanted to shake her, hold her, yell at her, make love to her…

'Tea?' he said, trying to get a grip.

'Made in a mug with a tea bag, milk from a cow

and two heaped spoons of sugar.' She managed a rueful smile. 'Stirred, not shaken.'

'I'm glad your sense of humour survived intact,' he said.

'My sense of humour and everything else.' She lifted her shoulders in a simple up and down shrug. 'I've only come that close to losing my virginity once before, Kal. I'm beginning to think I'm destined to be an old maid and the really bad news is that I'm allergic to cats.'

Better make that two cups of hot, sweet tea, he thought, picking up the phone.

CHAPTER TEN

'WHO are you?'

Lydia, her hands around the mug of tea he'd rustled up for her, was sitting in the shuttered balcony of her room, bars of sunlight slanting through into a very private space and shimmering off Kal's naked shoulders.

'What are you?'

'Lydia. Lydia Young. I've been a professional lookalike pretty much from the moment that Lady Rose made her first appearance.'

'Lydia.' He repeated her name carefully, as if memorising it. 'How old were you?'

'Fifteen. I'm a few months younger than Rose.' She sipped at the hot tea, shuddering at the sweetness. 'How did you know?' Then, because it was somehow more important, 'When did you know?'

'I think that on some level I always knew you weren't Rose.' He glanced at her. 'I sensed a dual personality. Two people in the same body. And you have an unusual turn of phrase for a young woman with your supposedly sheltered upbringing. Then there was the Marchioness slaving over Sunday lunch. And Mrs Latimer.'

'Year Six French.' She took another sip of tea. 'I knew you'd picked up on that. I hoped I'd covered it.'

'You might have got away with it but once that text arrived you were in bits. It wasn't difficult to work out that you'd be heading for the beach as soon as you'd got rid of me so, while I waited for you to show up, I took a look at the Internet, hoping to pick up some clue about what the hell was going on.'

'What was the clincher?' she asked. Not a Lady Rose word, but she wasn't pretending any more.

'You made the front page in that cute little hat you were wearing. The caption suggested that after recent concerns about your health you appeared to be full of life. Positively glowing, in fact. Fortunately for you, they put it down to true love.'

She groaned.

'I should have done more with my make-up, but we were sure the veil would be enough. And it was all going so well that I might just have got a bit lippy with the photographers. What an idiot!'

'Calm down. There was nothing in the stories to suggest that you were a fake,' he assured her. 'Just a recent photograph of Rose with Rupert and some salacious speculation about what you'd be doing here.'

'But if you had no trouble spotting the difference—'

'Only because I've become intimately acquainted with your face, your figure,' he said. 'I don't pay a lot of attention to celebrity photographs, but the "people's angel" is hard to miss and I expected someone less vivid. Not quite so…' He seemed lost for an appropriate adjective.

'Lippy?' she offered helpfully.

'I was going to say lively,' he said, his eyes apparently riveted to her mouth. 'But lippy will do. One look at the real thing and I knew you were someone else.' Then, turning abruptly, he said, 'So what's going on? Where is Rose Napier? With Rupert Devenish?'

'Good grief, I hope not.'

'Strike two for Rupert. Lucy isn't a fan either. I take it you've met him?'

'I've seen him with her. He's an old style aristocrat. Her grandfather,' she explained, 'but thirty years younger.'

'Controlling.'

She thought about it for a moment, then nodded. 'Rose and I met by chance one day. I'd been booked for a lookalike gig, a product launch at a swanky hotel. I had no idea Rose was going to be a guest at a lunch there or I'd have turned it down, but as I was leaving we came face to face. It could have been my worst nightmare but she was so sweet. She really is everything they say she is, you know.'

'That's another reason I saw through you.' He reached out, wiped the pad of his thumb across her mouth. 'You're no angel, Lydia Young.'

She took another quick sip of her tea.

'How is it?'

'Just what the doctor ordered. Too hot, too sweet. Perfect, in fact.'

'I'll remember the formula.'

She looked at him. Remember? There was a future?

Realising just how stupid that was, she turned away. Just more shocks, she decided, and concentrated on getting through her story.

'Rose spent a little too long chatting with me for Rupert's liking and when he summoned her to heel she asked me how much I charged. In case she ever wanted an evening off.'

'How much do you charge?' he asked pointedly.

'This one is on the house, Kal. I owe Rose. My father was killed in a car accident when I was ten years old. My mother was badly injured—'

'Your brave, determined mother.'

'She lost the man she loved, the use of her legs, her career in the blink of an eye, Kal.'

'I'm sorry.'

She shook her head. It was a long time since she'd cried for the loss and when he reached out as if to take her hand, offer comfort, she moved it out of reach. Right now, comfort would undo her completely and she was in enough trouble without that.

'Is this what you do? I mean, is it a full-time job?'

'Hardly. Two or three gigs a month at the most. The day job is on the checkout at a supermarket. The manager is very good about me swapping shifts.' She was going to tell him that he wanted her to take a management course. As if that would make any difference... 'The money I earn as Rose's lookalike has made a real difference to my mother's life.'

The electric wheelchair. The hand-operated sewing machine. The car she'd saved up for. And the endless driving lessons before she'd eventually passed her test.

'So, like Rose, you have no other family?'

She shook her head.

'And, like her, no lover? You are a beautiful, vivid woman, Lydia. I find that hard to believe.'

'Yes, well, I live a rather peculiar life. My day job is in a supermarket, where staff and customers alike call me Rose despite the fact that I wear a badge with my real name on it. Where most of them can't quite decide whether I'm fish or fowl. The rest of the time I'm pretending to be someone else.'

'And taking care of your mother. I imagine that takes a chunk out of your time, too. Who is with her while you're here?'

'A friend stays with her sometimes so that I can take a holiday. And I'm not totally pathetic. I do get asked out. Of course I do. But I'm never sure exactly who they think they're with.'

'Someone must have got through. If we… If I… If that was the second time.'

She nodded. 'He said he was a law student. He always came to my checkout at the supermarket. Chatted. Brought me tiny gifts. Wooed me with sweet words and posies, flattery and patience. Endless patience. It was weeks before he asked me out.'

Months before he'd suggested more than a kiss. So long that she'd been burning up with frustration. Ready to go off like a fire-cracker.

'It was the patience that did it,' she said. 'The understanding. How many men are prepared to put up with the missed dates, always coming second to my mother, the job, the gigs? To wait?'

'A man will wait for what is precious,' Kal said.

'And who could resist that?' Not her. She'd fallen like a ton of bricks. 'It was that flash, bang wallop love thing that you so distrust, Kal. In this case with good reason because when I say precious, I do mean precious. My worth, it seems, was above rubies.'

She could have made a lot of money selling the story to the newspapers but she'd never told anyone what had happened. Not her mother. Not her friends. Not even the agency that employed her. But, sitting here in this quiet space above a beautiful garden carved out of the desert, nothing but the truth would do. She had lied to Kal, hidden who she was, and if she was to win his trust now, win him over so that she could fulfil her promise to Rose, she had to strip herself bare, tell him everything.

'When he asked me to go away for the weekend I felt like the sun was shining just for me. He made it so special, booked the honeymoon suite in a gorgeous hotel in the Cotswolds. I suppose I should have wondered how a student could afford it, but I was in love. Not thinking at all.'

'So what went wrong?'

'Nothing, fortunately. The "Lady Rose" effect saved me.'

He frowned. Well, why wouldn't he? Unless you'd lived it, how would anyone know?

'An elderly chambermaid—a woman who'd seen just about everything in a long career making beds—thought I was Rose and she waylaid me in the corridor to warn me, told me where to find the hidden cameras.'

She swallowed. Even now the memory of it chilled her.

'When I confronted my "student" he confessed that he was an actor who'd been hired to seduce me by a photographer who intended to make a fortune selling pictures of "Lady Rose" losing her virginity with some good-looking stud. Someone who worked in the hotel was in on it, of course. He even offered me a cut of the proceeds if I'd go ahead with it since, as he so eloquently put it, "I was gagging for it anyway". I declined and since then…' she shrugged '…let's say I've been cautious.'

'And yet you still believe in love?'

'I've seen it, Kal. My parents were in love. They lit up around each other and my mother still has a dreamy look whenever she talks about my dad. I won't settle for less than that.' She looked at him. 'I hope that Rose won't either. That this week away from everyone, being anonymous, will help her decide. Will you let her have that?'

'She's safe?' Kal asked, reserving judgement.

'She's been wrapped in cotton wool all her life. I've loaned her my car and right now she's as safe as any anonymous woman taking a few days to do something as simple as shopping without ending up like the Pied Piper of Hamelin, or appearing on the front page of next day's newspaper eating a hot dog.'

'So what was the panic this morning?'

'I think someone must have said something that panicked her. She's not as used to people commenting on the fact that she looks like Lady Rose as I am.' She used her free hand to make little quotes, put on a quavery voice. '"Has anyone ever told you you look a bit like Lady Rose, dear?"'

Kal smiled, but wondered what it must be like to always be told you look like someone else. Whether she sometimes longed for someone to say that Lady Rose looked like her.

'I'll bet that gets old. How do you cope?'

'It depends. If some old biddy whispers it to me in the supermarket, I whisper back that I really am Lady Rose and I'm doing undercover research into working conditions. Warn her not to tell a soul, that she's spotted me. Then wait to see how long it takes before she points me out to someone.'

'That's really bad.'

'You said it, Kal. I'm no angel.'

And for a moment he thought only about the touch of her lips beneath his fingers, the taste of them beneath his mouth. Then forced himself to remember that she had deceived him. Put his own mission in jeopardy. If the Emir, the Princess ever discovered the truth…

'Sometimes I do a flustered "good heavens, do you really think so, no one has ever said that before" routine,' she said, distracting him with the whole surprised expression, fluttery hand to chest routine.

'I like that one,' he said, which brought that light-up-the-day smile bubbling to her face.

'My favourite is the one where I put on a slightly puzzled smile…' she did a perfect version of the world famous luminous smile that was about a hundred watts less bright than her natural one '…and say "Only a bit?" and wait for the penny to drop.'

'You're a bit of a clown on the quiet, aren't you, Lydia Young?'

'Quiet?' she repeated.

He'd caught glimpses of this lively woman beneath the Rose mantle, but in full flood she was irresistible. Now that she'd stepped out of the shadows, was wholly herself, he knew that it was the lippy woman desperate to break out of the restraints of being Lady Rose that he desired, liked more and more. Her laughter lit him up, her smile warmed him. Even when he was furious with her he wanted to kiss her, wrap her up in his arms and keep her safe, love her…

'Maybe that wasn't the most appropriate word,' he said quickly. 'Did you never consider a career as an actress?'

'No.'

One minute they were laughing, the next they weren't.

'No more,' she said. 'I can't do this any more, Kal. I shouldn't be here. Rose shouldn't be hiding and I shouldn't be living a pretend life.'

'No.' Then, 'You've stopped shivering.'

'Nothing like tea for shock,' she said.

'I'm sorry if I frightened you.'

'Only for about a millisecond. Then I knew it was you.'

'I was angry,' he said.

Lydia swallowed, nodded. Of course he was angry. He'd been charged with protecting her—protecting Rose—and she had sneaked off the minute his back was turned.

'You had every right,' she said. 'But you stuck around to look out for me, even when you knew I wasn't Rose.'

Long after her momentary fear had been forgotten, she'd still feel his strong, protective arm as he'd held her against him. She recalled the warm scent of his skin.

She wouldn't need a shell or anything else to remember that. Remember him.

'So,' she said, sensing the weight of unspoken words between them and, recalling his earlier tension, she repeated the question she'd asked him then, 'what's your problem, Kal? What aren't you telling me?'

'Not just lovely, not just cool under pressure and a loyal friend, but smart, too,' he said, not looking at her. 'You're right, of course. I have a confession to make.'

'You got me at lovely,' she said. Then, because when a man needed to confess, it was never going to be good news, she summoned up all the flippancy at her command and said, 'Don't tell me. You're married.'

No one would have guessed that, in the time it took him to answer, her heart had skipped a beat. Two. Maybe he was right. She should take up acting.

'No, Lydia, I'm not married.'

'Engaged?' This time the pause was longer, but he shook his head.

'That wasn't totally convincing,' she said.

'I am not in a relationship of any kind.'

Better, but there was something he wasn't telling her. Maybe if she shut up and let him get on with his 'confession' in his own way it would all become clear.

It took another half a dozen heartbeats before he said, 'I want you to understand that Lucy was truly concerned for Rose. Her grandfather tried to talk her into withdrawing the invitation, said there had been a threat of some kind.'

'A threat? What kind of threat?' she asked, alarmed.

'Lucy was certain there was nothing, that it was just a ploy to keep her under his control, but she had to do something to pacify the Duke so she told him that the Emir's nephew would be in charge of his granddaughter's security.'

'That would be you. And he was happy with that?'

'No, but he couldn't object without offending the Emir.'

'And what about the Emir? Wasn't Lucy afraid of offending her father-in-law?'

'She saved Hanif. She can get away with things that no one else would dare to. Even be my friend. My grandfather is dying, Lydia. He lives only to return to Ramal Hamrah to die in the house where he was born.'

Her hand found his and she squeezed it, knowing how much he loved the old man.

'Lucy knew that Princess Sabirah would want to pay her respects to Rose and she seized the chance to put me where I could make a personal appeal to her, beg her to intercede with her husband.'

'And?'

'That first. Above everything…'

'But, once he has been allowed home, you hope the rest will follow. That you can become a Khatib again. With everything that entails.' His name, his title…

'It is as if I have been cut off from half my life. I have the language, I have property here, can study the culture, the history, but without my family…'

The metaphorical clock struck twelve. Time for the coach to turn back into a pumpkin, for Cinderella to go back to the checkout and check out the alternatives to getting a cat. Maybe a rabbit or a guinea pig, she thought. Or half a dozen white mice. Just in case the fairy godmother ever dropped in again.

'Not just your name, your title, but you want the ultimate prize of an arranged marriage to one of the precious daughters of a powerful Ramal Hamrahn family.'

His silence was all the answer she needed.

'That was why you stopped.' She swallowed. 'Would not make love with me.'

'Honour would not allow it,' he agreed.

Honour. What a rare word, but this man who'd been raised in the west was steeped in the culture that had excluded him.

'Absolutely,' she agreed. The kitchen telegraph would be humming to news of an affair before they disturbed the sheets. Princess Sabirah would suddenly find herself too busy to call and all Kal's hopes and dreams would fly right out of the window. 'Good call.'

Lydia stood up, pushed open one of the shutters, looked out over the garden, needing a little space to recover, put the smile back on.

'I'm glad that we were able to be honest with one another, Kal.'

Honest.

This was honest?

This was honour?

Lydia was pretending to be someone she was not, while he was about to collude with her deception, not just of the world's press but the Emir of Ramal Hamrah.

She turned to him.

'Will you take me to the souk tomorrow? I'd like to buy a gift for my mother.'

The request was simple enough, but that wasn't the question she was asking. They both knew it and when, after the briefest pause, he responded in the affirmative with a slight but formal bow, he was confirming that there would be a tomorrow for 'Lady Rose' at Bab el Sama.

What choice did he have?

He had been prepared to be patient, wait for those precious things he wanted for himself, no matter how long it took. But for his grandfather time was running out, leaving him with no choice but to seize the chance Lucy had given him.

She wasn't sure that honour had much to do with it, but love was there in abundance.

'You should believe in love, Kal,' she said. 'You are living proof of its existence. Your love of your family shines through when you talk of them. You yearn with all your heart for this country, for everything that you have lost here and yet you would risk it all on this chance to bring your grandfather home. That's love at its finest. Unselfish, pure, the real thing.'

'I am asking a great deal of you, Lydia. I would understand if you said you could not go through with it.'

'We both have debts, Kal, and to pay them we

need each other.' Then, 'You'll excuse me if I ask you to leave now? I need to change.'

Kal watched her wrap herself in the figurative mantel of Lady Rose Napier. Stand a little taller, inject the crispness back into her voice as she distanced herself from him. And where he had been warmed by her smile, her presence, a touch as she'd reached out without thinking, there was now an icy chill.

'Will you come to the stables in the morning?' he asked.

He saw her neck move as she swallowed, glimpsed a momentary longing for the closeness that would give them as he lifted her to the saddle, fitted her feet in the stirrups, placed her hands just so on the reins.

Then she shook her head just once and said, 'Lady Rose is afraid of horses.'

'And Lydia?'

'It's safer to stick to Rose, don't you think?'

He wasn't thinking. That was the problem. He'd set out on a quest that he'd believed nothing in the world could distract him from. How wrong could one man be?

He leaned forward, kissed her cheek. 'I'll send Yatimah to you.'

When Yatimah arrived, Lydia was filling the huge sunken bath.

'*Sitti!*' she declared. 'I must do that for you.'

Then, 'Bin Zaki says that you are going to the souk tomorrow. I will bring you an *abbayah* to keep the dust from your clothes,' she said as she ladled something into the bath that foamed magically, filling the air with an exotic, spicy fragrance. 'Would you like me to wash your hair?'

'Not tonight. I'm really tired so I'll just take a bath and then go to bed.'

She closed the bathroom door, locked it. Leaned back against it. Lifted her hand to her cheek.

Flash, bang, wallop...

Kal walked along the shore that she had walked, but went much further before sitting on a rock and calling his grandfather in London. He didn't ask how he was feeling. He knew he would be in pain because he refused to slide into the morphine induced coma that would lead to death.

Instead, he described the scene before him. The lights along the far shore, the boats riding on the water, the moon rising, dripping, from the ocean so that he could, in his heart, be here with him.

He called his mother, who'd complained of a cold the last time they'd spoken, listened to her news, her happiness at becoming a grandmother again. She demanded to know when he was going to settle down and add to her joy.

Talked to a brother who was struggling at university. Made a promise to go and see him soon.

This was what Lydia called love, he thought. Joint memories that needed only a word to bubble to the surface. Shared connections, history. To know that you could reach out and there would be a hand waiting.

Without that, how would you ever know how to see beyond the fireworks and make a marriage?

How could you ever know for sure?

He was still holding the phone and he scrolled through his contact list until he found 'Rose'.

'Kal?'

Was that it? When just the sound of her voice made your heart sing?

'Where are you, Kal?'

'On the beach, watching the moon rise. I called my grandfather so that he could share it.'

'And now you're sharing it with me?' she asked, still distant, still 'Rose'.

'I'm making a memory, Lydia.' One that, for the rest of their lives, whenever either of them looked at the rising moon would bring back this moment. 'Go onto your balcony and you will see it rise above the trees.'

He heard her move. A door opening. A tiny breath that was not quite a gasp, not quite a sigh. 'It's there,' she said. 'I can just see the top of it.'

'Be patient…'

Was it when you could sit miles apart watching the same spectacle and words weren't necessary?

'Thank you, Kal,' she said, minutes later when it was high enough to have cleared the trees around Bab el Sama. Her voice softer. Pure Lydia.

'*Afwan ya habibati, hada mussdur sa'adati,*' he replied. Then, when she'd broken the connection, 'It is the source of my pleasure, beloved.'

Lydia stood on the terrace at dawn, sipping the orange juice that Dena had brought her, staying to watch Kal ride along the beach.

'He is faster this morning,' Dena said enigmatically. 'The demons must be getting closer.'

'Yes,' she replied without thinking. 'They are.'

She'd scarcely slept—at this rate she would soon look exactly like Rose—and had watched the sky grow light, barely able to stop herself from going to the stables, just to be near him.

'Come, *sitti*, I will prepare you.'

Two hours later, resolved to keep her distance and wearing a feather-light black silk wrap, she and Kal crossed the creek to visit the souk.

It started well enough. They'd kept a clear foot between them and the conversation safely on topics such as the weather, Arabic vocabulary, followed by a whole lot of incoherent babbling as she'd seen the amazing array of colourful spices that came in dustbin-sized containers instead of tiny little glass jars.

Neither of them had mentioned the full moon they'd watched rising from the far ends of Bab e Sama. Apart and yet more intensely together than if they had been in each other's arms.

'Would you like the full tour?' he asked, 'or shall we go straight for the good stuff?'

She gave him a 'Lady Rose' look and said, 'The full tour. I want to see everything.'

Maybe that was the wrong answer. The area where the blacksmiths worked was noisy, hot and sparks flew everywhere. There were tinsmiths hammering away too and carpenters repairing furniture.

Once they turned into an area where tailors were waiting to run her up a dress in an hour or two things improved. There were tiny shops containing all kinds of strange and wonderful foods that weren't on the shelves of the supermarket that was her second home. She tasted Turkish delight flavoured with cardamom, a glass of tea from a man wandering about with an urn, little sticky cakes from a stall.

It was a different world and she sucked up every experience, her guard dropping long before they reached the stalls piled high with gorgeous silks.

Once there, she realised that she was not alone in wearing western clothes beneath the *abbayyeh* There were plenty of woman who, when they leaned forward to look at the goods on display revealed business suits, trousers, simple dresses beneath them. And although her pale hair and blue eyes made her an obvious foreigner, no one took much notice.

'They're used to Lucy and her friends,' Kal said. 'And another cousin, Zahir, is married to an English woman, too. A redhead in his case.'

'I read about it,' she said. 'It caused quite a sensation but I had no idea he was your cousin. Do you know him?'

'Our paths have crossed,' he said. 'We're in the same business.' He shrugged. 'My planes carry freight. His carry passengers.'

'Air freight? When you said you'd hadn't quite broken the habit of acquiring planes, you weren't joking, were you?'

'I ran out of room, so I had to keep some of them in the air,' he said. Joking, obviously. He had to be joking. 'Have you decided what you want?' he asked.

'It's impossible, but I've narrowed it down to three,' she said.

'I thought you were looking at this one?' He lifted the edge of a rich, heavy cream silk that would be perfect for a wedding dress.

'It's lovely,' she said, 'but I have no use for it.'

'Why do you have to have a use for something?' With a gesture that took in all four fabrics, he spoke briefly to the stallholder. Moved on.

'Kal,' she protested. 'I haven't paid. I haven't

told him how much I want. And what about my parcels?'

'He'll deliver them. And Dena will settle with him. Unless you want to haggle?'

Giving it up as a lost cause, she said, 'No, thanks. I'd rather hear more about this air freight business of yours. Does it have a name?'

'Kalzak Air Services.'

'Kalzak? That's your company?' Even she'd heard of them. Everybody had heard of them. 'I…um…hadn't made the connection. It's not exactly a hobby, then?'

'No,' he admitted. 'It's not a hobby. But I wasn't interested in the family business.'

She frowned. He hadn't mentioned a family business but there must be one or how else had they supported all those wives, children?

'Exiled playboy?' he prompted.

'I'm sorry—'

He stopped her fumbling apology with a touch to the elbow. 'It's okay. My grandfather lost his throne, but his father made a generous financial settlement—probably out of guilt.'

'And his brother didn't take that away?'

'He couldn't have, even if he'd wanted to, but I imagine he thought he was less dangerous playing with his racehorses and women than taking to the hills and fermenting more trouble.'

'You said he was the clever one.'

She thought that Kal was a lot more like his great-uncle, with his work ethic and philanthropy, than the grandfather he adored.

'Well, you and your cousin have something in common. Isn't that a starting place?'

'I help Lucy out when she needs to move disaster relief supplies. Zahir al-Khatib suggested I was taking advantage of her and offered to carry anything she needed so that she wouldn't have to turn to me for help.'

'Oh…'

And then, just when she was feeling desperately sorry for him, he gave her one of those slow smiles calculated to send her hormones into a dizzy spin.

'She probably shouldn't have told him that I had more aircraft, fewer family commitments. That I could afford to bear the cost more easily. His airline is very new,' he explained. 'But she wanted him to understand that my participation wasn't a matter for discussion.'

'Honestly,' she declared, 'I was just about to open up my heart and bleed for you.'

'I know.' And he touched the spot just by her mouth where she had pointed out his own giveaway muscle. 'You probably shouldn't ever play poker unless you're wearing a full face mask, Lydia,' he said softly. Then, as if nothing had happened, 'Gold next, I think.'

She followed him on rubbery legs to the glittering gold souk where the metal shone out of tiny shop windows and the air itself seemed to take on a golden glow.

It was a stunning spectacle and she could have spent hours there, but she quickly chose a pair of earrings, a waterfall of gold and seed pearls for her mother—who wore her hair up and adored dangly earrings—and a brooch set with turquoise for Jennie for looking after her.

'You will not choose something for yourself?'

He lifted the heavy rose pendant she was wearing at her throat. 'I imagine you'll have to give this back?'

'You imagine right.' But she could read him too, and she shook her head. 'Don't!' Then, 'Please, don't even think it…' she said, and walked quickly away in the direction of the harbour and the launch that had brought them across the creek, knowing that he had no choice but follow.

But later that afternoon four bolts of cloth were delivered to her room. And when she asked about paying for them Dena simply shrugged and suggest that she ask 'bin Zaki.'

Lydia didn't know much about the protocol in these things, but she was fairly certain that a man on the lookout for a bride was not supposed to buy another woman anything, let alone something as personal as cloth she would wear next to her skin.

Easy to see, in retrospect, that the spark that

flared between them had been lit in the first moment they had set eyes on one another and for a moment it had burned so intense that, even while he was single-mindedly focused on his future, he had still come close to losing control.

There could be nothing 'little' between them and she was holding herself together with nothing but willpower.

CHAPTER ELEVEN

LYDIA wanted this over. Was desperate for Princess Sabirah to pay her call and the week to be over so that she could just stop pretending and go home.

Stop pretending to be Rose. Stop pretending that she felt nothing for Kalil. Not that that worked. He'd only had to call in the darkness. She only had to hear his voice. If she hadn't cared she would have hung up, not stood there with her phone pressed to her ear, imagining she could hear him breathe while that huge moon rose above them.

Why had he done that?

He was the one who'd stepped back from the brink, broken the most intense, the most intimate connection there could ever be between a man and a woman even when it was obvious he'd wanted her as much as she'd wanted him.

Trapped, like her, committed to a course from which there was no escape but unable to stop himself from touching her. Calling her. Making love to her with words.

Breaking her heart.

She had taken lunch alone, keeping her nose firmly in a book until the words all ran together in a smeary blur, swam fifty lengths of the pool just to stop herself from thinking about him.

Except that when she emerged, slightly dizzy with the effort, he was waiting to wrap a towel around her.

'You shouldn't be here,' she said.

'I am your bodyguard. It is my duty.'

'I'm not in any danger.'

Only from falling in love with a man who didn't believe in love. Who thought marriage was no more than a convenient contract arranged by two families for their advantage. Maybe the girls did have some say, but the pressure had to be intense to make a 'good' marriage. Scarcely any different from the way that medieval barons gave their daughters to men whose land marched with theirs, or who could bring them closer to the King.

'Please…' She grabbed the towel and ran from the poolside to her room. Sat with it pressed to her face.

'Be strong, Lydie. You have to be strong…'

But, no matter how she ignored him, Kal's presence permeated the house.

Everywhere she went, she was sure he'd been there a second before. She couldn't escape the woody scent that clung to him, the swish of freshly laundered robes, the gentle flapping sound of leather thongs against marble floors.

The thrumming beat of hooves against sand.

It was all in her head, she knew, but she retreated to her room, allowing Yatimah to pamper her with facials, massage the tension out of her shoulders, paint more ornate patterns on her hands and feet with henna.

She caught sight of them as she reached for the phone, hoped they would wear off before she went back to work or they'd cause a few comments from the regulars as she swished their weekly shop over the scanner.

She checked the caller ID and, when she saw it was Kal, considered not answering. But then he'd come looking for her.

She took a deep breath, composed herself.

'Kal?' she queried, ice-cool.

'Just checking. I haven't seen you all day. Are you hiding from me?'

Reckless, bold, dangerous Bagheera, whose skin shimmered like watered silk, whose mouth tasted like wild honey—only a fool wouldn't hide.

'Just putting my feet up, taking it easy while I plan my future,' she said.

'Oh? What did you have in mind?'

'Well,' she said, her fingers lingering on the bolt of cream silk on the table beside her, 'now I'm giving up the lookalike business I thought I might set myself up in the rag trade,' she said. 'Costing is tricky, though. I need to know how much to budget for material.'

'Oh, I see. This is about the silk...'

'I can't wear it all myself,' she pointed out. Not unless she made a wedding dress with a thirty foot train. 'I need to know how much it cost.'

'You must ask Dena. She dealt with the merchant.'

'She told me to ask you.'

'Then it's a mystery,' he said with an infuriating hint of laughter in his voice that undid all her good intentions, all her cool.

'Kal!' she exploded. 'I just wanted a few metres for a suit or dress. I can't take all that home with me.'

'No problem.' Now he was enjoying himself. 'I'll deliver.'

'Deliver them to your bride,' she snapped. 'Yatimah was telling me that's what a groom is supposed to do. Send jewels, cloth, carpets, the biggest flat screen television you can afford.'

'Yatimah has altogether too much to say for herself,' he snapped back and she rejoiced in having rattled him out of his teasing. He had no right to tease her. No right to call her and make her want him... For a moment neither of them spoke and the only sound was of raised breathing. Then, after a moment, his voice expressionless, his manner formal, Kal said, 'Lucy phoned to check up on how well I've been looking after you, *sitti*.'

'Tell her what you like,' Lydia replied, not even trying for cool. 'I won't tell tales. And cut out the *sitti*.' It was one thing having Dena or Yatimah calling her 'lady', quite another from Kal.

'I can't tempt you to come on a picnic?'

Oh, the man knew how to tempt.

She refused without having to think twice. Well, maybe twice, but she knew the attraction between them was too great to risk another close encounter. And that even while he was paying lip service to honour, his frustrated libido was refusing to quit.

'Sorry, Kal, but I'm planning a walk on the beach this afternoon and, unlike you, I'm happy with my own company,' she said, knowing how much that would infuriate him. But she was angry with him for putting her through this, with herself for aching for something so far out of reach. For bringing tears stinging to her eyes. 'But you're welcome to stand and watch if you like. Just remember how handy I am with a shell.'

She didn't wait for him to command her not to do it, but hung up. Then had to hold herself together. Physically wrap her arms around herself, holding her breath, just to stop herself from falling apart.

* * *

Kal took himself to the stables in the foulest, blackest mood.

He was behaving like a man who didn't know his own mind. Who had lost control of his senses.

It wasn't true. When he could have taken Lydia, he had known it was wrong. That, without commitment, honour, such an act was beneath him, could only hurt her.

He'd hurt her anyway.

She could hide nothing from him and he'd seen her eyes in the moment she had realised why he had refused the greatest gift a woman could bestow on any man. Had seen her pain in the way she'd moved as she'd taken herself away from him in the souk, when all he'd wanted to do was shower her with gold, pearls. Put diamonds in her ears, on every one of the fingers he had taken to his lips. When, seeing that in his face, she had begged him not even to think it.

He was furious because, even as he weakened, unable to stay away, she grew stronger, keeping him at arm's length when he needed them around her.

A nagging, desperate need that came from somewhere deep inside, from a place he hadn't, until that moment, known existed. All he knew was that he was ready to consign common sense, five years of patient planning along with everything he had learned about the fleeting nature of 'love' from his grandfather, his father, to the deep blue sea.

And still she had turned him down. Not because she didn't want to go. He was attuned to every nuance in her voice, every hesitation and he'd heard the unspoken longing in a whisper of a sigh before she had said no to his picnic.

But, even when he was losing control, she was strong enough to save him from himself.

Lydia Young might not be a princess, but she had all the attributes of one. Courage, dignity that would become a queen. A spirit that was all her own. He wanted her with a desperation that was driving every other thought from his head.

At home he would have taken up the small biplane he used for stunting, shaken off his mood in a series of barrel rolls, loops. Here, the closest he could get to a release in the rush of power was on one of Hanif's fine stallions but, as he tightened the girth, the horse skipped edgily away from him, sensing his frustration.

But it wasn't simply his out of control libido, the sense of being too big for his skin. This was a need that went much deeper, challenging everything he believed in.

He'd spent the last five years planning the perfect life but Lydia was forcing him to face the fact that life wasn't something that you could plan. It happened. Some of it good, some of it bad, none of it 'safe'.

He had arrogantly assumed that his grandfather,

his father had wasted their lives but, while their families were scarcely conventional, their quivers were full of the children of their youth and they were, he realised with a shock, happy men. That, wherever his grandfather died, he would be sur-rounded by his children, grandchildren, people who loved him.

He lay his hand on the neck of the horse, gentling him with soft words, even while he yearned for the sound of Lydia's voice. The sweet scent that clung to her, as if she had been brushing her hands over jasmine. The touch of her hands against his skin.

Wanted to see her face, her eyes lighting up, her mouth softening, her hands describing what her lips were saying. Her quickness with a tender touch to show that she understood. Her laugh. The swiftness with which she melted to his kisses.

While he kept the world at bay, carefully avoiding the risk, the pain that was an inevitable part of what Lydia called 'love', she held nothing back.

She had answered every question he had asked of her with not just her body, but her heart and her soul and he wanted to shower her with gifts, buy her every bolt of cloth in the market, heap up gold, pearls, gems in a dower that she could not ignore.

Except, of course, she could and would. She had told him so. Her price was above rubies. Only his heart, freely given in an avowal of love, without negotiations, conditions, guarantees would win her acceptance.

She would not settle for less and neither, he knew now, would he. Because the nearest a man could come to perfection was to take every single moment and live it to the full. With love. And she was right. He was not a stranger to the emotion. Love for his family was part of who he was.

But this was new. This love for a woman who, from the first moment he had set eyes on her, had made the lights shine more brightly.

He'd lost the perfect moment, had hurt her. Now, to show her how he felt, he had to give her not just his heart but his world. Everything that made him who he was. And there was only one way he could do that, could win her trust.

The horse snorted impatiently, eager to be off, but he left the groom circling the yard as he made the calls that would change his life.

Lydia stepped onto the beach, kicking off her sandals. It was cooler today and she was wearing cotton trousers, a white shirt, a cashmere sweater knotted at her waist.

There were clouds gathering offshore and the wind coming off the sea was sharper, whipping up little white horses on the creek and, as she strode along the beach, hanging onto her temper by a thread, she glowered at the photographer's

aunch, bobbing on the waves, hoping that he
vas seasick.

She doubted that. There hadn't been pictures in
he papers for a day or two. A sighting of Rupert
Devenish at a business meeting in the States had
downgraded interest in Bab el Sama and he would
have packed up his telephoto lenses and gone in
earch of more lucrative prey.

It hadn't been a great week for anyone, she
thought, her hand tightening around the note from
Princess Sabirah's secretary that Dena had deliv-
red to her as she'd left for her walk.

It was brief and to the point, informing her, re-
gretfully, that the Princess had a cold and was
unable to travel this week. Wishing her a pleasant
tay and the Princess's sincere hope that they
would meet soon in London.

Somewhere where there was no chance that Kal
al-Zaki would pop out of the woodwork, presumably.

That the illness was diplomatic, she had no
doubt, and she let out a very unladylike roar of
outrage that all Kal's hopes and dreams had been
crushed without even a chance to put in a plea for
his grandfather.

What on earth was the matter with these people?
t had all happened fifty years ago, for heaven's
sake.

'Get over it!' she shouted to the sky, the seabirds
whirling overhead.

He had to know. She would have to tell him and the sooner the better. Maybe there was still something he could do. She could do…

If she really had been Rose, she could have gone to Rumaillah by herself, taken some flowers to the 'sick' Princess. On her own, she would have been admitted. Could have pleaded for him.

She stopped, stood for a moment staring at the phone in her hand as she realised something else. That with his mission dead he would turn to her for comfort, would be free to love her…

She stopped the thought dead, ashamed even to have given it room in her head, and quickly scrolled down the contact list and hit 'dial'. Unexpectedly, it went straight to voicemail…

'Kal,' she began uncertainly, hating to be the bearer of such bad news. Then, as she hesitated above the buffeting of the wind she heard another sound. The pounding of hooves. She swung round and saw him riding towards her astride a huge black horse, robes flying behind him, hand outstretched. Before she could think, move, there was a jolt as he swooped low, caught her round the waist, lifted her to his saddle.

It was the dream, she thought crazily as she clung to him, her face pressed against his pounding heart.

She'd reached out to him as she'd watched him from above, wanting to be lifted to the stars.

There were no stars and she knew that at any moment he would slow down, berate her for taking unnecessary risks.

But he didn't stop, didn't slow down until Bab el Sama was far below them, the horse rearing as he brought it to a halt, turned, slid to the ground with her.

'Did your English heart beat to be swept onto my horse, *ya habibati?*' He smiled as he curved his hand around her face. 'Did you feel mine, beloved?' He took her hand and placed it against his chest. 'Feel it now. It beats for you, Lydia Young.'

Beloved…

He had called her his beloved and as his lips came down on hers she was lost.

'This is kidnapping,' she said when he carried her to a waiting four-by-four. 'Where are you taking me?'

'You will see,' he said as he fastened the seat belt and climbed in beside her. 'Then I will ask you if you wish me to take you back.'

'But what about…?'

He silenced her protest with a kiss.

'The groom will take him back,' he said and she realised that this had not been a spur of the moment escapade but was a carefully arranged assault on her defences by a man who when he offered a treat refused to take no for an answer. No doubt there would be a picnic waiting for her at the side of th[e] river, or some archaeological treasure.

But when he stopped there was nothing but distant view.

'There,' he said. 'Do you see it?'

She could see something shimmering throug[h] the dust haze like a mirage. A tower, a shimmer o[f] green above high walls, and she knew withou[t] doubt that she was looking at Umm al Sama.

'I see it,' she said. Then, turning to him, 'I se[e] you, Kalil bin Zaki.'

'Will you go there with me?'

He had brought her to the place where his grand[-] father had been born. The place he called home. N[o]t home as in the place where he lived, like the apar[t-] ments in Rumaillah, London, New York, but th[e] home of his heart. The place that an exile, generation[s] on, still carried deep in the memory, in his soul.

That he would keep for a woman who mear[t] more than a brief affair. This was the home he ha[d] been preparing not just for the return of his grand[-] father, but for the bride he would one day brin[g] here and, even though he knew who she was, Lydi[a] Young, he was offering it to her.

Words for a moment failed her, then a phras[e] came into her head, something from long ag[o,] Sunday School...

'Whither thou goest, I will go; and where tho[u] lodgest, I will lodge...'

Kal knew this was a perfect moment. He had offered the woman he loved all that he was and she had replied with words that touched his soul and as he reached for her, embraced her, sealed their future with a kiss, he knew he owned the world.

Kal led her through Umm al Sama by the hand, through gardens that had run wild, but were being tamed. Beside pools that had been cleaned and reflected the blue of a sky that had magically cleared above them. Through arched colonnades decorated with cool blue and green tiles.

Showed her a wind tower that funnelled the air down to a deep cooling pool below ground. Buildings that had been beautiful once and would be beautiful again when he had finished restoring them.

One building, smaller than the rest, was finished. Kal watched her from the doorway as she walked around an exquisite sitting room touching fine tables, running a finger over the smooth curves of fine porcelain.

'This is so beautiful, Kal. So special.' She looked at him. 'What was this?'

Kal had not touched Lydia since they'd arrived at Umm al Sama. Outside, in the garden, where they might be seen, he'd kept a discreet distance between them. Showing her respect. He had not brought her here to make love to her, but to give her his heart. To give her this.

'My great-grandfather's wife lived here before they moved to the new palace at Rumaillah.'

'Leaving it to the heir apparent?'

'No one has lived here since my grandfather was banished. If you go upstairs, there should be something to eat on the balcony.'

'All this and food too?'

'I invited you on a picnic,' he reminded her, leading the way to a wide covered balcony with carved shade screens that ran the length of the building.

She stared for a moment at the distant view of the mountains, then pushed open a door to reveal the private apartment of a princess.

The polished floor was covered with rare carpets, the walls hung with vivid gauzy silk, as was the great bed at its heart.

Lydia looked back at him. 'Are you expecting Scheherazade?'

'Only you. Come, *ya habibati,*' he said, extending his hand to her. 'You must be hungry.'

'I'm starving, Kal.' As she raised her hand to meet his, she came into his arms, lifted her lips to his. 'Feed me.'

As she breathed the words into his mouth he shattered. The man who had been Kalil al-Zaki no longer existed. As he shed his clothes, fed Lydia

Young, the wife of his heart, with his touch, his mouth, his body, she rebuilt him with her surprise, her delight, tiny cries of pleasure at each new intimacy and finally with her tears as they learned from each other and finally became one.

'I have to go back to Bab el Sama, Kal,' she protested the following morning as she lay in bed while he fed her pomegranate seeds and dates for breakfast. 'I have no clothes here.'

He kissed her shoulder. 'Why do you need clothes?'

'Because otherwise I can't leave this room.'

He nudged the edge of the sheet, taking the kiss lower. 'I repeat, why do you need clothes, *ya rohi, ya hahati?*'

He'd showered her with words she did not understand as he'd made love to her, but she refused to be distracted.

'Dena will be concerned.'

'Dena knows that you are with your bodyguard. Am I not guarding your body?' And his smile, his touch, made everything else go away.

Thoroughly and completely distracted, it was gone noon when she stirred again. She was alone in the great bed they'd shared and, wrapping the sheet around her, she went to the balcony, expecting to find him there waiting for her to wake.

The balcony was deserted but her clothes,

freshly laundered, were waiting for her on dresser with a note from Kal.

Ask for whatever you want. Umm al Sama is yours. I will back soon.

She held it to her breast, smiling. Obviousl' he'd gone to fetch her clothes, explain thei absence, and she bathed, washed her hair, dressed The note from the princess's secretary, forgotte in the wild excitement of her abduction, of Umn al Sama, of Kal, was at the bottom of the pile. Tha had been ironed, too.

She should have told him about that. As she pu on Rose's watch she wondered what time he'd left How long it would be before he returned.

Maybe he'd rung. She checked her message but there was nothing. Tried his number but it wen straight to voicemail but this wasn't news sh could dump on him that way. And leaving a *Whe will you be back?* message seemed so needy...

A servant brought her food. She picked at it Took a walk in the garden.

Checked her phone again. With nothing to read no one to talk to, she switched to the Net an caught the urgent flash of a breaking news stor and her blood ran cold.

Lady Rose kidnapped...

Rose...

But it wasn't Rose.

Of course it wasn't. It was her in the picture.

Make that a whole series of pictures.

Alone on the beach. Kal riding her down. Lifting her to his saddle. Disappearing into the distance.

The photographer hadn't gone anywhere, she realised. Or had he been tipped off because he'd had all the time in the world to get the whole story in pictures...?

No question by whom.

There was only one person at Bab al Sama who wanted to be visible.

Well, two. She had wanted to be visible and maybe she'd given Kal the idea. Because when he'd realised that the princess wasn't coming— Dena had no doubt had her own note from the palace and would certainly have told him—he must have been desperate.

Not for himself. Whatever happened, he'd thrown away his own hopes and dreams the minute he'd picked her up from the beach. The family name, the title, the bride. Five years of quiet diplomacy, of being invisible.

He'd done this solely out of love for his grand-father.

For love, she reminded herself as she stared at the pictures for one last moment.

One thing was certain—with the world's press on the case, he was no longer invisible. The Emir could no longer pretend he did not exist. On the contrary, he had probably sent his guard to arrest him, lock him up. That would explain his lengthy absence. Why his phone was switched off.

And only she could save him.

She resisted the temptation to leave him to cool his heels for a night in the cells and went to find someone to take her to Rumaillah.

All he'd planned was a photo opportunity followed by a picnic. She was the one who'd got completely the wrong end of the stick, responding to his polite invitation to visit his family home with a declaration of eternity. Led all the way with her desperate *'I'm starving…feed me'*. What on earth was a man to do faced with that? Say no, thanks—again?

Once she was on her way—and had stopped blushing long enough to think straight—she called Rose. She couldn't have picked up the story yet, or she'd have been on the phone herself. She growled with frustration as her call went straight to voicemail and she left a reassuring message.

Then she called her mother, not because she'd be worried, but because she really, really needed to hear her voice.

Kal left his beautiful Lydia sleeping. He could have asked for her things to be sent to Umm al Sama, but he wanted to visit the souk.

While she had clearly understood the significance of his taking her to Umm al Sama, that no one but his bride would ever sleep in that bed, he wanted to buy her at least one of the diamonds that he would shower on her.

He left Yatimah to pack their bags while he crossed the creek in search of a perfect solitaire. A stone that would say the things that words could never say. A pledge. A promise of forever.

Then he called his grandfather to tell him that he must not be in such a hurry to die. That, if he was patient, he would see not only a wedding at Umm al Sama but a great-grandson born there, too.

It was after lunch before he arrived home to be told that the *sitti* had insisted on being taken to Rumaillah. To the palace.

Rumaillah...

Had there been a call? A summons from the Princess? No. She would not have made a formal visit wearing a pair of cotton trousers and a shirt. This was something else. He took the stairs two at a time as he raced to the room where they had spent the night in blissful discovery of each other, certain that she must have left a message.

There was nothing.

Only the message he had left for her.

And a note from the palace with Princess Sabirah's regrets...

Dena had told him that she'd been unwell; it

was why she hadn't come earlier. This must have been in Lydia's pocket when he'd taken her from the beach. It couldn't have anything to do with her racing off to Rumaillah.

Unless…

He flipped to the Net, saw the breaking news story. And swore long and inventively in several languages. He'd had the photographer warned off but he'd either come back or this was another one. It made no difference.

He knew exactly what Lydia must be thinking.

She'd assume that he'd known that the Princess was not coming and that he had used her to force the Emir to notice him.

That she'd trusted him with all that she was, given him her most precious gift, and he had betrayed her.

Lydia stood at the door to the *majlis*. She'd borrowed an *abbayeh* from one of the women at Umm al Sama but she was the only woman in the group of people who had arrived to petition the Emir. She was aware of a rumbling of disapproval, a certain amount of jostling, but she stood tall, refused to turn tail and run, and waited her turn.

The room was vast. At one end the Emir sat with his advisors. Along each wall men, drinking coffee from tiny cups, sat on rows of sofas.

As she kicked off her sandals, stepped forward

the *abbayeh* caught—or maybe someone was standing on it—and slipped from her hair and every sound died away.

The Emir rose, extended a hand in welcome and said, 'Lady Rose. We were concerned for your safety. Please…'

He gestured her forward.

She walked the length of the room. Bowed. Said, 'Thank you, Excellency, but as you see I am safe and well. If you have seized Kalil al-Zaki, have him locked in your cells, I must ask you to release him.'

There was a buzz, silenced by a look from the Emir.

'Who is Kalil al-Zaki?' he asked.

She gasped, snapped, 'Who is he? I don't believe you people! It's been fifty years since his grandfather was exiled. Was stripped of everything he cared about. Your nephew has an apartment in this city, yet you treat him as if he did not exist.'

Now there was silence. Pin drop silence, but she was too angry to care that she was flouting royal protocol. Even an Emir needed to hear the truth once in a while.

'Kalil al-Zaki is a man of honour, a man who cares for his family, who has built up an international business that would grace any nation. He wants nothing from you but to bring his grandfather home to die. You would grant that to a dog!'

Then, in the ringing silence that followed this outburst, 'And, by the way, my name is Lydia Young. Lady Rose has taken a holiday in a place where she won't be photographed twenty-four hours a day!'

Then, because there was nothing left for her, she sank to her knees before him.

'The son of your great-grandfather is dying, Excellency. Will you not let him come home?'

Kal was too late to stop her. He was blocked at the doorway by the Emiri guard, forced to watch as she berated the Emir.

But, in the deathly silence that followed her appeal for mercy, even they were too stunned to stop him and he pushed the man aside, lifted her to her feet, then touched his head, his heart and bowed to her.

'*Ya malekat galbi, ya rohi, ya hahati.* You are beautiful, my soul, my life. Ahebbak, ya tao'am rohi. The owner of my heart. *Amoot feeki.* There is no life without you.' Then, 'I did not know, Lydia. Please believe me, I did not use you. I did not know.'

She would have spoken, but the Emir stepped forward. 'I have listened to your appeal, Lydia Young.'

That she was dismissed, neither of them were in any doubt, but as he turned to leave with her, caring only that she should believe him, the Emir said, 'I have not heard from you, Kalil al-Zaki.'

She touched his hand, said, 'Stay.'
'No…'
'For heaven's sake, Kal. This is what you wanted. Your chance. Don't blow it now.'
Then she turned and walked away.

Lydia had been taken to the Princess's quarters. She'd been fed and given a change of clothes and then, having asked to be allowed to go straight home, the British Consul had been summoned to provide her with temporary papers since her passport was with her belongings and only Kal knew were they were.

She arrived home to a dozen messages from newspapers wanting her story and one from a famous publicist who warned her to sign nothing until she'd talked to him. And reporters knee-deep on the footpath outside her mother's flat.

Her mother didn't say a word. Just hugged her.
Numb until then, she finally broke down and cried.
Rose called to make sure she was really all right. To apologise for the publicity. To thank her.
'You've changed my life, Lydia. Words cannot express my gratitude. You should sell your story, make a mint.'
'There is no story, Rose.' Then, 'Is there any chance of getting my car back soon? I'm due back at work the day after tomorrow.'
'That's a bit of a bad news, good news story, I'm

afraid. The bad news is that I had a little bit of an accident,' she confessed.

'Oh.' The car had been her pride and joy. It had taken her forever to save up for it... 'Is it in the garage?'

'Er...a little bit more of an accident than that,' she admitted. 'It's nothing but a cube of metal in a scrapyard, but the good news is that George has arranged a replacement for you. A rather jolly red Beetle. I'll make sure it's delivered tomorrow.'

'Thank you. And Rose. Congratulations. I hope you will be really happy.'

'I'll send you and your mother an invitation to the wedding.'

There was nothing from Kal and, since she didn't want to hear from the reporters, the newspapers or the publicist, she unplugged the phone and turned off her mobile.

She sent an email to the lookalike agency, informing them that she would no longer be available and asking them to take her off their books.

Deleted dozens from newsmen offering interviews, and weirdos who just wanted to be weird.

She didn't open the door to the manager of the local garage who came to deliver a brand-new red VW Beetle, which she knew cost about three times what she'd paid for her car, until he put a note through the door explaining who he was.

There was no missing the black and gold livery of

the Kalzak Air Services courier who pulled up outside and delivered her luggage. All those lovely clothes, the cosmetics, the scent, the four bolts of silk.

She gave her mother and Jennie their gifts.

And then, in the privacy of her room, she cried again all over the cream silk.

The Emir had given Kal a hard time. Made him wait while he consulted his brothers, his sons, his nephews. Hanif had supported him and so, unexpectedly, had Zahir and all the time he had been berating himself for letting Lydia walk away. Fly away.

She had thought he was in trouble and had come to help. Had begged for him.

Only her 'stay' had kept him here while members of a family he did not know video-conferenced from all over the world, deciding the fate of his grandfather, eventually deciding that compassion required that he should be allowed to return to Umm al Sama. And that, after his death, his family could use the name Khatib.

Kal told the Emir that he would bring his grandfather home but under those terms they could keep their name. He didn't want it. Lydia deserved better from him than acceptance of such a mealy-mouthed offer.

And the Emir smiled. 'I remember him. You are just like him.'

'You honour me, Excellency.'

At which point His Excellency had thrown up his hands and said, 'Let the old man have his name and his title.'

'Will you permit Dena to return to London with me to fetch him, travel back with him and his nurses?'

'If she is agreeable.' Then, with heavy irony, 'Is there anything else you want, Kalil bin Zaki al-Khatib? One of my granddaughters as a bride, perhaps, now that you are a sheikh?'

'I am very conscious of the honour you bestow, Excellency,' he replied, 'but, like my grandfather, I have chosen my own bride. You have had the honour of meeting her.'

And this time the Emir laughed appreciatively.

'She is all fire, that one. You will have your hands full.' He did not appear to believe that this was a bad thing.

Since there was no other way to get rid of them, Lydia finally faced the newsmen, standing on the pavement outside her home giving an impromptu press conference, answering their questions.

'Who was the horseman?'

'A bodyguard rescuing me from intrusive photographers.'

Laughter.

'Lady Rose has cut her hair. Will you do that?'

'No.'

'When did you meet?'

'Will you be seeing her?'

'Have you met her fiancé?'

No. No. No.

She kept a smile pinned to her face, didn't lose her temper, even at the most intrusive questions, and eventually they ran out of things to ask.

And since she wasn't Lady Rose, it didn't take long for the madness to die down. One moment the pavement in front of their flat had been mobbed, the next there was no one.

The agency was still pleading with her to reconsider her decision. They'd been inundated with requests for appearances since Rose had announced her engagement. But the publicist, who'd been so keen to negotiate a contract for her to 'write' the story of her career as Rose's lookalike—with the titillating promise to reveal who had really swept her away on that black stallion and what had happened afterwards—finally accepted that she meant it when she said 'no'.

With the excitement of Rose's engagement to occupy the gossip pages, she quickly became old news.

The story about the exiled Sheikh who had been pardoned by the Emir and allowed to return home to die probably wouldn't have made the news at all, except that Ramal Hamrah was where that very odd incident had taken place, when everyone thought Lady Rose had been kidnapped.

She had heard nothing from Kalil.

No doubt he had his hands full taking care of his grandfather, transferring him to Umm al Sama. Getting to know a whole new family.

She winced as *White Christmas* began to play for the fiftieth time that week on the seasonal tape. Turned to smile at yet another harassed mother doing her Christmas shop. Reached for yet another turkey.

Kal quietly joined the checkout queue.

All his duties done, he had come straight from the airport to find Lydia. Had gone to her home. He'd met her mother and, with her blessing, he had come to claim his love publicly, in her real world. Wanted her to know that there was no misunderstanding between them. That he knew who she was. That it was not some icon he had fallen in love with but Lydia Young.

Not the aristocrat in the designer suit, but the ordinary girl on the supermarket checkout wearing an overall and a ridiculous hat.

She looked exhausted. There were dark shadows beneath her eyes, her cheeks were hollow and had lost their glow, but the smile never faltered.

She greeted regular customers as friends. Asked what they were doing for the holiday and, as she listened with every appearance of interest, they lost a little of their tension as she swiftly dealt with their purchases. He watched her pack the shopping for one old lady whose hands were crippled with arthritis, helped her count out the money.

He made an instinctive move forward to help as she heaved a heavy bag of potatoes over the scanner, got a glare from the woman in front who was fiddling with a mobile phone. She was trying to take a picture of Lydia, he realised, and he leaned forward and said very quietly, 'Don't do that.'

About to tell him to mind his own business, she thought better of it and, muttering something about forgetting something, melted away.

Next in line was a woman with a toddler and a small baby who was grizzling with exhaustion.

Lydia whizzed the goods through, packed the bags, then took the baby, put it to her shoulder as the woman searched helplessly for her wallet. Reassuring the woman, patting the baby. The baby fell asleep, the wallet was found.

'Can I take you home with me?' the woman asked as she retrieved her baby.

He'd seen her dressed in designer clothes, every inch the Lady with a capital L.

He'd seen her sweetness with Yatimah, her eyes hot with passion, soft with desire. Seen her berate the Emir in a room filled with hostile men. Seen her on her knees begging for him…

Beauty was a lot more than skin-deep and with each revelation he'd fallen deeper in love with Lydia. And as he watched her kindness, her compassion, her cheerful smile even though she was exhausted, he fell in love with her all over again.

She lifted her hands to her face and rubbed it, turned as someone came alongside her. 'Your shift is nearly up. Just this last one and then I'll take over.'

His cue to place the basket he was carrying on the shelf, take out the single item it contained and place it on the conveyer.

He saw her gather herself for one last effort. Put the smile back in place, turn to wait for the goods to reach her. Saw the smile falter, the frown pucker her brow as she watched the tiny dark blue velvet-covered box move slowly towards her. The diamond solitaire at its heart sparking a rainbow of light.

Confused, she looked up. Saw him standing at the far end of the conveyer as, behind him, half a dozen shoppers stared open-mouthed. Rose slowly to her feet.

'Kal…'

'The ring was in my pocket when I returned to Umm al Sama, Lydia. I was sure that you knew, understood that the only woman I would take there would be my bride. But I wanted to give you a tangible token of my love. Something more than a dream.'

'I am not what you wanted.'

'Until I met you I didn't know what I wanted, but love is the star to every wandering bark, Lydia. You taught me that. I had been wandering all my life, without a star to guide me...' He sank to his knees. '*Ahebbak,* Lydia. I love you. I am begging you to marry me, to be my princess, my wife, my lover, the mother of my children, my soul, my life.'

The growing crowd of onlookers broke out into a spontaneous round of applause but it was Lydia who mattered.

'How is he?' she asked. 'Your grandfather?'

'Happy to be home. Thanks to you.'

'Then you have everything.'

'Everything but you.' He stood up, took the ring from the box, held it up, then touched it to each finger of her left hand, counting slowly in Arabic... '*Wahid, ithnan, thelatha, arba'a, khamsa...*'

'*Ithnan, ya habibi*—my beloved,' she said. '*Ahebbak,* Kalil. I love you.'

He slipped the ring onto the ring finger of her left hand, then walked around the checkout, took her in his arms and kissed her.

By this time they had brought the entire row of checkouts to a standstill. And the entire store was clapping.

'Maybe we had better leave, my love,' he said. 'These good people need to finish their shopping. And we have a wedding to arrange.'

Daily Chronicle, 2nd March 2010

LADY ROSE LOOKALIKE MARRIES HER LORD

Lydia Young, who for ten years made regular appearances as a Lady Rose lookalike, was married today at Umm al Sama in Ramal Hamrah to Sheikh Kalil bin Zaki al-Khatib, nephew of the Emir.

Sheikh Kalil, who founded the international air freight company Kalzak Air Services, met Miss Young before Christmas and proposed after a whirlwind romance.

The bride's mother Mrs Glenys Young, who was formerly a seamstress for a London couturier, made her daughter's wedding dress from a bolt of cream silk that was a gift from the groom.

Four of the groom's sisters were attendants and his brother was best man. Family members and guests flew in from all over the world to be present at the ceremony, amongst them Lady Rose Napier and her fiancé billionaire businessman George Saxon. The groom's grandfather, who is gravely ill rallied sufficiently to make a short speech at the reception.

The couple will spend their time between homes in London, Paris, New York and Ramal Hamrah.

AND THE BRIDE WORE RED

BY
LUCY GORDON

® MILLS & BOON®

*This book is dedicated to my friend Xin Ying,
who lives in Beijing and whose assistance
with Chinese social customs was invaluable.*

First published in Great Britain 2009
Harlequin Mills & Boon Limited,
Eton House, 18-24 Paradise Road, Richmond, Surrey TW9 1SR

© Lucy Gordon 2009

ISBN: 978 0 263 86962 0

Set in Times Roman 12¾ on 14 pt
02-1209-49436

Printed and bound in Spain
by Litografia Rosés, S.A., Barcelona

Dear Reader

A couple of years ago I visited China, and was overwhelmed by its beauty, its magnificence and above all its mystery. In Beijing I saw the Forbidden City, where the Emperors lived and where their concubines had their apartments. Later I visited the Terracotta Warriors. I'd heard so much about them, but nothing could have prepared me for their breathtaking, lifelike reality.

After that came a cruise along the Yangtze River, marvelling at the high banks that rise on each side, giving the feeling of being enclosed in a separate world. It could be a perfect place for lovers, as my hero and heroine Lang and Olivia discovered. But at last the outside world intruded, facing them with decisions that threatened to tear them apart.

When they finally found their destiny it was because they were true to themselves, and also because they had answered the magical call of China. It was a call that would always draw them back—just as it has drawn me back, and will do again.

Warm wishes

Lucy Gordon

Lucy Gordon cut her writing teeth on magazine journalism, interviewing many of the world's most interesting men, including Warren Beatty, Charlton Heston and Roger Moore. She also camped out with lions in Africa, and had many other unusual experiences which have often provided the background for her books. Several years ago, while staying in Venice, she met a Venetian who proposed in two days. They have been married ever since. Naturally this has affected her writing, where romantic Italian men tend to feature strongly.

Two of her books have won the Romance Writers of America RITA® award: SONG OF THE LORELEI in 1990, and HIS BROTHER'S CHILD in 1998, in the Best Traditional Romance category.

You can visit her website at www.lucy-gordon.com

CHAPTER ONE

'OLIVIA, come quickly! There's been a terrible disaster!'

Olivia looked up from the school books she was marking to where Helma, the young teaching assistant, stood in the doorway. She was only mildly alarmed by the girl's agitated words. Helma had a wild sense of drama and 'a terrible disaster' might mean no more than the school cat making off with someone's lunch.

'It's Yen Dong!' Helma wailed.

Ten-year-old Dong was the brightest pupil in Olivia's class at the Chang-Ming School in Beijing. He was also the most mischievous, using his impish charm to evade retribution for his many escapades.

'What's he done now?' Olivia asked. 'Set a booby trap for the headmistress?'

'He's climbed a tree.'

'Again? Then he can just come down. It's almost time for afternoon lessons.'

'But he's ever so high and I don't think he can get down.'

Olivia hurried out into the garden that formed the school's playground and looked up. Sure enough, there was the little rascal, high on the tallest tree, looking cheerful even while hanging on for dear life.

'Can you climb down?' Olivia called.

He ventured a step, but his foot slid on the next branch and he backed off hastily.

'All right, not to worry,' Olivia said, trying to sound more confident than she felt. 'I need a ladder.'

One was fetched immediately, but to everyone's dismay it fell short of Dong by several feet.

'No problem,' Olivia sang out, setting her foot on the bottom rung.

Luckily she was wearing jeans, which made climbing easier, and reaching the top of the ladder wasn't too hard. But the next bit didn't look so easy. Taking a deep breath, she set her foot on a branch. It trembled but held, and she was emboldened to haul herself up. In another moment she had reached Dong, who gave her a beaming smile.

'It is very nice up here,' he said in careful, perfect English. 'I like climbing trees.'

Olivia looked at him askance. At any other time she would have been delighted with his command of her language. In the six months she'd spent teaching English at the Chang-Ming School, she'd found that Dong was the one who grasped everything first. She was proud of him, but right now she had other things to worry about.

'I like climbing trees too,' she said. 'But I also like getting down safely. So let's try to do that.'

She began to edge down, encouraging him to follow her so that he descended into the safety of her arms. One branch, then two, then three and finally, to her immense relief, the top rung of the ladder.

'Just a little further,' she said. 'Nearly there.'

But it was the ladder which failed them, sliding away from the tree suddenly and depositing them on the ground with a bump.

Olivia gasped as she felt the bark scrape painfully against her arm, but her real fear was for Dong.

'Are you hurt?' she asked worriedly.

He shook his head, refusing to be troubled by a few bruises, and bounced back onto his feet.

'I am well,' he pronounced.

Clearly this was true, but Olivia knew she had to be sure.

'I'm getting you to a doctor,' she said.

The headmistress had arrived on the scene in time to hear this. She was in her late forties with an air of common sense.

'That's a good idea,' she said. 'He seems fine, but let's take no chances. There's a hospital ten minutes away. I'll call a taxi.'

A few minutes later they were on their way to

the hospital. Olivia kept an anxious eye on Dong, but he was grinning, completely happy with the result of his escapade.

In the hospital someone showed them the way to the clinic, and they joined a short queue. A nurse gave Olivia some forms, and she filled them in while they waited to be seen.

A notice on the wall informed her that today's clinic was being taken by Dr Lang Mitchell. Briefly she wondered about that name; 'Mitchell' suggested that he might come from the West, but 'Lang' held a hint of Chinese.

After a few minutes the buzzer announced that the doctor was free, and they went in. Olivia saw a tall young man in his early thirties, with dark hair and eyes, and good-looking features that were mostly Western, yet with an intriguing hint of something else.

'What have you two been doing to yourselves?' he demanded, smiling and eyeing the state they were in.

'Miss Daley climbed a tree,' Dong said irrepressibly, 'and I went up to help her when she got stuck.'

Olivia looked aghast, which made Dr Mitchell grin in perfect comprehension.

'Perhaps it was the other way around?' he suggested.

'It certainly was,' Olivia declared, recovering

her dignity. 'On the way down the ladder slipped, and we landed in a heap.'

He studied the forms. 'You are Miss Olivia Daley, a teacher at the Chang-Ming School?'

'That's right. Yen Dong is one of my pupils. I don't think he's hurt, but I have to be sure when I hand him back to his mother.'

'Of course. Let's have a look.'

After a thorough examination of Dong, he said, 'I agree that it doesn't look serious, but we'll have an X-ray just to be on the safe side. The nurse will take him.'

'Perhaps I should go too.'

But Dong shook his head, informing her that he was grown up and didn't need to be protected all the time. When he'd left with the nurse, the doctor switched to English to say, 'Let's see about your injuries.'

'Thank you. But I really don't need much done.'

Smiling, he said gently, 'Why don't you let me decide that?'

'Sorry,' she groaned. 'I just can't help it. My aunt says if I'd shut up occasionally I might learn something.'

He smiled again but didn't answer directly. Then he frowned, saying, 'It might be worse than you think.'

Now she saw the true extent of the damage. The final slide against the bark of the tree had not merely scratched her flesh but torn the top of her sleeve so that it was barely hanging on.

'I'm afraid I'll need to remove your blouse,' Dr Mitchell said. 'The scratches seem to go further than your arm. Don't worry, a nurse will be present.'

He went to the door and called, 'Nurse.' A smiling young woman entered, removed Olivia's blouse gently and remained while he studied her abrasions. He eased her arm this way and that with movements that were as neat as they were skilful. His hands were large and comforting, both gentle and powerful together.

Disconcertingly she found herself becoming self-conscious. The blouse was high-necked and modest, even severe, as befitted a teacher, but beneath it she wore only a bra of fairly skimpy dimensions. She had breasts to be proud of, an unusual combination of dainty and luscious. Every bra she possessed had been designed to reveal them to one man, and although he was no longer part of her life she had never discarded them.

It had briefly crossed her mind to substitute underwear that was more sober and serious, but she'd rejected the thought as a kind of sacrilege. Now she wished she'd heeded it. Her generous curves were designed to be celebrated by a lover, not viewed clinically by a man who seemed not to notice that they were beautiful.

But that was as it should be, she reminded

herself. The doctor was being splendidly professional, and deserved her respect for the scrupulous
way he avoided touching her except when and
where necessary. It was just disturbing that his restraint seemed to bring her physically alive in a
way that only one man's touch had before.

He was cleaning her arm, swabbing it gently
with cotton wool anointed with a healing spirit.

'This will sting a little,' he said. 'I'm sorry, are
you all right?'

'Yes, I—'

'You jumped. I guess it stings more than I
thought. Don't worry, I'll soon be finished.'

To her own dismay she'd sounded breathless.
She hoped he didn't guess the reason, or notice the
little pulse beating in her throat.

'Your diagnosis was quite correct,' he said after
a while. 'Just a light dressing, I think. Nurse?'

The nurse did the necessary work, then helped
Olivia back on with her ruined blouse and
departed. Dr Mitchell had retired behind his desk.

'How are you going to get home?' he asked,
eyeing the tear.

'I look a bit disreputable, don't I?' she said with a
laugh. 'But I've got this.' She took a light scarf from
her bag and draped it over the spot. 'And I'll take a
taxi. Just as soon as I know that Dong is all right.'

'Don't worry about him. I never saw such a
healthy child.'

'I know,' she said with a shaky laugh. 'He's a rascal, I'm glad to say. No power on earth stops him getting up to mischief. He couldn't see the highest tree in the playground without wanting to climb it.'

'And that can be good,' Dr Mitchell said. 'Except that other people have to pick up the pieces, and often it is they who get hurt. I was much the same as a boy, and always in trouble for it. But I only recall my teachers reproving me, not risking their own safety to rescue me.'

'If he'd been seriously hurt, how could I have faced his mother?'

'But he isn't seriously hurt, because he had a soft landing on top of you.'

'Something like that,' she said ruefully. 'But nothing hurts me. I just bounce. And I should be getting him back to school soon, or he'll be late going home.'

'What about when you go home?' he asked. 'Is there anyone there to look after you?'

'No, I live alone, but I don't need anyone to look after me.'

He paused a moment before saying, 'Perhaps you shouldn't be too confident of that.'

'Why not?'

'It—can sometimes be dangerous.'

She wanted to ask him what he meant. The air was singing as though two conversations were happening together. Beneath the conventional words, he was speaking silently to a part of her that had never listened before, and it was vital to know more. She drew a breath, carefully framing a question…

'Here I am,' came a cheerful voice.

Suddenly she was back on earth, and there was Dong, trotting into the room, accompanied by the nurse with the X-ray.

'Excellent,' Dr Mitchell said in a voice that didn't sound quite natural to Olivia's ears. But nothing was natural any more.

As predicted, the X-ray showed no injury.

'Bring him back if he seems poorly,' Dr Mitchell told her, his tone normal again. 'But he won't.'

He showed her out and stood watching as she vanished down the corridor and around the corner. Closing the door, he reached automatically for the buzzer, but stopped. He needed a moment to think before he saw another patient.

He went to stand at the window. Here, two floors high, there was a close-up view of the trees hung with cherry blossom; the promise of spring had been gloriously kept, and still lingered.

Here in China cherry blossom was a symbol of feminine beauty; seemingly delicate, yet laden with hope and promise. Now he saw that wherever he looked it was the same, as fresh new life returned after the cold, bringing hope and joy for those who were eager to embrace it.

On the surface nothing very much had

happened. Olivia Daley was strong, independent, concerned not for herself but those in her care, much like the kind of woman a medical man met every day. It might only have been his imagination that beneath her composure was someone else— someone tense, vulnerable, needing help yet defiantly refusing to ask for it.

He could hear her again, insisting, *Nothing hurts me. I just bounce.*

He wondered if she truly believed herself so armoured to life. For himself, he didn't believe a word of it.

A few minutes they'd been together, that was all. Yet he'd seen deep into her, and the sad emptiness he'd found there had almost overwhelmed him. He knew too that she'd been as disconcertingly alive to him as he had been to her.

He'd smothered the thought as unprofessional, but now it demanded his attention, and he yielded. She was different from other women. He had yet to discover exactly how different, and caution warned him not to try. Already he knew that he was going to ignore caution and follow the light that had mysteriously appeared on the road ahead.

It was a soft light, flickering and uncertain, promising everything and nothing. But he could no more deny it than he could deny his own self.

'Is everything all right?' asked the nurse from the doorway. 'You haven't buzzed.'

'I'm sorry,' he said with an effort. 'I just—got distracted.'

She smiled, following his gaze to the blossom-laden trees. 'The spring is beautiful, isn't it?'

'Yes,' he murmured. 'Beautiful.'

They arrived back at the school to find Mrs Yen, Dong's mother, waiting with a worried look that cleared as soon as she saw him waving eagerly.

'Perhaps you should take tomorrow off?' Mrs Wu, the headmistress, asked when they were finally alone.

'Thanks, but I won't need to.'

'Well, be sure. I don't want to lose one of my best teachers.'

They had been friends since the day Olivia had joined the school, charged with instructing the children in English. Now Mrs Wu fussed over her kindly until she went to collect her bicycle and rode it to her apartment, ten minutes away.

She had moved in six months ago, when she'd arrived to work in Beijing. Then she had been distraught, fleeing England, desperately glad to be embraced by a different culture which occupied her thoughts and gave her no time to brood. Now her surroundings and her new life were more familiar, but there were still new discoveries to be made, and she enjoyed every day.

She had a settled routine for when she arrived

home. After a large cup of tea, she would switch on the computer and enter a programme that allowed her to make video contact with Aunt Norah, the elderly relative in England to whom she felt closest.

London was eight hours behind Beijing, which meant that back there it was the early hours of the morning, but she knew Norah would be ready, having set her alarm to be sure.

Yes, there she was, sitting up in bed, smiling and waving at the camera on top of her computer screen. Olivia waved back.

Norah was an old lady, a great-aunt rather than an aunt, but her eyes were as bright as they'd been her youth, and her vitality was undimmed. Olivia had always been close to her, turning to her wisdom and kindness as a refuge from the self-centred antics of the rest of her family.

'Sorry I'm late,' she said into the microphone. 'There was a bit of a kerfuffle at school today.'

She outlined the events of the afternoon, making light of them.

'And the doctor said you were all right?'

'He says I'm fine. I'll have an early night and be fit as a fiddle.'

'Are you going out with anyone?'

'You asked me that last night, and the night before. Honestly, Auntie, it's all you ever think of.'

'So I should hope. You're a pretty girl. You ought to be having a good time.'

'I'm having a wonderful time. And I do have dates. I just don't want to get serious. Now, tell me about yourself. Are you getting enough sleep?'

There was more in the query than just a desire to change the subject. Norah was in her seventies, and the only thing that had made Olivia hesitate about coming to China was the fear of possibly not seeing her again. But Norah had assured her that she was in the best of health and had urged her to go.

'Don't you dare turn down your chance because of me,' she'd insisted.

'I'm just trying to be sensible,' Olivia had protested mildly.

'*Sensible?* You've got the rest of your life for that sort of nonsense. Get out there, do things you've never done before, and forget that man who didn't deserve you anyway.'

Norah could never forgive the man who'd broken Olivia's heart.

'I'm sleeping fine,' Norah said now. 'I spent yesterday evening with your mother, listening to her complaining about her latest. That sent me right off to sleep.'

'I thought Guy was her ideal lover.'

'Not Guy, Freddy. She's finished with Guy, or he finished with her, one of the two. I can't keep up.'

Olivia sighed wryly. 'I'll call her and commiserate.'

'Not too much or you'll make her worse,' Norah said at once. 'She's a silly woman. I've always said so. Mind you, it's not all her fault. Her own mother has a lot to answer for. Fancy giving her a stupid name like Melisande! She was bound to see herself as a romantic heroine.'

'You mean,' Olivia said, 'that if Mum had been called something dull and sensible she wouldn't have eloped?'

'Probably not, although I think she'd have been self-centred whatever she was called. She's never thought of anyone but herself. She's certainly never thought of you, any more than your father has. Heaven alone knows what he's doing now, although I did hear a rumour that he's got some girl pregnant.'

'Again?'

'Yes, and he's going about preening as though he's the first man who's ever managed it. Forget him. The great fool isn't worth bothering with.'

Thus she dismissed her nephew—with some justice, as Olivia had to admit.

They chatted for a while longer before bidding each other an affectionate goodnight. Olivia delayed just long enough to make herself a basic meal, then fell thankfully into bed, ready to fall asleep at once.

Instead she lay awake, too restless for sleep.

Mysteriously, Dr Mitchell had found his way into her thoughts, and she remembered him saying, *Other people have to pick up the pieces, and often it is they who get hurt.*

He'd given her a look full of wry kindness, as if guessing that she was often the person who had to come to the rescue—which was shrewd of him, she realised, because he'd been right.

As far back as she could remember she'd been the rock of stability in her family. Her parents' marriage had been a disaster. They'd married young in a fever of romance, had quickly been disillusioned by prosaic reality and had headed for divorce. Since then her mother had remarried and divorced again before settling for lovers. Her father had moved straight onto the lovers.

She herself had been passed from pillar to post, depending on whichever of them had felt she could be most useful. They had lavished noisy affection on her without ever managing to be convincing. Their birthday and Christmas gifts had been expensive, but she'd realised early on that they were aimed at scoring points off each other.

'Let's see what your father thinks of that,' her mother had said, proudly revealing a state-of-the-art, top-of-the-range, laptop. But she'd been too busy to come and see Olivia in the school play, which would have meant far more.

The person who'd always come to school functions was Norah, her father's aunt. When both her parents had been busy, Olivia had gone to Norah for long visits and found that here was someone she could talk to. Norah had encouraged her to say what she was thinking. She would argue, forcing the girl to define her ideas then enlarge on them, until Olivia had begun to realise that her own thoughts were actually worth discussing—something she'd never discovered with her parents, who could talk only about themselves.

There'd always been a bedroom for her in Norah's home, and when she'd turned sixteen she'd moved into it full-time.

'How did that pair of adolescents you call parents react to the idea?' Norah demanded.

'I'm not sure they quite realise that I've gone,' Olivia said. 'He thinks I'm with her, she thinks I'm with him. Oh, what do they matter?'

It was possible to cope with her parents' selfish indifference because Norah's love was there like a rock. Even so, it was painful to discover yet again how little they really cared about her.

Eventually her mother asked, 'Will you be all right with Norah? She's a bit—you know—' she'd lowered her voice as though describing some great crime '—*fuddy-duddy*.'

It crossed Olivia's mind that 'fuddy-duddy' might be a welcome quality in a parent, but she said nothing. She'd learned discretion at an early age. She assured her mother that she would be fine, and the subject was allowed to die.

Before leaving, Melisande had one final request. 'Would you mind not calling me Mum when there are people around? It sounds so middle-aged, and I'm only thirty-one.'

Olivia frowned. 'Thirty-three, surely? Because I was born when—'

'Oh, darling, must you be so literal? I only *look* thirty-one. In fact, I've been told I look twenty-five. Surely you understand about artistic licence?'

'Of course,' Olivia agreed with a touch of bitterness that passed her mother by. 'And if I start claiming you as my mother it spoils the effect.'

'Exactly!' Melisande beamed, entirely missing the irony in her daughter's voice. 'You can call me Melly if you like.'

'Gosh, thanks, Mum.'

Her mother gave her a sharp look but didn't make the mistake of replying.

That evening, she told Norah, who was disgusted.

'Fuddy-duddy! She means I don't live my life at the mercy of every wind that blows.'

'She just thinks you know nothing about love,' Olivia pointed out.

When Norah didn't answer, she persisted, 'But she's wrong, isn't she? There's someone you never talk about.'

That was how she'd first heard about Edward,

who'd died so long ago that nobody else remembered him, or the volcano he'd caused in the life of the girl who'd loved him. Norah told her only a little that night, but more later on, as Olivia grew old enough to understand.

Norah had been eighteen when she'd met Edward, a young army-officer, nineteen when they'd celebrated his promotion by becoming engaged, and twenty when he'd died, far away in another country. She had never loved another man.

The bleak simplicity of the story shocked Olivia. Later she learned to set it beside her own parents' superficial romances, and was equally appalled by both.

Had that lesson hovered somewhere in her mind when she too had fallen disastrously in love?

Looking back, she could see that her life-long cynicism about emotion, far from protecting her, had left her vulnerable. She'd determinedly avoided the youthful experiences on which most girls cut their romantic teeth, proud of the way her heart had never been broken because she'd never become involved. But it meant that she'd had no yardstick by which to judge Andy, no caution to warn her of signs that other women would have seen. Her capitulation to him had been total, joyful, and his betrayal had left her defenceless.

She'd fled, seeking a new life here in China, vowing never to make the same mistake again.

From now on men would no longer exist. Neither would love, or anything that reminded her of 'the whole romantic nonsense' as she inwardly called it. And so she would be safe.

On that comforting thought, she fell asleep.

But tonight her sleep was mysteriously disturbed. Phantoms chased through her dreams, making her hot and cold by turns, causing her blood to race and her heart to pound. She awoke abruptly to find herself sitting up in bed, not knowing when it had happened, not knowing anything, except that suddenly there was no safety in all the world.

CHAPTER TWO

THE next day Olivia felt down from the moment she awoke. The sight of herself in the bathroom mirror was off-putting. Where was the vibrant young woman in her twenties with a slender figure, rich, honey-coloured hair and large blue eyes that could say so much?

'I don't think she ever really existed,' she informed her reflection gloomily. 'You're the reality.'

She wondered if she might still be in shock from her nasty fall, but dismissed that as just making excuses.

'I'm a hag,' she muttered. 'I look older than I am. I'm too thin, and my hair is just plain drab. I'll be going grey next.'

The woman in the mirror stared back, offering not a glimmer of sympathy. Normally Olivia wore her wavy hair long and bouncy but today she pulled it back into an efficient-looking bun. It suited her mood.

The day continued to be glum for no apparent reason. Her students were attentive and well-behaved, lunch was appetizing and her friends on the staff made kindly enquiries as to her health. Mrs Wu even tried to send her home.

'It's a reaction to that fall,' she said. 'Go home and rest.'

'Dong doesn't seem to need rest,' Olivia pointed out. 'I actually had to stop him trying to climb that tree again.'

'It's up to you,' the headmistress said sympathetically. 'But feel free to leave when you feel like it.'

She stuck it out to the end of the day, tired and grumpy, wanting to go home yet not looking forward to the empty apartment. Finally she delivered some papers to the headmistress and slipped out of the building by a side door, instead of the main entrance that she would normally have used. Then she stopped, arrested by the sight that met her eyes.

Dr Mitchell was there.

Now she knew that this moment was always meant to happen.

He was sitting on a low wall near the main entrance. Olivia paused for a moment just as he rose and began to pace restlessly and look at the main door as though expecting somebody to come through it. Occasionally he consulted his watch.

She backed off until she was in shadow under the trees, but still able to see him clearly. She realised that her view of him the day before had been constricted by the surroundings of his office. He was taller than she remembered, not muscular, but lean with a kind of casual elegance that yet hinted at tension and control.

Yesterday he'd been in command on his own territory. Now he was uncertain.

She began to walk towards him, calling, 'Can I help you?'

His face brightened at once, convincing her that she was the one he'd been awaiting. Mysteriously the day's cares began to fall away from her.

'I thought I'd drop in to see how my patients are,' he said, moving towards her.

'Do you always do follow-up visits from the clinic?'

He shook his head. His eyes were mischievous.

'Just this time,' he said.

'Thank you. Dong has already gone home, but he's fine.'

'But what about you? You were hurt as well.'

'It was only a few scratches, and I was cared for by an excellent doctor.'

He inclined his head in acknowledgement of her compliment, and said, 'Still, perhaps I should assure myself that you're really well.'

'Of course.' She stood back to let him enter the building, but he shook his head.

'I have a better idea. There's a little restaurant not far from here where we can talk in peace.'

His smile held a query, asking if she would go along with his strategy, and she hurried to reassure him, smiling in return and saying, 'What a lovely idea!'

'My car's just over there.'

To her pleasure he drove to a place that had a look that she thought of as traditionally Chinese. Much of Beijing had been rebuilt in a modern style, but she yearned for the old buildings with their ornate roofs turning up at the corners. Here she found them glowing with light from the coloured lamps outside.

The first restaurant they came to was full. So was the second.

'Perhaps we should try—'

He was interrupted by a cheerful cry. Turning, they saw a young man hailing him from a short distance away, and urgently pointing down a side street. He vanished without waiting to see if they followed him.

'We're caught,' her companion said ruefully. 'We'll have to go to the Dancing Dragon.'

'Isn't it any good?'

'It's the best—but I'll tell you later. Let's go.'

There was no mistaking the restaurant. Painted dragons swirled on the walls outside, their eyes alight with mischief. Inside was small and bright, bustling with life and packed.

'They don't have any tables free,' she murmured.

'Don't worry. They always keep one for me.'

Sure enough the man from the street reappeared, pointing the way to a corner and leading them to a small, discreet table tucked away almost out of sight. It had clearly been designed for lovers, and Lang must have thought so too, because he gave a hurried, embarrassed mutter, which Olivia just managed to decipher as, 'Do you have to be so obvious?'

'Why not?' the waiter asked, genuinely baffled. 'It's the table you always have.'

Olivia's lips twitched as she seated herself in the corner, but she controlled her amusement. Dr Mitchell was turning out to be more interesting than she would have guessed.

The restaurant was charming, the lanterns giving out a soft, red light, the walls covered in dragons. She regarded them in delight. Dragons had been part of her love affair with China ever since she'd discovered their real nature.

Raised in England, the only dragon she'd heard of had been the one slain by St George, a devil breathing fire and death, ravaging villages, demanding the sacrifice of innocent maidens, until the heroic knight George had overcome him and become the country's patron saint as a result.

In China it was different. Here the dragon had always been the harbinger of good luck, wealth, wisdom, a fine harvest. Delightful dragons popped up in every part of life. They danced at weddings, promenaded in parades, breathing their friendly fire and spreading happiness. They were all around her now.

Perhaps that was why she suddenly felt better than she'd done all day. There surely couldn't be any other reason.

Looking at a dragon painted onto a mirror, she caught sight of her own reflection and realised that her hair was still drawn back severely, which no longer felt right. With a swift movement she pulled at the pins until her tresses were freed, flowing lusciously again, in keeping with her lighter mood.

The dragon winked at her.

While Dr Mitchell was occupied with the waiter, Olivia remembered a duty that she must perform without delay. Whenever she was unable to make computer contact with Norah she always called to warn her so that the old woman wouldn't be left waiting in hope. Quickly she used her mobile phone and in a moment she heard Norah's voice.

'Just to let you know that I'm not at home tonight,' she said.

'Jolly good,' Norah said at once, as Olivia had known she would say. 'You should go out more often, not waste time talking to me.'

'But you know I love talking to you.'

'Yes, I do, but tonight you have more important things to think of. At least, I hope you have. Goodnight, darling.'

'Goodnight, my love,' Olivia said tenderly.

She hung up to find her companion regarding her with a little frown.

'Have I created a problem?' he asked delicately. 'Is there someone who—' he paused delicately '—would object to your being with me?'

'Oh, no! I was talking to my elderly aunt in England. There's nobody who can tell me who to be with.'

'I'm glad,' he said simply.

And she was glad too, for suddenly the shadows of the day had lifted.

'Dr Mitchell—'

'My name is Lang.'

'And mine is Olivia.'

The waiter appeared with tea, filling Olivia's cup, smiling with pleased surprise as she gave the traditional thank-you gesture of tapping three fingers on the table.

'Most Westerners don't know to do that,' Lang explained.

'It's the kind of thing I love,' she said. 'I love the story too—about the emperor who went to a teahouse incognito with some friends and told them not to prostrate themselves before him because it would give away his identity. So they tapped their fingers instead. I don't want to stand out. It's more fun fitting in.'

When the first dishes were laid out before them, including the rice, he observed her skill using chopsticks.

'You really know how to do that,' he observed as they started to eat. 'You must have been in China for some time.'

He spoke in Mandarin Chinese and she replied in the same language, glad to demonstrate that she was as expert as he.

'About six months,' she said. 'Before that I lived in England most of the time.'

'Most?'

'I've always travelled a lot to improve my languages. They were all I was ever good at, so I had to make the most of them.'

'How many languages do you speak?'

'French, German, Italian, Spanish…'

'Hey, I'm impressed. But why Chinese?'

'Pure show-off,' she chuckled. 'Everyone warned me it was difficult, so I did it for the fun of proving that I could. That showed 'em!'

'I'll bet it did,' he said admiringly, reverting to English. 'And I don't suppose you found it difficult at all.'

'Actually, I did, but I kept that to myself.

You're the only person I've ever admitted that secret to.'

'And I promise not to reveal it,' he said solemnly. 'On pain of your never speaking to me again.'

She didn't have to ask what he meant by that. They both knew that the connection between them had been established in those few minutes of devastating consciousness in his surgery, and today he'd come looking for her because he had to.

Olivia thought back to last night, to the disturbance that had haunted her dreams, waking her and refusing to let her sleep again. Instinct told her that it had been the same with him.

They might spend no more than a few fleeting hours in each other's company, or they might travel a little distance along the road together. Neither could know. But they had to find out.

'So you came out here to improve your Chinese?' he asked in a tone that suggested there must be more to it.

'Partly, but I needed to get away from England for a while.'

He nodded, understanding at once. 'Was he a real louse?'

'I thought so at the time, but I think now I had a lucky escape. He almost made me forget my prime directive. But when I discovered what a louse he really was, I realised that the prime directive had been right all the time.'

'Prime directive,' he mused, his eyes glinting with amusement. 'Now, let me see—what would that be? "Only learning matters." "Life can be reduced to graphs on a page." How am I doing?'

'You're part of the way there, but only part. Beware people, beware relationships—'

'Beware men!'

'Hey, you guessed.'

'It was obviously what you were building up to. Are we all condemned?'

'It's not that simple. I don't just condemn men, I blame women, as well.'

'Well, that seems to take care of the entire human race. Having disposed of the whole lot of them, let's go on eating.'

His wryly mocking tone made her laugh.

'My parents were both wild romantics,' she went on, 'and I can't tell you what a misfortune that is.'

'You don't need to. Romance isn't supposed to be for parents. Their job is to be severe and straight-laced so that their kids have a safety net for indulging in mad fantasies.'

'Right!' she said, relieved at his understanding. 'According to Aunt Norah it was love at first sight, then a whirlwind romance—moon rhyming with June. All that stuff.'

Lang regarded her curiously. Something edgy in the way she'd said *all that stuff* had alerted him.

'What happened?'

'She was seventeen, he was eighteen. Nobody took it seriously at first, just kids fooling around. But then they wanted to get married. The parents said no. He had to go to college. So she got pregnant—on purpose, Norah thinks. They ended up making a runaway marriage.'

'Wonderfully romantic,' Lang supplied. 'Until they came down to earth with a bump. He had to get a job, she found herself with a crying baby....'

'Apparently I cried more than most—for no reason, according to my mother.'

'But babies can sense things. You must have known instinctively that she was dissatisfied, wanting to go out and enjoy herself, and your father probably blamed her for his blighted career-prospects.'

She stared at him, awed by this insight.

'That's exactly how it was. At least, that's how Norah says it was. I don't remember, of course, except that I picked up the atmosphere without knowing why. There was lots of shouting and screaming.

'It got worse because they both started having affairs. At last they divorced, and I found I didn't really have a home. I stayed with her, or with him, but I always felt like a guest. If there was a new girl-friend or new boyfriend I'd be in the way and I'd stay with Norah. Then the romance would break up and my mother would cry on my shoulder.'

'So you became *her* mother,' Lang observed.

'Yes, I suppose I did. And, if that was what romance did to you, I decided I didn't want it.'

'But wasn't there anyone else in your family to show you a more encouraging view of love? What about Norah?'

'She's the opposite to them. Her fiancé died years ago. There's been nobody else for her since, and she's always told me that she's perfectly content. She says once you've found the right man you can't replace him with anyone else.'

'Even when she's lost him?'

'But according to Norah she hasn't lost him. He loved her to the end of his life, so she feels that they still belong to each other.'

'And you disapprove?' he asked, frowning a little.

'It sounds charming, but it's really only words. The reality is that it's turned Norah's life into a desert that's lasted fifty years.'

'Perhaps it hasn't. Do you really know what's inside her heart? Perhaps it's given her a kind of fulfilment that we can't understand.'

'Of course you could be right, but if that's fulfilment…' She finished with a sigh. 'I just want more from life than dreaming about a man who isn't there any more. Or,' she added wryly, 'in my mother's case, several men who aren't there any more.'

'But what about the louse? Didn't he change your mind?'

For the first time he saw her disconcerted.

'I kind of lost the plot there,' she admitted. 'But it sorted itself out. Never mind how. I'm wiser now.'

She spoke with a shrug and a cheerful smile, but she had the feeling that he wasn't fooled. Some instinct was telling him the things she wouldn't, couldn't say.

She'd been dazzled by Andy from the first moment. Handsome, charming, intelligent, he'd singled her out, wooed her passionately and had overturned all the fixed ideas of her life. For once she'd understood Norah's aching fidelity to a dead man. She'd even partly understood the way her mother fell in love so often.

Then, just when she'd been ready to abandon the prejudices of a lifetime, he'd announced that he was engaged to marry someone else. He'd said they'd had a wonderful few months together but it was time to be realistic, wasn't it?

The lonely, anguished nights that had followed had served to convince her that she'd been right all the time. Love wasn't for her, or for anyone in their right mind. She couldn't speak of it, but there was no need. Lang's sympathetic silence told her that he understood.

'Tell me about you,' she hastened to say. 'You're English too, aren't you? What brought you out here?'

'I'm three-quarters English. The other quarter is Chinese.'

'Ah,' she said slowly.

'You guessed?'

'Not exactly. You sound English, but your features suggest otherwise. I don't know—there's something else…'

She gave up trying to explain. The 'something else' in his face seemed to come and go. One moment it almost defined him, the next it barely existed. It intrigued and tempted her with its hint of another, mysterious world.

'Something different—but it's not a matter of looks,' she finished, wishing she could find the right words.

He seemed satisfied and nodded.

'I know. That "something different" is inside, and it has always haunted me,' he said. 'I was born in London, and I grew up there, but I knew I didn't quite fit in with the others. My mother was English, my father was half-Chinese. He died soon after I was born. Later my mother married an Englishman with two children from a previous marriage.'

'Wicked stepfather?' Olivia enquired.

'No, nothing so dramatic. He was a decent guy. I got on well with him and his children, but I wasn't like them, and we all knew it.

'Luckily I had my grandmother, who'd left China to marry my grandfather. Her name was Lang Meihui before she married, and she was an astonishing woman. She knew nothing about

England and couldn't speak the language. John Mitchell couldn't speak Chinese. But they managed to communicate and knew that they loved each other. He brought her home to London.'

'She must have found it really hard to cope,' Olivia mused.

'Yes, but I'll swear, nothing has ever defeated her in her life. She learned to speak English really well. She found a way to live in a country that probably felt like being on another planet, and she survived when her husband died ten years later, leaving her with a son to raise alone.

'He was called Lang too. She'd insisted on that. It was her way of keeping her Chinese family-name alive. When I was born she more or less bullied him into calling me Lang, as well. She told me later that she did it so that "we don't lose China."

'My father died when I was eight years old. When my mother remarried, Meihui moved into a little house in the next street so that she could be near me. She helped my mother with the children, the shopping, anything, but then she slipped away to her own home. And in time I began to follow her.'

He gave her a warm smile. 'So you see, I had a Norah too.'

'And you depended on her, just as I did on mine.'

'Yes, because she was the only one who could make me understand what was different about me.

She taught me her language but, more than that, she showed me China.'

'She actually brought you here?'

'Only in my head, but if you could have seen the fireworks she set off in there.' He tapped his forehead. 'She used to take me out to visit London's Chinatown, especially on Chinese New Year. I thought I was in heaven—all that colour, the glittering lights and the music—'

'Oh, yes, I remember,' Olivia broke in eagerly. 'You saw it too?'

'Only once. My mother visited some friends who lived near there, and they took us out a couple of nights to see what was happening. It was like you said, brilliant and thrilling, but nobody could explain it to me. There was a lot of red, and they were supposed to be fighting somebody, but I couldn't tell who or what.'

'Some people say they're fighting the Nian,' Lang supplied. 'A mythical beast rather like a lion, who devours crops and children. So they put food out for him and let off firecrackers, because he's afraid of loud noises and also of the colour red. So you got lots of red and fireworks and lions dancing. What more could a child want?'

'Nothing,' Olivia said, remembering ecstatically. 'Oh, yes, it was gorgeous. So much better than the English New Year celebrations, which always seemed boringly sedate after that.'

'Me too. It was the one thing I refused ever to miss, and that drove my mother mad, because the date was always changing—late January, mid-February—always lasting fifteen days. Mum complained that she couldn't plan for anything, except that I'd be useless for fifteen days. I said, "Don't worry, Mum, I'm always useless".' He made a face. 'She didn't think that was at all funny.'

'Your grandmother sounds wonderful,' Olivia said sincerely.

'She was. She told me how everyone is born in the year of an animal—a sheep, an ox, a rat, a dragon. I longed to find I was born in the year of the dragon.'

'And were you?'

He made a face. 'No, I was born in the year of the rabbit. *Don't laugh!*'

'I'm not laughing,' she said, hastily controlling her mirth. 'In this country, the rabbit is calm and gentle, hard-working—'

'Dull and plodding,' he supplied. 'Dreary, conventional—'

'Observant, intelligent—'

'Boring.'

She chuckled. 'You're not boring, I promise.'

It was true. He delighted her, not with any flashy display of personality, but because his thoughts seemed to reach out and take hers by the hand in a way that, she now realized, Andy had never done.

He gave her a rueful grin.

'Thank you for those kind words, even if you had to scrape the bottom of the barrel to find them.'

'According to everything I've read, there's nothing wrong with being born in the year of the rabbit.'

'And you've obviously read a lot, so I guess you know your own year.' He saw her sheepish look and exclaimed, 'Oh, no, please don't tell me—!'

'I'm sorry, I really am.'

'The year of the dragon?'

'It not my fault,' she pleaded.

'You know what that means, don't you?' He groaned. 'Dragons are free spirits, powerful, beautiful, fearless, they soar above convention, refusing to be bound by rules and regulations.'

'That's the theory, but I never felt it quite fitted me,' she said, laughing and trying to placate him. 'I don't see myself soaring.'

'But perhaps you don't know yourself too well,' he suggested. 'And you've yet to find the thing that will make you soar. Or the person,' he added.

The last words were spoken so quietly that she might have missed them, except that she was totally alive to him. She understood and was filled with sudden alarm. Things were happening that she'd sworn never to allow happen again.

She would leave right now and retreat into the old illusion of safety. All she had to do was rise, apologise and leave, trying to avoid his eyes that saw too much. It was simple, really.

But she didn't move, and she knew that she wasn't going to.

CHAPTER THREE

'THE trouble with soaring,' she murmured, 'is that you fall to earth.'

'Sometimes you do,' he said gently. 'But not always.'

'Not always,' she murmured. 'Perhaps.'

But it was too soon. Her nerve failed her and in her mind she crossed hastily to the cautious side of the road.

'What about your grandmother? What was her year?'

Tactfully he accepted her change of subject without demur.

'She was a dragon too,' he said. 'With her courage and sense of adventure she couldn't have been anything else—a real dragon lady. Everything she told me about this country seemed to bring me alive, until all I could think of was coming here one day.

'We planned how we'd make the trip together,

but she became very ill. I'd qualified as a doctor by then, and I knew she wasn't going to recover, but she still talked as though it would happen soon.

'At last we had to face the truth. On her deathbed she said, "I so much wanted to be there with you." And I promised her that she would be.'

'And she has been, hasn't she?' Olivia asked, marvelling.

'Every step of the way,' he confirmed. 'Wherever I go, I remember what she told me. Her family welcomed me with open arms.'

'Did you find them easily?'

'Yes, because she'd stayed in touch. When I landed at Beijing Airport three years ago there were thirty people to welcome me. They recognised me at once from the pictures she'd sent them, and they all cheered.

'It's an enormous family. Not all of them live in Beijing, and many of those who lived further out had come in especially to see Meihui's grandson.'

'They weren't put off by your being three-quarters English?'

He laughed. 'I don't think they even see that part of me. I'm one of the Lang family. That's all that counts.'

'It was clever of your grandmother to name you and your father Lang,' Olivia mused. 'In England it's your first name, but here the family name comes first.'

'Yes, my uncles are Lang Hai and Lang Jing, my great uncle is Lang Tao, my cousin is Lang Dai, so I fitted in straight away.'

A sudden look of mischief crossed her face. 'Tell me something—have your stepbrothers given you any nephews and nieces?'

He looked puzzled. 'Three, but I don't see...'

'And I'll bet they call you Uncle Lang.'

'Yes, but—'

'And what do the children of the Lang family call you? It can't be Uncle Lang, because that would be nonsense to them. So I guess they must call you Uncle Mitch.'

A glazed look came into his eyes and he edged away from her with a nervous air that made her laugh.

'Are you a witch to have such second sight?' he demanded. 'Should I be scared?'

'Are you?' she teased.

'A bit. More than a bit, actually. How did you know that?'

'Logical deduction, my dear Watson. Second sight doesn't come into it.'

He could see that she was right, but it still left him with an enchanted feeling, as though she could divine what was hidden from others. A true 'dragon lady', he thought with delight, with magic arts to entice and dazzle a man.

'You're right about my grandmother,' he said. 'In her heart, she never really left China.'

'How did her relatives feel about her marrying an Englishman and leaving the country?'

'They were very supportive, because it's in the family tradition.'

'You all believe in marrying for love?'

'Much more than that. Marrying in the face of great difficulties, putting love first despite all obstacles. It goes back over two-thousand years.'

'Two thou...?' She laughed in astonishment. 'Are you nobility or something?'

'No, just ordinary people. Over the centuries my family has tilled the land, sold farm produce, perhaps made just enough money to start a little shop. We've been carpenters, wheelwrights, blacksmiths—but never noble, I promise you.'

The arrival of the waiter made him fall silent while plates were cleared away and the next course was served. It was fried pork-belly stewed in soy and wine, and Olivia's mouth watered at the prospect.

'We're also excellent cooks,' Lang observed, speaking very significantly.

'You mean...?'

'This was cooked by my cousin Lang Chao, and the guy who served it is his brother, Lang Wei. Later Wei's girlfriend, Suyin, will sing for us.'

'Your family own this restaurant?'

'That's why they virtually hijacked us. I wasn't planning to bring you here because I knew we'd be stared at—if you glance into the corner you'll see Wei sneaking a peek and thinking we can't see him—but they happened to spot me in the street, and after that we were lost.'

'We seem to be providing the entertainment,' she said, amused. 'Wei's enjoying a good laugh over there.'

'I'm going to strangle him when I get home,' Lang growled. 'This is why I didn't want them to see you because I knew they'd think— Well…'

'That you'd brought one of your numerous girl-friends here?' Olivia said.

She was teasing but the question was important.

'I occasionally bring a lady here to dine,' he conceded. 'Purely in a spirit of flirtation. Anything more serious, I wouldn't bring her here. Or at least,' he added, grinding his teeth and glaring at the unrepentant Wei, 'I'd *try* not to.'

'No problem.' Olivia chuckled. 'You tell him that he's completely wrong in what he's thinking, that we're just a pair of fellow professionals having a quiet meal for companionship. There's no more to it than that.'

'No more to it than that,' he echoed in a comi-cally robotic voice.

'*Then* you can strangle him.'

'That sounds like a good idea. But what do I tell him when I take you out again?'

'Tell him to mind his own business?' she sug-gested vaguely.

'I can see you've never lived with a family like mine.'

'Wait a minute, you said when you "get home"? You don't live in the same house, do you?'

'Sometimes. I have a room there, but also a little place of my own near the hospital where I go if I've done a long stint at work and need to collapse. But if I want warmth, noise and cousins driving me crazy I go to the family home, so they tend to know what I do. But next time we'll avoid this place and have some privacy.'

'Look—'

'It's all right.' He held up a hand quickly. 'I don't mean to rush you. I know you haven't decided yet. But, when you do, let me know where you want to go.'

Her eyebrows rose at this quiet assurance but his smile disarmed her, making her complicit.

'I didn't finish telling you about our tradition,' he said.

'Yes, I'm curious. How did a family that had to work so hard come to put such a high value on romantic love? Surely it made more sense for a man to marry the girl whose father owned a strip of land next to his own?'

'Of course, and many marriages were made for such practical reasons. But the descendants of Jaio and Renshu always hoped for more.'

'Who were they?'

'They lived in the reign of the Emperor Qin, of whom I'm sure you've heard.'

She nodded. In reading about China, she'd learned about the time when it had been divided into many states. Qin Shi Huang, king of the state of Qin, had conquered the other states, unifying them into one gigantic country. Since Qin was pronounced 'chin' the country had come to be called China. Qin had proclaimed himself emperor, and on his death he'd been buried in a splendid mausoleum accompanied by any of his concubines who hadn't born him a child.

'One of those concubines was Jaio,' Lang told her now. 'She didn't want to die, and she was in love with Renshu, a young soldier who also loved her. Somehow he managed to rescue her, and they fled together. Of course, they had to spend the rest of their lives on the run, and they only had about five years before they were caught and killed. But by then they'd had a son, who was rescued and spirited away by Jaio's brother.

'Nobody heard anything for years, but when the son was an old man he revealed the writings that Jaio and Renshu had left, in which they said that their love had been worth all the hardship. Of course, they had to be kept secret, but the family protected them and still has them to this day.

'Because of this the Langs have always cherished a belief in love that has seen them through many hard times. Often their neighbours have thought them mad for trusting in love when there were so many more *important* things in life, but they have clung to their ideals. It was that trust that made Meihui leave China and follow John Mitchell to England. And she never regretted it. She missed her homeland, but she always said that being with the man she loved mattered more than anything in life.'

Hearing these words, Olivia had a strange sense of familiarity. Then she realised that this was exactly what Norah would have said.

She sipped her wine, considering what she had just been told. On the surface it was a conventional legend—charming, a tad sentimental. What made it striking was that this serious man should speak as though it had a deep meaning for him.

'It's a lovely story,' she said wistfully. 'But did it really happen that way?'

'Why not?' he asked, giving her a quizzical smile.

She suppressed the instinct to say, *Because it's too absurdly romantic to be real*, and said, 'I only meant that two-thousand years is a terribly long time. So many things get lost in the mists, and you could never really know if they were true or not.'

'It's true if we want it to be,' he said simply. 'And we do.'

For a moment she almost queried who 'we' were, and then was glad she hadn't, because he added, 'All of us, the whole family—my aunts, great-aunts, my uncles, cousins—we all want it to be true. And so it is—for us.'

'That's a delightful idea,' she mused. 'But perhaps not very practical.'

'Ah, yes, I'd forgotten that you must always be practical and full of common sense,' he teased.

'There's a lot to be said for it,' she protested defensively.

'If you're a schoolteacher.'

'Doesn't a doctor need common sense, as well?'

'Often, but not always. Sometimes common sense is a much over-rated virtue.'

'And sometimes it can come to your rescue,' she said wryly.

She didn't realise that she'd spoken aloud until she saw him looking at her with a question in his eyes.

'Has it rescued you very often?' he asked gently.

'Now and then. It's nice to know I can always rely on it.'

'That's just what you can't do!' he said with sudden urgency. 'You must never rely completely on your head, because sooner or later it will always let you down.'

'And you think the heart doesn't?' she retorted with a touch of indignation. 'We're not all as lucky as Meihui.'

'Or Norah.'

'I'd hardly call her lucky.'

'I would,' he said at once. 'The man she loved died, but he didn't betray her. That makes her luckier than many women, and men too, who live for years with the shadows of failed love, bad memories, regrets. Or the others, who never dared risk love at all and have only thoughts of what might have been if only they'd had a little more courage.'

'That sounds very fine,' she said. 'But the fact is that most people are unlucky in love. Is there really much to choose between taking the risk and regretting it, and deciding not to take it at all?'

'And regretting that?'

'And living free,' she said defiantly. 'Free of regrets, free of pain—'

'Free of joy, free of the sense that life is worth living or ever has been?' he interrupted her firmly. 'Being free of pain can come at a heavy price.'

How had they strayed into this argument? she wondered. And why? The conversation was becoming dangerous, and she acted instinctively to get back into control.

'I see Wei coming towards us,' she said brightly.

If he noticed her abrupt change of subject he didn't say so. Instead he turned sardonic eyes on his cousin, who bustled forward eagerly, his gaze darting between the two of them.

'We'd like some fruit, please,' Lang said firmly. 'And then, *vanish*!'

Wei gave him a hurt look and departed with dignity. Lang ground his teeth.

'Sometimes I think I should have stayed well clear of my family,' he said.

Fruit was served, then tea, and then it was time for the entertainment. Two girls identically dressed in white-embroidered satin glided in. One, holding a small lute, seated herself, ready to play. The other stood beside her.

The lights dimmed except for the one on the performers. The first notes came from the lute and the singer began to make a soft crooning noise, full of a poignancy that was like joy and sadness combined. As Olivia listened an aching feeling came over her, as though the music had sprung all the locks by which she protected herself, leaving her open and defenceless as she had sworn never to be again.

The girl was singing in a soft voice:

'The trees were white with blossom.
We walked together beneath the falling petals.
But that is past and you are gone.
The trees do not blossom this year.
Aaaii-eeeii!'

That was how it had been; the trees hadn't blossomed this year and she knew they never would again. Andy had been an abject lesson in the need to stay detached. In future no man would hurt her like that because she wouldn't let it happen.

'The bridge still leads across the river,
Where we walked together.
But when I look down into the water,
Your face is not beside me.
Never again...'

Never again, she thought, not here or anywhere. She closed her eyes for a moment. But suddenly she opened them again, alerted by a touch on her cheek.

'Don't cry,' Lang said.

'I'm not crying,' she insisted.

For answer he showed her his fingertips, wet with her tears.

'Don't weep for him,' he said softly.

It would have been useless to utter another denial when he hadn't believed the first.

'I get sentimental sometimes.' She tried to laugh it away. 'But I'm really over him.'

In the dim light she could see Lang shake his head, smiling ruefully.

'Perhaps you belong together after all,' he said. Suddenly he reached into his pocket, took out his mobile phone and pushed it towards her, then he leaned close to murmur into her ear without disturbing the singer.

'Call him. Say that your quarrel was a mistake, and you love him still. Go on. Do it now.'

The dramatic gesture astonished and intrigued her. With a gasp of edgy laughter, she pushed the phone back to him.

'Why are you laughing?' he demanded.

'I was just picturing his face if he answered the phone and found himself talking to me. There was no quarrel. He left me for someone else. She had a lot of money, so he obviously did the right thing. I believe they're very happy. She bought him a posh car for a wedding present.'

'And that makes it the right thing?' he enquired.

'Of course.'

'So if a millionaire proposed you'd accept at once?'

'No way! He'd have to be a billionaire at least.'

'I see.' The words were grave but his lips were slightly quirked, as if he were asking who she thought she was fooling.

But he said nothing more. The music had ended. The singer bowed to the heartfelt applause and embarked on another song, slightly more cheerful. Lang turned his head towards the little stage, but reached back across the table to take hold of Olivia's hand, and kept it.

She found that her nostalgic sadness had vanished, overtaken by a subtle pleasure that seemed to infuse the whole evening. Everything was a part of it, including the man sitting opposite her, looking away, giving Olivia the chance to study him unobserved.

She could appreciate him like this. His regular features were enough to make him good-looking, but they also had a mobility that was constantly intriguing. His eyes could be bland and conventional or wickedly knowing in a way that gave him a disconcerting charm. She wondered if there was anyone he regretted from his own past. A warm-natured man in his thirties, with a deep belief in the value of romantic love, had surely not reached this point without some sadness along the road.

She began to muse on the subject, wondering if there was a way to question him without revealing too much interest. There wasn't, of course, and an alarm bell sounded in her head. This was just the kind of atmosphere she'd learned to fear—seductive, romantic, lulling her senses and her mind in dangerous harmony.

It was time for common sense to take over. In a few minutes she would suggest that the evening should end soon, phrasing it carefully. She began to plan the words, even deciding what she would say when he protested.

Lang was beckoning to Wei, paying the bill, and ordering him to stop giggling and make himself scarce. Wei departed jauntily. Olivia took a deep breath to make her speech.

'We'd better go,' Lang said.

'Pardon?'

'We both have to work tomorrow, so I'll get you home quickly. I'm sorry to have kept you out so late.'

'Don't mention it,' she said faintly.

On the journey she wondered what was going to happen now. Lang had recognised that she wasn't ready for a decision, while subtly implying that he was attracted to her. He was charming and funny, with a quiet, gentle strength that appealed to her, perhaps because she could sense something quirky and irreverent beneath it.

A light-hearted flirtation could be agreeable, but if he wanted more, if he planned to end the evening in her arms—or even in her apartment— what then? A gentle let-down? How did you half-reject someone you more than half-liked? Again she began to think about what she would say to him.

When they arrived, he came with her to the apartment block.

'How far up are you?' he asked.

'Second floor.'

He rode up with her and came to her door.

'Lang?' she began uneasily.

'Yes?'

She lost her nerve. 'Would you care to come in for a drink?'

'I certainly want to come in, but not for a drink.

Let's get inside and I'll explain, although I'm sure
you know what the problem is.'

Once inside he took off his jacket and helped her
off with hers.

'You'll need to remove your blouse as well,' he
said, beginning to work on her buttons.

'Lang…'

He took no notice, opening the buttons one by
one until he could remove the blouse, revealing her
as he had the day before. She was astonished at his
effrontery. Did he think he could simply undress
her, seduce her, do as he liked with her?

'Now let me look at that arm,' he said.

'My arm?' she echoed, thunderstruck.

'That's why I came to find you tonight, isn't it?'

'Oh, yes—I remember.'

She had a horrible feeling that she sounded
idiotic, but that was how she felt. He hadn't come
here to seduce her, but to tend her. Her wild
thoughts had been nonsense. She felt herself
blushing from head to toe.

Then she thought she caught a gleam of mischief
in his eyes, although it was gone before she could
be certain.

With her blouse removed, he held her arm up,
moving his head this way and that without appearing to notice anything but her injury. He had no eyes
for the peachy, youthful glow of her skin, the way

her waist narrowed and the lamp threw shadows between her breasts. It was almost insulting.

'This is the last time it will need covering,' he said. 'It's healing nicely.'

He'd brought a small bag in with him, and from it he took replacement dressings. He covered the grazes lightly, and fixed everything in place.

'Now get a good night's sleep,' he instructed.

Then he was heading out of the apartment, without having touched her, except as a doctor.

'Wait,' she said desperately. 'What did you mean about "the problem"?'

He paused in the doorway.

'The problem,' he said, 'is that you're still my patient. Later…'

'Later?'

His gaze moved over her slowly, lingering just a little on the beauty he had so dutifully ignored.

'Later you won't be. Goodnight.'

The school term was nearly over. Olivia was busy writing reports, talking to parents and consulting with the headmistress, who looked in on her on the penultimate day.

'I'm just making plans for next year,' she said cheerfully. 'I'm so glad you're staying.'

'Staying?' Olivia echoed vaguely.

'You originally came for six months, but when

I asked if you were going to stay on you said you would. Don't you remember?'

'Oh, yes—yes.'

'You really sound in need of a holiday,' Mrs Wu said kindly.

'It's just that I've been wondering if I should go home.'

'But you can do that and still come back next term. From all you've told me about Norah, she wants you to stay here and spread your wings. I hope you come back. You're doing such a good job. But you've got my number if you have a last-minute change of mind.'

Olivia went home, thoughtful. Everything that had seemed simple only a short while ago had suddenly become complicated.

It was true that Norah showed no sign of wanting her early return. Only last night she'd been at her most lively, talking furiously about Melisande's latest lover.

'You mean, Freddy?' Olivia had queried.

'No. Freddy's finished since she caught him sleeping with a pole dancer. It's your father.'

'Mum and Dad? What are they playing at?'

'I gather he went to see her, seeking solace from a broken heart.'

'I thought you said he'd made some girl pregnant.'

'He thought he had, but apparently it's not his so he went to cry on your mother's shoulder.

because, and I quote, "she's the only one who understands".'

'Give me patience!'

'That's what I said. Anyway, it seems that they looked at each other across the barrier of years, heart spoke to heart as though time and distance had never been…'

'What?'

'I told her to get out before she made me ill. It's just her putting herself centre-stage again, as always.'

Olivia had had to agree. She'd seen, and suffered from, enough of her parents' selfish grandstanding to dismiss this great romance as just another show in the spotlight.

You could say much the same of all great romances, she thought. Her father would let her mother down again, because that was what men did. It was what Andy had done. And who cared if Lang called her or not?

Several days had passed since their last meeting. After talking so significantly he had fallen silent, and with every passing hour Olivia had condemned herself more angrily as a fool.

It wasn't as if she hadn't been warned, she told herself crossly. When Andy had appeared in her life, she'd abandoned the caution so carefully built up over a lifetime because she'd convinced herself that *this* man was different.

But no man was different, as she'd learned in

anguish and bitterness. She'd vowed 'never again', but then she'd been tricked into ignoring those resolutions because Lang had charmed her.

No, it was more than charm, she admitted. It was the sense of quiet understanding, the feeling that his mind and heart were open to hers, and that she would find in him generosity and understanding.

Heart spoke to heart as though time and distance had never been.

Her mother's melodramatic words shrieked a warning in her head. She and Lang had met only a couple of times, and came from different worlds, yet time and distance did not exist, hadn't existed between them from the first moment.

Which meant that she would fight him all the harder. If she made the foolish mistake of falling in love with Lang, the misery would be far greater than before.

It was useful that he'd shown his true colours in time to prevent a disaster. She repeated that to herself several times.

But no way would she stay here, pining. If she didn't return to England, she'd go somewhere else. She got a brochure advertising cruises along the great Yangtze River and booked herself a cabin. She would board the boat at Chongqing, leave it at Yichang and travel on to Shanghai. After that, who could tell where she would travel? And what did it matter? What did anything matter as long as she had no time to think?

CHAPTER FOUR

ON THE last day of term Olivia counted the minutes
until it was time to go. Just a little longer and she
need never think of Lang again. *Concentrate on the
Yangtze. Think of Shanghai.*

The last pupil had gone home. She was gathering up her things when a buzz made her look at her
mobile phone, where there was a text: *I'm outside*.

For a brief moment her heart leapt, then indignation took over. Cheek! Like he only had to
announce his presence and she must jump.

She texted back: *I'm busy*.

The reply came at once: *I'll wait*.

Mrs Wu looked in to say goodbye and they left
the building together.

'Have a good holiday,' she said. 'And please
dispose of that young man hanging around the
gate. Loiterers are bad for the school's reputation.'

'He's nothing to do with me.'

'Of course he isn't. That's why his eyes are fixed
on you. Goodbye for now.'

Lang was leaning against the wall as though there was all the time in the world, which did nothing to improve her mood. She advanced on him in a confrontational mood, and thrust out her arm, from which she'd removed the dressing.

'Just a few scratches and healing nicely, thank you,' she said in a formal voice.

'You don't know how glad I am to hear that.'

'And the headmistress says I'm to get rid of you. You're giving the place a bad name.'

'In that case, let's go.'

'I don't think—'

'Let's not waste any more time.' He already had hold of her arm and was ushering her into his car, which he started up quickly, as though afraid to give her time to think.

Had he known it, she was beyond coherent thought, beyond anything but wild emotion. He hadn't abandoned her, hadn't turned away, leaving her desolate. He had come for her because he could no more escape the bonds tightening around them than she could.

She knew she should try to control the heady, idiotic feeling that pervaded her. It was too much like joy: terrifying, threatening, destructive, glorious joy.

At last she managed to speak and ask where they were going. At least, that was what she thought she'd asked. She was too confused to be sure.

'I'm taking you somewhere that will help you get over being grumpy,' he replied.

'I'm not grumpy.'

'Yes you are. When you saw me outside the school, you glared hard enough to terrify the devil.'

'Well, it was very inconsiderate of you to arrive in the last five minutes.'

'You couldn't possibly have been hoping to see me earlier?'

'Certainly not. You just disrupted my schedule. I like things done in the proper order.'

'Just as I said, grumpy. Meihui used to have a way of dealing with my bad moods—several ways, actually—but this was our favourite one.'

More than that he would not say, but he drove for half an hour in silence, glad of the chance to say nothing and collect his thoughts. Unusually for him, they were chaotic.

After their last meeting he'd resolved not to approach Olivia again, at least, not soon. He was an ambitious man, and his career was beginning to look promising. He needed no distractions, and the sensible course would be to let the summer vacation pass before they met again. The passage of a little time would put him in control of himself again.

It had all been very simple. Until today.

The summer break from his job had already started, which was unlucky, because if he'd been at work he couldn't have yielded to temptation. As it was, the realisation that she would be leaving any minute had galvanised him. Suddenly his resolutions were rubbish, his strength of will non-existent. He'd barely made it to the school in time.

Now he was calling himself names, of which 'weakling' was the kindest. But the abusive voice was bawling only from the back of his head; the front was full of relief that he'd made it in time.

There was another voice too, not yelling, but muttering. This was his conscience, warning him that there was something he must confess to her without delay. He wasn't sure what her reaction would be. That troubled him more than anything.

'Here we are,' he said, drawing up outside a huge gate.

'You've brought me to a zoo?' she said, astounded.

'Meihui said nobody could stay cross in a zoo. So let's go in.'

He was right, after only a few minutes of wandering around the animals, her spirits lightened. Who cared about anything else when there were lions to be viewed, bears to watch, exotic birds?

Lang was like no other man. When was the last time anyone had taken her to a place like this? she wondered as they gazed at the giant pandas.

'I've never seen anything so beautiful,' she murmured.

'They're magnificent, aren't they?' he agreed warmly.

'But how do you tell one from the other? Pandas all look exactly alike.'

'The one over there on her own in the tree is the female. Earlier this year she was in heat for a couple of days, and had all the males swooning after her. Now she's safely pregnant, and they can go and jump in the lake for all she cares.'

'I wonder which male she favoured.'

'The highest ranking one. He proved his status by knocking seven bells out of the competition.'

'Very sensible,' Olivia said. 'None of that sentimental nonsense. If ever I'm reborn, I shall come back as a panda.'

He laughed but said, 'Why do you have to be so severe?'

'I'm not severe.'

'You are from where I'm standing.'

'Oh, I see, a *male* version of severe—meaning a woman who doesn't collapse in a sentimental heap at the mention of *lurve*.' She gave the word a satirical inflection that made him wince. '*That* kind of severe.'

'You put it very crudely,' he complained.

'The truth is usually crude, and definitely unromantic. Like life. We just have to face up to it.'

She was saying the first thing that came into her head and enjoying the sight of his face. For once the confident Dr Mitchell was struggling for words, and that was fun.

'Why are you so determined not to believe in love?' he asked. 'I know you had a bad experience, but so have most people, and they don't abandon hope. I didn't give up when Becky Renton told me it was all over.'

'Oh, yes? And I'll bet the two of you were about twelve when that happened.'

He grinned. 'A little older than that, but you've got the right idea.'

She wondered if this handsome, assured man had ever been dumped in his life. Not by anyone he really cared about, she would have bet on it.

'Joking apart,' he resumed, 'people really do do things for love. I know you don't believe it, but it's true.'

'If you're talking about your romantic ancestors, allow me to point out that there's no reason to believe that Jaio was ever in love. They were going to lock her in the tomb and Renshu offered escape. She might simply have thought that going with him was better than dying.'

'But what about him? He must have loved her a lot because he sacrificed everything to be with her.' Lang added provocatively, 'Perhaps it really means that a man can love more deeply than a woman. It could even be doubted that women know how to love at all. They believe in logic rather than sentiment—like pandas.'

Olivia eyed him askance. 'Did you say that just to be annoying?'

'No, I think it's an interesting theory.' Catching her expression, he couldn't resist adding, 'But I must admit I also enjoy annoying you.'

'You'll go too far.'

'I hope so. Better too far than not far enough.'

His grin was her undoing, leaving her no choice but to smile back.

'Let's find the snack bar,' he said, slipping an arm around her shoulders.

As they sat down over coffee, Lang suddenly said, 'I hope you can forgive my clumsiness.'

'About what?'

'That remark about choosing a mate through logic rather than sentiment. It's exactly what your louse boyfriend did, isn't it? I'm sorry. I didn't mean to hurt you.'

'You didn't,' she said, realising that it was true. She hadn't even thought about Andy. Nor, now she thought of it, had she ever enjoyed such a day as this, strolling calmly through pleasant gardens, teasing and testing each other.

There had been no jokes with Andy, only passion and violent emotion, which at the time she'd thought was enough. But with Lang she was discovering how emotion could be tempered with humour. He was a patient man who knew when to back off. It made him a restful companion, as well as an exciting one, and that too was a new pleasure.

'I've dismissed Andy from my mind,' she told him, adding with a flourish, 'It was the common sense thing to do.'

'That easy, huh?'

'Of course. Logic over sentiment any day. I reckon the female panda knows exactly what she's doing.'

'Then I'm glad I'm not a panda,' he said, matching her flourish with one of his own.

Before they left the zoo he took her to the gift shop and bought her a small soft toy in the shape of a panda.

'She's a female,' he declared.

'How can you tell?'

'Because that's what I want her to be,' he said, as though explaining the obvious. 'Her name is Ming Zhi. It means wise.' His eyes gleamed with mischief. 'It was the nearest I could get to logic and common sense.'

'Then she and I will get on very well,' Olivia declared, taking the delightful creature and rubbing her face against its soft black-and-white fur. 'If I forget what's important, she's bound to remind me.'

'To the victory of logic,' he proclaimed.

'Every time.'

'Let's go and have some supper.'

They found a small, old-fashioned restaurant.

'Why were you in such a bad mood when we met earlier?' he asked when they were settled. 'Is it me you're annoyed with?'

'No, my parents. According to Norah, they've rediscovered each other, acting like love's young dream.'

'Which could be charming.'

'If it was anyone else, it could, but this pair of raging play-actors are heading for disaster.'

'Don't be so sure,' Lang said. 'Maybe they just married too young and were always meant to find each other again.'

She gave him a look.

'Maybe not,' he said hastily.

'In the end it'll collapse in lies, as it did the first time.' Olivia sighed. 'And there's nothing so fatal as deception.'

'Sometimes a deception can be fairly innocent,' Lang observed casually.

'But it's always destructive,' she insisted. 'Once you know he hasn't been straight with you, it's over, because—I don't know. I'm going to eat.'

Concentrating on her chopsticks, she didn't see the uncomfortable look that came over Lang's face.

'This food is nice,' she said after a while. 'But not as nice as at the Dancing Dragon.'

To her surprise he didn't respond to the compliment. He seemed sunk in thought, and strangely uneasy.

'Is everything all right?' she asked.

'No,' he said with an effort. 'There's something I have to tell you.'

There was a heaviness in his voice that filled Olivia with foreboding.

'I must admit that I've been putting this moment off,' Lang continued awkwardly. 'I was afraid it would make you think badly of me. I know I've done wrong, but I didn't want to risk not seeing you again.'

Now she knew what he was trying to say: he had a wife.

Impossible. In that case he would never have taken her to the Dancing Dragon where they would be seen by his family. But perhaps the family's attitude had simply been curiosity that their foreign relative was playing around. She tried to recall exactly what they had said, and couldn't.

'Will you promise to let me finish explaining before you condemn me?' he asked.

By ill luck, Andy had said much the same thing: 'If only you'd let me explain properly, it really wasn't my fault…'

A chill settled over her heart.

'Go on then,' she said. 'Tell me the worst.'

Lang took a deep breath and seemed to struggle for words.

'The fact is—' he began, stopped then started again. 'When we met—' He was floundering.

'Look,' she said edgily, 'why don't we just skip it and go home?'

'Don't you want to know what I have to say?'

'I probably already know what you're going to say,' she observed with a faint, mirthless laugh.

'You guessed? I don't see how you could have done.'

'Let's say I have a nose for some things. Call it my cynical nature.'

'I don't think you're as cynical as you try to pretend.'

Her temper flared. 'And I don't think you know anything about me.'

He stared. 'All right, don't jump on me. I'm harmless, I swear it. I'll believe that you're anything you say—hard, cynical, unfeeling…'

'Ruthless, unforgiving, cold-hearted,' she supplied. 'I'm glad you understand.'

'I wish you hadn't said unforgiving,' he observed gloomily.

'Well, I did say it. I never give second chances. Now, if we've got that settled, what were you going to confess? Something unforgivable, obviously.'

'Well, you might think so.'

Her dismay increased. 'All right. I'm listening.'

'It's like this. When we met in that clinic—I wouldn't normally be there. I work in another part of the hospital, and I'd just started a vacation. But a friend who does work in the clinic got a stomach upset and had to take time off. They were short staffed, so I filled in.'

'But what's so terrible about that?' she asked, trying to think straight through the confusion of reactions storming through her.

'The thing is, he was back next morning. I did try to persuade him that he needed another day off, but he got an attack of heroics and insisted on returning.' Lang sighed and added distractedly, 'A man can't trust his friends for anything, not even to be ill when he needs them to be.'

'What on earth are you—?'

'So when I came to see you next day I wasn't working in the clinic any more, and strictly speaking you were no longer my patient.'

Olivia stared at him in mounting disbelief. 'Are you saying…?'

'That I lied to you,' he said mournfully. 'I approached you under false pretences, claiming that you were my patient when you no longer were. I deceived you.'

Olivia met his eyes and drew a quick breath at what she saw there, a look of suspiciously bland innocence that masked something far from innocent. This man wasn't worried about being in trouble. He was inviting her into a conspiracy.

'You're overdoing it,' she said wryly.

'No, honestly! On the pretext of medical privilege, I gained access to your body.'

'To my—? Oh, yes, you saw my bare arm, didn't you?' she said sardonically. 'How could I have forgotten that? Shocking!'

'It was a little more than your arm,' he reminded her. 'If you want to report me to the medical authorities, well, I'll just have to accept it, won't I?'

'And if I kicked your shins you'd just have to accept that, wouldn't you?' she said sweetly.

'It would be my just deserts.'

'Don't get me started on your just deserts or we'll be here all night.'

'Would we? Tell me more.'

'Let's just say that you're a devious, treacherous— I can't think of anything bad enough.'

'I'll wait while you think of something. After all, it was shocking behaviour on my part.'

'I didn't mean that. I meant just now, making me think—'

'What?'

She pulled herself together. 'Making me think it was something really serious, instead of just fooling.'

She could barely speak for the confusion of relief and fear that warred in her: relief that he was a free man, fear that it mattered so much. She tried to bring herself under control lest he guess the truth.

Or did he already know? He was watching her

intently but cautiously, as though trying to discover
something that was important to him.

'I wanted to see you again,' he said simply. 'And
that was the best excuse I could find.'

The storm died down. The relief was still there,
but now tinged with laughter. The world was
bright.

'Well, I guess I'm glad you thought of something,' she admitted.

He took her hand. 'So am I.'

'I'm still annoyed with you, but I forgive you—
on a purely temporary basis.'

'That's all I ask.'

'So what is your job in the hospital?'

Lang shrugged. 'I fill in a lot, do the stuff
nobody else wants.' He squeezed her hand gently.
'Sometimes I get a good day.'

He didn't pursue the subject and she was glad.
The attraction between them was growing slowly,
delicately, and she liked it that way. Any sudden
movements might be fatal.

He was looking down at her hand, rubbing his
fingers against it softly, and she had the feeling that
he was uneasy again.

'What is it?' she asked. 'What terrible crime do
you have to admit now?'

'We-ell…'

'Be brave. It can't be worse than you've already
confessed.'

'The fact is there have been some repercussions to the other night. Wei, the great blabbermouth, went home and sounded off to my family, telling them all about you.'

'But he doesn't know anything about me—unless, of course, you've told him, which would be another abuse of medical privilege.' She considered him, her head on one side. 'You really are proving to be a disreputable character. Interesting, but disreputable.'

'This time I plead not guilty. Anything I know about you—which is frustratingly little—I keep firmly to myself. Wei's method is to invent what he doesn't know. The family's curiosity is aroused, and now there'll be no peace until I take you home for dinner.'

'Let me get this straight. You want to take me home just to save yourself from nagging?'

'That's about the size of it.'

'It's got nothing to do with wanting my company?'

'Certainly not,' he said in a shocked voice.

'It wouldn't mean that you were glad to be seen with me, liked me for myself, and maybe, I don't know…?'

'Maybe thought you were the prettiest girl I'd ever seen and the nicest I'd ever been out with?' he supplied helpfully. 'No, nothing like that. Don't worry.'

'You relieve my mind,' she said gravely.

He raised her hand and brushed his cheek against the back of her fingers.

'I think we should stay level-headed,' he said. 'I wouldn't want to offend you by indulging in the kind of sentimental behaviour I know you despise.'

'That's thoughtful of you. On the other hand, your family are going to expect us to seem at ease with each other. We mustn't disappoint them by being too distant.'

He nodded as though giving this judicious consideration.

'True. We need to get it just right.'

Before she knew what he meant to do, he leaned across the table and laid his lips softly against hers.

It was the briefest of contacts. No sooner was his mouth there than it was gone again. It might never have happened, yet it went through her like lightning, making nonsense of logic and control, leaving her changed and the world a different place.

She tried to smile with careless unconcern, but her heart was thumping, and there was no way she could seem indifferent. To hide her confusion she looked down, but when she raised her head again everything was more confusing, because now she could see that Lang was startled too.

'That should be about right,' she managed to say.

She was lying. It wasn't about right, it wasn't

nearly enough. One whispering touch and something inside her had sprung to life, making her tingle with frustration. She wanted more, and so did he. His expression had told her that. Yet here they were, two well-behaved dolls, bound and gagged by the constraints that they had set themselves. Only a moment ago it had seemed amusing.

'So what can I tell the family?' he asked, and she wondered if she only imagined that his voice was shaking.

'I'd be delighted to accept their kind invitation when I return from my travels.'

'You're going away? When? Where?'

'I'm taking a cruise down the Yangtze.'

'But not tomorrow?'

'No, in three days but—'

'Fine, that gives us plenty of time.' He whipped out his mobile phone and dialled hurriedly. 'Better do this before you can change your mind. You're a very confusing person. I never know where I am with you.'

After the days she'd spent longing to hear from him—which she now admitted to herself she had—this left her speechless with indignation. While she was still trying to think of something bad enough to call him, he began talking into the phone.

'Hallo, Aunt Biyu? Olivia says she'd be delighted. Yes, yes.' He looked back at Olivia. 'Do you like dumplings?'

'I love them,' she said promptly.

'She loves them, Aunt Biyu— What's that? All right, I'll ask her. Do you prefer meat or vegetables?'

'I'm happy with either.'

'She's happy with either. Oh, yes, that sounds nice.' To Olivia he said, 'Shrimp and bamboo, OK?'

'Yes, splendid,' she said, slightly confused.

Lang turned back to the phone. 'Olivia is thrilled with shrimp and bamboo. Tomorrow evening?' He raised an eyebrow and Olivia nodded. 'Tomorrow's fine. Goodnight.'

He hung up. 'Aunt Biyu is married to Uncle Hai. She's preparing you the best shrimp and bamboo you ever tasted, and the whole family is helping. You're a very important guest.'

She knew enough about Chinese culture to recognise that this was true. In the old days of poverty, dumplings had been the staple food, and had subsequently acquired a place of honour. To lay out a banquet of dumplings for a guest was to pay a compliment.

She began to wonder exactly what Lang had told them. As he drove her home later, he was smiling.

At her apartment block he saw her to the main front door, but didn't try to come any further.

'I'll collect you at six o'clock tomorrow evening,' he said.

'Yes. Goodnight.'

'Goodnight.'

He hesitated for a moment, then leaned forward suddenly and gave her the briefest possible kiss before hurrying away.

Olivia was thoughtful as she entered her apartment. Nothing in the world seemed clear or simple, and it was because of Lang, a man she'd met only three times.

Reaching into her bag, she felt something soft and silky, and realised that she'd forgotten all about Ming Zhi. The little panda regarded her severely, reminding her that she was a sensible woman who had renounced love in favour of logic.

'Oh, shut up!' Olivia said, tossing her onto the bed. 'I don't care if he did give you to me. You're a pain in the whatsit. And so is he.'

That night she slept with Ming Zhi in the crook of her arm.

CHAPTER FIVE

NEXT morning she went online to Norah and was rewarded by the sight of the old woman waving and smiling at the camera.

'So, what are you going to do with your holidays?' she asked. 'Did you book that cruise?'

'Yes, I'll be off in a few days.'

'And?' Norah probed, for Olivia's tone clearly hinted at something else.

'I've met this madman…'

She tried to describe Lang. It wasn't easy, for he seemed to elude her even as she spoke. Calling him a madman was the truth, but far from the whole truth, and she was still discovering the rest.

'He can make me laugh,' she said.

'That's always a good beginning.'

'And he gave me this.' She held up Ming Zhi. When we went to the zoo.'

'Now, that looks like getting serious. When are you seeing him again?'

'This evening. He's taking me to have dinner with his family.'

'Already? My dear, he's moving very fast.'

'No, it's not like that. One of his relatives saw us together and the family got curious. He's only taking me home to shut them up.'

'Is he a wimp, that he can't stand up to them?'

'No, he's not a wimp,' Olivia said, smiling and remembering how Lang gave the impression of being quietly in command, except when he was being jokingly deferential to make her laugh. 'He pretends to be sometimes, but that's just his way of catching me off-guard.'

'And does he often succeed?'

'Yes,' Olivia admitted wryly. 'He does.'

'Then he must be a very clever man indeed. I look forward to meeting him.'

'Norah, please! You're going much too fast. Lang and I have only met a few times. I'm not looking for anything serious. We'll enjoy a brief relationship and then I'll come home. In fact—'

'Don't you dare start that again. You stay where you are, and *live* your life. Don't throw it away.'

'All right, I promise,' Olivia said. She was slightly startled by Norah's intensity; a kind of anguish almost seemed to possess her.

'You spend as much time with Lang as you can. He sounds nice. Is he good-looking?'

'Yes, he's good-looking?'

'*Really* good-looking?'

'Well…'

'On a scale of one to ten?'

'Seven. Oh, all right—eight.'

'Jolly good,' Norah said robustly. 'Now, go and buy a really nice, new dress. Splash out, do you hear?'

'Yes, Aunt,' Olivia said meekly, and they laughed together.

After a hasty breakfast she headed out to the shops, meaning to choose something from the Western fashions that were now available in Beijing. But before long her eye fell on a *cheong-sam*, the traditional Chinese dress that was so flattering to a woman with a good figure. The neckline came modestly up to the throat, and there was a high-standing collar, but it was also figure-hugging, outlining her tiny waist, flared hips and delicately rounded breasts in a way that left no doubt that her shape was perfect.

It was heavily embroidered and made of the highest-quality silk, at a price that made her hesitate for half a second. But when she tried it on and saw what it did for her she knew she was lost. When she combined it with the finest heels she dared to wear, the effect was stunning.

She wondered if Lang would think so. Would he compliment her on her appearance?

* * *

He did not. Calling for her punctually at six, he handed her into the car without a word. But she'd seen the way his eyes had lingered on the swell of her breasts, so perfectly emphasised by the clinging material, and she knew he had remembered their first meeting. His expression told her all she wanted to know.

She settled down to enjoy herself. They were headed for the *hutongs*; she'd always been fascinated by these streets that had surrounded the Forbidden City for hundreds of years. A plentiful water supply had dictated the location, and the *hutongs* had always flourished, colourful places full of life and industry. Shops sprung up, especially butchers, bakers, fishmongers and anything selling domestic necessities. Change came and went. Other parts of the city had become wealthier, more fashionable, but the *hutongs'* vibrant character had ensured their survival.

Olivia had sometimes shopped there. Now for the first time she would see the personal life that lay behind the little stores. A *hutong* was a street formed by lines of quadrangles, called *siheyuans*, each *siheyuan* consisting of four houses placed at right angles to each other. Here large families could live with the privacy of their own home, yet with their relatives always within calling distance.

As they drove there, Lang described his family's *siheyuan*.

'The north house belongs to Grandfather Tao.

He's the centre of the family. Meihui was his kid sister and he remembers her as if it were yesterday. He says I remind him of her, but that's just affection, because I don't really look like her at all. Uncle Jing and his wife also live there, with their four children.

'One of the side houses is occupied by Uncle Hai, his wife and their two younger children. The one opposite is the home of their two elder sons and their wives. And the south house has been taken over by Wei. He's Jing's son, and he's living in the south house in preparation for his marriage.'

'He's the one I saw the other night? Married? He looks far too young.'

'He's twenty, but he's madly in love with Suyin, the girl who sang in the restaurant, and she seems to feel she can put up with him. Apart from him there are several other children, ranging from five to twelve. They're wonderful kids. Villains, mind you.'

'As the best youngsters always are.'

'Right,' he said, gratified.

'But how many people am I meeting?' she asked, beginning to be nervous.

'About eighteen.'

'Wow! I'm getting scared.'

'Not you. You're a dragon lady, remember? Brave, adventurous, ready for anything.'

'Thank you. But that big a family still makes me a bit nervous.'

'Eighteen isn't so many. There are at least another dozen in other parts of the country, and probably plenty more I have yet to meet.'

'Is that where you're going? You said something about travelling soon.'

'Something like that. Let's talk later. I must warn you that you're about to walk into the middle of a feud. Uncle Jing is furious with Uncle Hai because Hai's wife Biyu is cooking you dumplings. Jing thinks the privilege of cooking for you should have been his. He's a fishmonger, and also a wedding planner.'

'I've heard of that before,' Olivia said, much struck. 'It's because the words for fish and prosperity are so alike that fish gets served at weddings as a way of wishing the couple good luck. So fishmongers often plan weddings as well.'

'That's right. Hai does very well as an arranger of weddings, where of course he sells tons of his own fish. The trouble is he thinks he's entitled to arrange everything for everyone, and he's very put out about the dumplings.'

His solemn tone made Olivia burst out laughing.

'I promise to be tactful,' she said.

'Have I told you you're looking beautiful tonight?'

'Not a word.'

'Well, I'm being careful. If I said that deep blue does wonderful things for your eyes you'd find me very boring.'

'I might,' she said in a pensive voice. 'Or I might decide to forgive you.'

'Thank you, ma'am, but I feel sure you'd censure me for insulting you with that old-fashioned romantic talk. Heavens, this is the twenty-first century! Women don't fall for that kind of clap-trap any more.'

'Well, I wouldn't actually say any of that out loud,' she said, laughing.

'But you might think it silently, and that would be much worse. I'm wary of your unspoken thoughts.'

'But if they're unspoken you can't possibly know what they are,' she pointed out.

'You're wrong. I'm starting to understand the way you think.'

'That's an alarming prospect!' she observed.

'For which of us, I wonder?'

'For me,' she said without hesitation.

'Are you more alarmed at the thought of my getting it right, or getting it wrong?'

She considered this seriously. 'Right, I think. I don't mind you getting it wrong. I can always tread on your toes.'

'Good thinking.'

'But what woman wants to be understood too well by a man?' she mused.

'Most women complain that men don't understand them.'

'Then they're being foolish,' she said with a little smile. 'They should bless their luck.'

They both laughed and the moment passed, but she was left with the sense that beneath the banter they had really been talking about something else entirely. It was a feeling that often assailed her in Lang's company.

They continued the journey in companionable silence, until at last he said, 'Before we get there I'd better warn you of just how enthusiastically Wei has prepared them for you. I've explained that we barely know each other, and he mustn't run ahead, but he— Well…'

'Didn't take any notice?' Olivia finished sympathetically.

'And how!'

'All right, I'm prepared.'

'Grandfather Tao and Grandmother Shu have learned a few words in English, in your honour. The rest of the family speaks English, but those two are so old that they've lived a different kind of life. They've been practising all day to offer you this courtesy.'

'How kind.' She was touched. 'I know I'm going to love your family.'

At last she found herself in streets that she recognised.

'Weren't we here the other night?'

'Yes, that restaurant is just around the corner. Just a couple more streets, and here we are. Home.'

The car drew up before the north house of the *siheyuan*, and Olivia drew an astonished breath as she saw what looked like the entire family gathered to meet her. They spilled out of the doorway into the street.

In the centre stood an old man and woman: Grandfather Tao and Grandmother Shu. On either side of them were two middle-aged men—the uncles, their wives and children. Everyone was watching the car's arrival with delight, and two of the younger children dashed forward to open the door and provide Olivia with a guard of honour.

'My goodness!' she exclaimed.

Lang took her hand. 'Don't worry,' he whispered. 'I'm here, Dragon Lady.'

He slipped his arm protectively around her as they neared the family and it divided into two groups, with the oldest, Grandfather Tao and Grandmother Shu, at the centre. He took her to them first.

'Our family is honoured to meet you,' Tao said, speaking in careful, perfect English, and his wife inclined her head, smiling in agreement.

'It is I who am honoured,' Olivia said.

Tao repeated his compliment. The words and manner were formal but his and Shu's expressions were warm, and their eyes followed her when she moved on.

Strictly speaking they were the host and hostess, but because of their age and frailty they performed only the most formal duties, delegating anything more energetic to the younger ones.

Although brothers, Hai and Jing were totally unalike. Jing was a great, good-natured bull of a man, tall, broad and muscular. Beside him Hai was like a mountain goat next to a gorilla, small, thin and sprightly, with a wispy beard and bright eyes.

As the elder, Hai was introduced first, then his brother, then their wives—starting with Biyu, wife of Hai, and Luli, wife of Jing. They too greeted her in English, which she appreciated, but Lang immediately said in Chinese, 'No, she speaks our language. I told you.'

They repeated their greetings in Mandarin and she responded accordingly, which made them smile with pleasure.

'Mrs Lang—' Olivia started to say, but there was a burst of laughter from several Mrs Langs.

'You can't say that,' Hai's wife declared merrily. 'There are so many of us. Please, call me Biyu.' She introduced the others as Ting, Huan, Dongmei, and Nuo.

There seemed to be at least a dozen grown-up youngsters, young men who studied Lang's lady with politely concealed admiration, and young girls who considered her with more open interest. The fact that Olivia had the figure to wear a *cheongsam* was particularly appreciated among her contemporaries.

It was a warm evening, and the first part was to be spent in the courtyard flanked by the four houses. Here tables had been laid out with a variety of small edibles, a foretaste of the banquet to come. Before anything was served, Biyu led her into the south house where Lang lived with Wei, and opened the door to a bedroom with its own bathroom.

'Should you wish to retire for a few moments alone,' she said, 'you will find this place useful.' She saw Olivia glance around at the room's functional, masculine appearance, and said, 'When Lang stays with us, this is his room, but this evening it is yours.'

'Thank you. I'll just refresh my face.'

'I'll be outside.'

Left alone, Olivia was able to indulge her frank curiosity, although she learned little. There were several books, some medical, some about China, but nothing very personal. Lang had revealed as little as possible about himself.

She went out to find that he had joined Biyu, and together they escorted her to where everyone was waiting. Now it was the turn of the children to crowd round. Just as she'd predicted, they called Lang 'Uncle Mitch', and even his adult relatives referred to him as Mitchell.

Glancing up, she caught his eye and he nodded, reminding her of the moment on the first evening when she'd anticipated this.

'The dragon lady always understands before anyone else,' he said lightly.

The children demanded to know what he meant by 'dragon lady'. He explained that she'd been born in the year of the dragon, and they regarded her with awe. Her stock had definitely gone up.

The children were frankly curious, competing to serve her and to ask questions about England. She answered them as fully as she could, they countered with more questions and the result was one of the most satisfying half-hours that she had ever spent. By the time they went inside to eat, the atmosphere was relaxed.

Olivia soon understood what Lang had meant about a feud. From the start the food was laid out like a banquet being displayed to her, dumplings in the place of honour, and a multitude of fish dishes which Hai kept trying to nudge to the fore, only to be beaten back by fierce looks from Biyu. To please them both, Olivia ate everything on offer and was rewarded with warm looks of pleasure.

Then she had a stroke of luck. Enquiring politely about Tao's life, she learned that he had once been a farmer. It happened that one of her mother's passing fancies had owned a small pig-farm where they had spent the summer. The relationship hadn't lasted, her mother having been unable to endure the quiet country life, but the fourteen-year-old Olivia had loved it. Now she summoned memories of that happy time, and she and Tao were soon in animated discussion. Pigs had provided Tao with a good living, and Olivia had enjoyed feeding time.

'There was a huge sow,' she recalled. 'She had a litter of fifteen, but only fourteen teats, and terrible fights would break out between the piglets over the last teat. I used to take a feeding bottle to make sure I could give something to the one who missed out. He'd just drink his fill and then go back to the fight.'

Tao roared with laughter and countered with the tale of a vast pig he'd once owned, who'd fathered larger litters than any other pig, and whose services had been much in demand among his neighbours. Everyone else round the table watched them with delight, and Olivia knew she'd scored a success by impressing the head of the family.

When the meal was over, Biyu showed her around the other houses. She was eager to know about her first meeting with Lang, and laughed at the story of the mischievous child.

'We are so proud of Mitchell,' Biyu said. 'He works very hard, and he's a big man at the hospital.'

'What does he actually do there?' Olivia asked. 'He was taking a clinic when we met, but apparently he was just filling in because they were short-staffed. I understand that his real job is something quite different.'

'That's true. He's a consultant.'

'A consultant?' Olivia echoed, amazed. 'He's young for that.'

'Oh, yes, he's only a *junior* consultant,' Biyu amended hastily. 'He keeps insisting on that. He gets cross if I make him sound too important—but I say he's going to be very, very important, because they know he's the best they have. There's a big job coming soon.'

She gave a knowing wink.

'You think he'll get it?'

'He will if there's any justice,' Biyu said firmly. 'But he's superstitious. He thinks if he gets too confident then some great power above will punish him by taking the job away from him.'

'Superstitious,' Olivia mused. 'You wouldn't think it.'

'Oh, he acts as if nothing could worry him,' Biyu confided. 'But don't you be fooled.'

It struck Olivia that this was shrewd advice. Lang's air of cool confidence had cracks, some of which he'd allowed her to see. The rest he seemed to be keeping to himself while their mutual trust grew.

'You're very proud of him, aren't you?' she said.

'Oh, yes. It was a great day for us when he came to China. We already knew a lot about him because Meihui had kept in touch, sending us news, and to see him was wonderful. The best thing of all was that he wanted to come, and then he wanted to stay. Some men from his country would have ignored their Chinese heritage, but he chose to find it and live with it, because it's important to him.'

'He's going away soon, isn't he, to do some exploring?'

'Actually, I thought he'd be gone by now. He spoke as though— Well, anyway, I'm glad he decided to wait a little longer, or we might not have met you.'

She tensed suddenly as Lang's voice reached them from outside.

'We're here,' she called back, showing Olivia out into the courtyard where he was waiting.

'Grandfather wants to bring out the family photographs,' he said. 'He's got hundreds of them, all ready to show Olivia.'

'And I'm longing to see them,' she said.

The largest room in the north house had been laid out in preparation, with a table in the centre covered in photographs. To Olivia's amazement the pictures stretched back sixty years to when Meihui had been a beautiful young girl. She must have been about sixteen in the first one, sitting in the curve of Tao's arm. His face as he looked down on his little sister bore an expression of great pride, and Olivia thought she could still see it there now as he regarded her picture. He was almost in tears over the little sister who had meant the world to him, and who he'd last seen when she was eighteen, departing for ever with the man she loved.

'And that's him?' Olivia asked as an Englishman appeared in the pictures.

'That's John Mitchell, my grandfather,' Lang agreed.

He seemed about twenty-three, not particularly handsome but with a broad, hearty face and a smile that beamed with good nature. Meihui's eyes, as she gazed at him, were alight with joy.

Then there were photographs that she had sent from England: herself and John Mitchell, proudly holding their new-born son, Lang's father. Then the child growing up, standing between his parents, until his father vanished because death had taken him far too soon. After that it was just Meihui and her son, until he married, and soon his own son appeared, a toddler in his father's arms.

'Let's leave them,' Lang groaned.

'But you were a delightful child!' Olivia protested.

He gave a grimace of pure masculine embarrassment, and she hastily controlled her mirth.

It was true that he seemed to have been a pleasant youngster, but even then his face held a sense of resolution beyond his years, already heralding the man he would become.

There were some pictures with his parents, then with his mother after his father's death, but mostly they showed the young Lang with Meihui. Then he appeared with his new family after his mother's remarriage. Looking at them, Olivia understood what he'd meant about not having been at ease. His stepfather looked as though he had much good nature, but no subtlety, and his offspring were the same. Standing in their midst, the young Lang smiled with the courteous determination of a misfit.

He grew older, graduated from school and passed his medical exams. One picture especially caught Olivia's attention—it showed him sitting down while Meihui stood behind him, her hands on his shoulders, her face beaming with pride. At that moment she had been the happiest woman in the world. Instead of looking at the camera, Lang was glancing up, connecting with her.

'No wonder your family recognised you at the airport,' she murmured, drawing him slightly aside. 'Thanks to Meihui, they'd been with you every step of the way while you were growing up.'

'Yes, they said much the same. It made me feel very much at home.'

He spoke just loud enough for Biyu to hear, making her glance up and smile. He smiled back, yet strangely Olivia sensed a hint of tension in him, the last thing she'd expected. Now she thought about it, she felt there was a watchfulness about him tonight that wasn't usually there.

She wondered if she was the cause of his concern, lest she make a bad impression, but his manner towards her was full of pride. What was troubling him, then? she wondered.

As they left the room, Biyu announced, 'Now I'm going to show you our special place, devoted to Jaio and Renshu. I know Lang has told you about them.'

'Yes, it must be wonderful having such a great family tradition, going back so far.'

'It is. We have mementoes of them which normally we keep locked away for safety, but in your honour we have brought them out.' She gave a teasing smile. 'Lang tells us that you may need a little convincing.'

'Oh, did he? Just wait until I see him.'

'You mean, it isn't true?' Biyu asked.

'Of course— Well, I think it's a lovely story.'

'But perhaps a little unreal?' Biyu sighed. 'The world is so prosaic these days. People no longer believe in a love so great that it conquers everything. But few families have been as fortunate as we. We keep our mementoes because they are our treasures, not in the worldly way, but treasures of the heart. Come, let me show you our temple.'

Crossing the courtyard, she entered the south house that would soon belong to Wei and his bride.

'This is where we keep our temple,' she said, opening the door to a room at the back. 'Wei and his wife-to-be have promised to respect it.'

It was a small room. In the centre was a table on which some papers were laid out, and a piece of jade.

'These are our mementoes of them,' Wei said.

'Those papers,' Olivia said. 'They are actually the ones that—?'

'The very ones that were discovered after their deaths.'

'Two-thousand years ago,' Olivia murmured.

She tried to keep a touch of scepticism out of her voice. She liked Biyu, and didn't wish to seem impolite, but surely nothing could be certain at such a distance of time?

'Yes, two-thousand years,' Biyu said. 'We've had collectors offering us a lot of money for them, saying that they are valuable historical relics. They cannot understand why we will not sell. They say the money would make us rich.'

'But these are beyond price,' Olivia said.

Biyu nodded, pleased at her understanding.

'Their value is not in money,' she agreed.

'What do the papers say?' Olivia asked. 'Normally I can read Chinese but these are so faded.'

'They say "We have shared the love that was our destiny. Whether long or short, our life together has been triumphant. They say that love is the shield that protects us from harm, and we know it to be true. Nothing matters but that".'

'Nothing matters but that,' Olivia murmured.

How would it feel to know a love so all-embracing that it extinguished everything else in the world? She tried to remember her feelings for Andy, and realised that she couldn't recall his face. Now there was another face on the edge of her consciousness waiting to be allowed in, but only when she was ready.

A man with the gift of endless patience could be comforting, fascinating, perhaps even alarming. She hadn't yet decided.

'I will never forget the day we showed these to Lang,' her hostess said. 'He had heard of them from Meihui, but the reality was very powerful to him. He held them in his hands and kept saying, "It is really true".'

'I love the way you all feel so close to Lang,' Olivia said. 'You don't treat him differently at all.'

'But should we? Oh, you mean because he's a little bit English?'

'Three-quarters English,' Olivia said, laughing.

Biyu shrugged as if to say 'what is three quarters?'.

'That is just on the surface,' she said. 'In here—' she tapped her heart '—he is one of us.'

Lang came in at that moment and Olivia wondered if he'd heard these last words. If he had they must surely have pleased him, but it was hard to tell.

'There's a little more,' he said, indicating a side table where there were two wooden boxes and two large photographs which Olivia recognised as Meihui and John Mitchell.

'The boxes are their ashes,' Biyu confided, looking at Lang. 'He brought them.'

'Meihui kept John's ashes,' Lang said. 'And when she died I promised her that I would bring them both here.'

'We had a special ceremony in which we welcomed them both home and said that we would always keep them together,' Biyu said. 'And we laid them in this temple, so that Renshu and Jaio could always watch over them.'

She spoke with such simple fervour that Olivia's heart was touched. It didn't matter, she realised, whether every detail of the legend was exactly true. The family had taken it as their faith, and perhaps a trust in the enduring power of love was the best faith anyone could choose.

Silently, Biyu drew her attention to a hanging on the wall. It was a large sheet of parchment, and on it were written the words Jaio had spoken: *love is the shield that protects us from harm.*

In the end their love hadn't protected them from those who'd sought them out, but now Olivia knew that this wasn't the harm Jaio had meant. To live a lonely, useless life, separated from the one who could give it meaning—that was a suffering neither she nor Renshu had ever known. And, if there had been a price, they did not complain.

She began to understand a little more of the family's pride in Lang, the man who through his grandmother embodied the legend in the present day.

He was looking away at that moment so that she was able to observe him unseen. And it seemed to her that the mysterious 'something' in his face was now more evident than ever.

CHAPTER SIX

As IT grew dark the lanterns came on in the courtyard and everyone gathered to hear Suyin sing. After a while Olivia slipped away and went to Lang's room in the south house, glad of a moment alone to mull over what she'd learned tonight. She was beginning to understand Lang a little better—he was a man who hung back behind a quiet, even conventional mask, but who behind that mask was a dozen other men. Some of those men were fascinating, and some she should perhaps be wary of.

After giving her hair a quick brush, she left the room and found him waiting in the hall outside. She faced him with an air of indignation that was not entirely assumed.

'I've got a bone to pick with you,' she said.

'Are you mad at me? I've offended you?'

'Don't you give me that deferential stuff. I see right through it. You can't open your mouth without fooling me about something.'

'What have I done now?'

'I asked you about your job and you gave me the impression that you were little more than the hospital porter. Now I find out you're an important man.'

'I deny it,' he said at once.

'A consultant.'

'*Junior* consultant. It's just a title that's supposed to make me feel pleased with myself. The real big man is the senior consultant.'

'Oh, really? And when is the big man going to retire and let you step into his shoes?'

'That's a long story. We should be getting back before they come looking for us.'

He was still smiling, but she had a feeling that she'd touched a nerve. The hospital was one of the biggest and most important in Beijing. If he was seriously hoping for a major promotion after only three years, then he was more ambitious than he wanted anyone to know.

'They've already come to seek us out. There they are,' Lang said, indicating outside where Biyu could be seen watching, accompanied by Wei, Suyin and an assortment of children. 'From where they're standing, you can see in through the window, and they're waiting to see if we fulfil expectations.'

This was so plainly true that she chuckled. Some people would have found the blatant curiosity intrusive and dismaying, but Olivia—child of a fractured family where there had been much hysterical emoting but little genuine kindness—felt only the warmth of a large family welcoming her, similar to what Lang himself had felt, she guessed.

'Then you'd better put your arm around my shoulders,' she said.

'Like that?' His hand rested lightly on her shoulder.

'I think you might manage to be a little more convincing,' she reproved him. 'We're supposed to be giving them what they want, and I doubt if they can even see anything from there.'

'You're right,' he agreed. 'It has to look real.'

Tightening his arm, he drew her closer to him. Slowly he lowered his head until his lips were just brushing hers.

'Is this real enough?' he murmured.

'I think—I think we might try a little harder.'

That was all the encouragement he needed. Next moment his mouth was over hers forcefully. There was no hesitancy now, but a full-scale declaration of intent; his lips moved urgently, asking a question but too impatient to await the answer.

Olivia responded with an overwhelming sense of relief. She had wanted this, and it was only now that she knew how badly. Since their first meeting she'd been fighting him on one level, responding on another. Now she was no longer torn two ways and could yield to the delight that flowed through her with dizzying speed.

She'd demanded that he be more convincing, and he was following her wishes to the letter. But then he lifted his head for a moment and she saw the truth in his eyes. The one brief touch of lips that they'd shared the day before had given barely a hint of what awaited them, and now he was as stunned as she by the reality.

'Olivia…'

'Don't talk,' she said huskily, pulling his head down.

Then there was only a silence more eloquent than words. She'd studied his mouth, not even realising she was doing so, wondering how its shape would feel against her own. Her imaginings had fallen far short of this overwhelming awareness of leashed power combined with subtlety.

He released her mouth and dropped his head so that his breath warmed her neck softly. He was trembling.

She wanted to say something, but there was nothing to say. No words would describe the feelings that pervaded her, feelings that she wanted to go on for ever. Tenderly she stroked his head, turning slightly so that they could renew the kiss. She wanted that so badly.

But one of the children outside gave an excited squeal and was hastily shushed. The noise seemed to come from a distance, yet it shattered the spell ruthlessly. Stranded back on earth again, they regarded each other in bewilderment.

'I think,' Lang said unsteadily, 'I think we'd better—'

'Yes, I guess we should,' she replied, not having the least idea what she was talking about.

They walked out, bracing themselves for an ironic cheer, but the others had melted tactfully away. They'd seen all they needed to.

When it was time to leave, everyone embraced her warmly. Tao and Shu presented her with a glass pig, insisting that she must come again soon, and everyone stood outside to wave them off.

Lang drove in silence. Olivia wondered if he would speak about what had happened, but she was neither surprised nor disappointed when he didn't. It wasn't to be spoken of.

'Let's stop for a while before we go home,' he said at last. 'There's a little place just down here.'

It turned out to be a teahouse constructed on old-fashioned lines, several connected buildings with roofs that curved dramatically up at the corners. Red lanterns hung inside, and stretched out to a small garden. They went to an outside table where their tea was served in elegant porcelain cups.

Lang wished he knew what to say. He'd come here hoping for time to think after having been disconcerted all evening. He'd wanted Olivia to make a good impression on his family, but she'd done more than that. She'd been a knockout. He smiled, remembering how brilliantly she'd swapped pig memories with Grandfather Tao, and how his female relatives had been won over by her fashion sense.

He'd been astonished, but he should not have been. In the brief time he'd known her she'd taken him by surprise more often than he could count. It was alarming—it turned the world on its head in a way that constantly caught him off-guard—but it was also part of her charm.

As an attractive man he was used to having women put themselves out to get his attention. He wasn't conceited about it, he just didn't know any different. Now he was relishing an experience that nothing had prepared him for.

To find himself powerfully attracted to a woman who was fighting her own attraction to him, to have to persuade her and tease her into a sense of security so that he could convince her of the value of romantic love, intrigued him and made him wonder just where this road was leading.

Wherever it led, he knew that he was happy to go there, and that the time of decision had come. He must act now or lose what might be the most precious gift of his life.

The courtyard of the teahouse was enclosed on

three sides. On the fourth there was a small pond where ducks quacked for titbits, and a bridge where they could linger after drinking their tea.

'Oh, this is so nice.' Olivia sighed, enjoying deep breaths of the sweet air and tossing a crumb into the water. She'd taken a small cake from the table for this purpose, but had eaten none of it herself.

'Are you sure you don't want anything else?' Lang asked.

She laughed. 'No, the tea was delicious and I've had enough food to last me for a month. It was wonderful food. I'm not complaining.'

'I am,' he said frankly. 'It felt like being fattened for the slaughter. They were in competition to see which one of us they could make collapse first.'

'But they're so nice,' Olivia said. 'It was all so warm and friendly, just like a family should be.'

'I'm glad you felt that. I love them dearly, but I was afraid you might find them a little overpowering.'

'I did.' She laughed. 'But I don't mind being overpowered with kindness. Not one bit.'

She tossed another crumb into the water and watched the quacking squabble. At last she said, 'Biyu mentioned something strange—apparently they'd expected you to be gone before now.'

He hesitated a brief moment before admitting, 'I stayed because of you. I didn't mean to. I've been packed and ready to go for several days, but

I couldn't make myself leave, or even make up my mind to come and talk to you.'

She nodded. The discovery that his confusion matched her own seemed to draw them closer.

'When do you leave for the Yangzte cruise?' he asked.

'I join the boat at Chongqing in a couple of days.'

'I've been planning to go to Xi'an,' he said thoughtfully.

'To see the mausoleum that Jaio escaped?'

'In a way. It hasn't been excavated yet, so I can't go inside, but I can see the terracotta warriors nearby. They were based on the Emperor's army.'

'So one of them might be Renshu,' she supplied. 'It sounds a great trip, but if you've been in China for three years I can't understand why you haven't been there before.'

'I have. It was one of the first places I went. But since I've lived here for a while I see things with different eyes. Then I was still a stranger. Now I feel part of this country, and I want to retrace my steps and try to understand things better.' Suddenly he grasped her hand and said, 'Olivia?'

'Yes?'

He took a deep breath and spoke with the eagerness of a man who'd finally seen the way clear.

'Come with me. Don't say no. Ah, say you'll come.'

It was only when she heard Lang beg her that Olivia fully understood how desolate she would have been if he'd left without a backward glance at her.

Don't get flustered, said the voice within. You're a woman of the twenty-first century. Stay cool.

'You mean, to see the warriors?' she asked with a fair display of casualness.

'I want to find out if I can make you see them as I do. Or maybe you'll show me something I've missed.' He added reflectively, 'You have a way of doing that.'

'It's quite unconscious.'

'I know. That's why it's so alarming. It springs out at me suddenly, and I have no chance to guard against it.'

'Do you want to guard against it?'

'Sometimes.'

She waited, sensing that he had more to say, and at last he went on. 'Sometimes you take fright and want to flee back to your old, safe life where things follow a pattern and nothing is too unpredictable. But then you realise that that's a kind of death; the safety is an illusion, and there's nothing to do but take the next step—whatever it brings. And sometimes—' he made a rueful face '—you can't decide between the two.'

'I know,' she murmured, awed by his insight.

'I'm a coward,' he said. Looking up, he added, 'But maybe I'm not the only one.'

She nodded.

'Now and then,' she said slowly, 'what passes for common sense is only cowardice in disguise.'

'Does that mean you'll come with me or not?' he asked urgently. 'We could leave for Xi'an tomorrow, and go on to Chongqing afterwards, if you wouldn't mind my joining you on the cruise. And after that, well, we go wherever we fancy and do whatever we fancy.'

'Whatever we fancy,' Olivia murmured longingly. 'I wonder…'

He drew her down the far side of the bridge and under the trees. There in the shadows he could take her into his arms and remind her silently of the things that united them. She came willingly, letting her own lips speak of feelings for which there were as yet no words.

She ought to refuse; she knew that. Step by seemingly innocent step he was enticing her along a path she'd sworn never to tread again, a path on which the delight in one man's presence would silence all warnings until her life spun into turmoil. How virtuous it would be to be strong. How sensible. How justified! How impossible!

With every caress his mouth begged her to trust him with her heart and follow him to an unknown destination. Except that it wasn't really unknown. It was the place where he wanted to be with her, and no questions were needed.

He kissed her again and again, breathing hard as his urgency and need threatened to overcome his control.

'We'll have the whole summer together,' he managed to say. 'That is, if the idea pleases you.'

'It pleases me,' she said softly.

A violent tremor went through him. He was resting his forehead against her, his eyes closed while he fought to subdue himself. She held him with passionate tenderness, waiting, wondering what was happening behind his eyelids, and half-convinced that she knew.

At last he drew away and spoke in a shaking voice. 'Then let us make the arrangements quickly.'

He led her back to the table, took out his phone, and in a few brief calls changed her flights, booked her into his hotel in Xi'an, and just managed to grasp the last available place on the Yangtze cruise.

Then a silence fell. Both suddenly felt embarrassed, as though the emotion that had brought them thus far had abandoned them, leaving them stranded in alien territory where nothing looked the same.

'Perhaps we should go home and start getting ready,' he said awkwardly.

'Yes—packing.'

Lang had recovered his composure and gave her a mischievous look. 'Don't forget to include that dress you're wearing.'

'Oh, do you like it? I wasn't sure it suited me.'

'Stop fishing. You know exactly what it does for you. And if you didn't know at the start,' he added, 'you do now.'

'Yes,' she said, feeling her heart beat faster. 'I know now.'

'Let's go.'

At her door he said, 'I'll be here for you at midday tomorrow.'

He gave her a brief peck on the cheek and drove away.

She began her packing in a dissatisfied frame of mind and grew more dissatisfied as she lay wakeful overnight. Her mood was nothing to do with Lang and everything to do with the fact that her wardrobe was inadequate. The only really glamorous item she possessed was the *cheongsam*, and something had to be done—fast.

When buying the *cheongsam* she'd lingered over several other items, wanting them but too prudent to spend the money.

But now she was going away with Lang, and to blazes with prudence.

He wouldn't arrive until noon. The shop was three streets away, and a quick dash there and back in a taxi would enable her to collect what she needed and return before him. She took her suitcases down to the front door, and spoke to the tenant of the downstairs apartment.

'If a man calls for me, will you tell him I'll be back in ten minutes? Thanks.'

She called a taxi and waited for it outside, waving cheerfully at a little girl from one of the other apartments who was playing nearby. The taxi was prompt and she took off, managing to be back barely five minutes after midday. With luck, she thought, Lang wouldn't be there yet—but it wasn't really a surprise to find him ahead of her. What did surprise her was the volcanic look on his face.

'Where the devil have you been?' he demanded explosively.

'Hey, cut it out!' she told him. 'I'm a few minutes late. It's not the end of the world. I went to do a bit of last-minute shopping. I left you a message with the woman who lives downstairs. Didn't you see her?'

'The only person I've seen is a child who was playing here. She said you got into a taxi and went away *for ever*. That was her exact phrase.'

Olivia groaned. 'I know who you mean. She saw me get into the taxi but the rest is her imagination. I just went to buy something. I'm here now. Have you been waiting long?'

'Five minutes.'

She stared. 'Five minutes? That's nothing. No need to make a fuss.'

For answer he slammed his hand down hard on

the bonnet of the taxi, causing the driver to object loudly. While they sorted it out, Olivia dashed inside to retrieve her suitcases.

She was stunned at what she'd just seen. Lang was the last man she would have suspected of such an outburst. Here was a troubling mystery, but her dismay faded as she emerged from the building and saw his face. It was no longer angry, but full of a suffering he was fighting to hide.

The driver, placated by a large tip, helped them load the bags, and then they were off.

In the taxi Olivia took Lang's hand and rallied him cheerfully. 'We're going to have a great time. Don't spoil it by being mad at me.'

'I'm not. I'm mad at myself for making a mountain out of a molehill. After all, what's five minutes? That's the trouble with being a doctor, you get to be a stickler for time.'

He went on talking, turning it into a joke against himself. But Olivia knew it wasn't a joke really. It wasn't about five minutes; just what it was about was something she had yet to learn. In the meantime, she fell in with his mood, and they went to the airport in apparently good spirits.

The flight took two hours, and they reached the hotel in the evening.

'Is your room all right?' Lang asked as they went down to the restaurant.

'Yes, I'm going to sleep fine. Not that I plan to

do much sleeping. I've still got a lot of reading to do about the Emperor.'

'I saw you buried in a book on the plane. Good grief, you've brought it down here with you.'

'He fascinates me. He took the throne of Qin when he was only thirteen, unified all the states into one country, standardised money, weights and measures, built canals and roads. But he only lived to be fifty, and he seems to have spent the last few years of his life trying to find a way to avoid death.'

'Yes, he dreaded the idea of dying,' Lang agreed. 'He sent court officials all over the world with orders to find a magic elixir. Most of them simply vanished because they didn't dare go back empty-handed. He tried to prolong his life by taking mercury, but that's probably what killed him so soon.'

'Which makes it all the more ironic that he had over half a million men building his tomb for years.'

'That was the convention. The pharaohs in Egypt used to do the same thing—start building their pyramids as soon as they ascended the throne.'

'And in the end all those poor, innocent women were trapped in there with him.' She sighed. 'What a pity we can't see inside.'

So far the tomb had not been excavated, although radar investigations had suggested many things of interest, including booby traps and rivers of mercury. Olivia knew that it would probably be several years before visitors could go into the tomb and see the place where Jaio would have died if Renshu hadn't rescued her.

In the meantime there was the other great sight to be seen, the terracotta warriors, buried nearly a mile away from the tomb and discovered thirty-five years earlier by farmers who'd happened to be digging in a field. The inspiration for these statues had been the men who protected the Emperor, of whom Renshu was one.

'I wonder how they met,' she mused now. 'Weren't the concubines kept strictly away from other men, except eunuchs?'

'Yes. The story is that Renshu was part of a group of soldiers who escorted her from the far city where she lived. Even so, he wasn't meant to see her face, but he did so by accident. The other story is that he was on duty in the palace one evening and caught a glimpse of her.'

'But could that be enough?' Olivia asked. 'They see each other for just a moment and everything follows from that?'

'Just a moment can be more than enough,' Lang mused. 'You never know when it's going to happen, or how hard it's going to hit you. You don't get to pick the person, either. She's just there in front of you, and it's her. She's the one.'

He gave a faint smile, aimed mainly at himself.

'Sometimes you might wish that she wasn't,' he said softly. 'But it's too late for that.'

'Oh, really? And why would you wish that she wasn't?'

'Lots of reasons. She might be really awkward. She might get you in such a state that you didn't know whether you were coming or going. You could go to bed at night thinking, "I don't need this. How can I get her out of my hair?" But the answer is always the same. You can't.

'And you come to realise that whichever one of the deities decides these things isn't asking your opinion, just giving you orders…"There she is, she's the one. Get on with it".'

Olivia nodded. 'You say deity, but that voice can be more like a nagging aunt.'

'You too?' he asked slowly.

'Yes,' she said in a low voice. 'Me too. You try to explain to the aunt that she's got it all wrong— you weren't planning for anything like this guy— and all she says is, "Did I ask what you planned?"'

Lang laughed at her assumed hauteur. His eyes were warm as they rested on her.

'It's like being swept along by an avalanche,' Olivia continued. 'And sometimes you just want to go with it, but at other times you think—'

'Not yet?' Lang supplied helpfully.

'Yes. Just a little longer.'

She wished she could explain the sweet excitement he caused within her, and the caution she still had to overcome. But he came to her rescue, saying, 'I imagine Renshu felt the same when he fell in love with Jaio. He probably had a fine career in the army, and falling for the Emperor's concubine just spelled big trouble. He must have fought it, and maybe he kidded himself that he was succeeding, until her life was threatened, and then nothing else mattered. He knew he had to save her, and then he knew he had to be with her for ever—to love her, protect her, have children with her.'

His voice became reflective, as though he was just realising something.

'When he finally faced it, he was probably relieved. However hard the way ahead, he'd be at peace, because the big decision was made.'

'And yet he gave up so much,' Olivia mused. 'It was easier for her, she had nothing to lose, but he lost everything.'

'No, he gained everything,' Lang said quickly. 'Even though they didn't have very long together, she fulfilled him as nothing else ever could have done. And he knew that she would, or he'd never have gone to such lengths to make her his.'

'And yet think of how they must have lived,' Olivia said. 'On the run for the rest of their lives, never really able to relax because they were afraid of being caught.'

'I expect it was more than just being afraid,' Lang said. 'They probably knew for certain that one day they'd be caught and pay a heavy price.

And, when it came, they were ready. The story is that when the soldiers found them Renshu tried to make Jaio escape while he held them off, but she went to stand beside him and they died together.'

'But what about their son?' Olivia asked. 'Shouldn't she have tried to live for his sake?'

'Her son had been rescued by the family. If she'd gone after him she would only have led the soldiers to him. Her choice was either to die in flight, or die at Renshu's side. To her there was really no choice at all. They knew what was coming. That's why they left those writings behind. They wanted to tell the world while there was still time.'

Olivia gazed at him in wonder.

'You speak as though you knew them, as though they were real people here with you this minute.'

'Sometimes that's just how it seems,' he confessed. He gave her a wry smile. 'No doubt you think that's ludicrously sentimental, you being such a practical person!'

'But you're a practical person too,' she pointed out. 'How could a doctor not be?'

'Yes, I'm a doctor, but that doesn't mean I only believe in things that can be proved in a test tube.'

'So a doctor can be as daft as anyone else?' she teased.

'Emphatically, *yes*. More so, in fact, because he knows what a false god scientific precision can be, and so he's wiser if he—'

He broke off abruptly and she guessed the reason. He was moving faster than her, so fast that perhaps he even alarmed himself.

But her alarm was fading. With every minute that passed the conviction was growing in her that this was right. She didn't know what was lying in wait for them, but whatever it was she was ready, even eager, to find it.

CHAPTER SEVEN

At last he said, 'If you've finished eating I think we should go upstairs. We need plenty of sleep.'

At her door he bid her goodnight with a brief kiss on the cheek before hurrying away, leaving her wishing he'd stay the same person for five minutes at a time.

She went to bed quickly and read some more of the book until finally she put it down and lay musing. After their talk that evening Renshu and Jaio seemed strangely real, and she had the feeling that tomorrow she was going to meet them. Face to face she would hear their story, about their life, about the love that was stronger than death. And perhaps she would understand a little more about the man whose existence had sprung from that love at a distance of two-thousand years.

Olivia turned out the light and went to the window. Opening it, she stood gazing out at the mountains that were just visible in the moonlight, and a thin line of silver where a river followed a curving course.

In the room beside hers, Lang's window was closed. She could see that his light was still on and, by leaning out, she could just see his shadow coming and going. She was about to call out to him when his light went off. She hurried back to bed and was soon asleep.

She awoke early, going to sit by the open window to breathe in the cool air and enjoy the view over the mountains now bathed in early-morning light. On impulse she took out her laptop and set up the connection with Norah. In England it would be mid-afternoon, not their usual time, but she might still make contact.

She was in luck. Almost at once Norah's face appeared on the screen. When the greetings were over, Olivia said, 'We're going to see the terra-cotta warriors.'

'I've heard of them. They're very famous.'

'Yes, but we have a special reason.'

Briefly she told the tale of Jaio and Renshu. As she'd expected, Norah was thrilled.

'So Lang is descended from a warrior and a con-cubine. What fun!'

'You're incorrigible,' Olivia said, laughing. Then something made her stop and peer more closely at the screen. 'Are you all right? You look a bit pale.'

'I've been out doing some shopping. It was nice, but very tiring.'

'Hmm. Come closer, so that I can see you better.'

'Stop fussing.'

'I just want to take a look at you.'

Grumbling, Norah moved until Olivia could see her better.

'There,' she said. 'Now stop making a fuss.'

Suddenly there came a knock on Olivia's bedroom door.

'Don't go away,' she said, drawing the edges of her light bathrobe together and heading for the door.

Lang was standing outside in a towel robe. He too pulled the edges together when he saw her.

'Are you all right?' he said. 'I heard you talking, and I wondered if anything's wrong.'

'I'm talking to Aunt Norah by video link. I promised her I'd stay in touch. Come and meet her.'

She showed him to the window chair and made him sit where the camera could focus on him.

'Here he is, Aunt Norah,' she said. 'This is Dr Lang Mitchell.'

'How do you do, Dr Mitchell?' Norah said formally.

'Please, call me Lang,' he said at once, giving the old woman his most charming smile. She responded in kind and they beamed at each other across five-thousand miles.

'And I'm Norah.'

'Norah, I can't tell you how I've looked forward to meeting you.'

'You knew about me?'

'Olivia talks about you all the time. At our very first meeting she told me that you said if she ever shut up she'd learn something.'

Olivia gaped, outraged, and Norah beamed.

'And I have to tell you,' Lang continued confidentially, 'that after knowing her only a short time I realise what a good judge of character you are.'

The two of them rocked with laughter while Olivia glared.

'You can leave any time you like,' she informed him coolly.

'Why would I want to leave? I've just made a new friend.'

He and Norah chatted on for a few minutes and Olivia regarded them, fascinated by the way they were instantly at ease with each other.

At last Lang rose, saying, 'It was delightful meeting you, and I hope we talk again soon.' To Olivia he said, 'I'll see you downstairs for breakfast.'

He left the room quickly. He needed to be alone to think.

The Chinese had a saying: 'it is easy to dodge a spear thrown from the front, but hard to avoid an arrow from behind'.

In Lang's mind the spear from the front had

been the moment he'd arrived to collect Olivia and found that she'd already left, 'for ever'. For a few blinding, terrible minutes he'd been convinced that she'd changed her mind and left him, even fled the country, and that he would never see her again.

The moment when she'd appeared was burned into his consciousness with searing force. She hadn't left him. Everything was all right. Except that now he'd glimpsed a future that didn't contain her, and it appalled him.

He'd coped. He'd known already that his feelings for her were running out of control. It was only their extent that shocked him, and which had made him ultra-cautious in their talk over dinner the night before.

Harder to cope with were the arrows that struck unexpectedly. One had come out of nowhere earlier, giving him a bad fright.

He'd heard Olivia's voice as soon as he'd opened his window, and had smiled, thinking she was on the telephone. But the words, 'you look a bit pale' had told him this was no phone call. And while he'd been trying to take in the implications she'd added, 'Come closer, so that I can see you better.'

The idea of a video link hadn't occurred to him. He'd tried to stay cool, not to jump to the conclusion that she had a man in the room, but no power on earth could have stopped him knocking on her door to find out. Now he was feeling like the biggest fool of all time. Yet mixed in with embarrassment was delight that he'd been wrong. All was well.

The arrows would keep coming when he least expected them. He knew that now. But nothing could stop his mood rioting with joyful relief, and in the shower he gave vent to a yodelling melody. When he joined her downstairs, he was still lightheaded.

'I can see that Norah and I are going to be the best of friends,' he told her.

'Ganging up on me at every turn, I suppose.'

'Of course. That's half the fun. Did she say anything about me after I'd gone?'

'Not a word,' she declared loftily. 'We dismissed you from our minds.'

'As bad as that?' he said, nodding sympathetically.

'Worse. I couldn't get any sense out of her. She just wittered on endlessly about how handsome you are. Where she got that idea, I couldn't imagine.'

'The video quality is never very strong on those links.'

'Well, she likes you enormously.'

'Good. I like her too. Now, let's have a hearty breakfast and get revved up for the day.'

An hour later the coach called to collect them, plus several others from the hotel, and soon they were on the road to the warrior site.

'The thing I loved about it,' Lang said, 'was that they didn't build a separate museum and transport everything to it. They created the museum on top of the actual site of the dig where the figures were found.'

She saw what he meant as soon as they entered. The museum was divided into three huge pits, the first of which was the most astonishing. There in the ground were hundreds of soldiers standing in formation as though on duty. A gallery had been built all around so that the visitor could view them from every angle. This was exactly the place where they had been discovered and, as Lang had said, it made all the difference.

Not only men but horses stood there, patient unto eternity. After burial they had had only a short existence, for less than five years after the Emperor's death they had been attacked, many of them smashed and the site covered in earth. For over two-thousand years they had remained undiscovered, waiting for their time to come, silent and faithful in the darkness.

Now their day had dawned again. Some had been repaired and restored to beauty, although thousands still remained to be unearthed. Now they were world-famous, proud and honoured as they deserved to be.

Although Lang had been here before he too was awed as they walked around the long gallery.

'We've only seen a small part,' he said as he left. 'When we visit the rest you can study some of them close up. It's incredible how they were created so skilfully all that time ago—the fine details, the expressions.'

When Olivia saw the figures that were displayed in glass containers she had to admit that he was right. Not one detail had been skimped on the armour, and the figures stood or crouched in positions that were utterly natural. No wonder, she thought, that historians and art experts had gone wild about them.

But she wasn't viewing them as a professional. It was as men that they claimed her attention, and as men they were awesome, tall, muscular, with fine, thoughtful but determined faces.

'It's incredible how different they all are,' she mused. 'It would have been so easy to give them all the same face, but they didn't do it the easy way. How many of them are there?'

'Something like eight thousand when they've finished excavating,' Lang said. 'And I don't think they're all precisely individual. If you hunt through them you'll find the same face repeated now and then, but it's a long hunt.'

Their steps had brought them to a glass container with only one figure. He was down on one knee, but not in a servile way. His head was up, his back straight, his air alert, as though his whole attention was devoted to his duty.

'Whoever this was based on had a splendid career ahead of him,' she murmured. 'And he gave it all up.'

'You've decided that this was Renshu?' Lang asked, fondly amused.

'Definitely. He's by far the most handsome.'

Before finishing the tour, they went to the pavilion where there was a teahouse to refresh them.

'It's so real,' she said. 'I hadn't expected to find them so lifelike. You could almost talk to them and hear them talk back.'

'Yes, that's how I felt.'

'You know that story you told me—how he might have seen her when he was escorting her, or later in the palace—well, I've been thinking, and they could both be true. Renshu saw her face accidentally on the journey, and after that he knew he had to see her again, so he connived to get assigned to palace duty.'

'That's a very romantic suggestion,' Lang exclaimed. 'I'm shocked!'

'All right, I've weakened just a little. Now I've seen what a fine, upstanding man he must have been, I can understand why she fell in love with him.' Olivia laughed at the sight of Lang's expression. 'It's this place. Somehow the whole story suddenly seems so convincing. I can't wait to go back in.'

They spent the afternoon going over everything again, fascinated by the semi-excavated parts in pit one, where broken figures lay waiting to be reclaimed, and the places where they could study the work in progress. The day finished in the shop that sold souvenirs, and Olivia stocked up on books and pictures. Lang also was buying extensively.

'But you've got that book,' she said, pointing. 'I remember seeing it in your room.'

'It's not for me. It's a gift for my friend Norah.'

'That's lovely. She'll be so happy.'

Some of the other tourists were from their hotel and they all made a merry party, exchanging views on the way back. It was natural to join up again over the meal, and the evening passed without Lang and Olivia having a moment alone.

'When will you talk to Norah?' he asked later.

'Early tomorrow morning.'

'Make sure you call me so that I can talk to her.'

'Can I tell her you've bought her a present?'

'Don't you dare! I want to do that myself. Goodnight.'

'Goodnight.'

She contacted Norah early next morning and found her bright-eyed with anticipation.

'Where's Lang?' was her first question.

'Good morning, Olivia, how nice to speak to you,' Olivia said ironically. 'I gather I don't exist any more.'

'Let's say he rather casts you into the shade, my darling.'

'All right, I'll go and knock on his door.'

'Knock on his—? Do you mean he's in a different room?' Norah sounded outraged.

'Yes, we have separate rooms,' Olivia said through gritted teeth.

She hurried out, unwilling to pursue this subject further. After the way passion had flared between herself and Lang, it seemed inevitable that they would take the next step. But suddenly he seemed in no hurry, and hadn't so much as hinted that he might come to her at night.

Perhaps she had mistaken him and he wasn't as deeply involved as her, but both her mind and her heart rejected that thought as unbearable.

He returned with her and she witnessed again the immediate rapport between he and Norah as he showed her the gifts he'd chosen. For most of the conversation she stayed in the background.

'It's not like you to be lost for words,' he teased her when they had finished.

'I didn't want to spoil it for you two,' she teased back. 'You get on so well, I'm beginning to feel like a gooseberry.'

'Can you give me her address so that I can mail her present before we leave?'

She did so, and they parted, not to meet again until it was time to leave for the airport.

On the flight to Chongqing they fell into conversation with passengers on the other side of the aisle who were headed in the same direction, and before long several more joined in. Olivia brought out the catalogue showing *The Water Dragon*, the boat that would carry them down the Yangtze. It was a gleaming white cruise-liner, but smaller than an ocean vessel would be. It was ninety metres long and took one hundred and seventy passengers.

'That sounds just right,' somebody observed. 'Big enough to be comfortable, small enough to be friendly.'

'Yes, it's going to be nice,' Olivia agreed. She showed the catalogue to Lang. 'What do you think?'

'I think the restaurant looks good,' he said prosaically. 'I hope we get there soon. I'm hungry.'

When they landed a coach was waiting to take them the few miles to the river. Lang had fallen into conversation with an elderly lady who could only walk slowly, and he held back to assist her onto the coach, then sat beside her. Olivia settled down next to a young man who knew all about the river and talked non-stop.

At last the coach drew up at the top of a steep bank, at the bottom of which was the river, and *The Water Dragon*.

Olivia was first off and found herself swept forward by the crowd. Looking back, she saw that Lang was still helping the old lady. He signalled for her to go on without him, so she headed down the steps to the boat and joined other passengers milling around the chief steward. He gave them a smiling welcome, and declared that he was always at their service.

'Now I am going to show you to your cabins,' he said. 'You will find them all clean and comfortable, but if any of you should want something of a higher standard we have two upgrades available. Follow me, please.'

Out of the corner of her eye Olivia saw Lang, still with the old lady, giving her his kindest smile. She waved and turned away to follow the steward.

The cabins were, as he'd said, clean and comfortable, but on the small and spare side. Olivia sat on her narrow bed, looking around at her neat, efficient surroundings, and felt there was something lacking. Wasting no more time, she went looking for the steward.

'Can I see the upgrades, please?'

'I'm afraid only one is left.'

It was a luxurious suite with a living room, bathroom and a bedroom furnished with a huge bed that would have taken three. From the corridor outside came the sound of footsteps approaching. Someone else was going to inspect the place and she had one second to decide.

'I'll take it,' she told the steward.

He too had heard the footsteps and moved fast, whipping out a notepad and writing down her details. By the time the door opened, the transaction was complete.

'It's taken,' he sang out.

The newcomers, a man and a woman, groaned noisily and glared at Olivia.

'Can't we come to some arrangement?' the man demanded of Olivia. He was an oafish individual, built like an overweight walrus.

'Sorry, it's mine,' she told him.

'Aw, c'mon. You're on your own. What difference can it make to you?' he demanded belligerently. 'Here.' He flashed a wad of notes. 'Be reasonable.'

'Forget it,' she said firmly.

'Let me show you out,' the steward urged.

The man glared but departed. As he left she heard him say to his companion, 'Damned if I know what a woman alone needs with a place like this.'

It was a good argument, she thought wryly. Just what did she need with a huge double bed? She should stop being stubborn, admit that her own cabin was adequate and give up this delightful palace, possibly even take the money. That was what a sensible woman would do.

But suddenly she couldn't be sensible any more.

Lang, having been shown to his cabin, was also regarding it with dismay. When he'd suggested joining Olivia on the cruise, this functional little room wasn't what he'd had in mind. He considered taking an upgrade, but how was he to explain this to her? She would immediately suspect his motives, and the fact that her suspicions would be correct merely added to his problems.

But at last, annoyed with himself for dithering, he approached the steward, only to discover that he was too late. Both upgrade suites were taken.

'Surely there must be something?' he pleaded with the steward.

But this achieved nothing. He was left cursing himself for slowness, and generally despairing.

'You too?' said a man's voice behind him.

Lang turned and saw a large, belligerent-looking man scowling in frustration.

'They shouldn't give those upgrades to just anybody,' he snapped. 'We went for the top one— nothing but the best for the missus and me—but it had already been taken by some silly woman who didn't need it.'

'Maybe she did need it,' Lang said.

'Nah, she was on her own, so why does she want to bother with a double bed? Hey, that's her over there in the green blouse— All right, all right.'

His wife was tugging his arm. He turned aside to squabble with her, leaving Lang in a daze.

Olivia was watching him across the distance, a slight smile on her face. He returned the smile, feeling delight grow and grow until it had stretched to every part of him. She began to move forward until she was standing in front of him, looking up, regarding him quizzically.

'I'm not sure what to say,' he told her.

'Don't tell me I've made you speechless?' she said, teasing and serious together.

'You do it often.'

The oaf had seen her and turned back to resume battle.

'Look, can't we talk…?' He fell silent, realising that neither of them was aware of him. They had eyes only for each other.

'Oh, well,' he mumbled at last. 'If it's like that.'

He let his wife drag him away.

Lang didn't speak, but he raised an enquiring eyebrow as though the question was too awesome to be spoken aloud.

Olivia nodded.

'Yes,' she said softly. 'It's like that.'

From somewhere came the sound of footsteps, calls, engines coming to life, and there was a soft lurch as the boat began its journey.

'Let's go and watch,' he said.

She nodded, glad of the suggestion. The time was coming, but not quite yet.

Up on deck they watched as the boat glided gently into the middle of the river and started its journey downstream between the tall hills on either side. After a while they went to the rear where a blazing-red sun was beginning to set, sliding slowly down the sky.

To Olivia's eyes that setting sun seemed to be

prophetic, marking the end of one thing and the beginning of another. Now she could no longer equivocate about her feelings for Lang, either to herself or to him. By seizing the chance of the upgrade, she'd given herself away, and she was filled with gladness.

No more pretence, no more hiding behind barriers that offered no real protection, no more denial that he had won her heart. She wanted to sing for joy.

'Isn't it wonderful?' she murmured.

He was standing behind her, his hands on her shoulders. 'Wonderful,' he said. 'And you know what would be even more wonderful?'

She leaned back. 'Tell me.'

He whispered softly in her ear. 'Supper.'

She jumped. 'What did you say?'

'I told you I was ravenous, and that was hours ago. They must be opening the restaurant about now.'

The joke was on her. She'd thought they were going to float away in misty romance, and all he cared for was his supper. But it wasn't really a delusion; the tenderness in Lang's face as he gazed down at her told her that.

'Let's go and eat before I fade to nothing,' he said.

'We'll do anything you want,' she vowed.

At that moment she would have promised him the earth.

The restaurant was a cheerful place with large

tables where six people could crowd, calling cheerfully across at each other. But in one corner it was different. Olivia and Lang sat at a table small enough for only themselves, speaking little, sometimes looking out of the window at the banks gliding past in the gathering darkness.

He really was hungry, and ate as though his last meal had come. She left him to it, content to sit here in a haze of happiness thinking no further ahead than the night.

'I meant to get that upgrade too,' he said after a while. 'But it took me too long to pluck up the nerve.'

'Nerve? I always thought of you as a brave man.'

'About some things. Not everything.'

He poured her some wine before adding, 'You've always kept me wondering and I—don't cope with that very well. In fact, I'm beginning to think I don't cope with anything very well.'

She smiled at him tenderly. 'Do I look worried?'

'I don't think anything worries you, Dragon Lady. You're the most cool, calm and collected person I know.'

'It's an act,' she said softly. 'I'm surprised you were fooled.'

'Sometimes I was. Sometimes I hoped— Well, at first I was afraid to ask for the upgrade in case you felt I was rushing you.' He gave her a teasing smile. 'After all, we've only known each less than two weeks.'

Less than two weeks? Had it really only been over a week? Yet a lifetime.

'So maybe *I'm* rushing you?' she mused.

He didn't reply in words, but he shook his head.

As the diners came to the end of the meal the steward announced that they might like to gather in the bar where entertainment would be provided. The others hurried out leaving Lang and Olivia together. The steward approached, meaning to remind them cheerfully that they were missing the fun, but the words died unspoken as he became aware of the silence that united them.

Realising that they would never hear him, he moved quietly away. Neither of them knew he'd been there.

CHAPTER EIGHT

ALONE now, Lang and Olivia drifted up to the top deck. Darkness had fallen completely and the brilliant moon overhead showed the stark outline of the river.

Olivia had read about the Yangzte River; it was nearly four-thousand miles long and the third-longest river in the world. But nothing had prepared her for the reality.

Used to English waterways, where the sides were either gently sloping or completely flat, she was stunned by the height of these banks that loomed up almost like sheer cliffs on either side.

'They seem to go up for ever,' she said, leaning back against Lang. 'And they blot out everything. It's like a separate world.'

'Do you mind that?' he murmured against her hair. 'Do you want to go back to the other world where everything's in the right place?'

'And always the same place every time,' she

supplied. 'Until it isn't the right place any more. No, I don't want to go back to that.'

She sighed and raised her arms up to the moon that seemed to glide in a narrow river between the high cliffs.

'This is the world I want!' she cried. 'The one where I belong—but I never knew it.'

Lang dropped his head and she felt his lips against her neck. Yes, this was what a part of her had always known would happen. She'd thought herself safe in the tight little box she'd constructed to protect herself from feelings. And all the time the truth had been waiting for her, ready to pounce out of the darkness, catch her off-guard and fill her with joy.

Slowly she turned in his arms and looked up into his face, which she could just see in the ghostly light. Then he lowered his head and she forgot everything as his mouth touched hers, filling her with a delight that transcended anything she'd known before. All her life had been a preparation for this moment.

Their first proper kiss in his family's home had been thrilling, but it had contained a hint of performance for an audience. Their embrace in the teahouse garden had been sweet, but still they had lacked total privacy, and it hadn't been quite perfect.

Now they were alone with the moon, the sky and the mountains, alone in the universe, and the truth that was flowering between them was for no other eyes.

His kiss was gentle, his lips moving softly over hers, awaiting her response, then growing more urgent as he sensed her eagerness. She answered him in kind, exploring to see how much she tempted him, then relaxing as the answer became gloriously plain.

He kissed her mouth for a long time before moving to her eyes, her cheeks, even her chin. He was smiling.

'What is it?' she whispered.

'You've got such a pretty chin. I've always thought so. I promised myself that one day I'd kiss it.'

She laughed softly and felt his lips move down her neck to the base of her throat. The sensation was so pleasurable that she gave a long sigh of satisfaction and wrapped her arms about him, drawing him as close as possible.

They held each other in silence for a long time, then he stepped back, took her by the hand and together they went below deck.

The door into the suite opened noiselessly, and Olivia locked it behind them without turning on the light. For now they needed only the moonlight that streamed in through the window just behind the bedhead.

This man wasn't like other men. Even in the bedroom he didn't rush things, but took her into his arms again, kissing her slowly, giving her time to be ready for the next step. When he deepened the kiss she was ready, opening up to him from deep inside, eager for what they would exchange.

Slowly he drew her down onto the bed. She felt his fingers moving on the buttons of her blouse until it fell open and he was helping her remove it. When her breasts were free, he touched them almost reverently before dropping his head to caress them with his lips.

Olivia sighed with satisfaction and laid her hand on his head, letting her fingers run gently through his hair, tightening them slightly as the pleasure mounted then arching against him, inviting him to explore her further. He did so, starting to pull at the rest of her clothes, but not fast enough for her. She undid her own buttons, then his, opening his shirt wide and running her hands over his chest.

She had to discern it by touch and everything she found delighted her—the smoothness, the slight swell of muscles, the faint awareness of his heart beating.

'Tell me what you're thinking,' he murmured.

'I want you,' she said simply.

'I've always wanted you—is this really happening?'

'Yes. We can have anything—everything.'

As though the words were a signal, he hurriedly removed the last of his clothes and she did the same. They had known each other such a little time, yet they were both moved by the thought that they had been kept apart too long. Later they might talk about this, try to analyse it, but now there was only the urgency of leaping barriers, closing the distance, becoming one.

She opened her arms and he fell into them like a man coming home, loving her body and celebrating it with his lips and his hands, teasing and inciting her into an ecstasy of anticipation. Her head was spinning, her flesh thrumming with desire until at last they were united in one powerful movement, and she was claiming him as urgently as he claimed her.

She wanted it to last for ever, and for a few glorious moments anything seemed possible, but then it ended suddenly in an explosion of light and force that consumed her then threw her back to earth, gasping, reaching out into the darkness, no longer sure where she was or what was happening.

'Olivia…' Lang's voice reached her from a thousand miles away.

'Where are you?' she cried.

'Open your eyes, my love. Look at me.'

She did so, and found his face close to her. Even in the darkness she could sense his profound joy, feel the smile on his lips as he pressed them against her cheek.

She lay there, breathing hard, trying to come to terms with what had happened to her. It was a loving beyond anything that she'd known in her life before, something that possessed her completely, but only because she was willing to be possessed.

'Don't go away,' she whispered, tightening her arms about him.

'I'm always here, if you want me.'

'I want you,' she said passionately. 'I want you. Hold me.'

He did so, keeping her against him while they both grew calmer. She was suffused by a sense of well-being such as she had never known before, as though everything in the world was right. She was where she was always meant to be, in the arms of the man who had been made for her, as she had been made for him. Of that she had not the slightest doubt.

'Do you remember what you said?' he asked softly. 'That we could have everything?'

'Wasn't I right?'

He shook his head. 'No, I've just found out that it isn't possible. Because, when you think you have everything, you discover that there's something more and you'll never reach the end. There will always be something more in you for me to find. And I will always want to find it.'

She nodded slowly. 'And I'll always want you to.'

He moved back carefully, looking down, trying to read her face in the moonlight. She smiled, and something in that smile seemed to reassure him, for he relaxed.

'I wondered how it would be,' he murmured. 'I knew we belonged together from the first moment we met.'

She raised an eyebrow and surveyed him with a touch of mischief.

'Really? You were very sure of yourself.'

'No, I was never that. You scared me. I wanted you so much that I was haunted by the fear of not winning you. I thought maybe there was another man, and when I found that there wasn't I couldn't believe my luck. I waited for you outside the school and pretended I was there as a doctor.

'I tried to be sensible. You'd have laughed if you could have seen my mental contortions. I didn't call you for several days because I was trying not to be too obvious, but you must have seen right through me.'

'Not quite,' she said with a memory of herself growing frustrated because he hadn't phoned.

'I did it all wrong. I left it so long to call you that the school term came to an end and I thought you might have gone.'

'So that's why you came and haunted the gate?'

'And I practically kidnapped you. Didn't you notice?'

'I can't really remember. I was too busy for distractions.'

He regarded her in dismay. 'Really?'

She just laughed. Let him wonder.

'I thought you might have left early,' he resumed, 'and I'd have lost you through my own carelessness. I nearly fainted with relief when I saw you coming out of the school. After that, I did everything to make sure of you—asking you home to dinner—'

'*Asking?*'

'Yes, I didn't give you much chance to refuse, did I?' He grinned. 'But how could I? You might really have refused, and I couldn't chance that.'

'Then you were quite right not to take any risks. And when you *asked* me to go to Xi'an, and joined me on this boat, you didn't take chances about that, either. I barely had time to catch my breath.'

'That was the idea. I thought I'd got it all sewn up. I was insufferably pleased with myself, so I suppose I was really asking for fate to sock me on the jaw.'

'This I have to hear. How did it do that?'

'I arrived to collect you and you'd gone, "for ever".'

'It was just an accident.'

'I didn't know that. I thought you'd had enough of me and decided to get out fast. You might have left the country and vanished into thin air. I didn't know how to contact you in England, and I couldn't ask the school until term started weeks later. I nearly went mad.'

'You could have texted my mobile phone.'

'Not if you'd turned it off and blocked my calls,'

he said glumly. 'Which you'd do if you were running away from me.'

She stared at him, astonishment at his vulnerability mingling with happiness that she affected him so strongly.

'You've really got a vivid imagination, haven't you?' she said.

'You arrived just in time to stop me going crazy.'

Light dawned. 'Is that why you slammed your hand on the taxi?'

'I had to do something. It was that or a heart attack. I'm not usually violent, it's just—I don't know—it mattered. And until then I hadn't faced how *much* it mattered.

'But I could tell you didn't like me getting so worked up, so after that I backed off, played it cool, so as not to alarm you.'

'I thought you were having regrets,' she whispered.

He shook his head and said in a slow, deliberate voice, 'If there is one thing I will never regret, it is you. If I live to be a hundred I shall still say that this was the supreme moment of my life. If you leave me tomorrow, I'll still remember this as the greatest joy I ever knew. I say that with all my heart and soul. No, don't speak.'

He laid his hand quickly over her lips, silencing what she would have said.

'Don't say anything now,' he urged. 'I don't

want you to be kind, or say what you think I want to hear. I'll wait gladly until your feelings prompt you to speak. Until then, silence is better.'

She could have said everything at that moment, gladdening his heart with a declaration to match his own. But instinct warned her that his reticence sprang from a deep need, and the kindest thing she could do for him was to respect that need.

So she merely enfolded him in her arms, drawing him close in an embrace that was comforting rather than passionate.

'It's all right,' she whispered. 'It's all right. I'm here.'

In a moment they were both asleep.

She awoke in the early hours to find him still lying across her in the same position. Everything about him spoke of blissful contentment.

Then he opened his eyes, looking at her. The same contentment was there, like a man who'd come home. It became a joyous, conspiratorial smile, the meaning of which they both understood. They had a shared secret.

Light was creeping in through the curtains over the window behind the bed. She pulled herself up in bed and drew the curtains back a little, careful in case they were passing another boat. But the river was empty. There was nobody to see her nakedness, so she moved up further. He joined her and they sat together at the window, watching a soft, misty dawn come up on the Yangtze, drifting slowly past.

It was like a new day in which the shapes were ill-defined, changing from moment to moment, but always beautiful, leading them on to more beauty and happiness.

Could you really start a new life like this? she wondered. Or was it nothing but a vague dream, too perfect to be true? And did she really want to know the answer just yet?

She slid down into the bed again, stretching luxuriously, and he joined her, laughing. Then he saw something on the side table that made him stare.

'Hey, what's this? Ming Zhi?' He took the little panda in his hand. 'You brought her with you?'

'I like to have her near as a reminder not to get carried away,' Olivia said.

He raised eyebrows. 'What happened last night?'

'I gave her time off.'

He set Ming Zhi down again and lay back, wrapping Olivia in his arms.

'If she's still off-duty, perhaps I should make the most of it.'

He didn't wait for her to answer, but covered her mouth forcefully and proceeded to 'make the most of it' in a way that left her no chance to argue even if she'd wanted to.

It was a riotous loving, filled with the sense of discovery that two people know when they have answered the first question and are eager to learn the others. This was an exploration, with more sense of adventure than tenderness, and when it was finished they were both gasping.

'I need my breakfast,' Lang said in a faint voice. He was lying flat on his back, holding her hand. 'Then I think I'll come back to bed.'

'Nonsense!' she declared in a hearty voice that made him wince. 'When the boat makes its first stop we're going to get out and do some sensible sight-seeing.'

'Not me. I'm staying here.'

'All right. You stay and I'll go. It'll give me a chance to get to know that very tall young man who came aboard in the same group as us.'

'You're a cruel woman. Help me up.'

They became conventional tourists, joining the crowds to see the sights, but always chiefly aware of each other. They were the first back on board, declaring themselves exhausted and badly in need of a siesta. Then they vanished for the rest of the afternoon.

'What shall I wear tonight?' she mused as they were dressing for dinner.

She held up the figure-hugging *cheongsam* and, to her surprise, he shook his head.

'I thought you liked it.'

'I do,' he said. 'When we're alone. But if you

think I want every other man in the place gawping at you…'

'Fine, I'll wear it.'

From this he could not budge her. The ensuing argument came close to being their first quarrel, but the knowledge that he was jealous was like heady wine, driving her a little crazy.

When she was dressed, he growled, 'Don't even look at anyone but me,' clamping his arm around her waist to make his point.

'I wasn't going to,' she assured him. 'Unless, of course, I get up onstage.'

'Why should you do that?'

'They're having a talent contest for the passengers. I thought I'd do a striptease.'

'Try that and I'll toss you over my shoulder and carry you off caveman-style.'

'Mmm, is that a promise?'

'Wait and see.'

The boat was equipped with a tiny nightclub, with a stage just big enough for modest entertainment. One by one people got up and sang out of tune, to the cheers of their friends.

'Hey!' A young man tapped Lang on the shoulder. 'There's a group of us going to sing a pop song. Want to join us?'

'Thank you, but no,' Lang said. 'I can't sing.'

'Neither can we, but it won't stop us. Aw, come on. Don't you know how to have a good time?'

'I am having a good time,' Lang said, polite but unmoved.

The young man became belligerent. He had a good-natured, if slightly oafish face, but had drunk rather too much.

'You don't look it to me. It's supposed to be a party. Come on.'

Lang made no reply but merely sat with an implacable smile on his face. At last the oaf gave up and moved away, but not before one parting shot to Olivia.

'I feel sorry for you, luv, know what I mean? A wimp, that's what he is.'

Olivia could have laughed out loud at such a total misreading of Lang. But she only looked the man in the eye, smiled knowingly and shook her head. He understood at once and backed off.

'More to him than meets the eye, eh?' he queried.

'Much, much more,' she said significantly.

'Ah, well, in that case...'

He took himself off.

Lang eyed her. 'Thank you, dragon lady, for coming to my defence.'

'Don't give me that. You don't need me or anyone defending you.'

'True, but it's nice to know that you don't consider me a wimp. Our vulgar friend can think what he likes.'

'Well, you know exactly what he's thinking.'

He grinned. 'Yes, thanks to you he believes I'm a cross between Casanova and Romeo.'

'He's not the only one. Look.'

Their tormentor had joined his fellows on the stage and was whispering to them urgently, pointing in Lang's direction.

'Oh, no!' Lang groaned. 'What have you done?'

'Given you a really impressive reputation.' She chuckled. 'You should be grateful to me.'

'Grateful? Let's get out of here.'

He hastily set down his glass, grabbed her hand and drew her away with more vigour than chivalry. By now the entire audience seemed to be in the know, and they were pursued by whistles of envy and appreciation.

Lang almost dragged her down the corridor and into their suite, where he pulled her into his arms and kissed her fiercely, both laughing and complaining together.

'Olivia, you wretch! I'll never be able to show my face again.'

'Nonsense, you'll be a hero.' She chuckled, kissing him between words.

'Come here!'

He drew her firmly down on the bed and lay on top of her, pinning her down, his eyes gleaming with enjoyment.

'Perhaps we should discuss this,' he said.

'Mmm, I'd like that. But you know what?'

'What?' he asked with misgiving.

'You're acting in exactly the kind of he-man style that they're imagining.'

'Oh, *hell*!'

He rolled off her but she immediately followed until she'd rolled on top of him, thanking her lucky stars that the bed was wide enough for this kind of frolicking.

'Now it's my turn to be the he-man,' she informed him.

'I didn't think it worked that way.'

'It does when I do it.'

He gave her his wickedest look. 'I'm at your mercy, dragon lady,' he said with relish.

'You'd better believe it.'

She began to work on his shirt buttons, opening them swiftly until she could run her hands over his chest. By the violent tremors that went through him she could tell that he loved it, but he made no move to do the same for her.

'Are you going to just lie there?' she demanded indignantly.

'What else can I do? I am but a mere wimp, awaiting orders.'

'Well,' she said, breathing hard, 'my orders are for you to go into action.'

'Right!'

One swift, forceful movement was enough to

demolish the front of her dress. Then she was on her back, having the rest of her clothes ripped away.

'To hear is to obey,' he murmured, tossing aside his own clothes and settling on top of her.

They fought it out, laughing, loving, challenging, bickering amiably, then doing it all again until they fell asleep in each other's arms, happy and exhausted.

It was a good night.

Now and then the boat stopped and everyone went ashore for an excursion to a temple, or to view one of the famous Three Gorges dams. Lang and Olivia joined these expeditions but they were always glad to get back on board.

In the privacy of their suite they could enjoy not merely love-making but talk. To both of them it was a special joy that their pleasure in each other was not confined to passion. Huddled close, they could explore hearts and minds in sleepy content.

Olivia found herself talking about her fractured life as she'd never done before, except with Norah.

'You said once that I was my mother's mother, and you were right. My parents are just like a couple of kids. It can seem charming, until you see all the people they've let down.'

'Mostly you,' Lang said tenderly.

'Yes, but there's a queue that stretches behind me—Tony, my mother's second husband, her step-children by that marriage, her child by Tony—my half-brother. He's about fourteen now and beginning to realise what she's like. He calls me sometimes for advice. I do my best, but I've never told him the worst she's capable of.'

She fell silent. At last Lang said, 'Tell me, if you can.'

'I was about twelve. It was December and I was getting all excited about Christmas. I was staying with Norah, but Dad and I were going to Paris together. I got ready, everything packed, and waited for him. When he was late I went outside and sat on the wall, looking for his car to appear at the end of the road, but he didn't come.

'Norah called him, but all she got was the answer machine. We tried his mobile phone but it was switched off. I suppose I knew in my heart that he wasn't coming, but I wouldn't face it. At last, hours later, he called to see if I was having a great time with my mother. I said, "But I'm supposed to be with you." Then it all came out about Evadne, his new girlfriend. She'd begged him to take her to Paris instead of me, and been very persuasive, so he'd left a message on my mother's phone to say she'd have to have me. He seemed terribly surprised that she hadn't turned up.'

Lang swore violently and rolled over away from her, his hands over his face. Then he rolled back and took her in his arms. 'I will kill him,' he muttered over and over. 'Don't ever let me meet your father or I will kill him. Hold onto me—hold me.'

It felt so good to embrace him, to bury her head against his shoulder and blot out everything else, as though he had it in his power to put the world right.

'So you had to spend Christmas with your mother?' he said at last.

'Oh, no, she didn't get his message until she'd left to spend Christmas with her new boyfriend—at least, she said she didn't. So neither of them came for me and I spent Christmas with Norah.'

He seized her again and this time it was he who hid his face in her shoulder, as though her pain was unbearable to him.

'How did you survive?' he murmured.

'Part of me didn't. I learned not to trust people, especially when they talked about their feelings. I thought Andy was different, but he was just the same.'

'Was he the only one?'

'You mean, have I had other boyfriends? Oh, yes. I dipped my toe in the water a few times, but only my toe. I always got cautious before I went too far. It doesn't take much to turn me back into that little girl sitting on the wall, watching for someone who never appeared. In my heart—' she shuddered '—I always know that's going to happen.'

'Never,' he said violently. 'Never, do you hear

me? I'm yours for life. Or at least for as long as you want me. No, don't answer.' He laid a swift hand over her lips. 'You can't promise life, not yet. I know that. But I'll be patient. Just remember that I'm always here.'

'Always,' she murmured longingly.

Always? queried the voice in her head. If only.

But held in his arms she could believe in anything, and she clung to him in desperate hope.

CHAPTER NINE

SOMETIMES he teased her about her preference for good sense.

'If I really believed in good sense I'd never have come anywhere near you,' she said indignantly.

'You're trying to reform me. I realised that ages ago.'

'I'm not having much luck, am I? Sometimes I doubt myself. You know those marvellous roofs you see on old buildings, the ones that curve up at the corners? I read that it dates back to a Buddhist belief about evil residing in straight lines, so they should be avoided if possible.

'But another book talked about architecture and rainfall, and how the curve was precisely calculated to give maximum benefit to the building. I hated that. I like the Buddhist interpretation much better.'

Lang's response was to lift Ming Zhi from beside the bed, and address Olivia severely.

'You're slipping. That kind of sentimentality isn't what I engaged you for.'

They laughed, cocooned in the safe refuge they offered each other. Their laughter ended in passion.

Another time Olivia recalled the night she'd met the Langs, and had seen him in the context of both his families.

'They say a picture's worth a thousand words,' she murmured. 'You told me how out of place you felt with your English family, but it only became real when I saw the photograph of you all together. You looked exactly like them, but I could still see you were a fish out of water.'

'That's putting it mildly,' he said. 'But, looking back, I feel sorry for them.'

'Sorry for *them*?'

'I know I was difficult. In some ways I'm not a very nice character. You said I looked like a misfit with them, and that was how I felt. But in my mind it was they who were the misfits, and I was the one who'd got it right, which isn't very amiable in a fifteen-year-old boy.'

'No, but it *is* very typical of fifteen-year-old boys,' she riposted. 'So you were a grumpy adolescent—join the club.'

'That's one way of looking at it,' he said with a self-mocking smile. 'The other way is that I'm stubborn, inflexible and set on my own way. Once I want something I won't give up. Everyone else becomes the victim.' He tightened his arms around her. 'As you have cause to know.'

'Mmm, I'm not complaining.'

'Good, because I've got you and I'm going to keep you.'

'Do I get a say about that?' she teased.

'Nope, you have nothing to say about it. You belong to me, understand?'

She couldn't resist saying, 'You mean, like Jaio belonged to the Emperor Qin?'

'No way. She escaped. You'll never escape me.'

'What, no gallant warrior to ride to my rescue?'

'The man who could take you away from me hasn't been born.'

'What happened to being patient and letting me decide in my own time?'

'That was then. This is now.'

She chuckled. 'That's all right, then. I'll forgive you if you're a bit overbearing, or even a lot overbearing. Which you most definitely will be. Anything else you want to warn me about?'

He kissed her, adding thoughtfully, 'Plenty. Take my career—I want to be the best. I have to be the best, whatever it means.'

'This job that's coming up?'

'Yes. I've set my heart on it.'

'But you've only been here three years. Aren't you rushing it?'

'I know the other likely candidates and they

don't worry me. Besides, the present incumbent hasn't retired yet, and probably won't for another year. I'll be patient until then.'

The unconscious arrogance of that 'I'll be patient' told her he was speaking the truth about himself. He was still the man who'd won her heart, gentle, charming, humorous. But she was learning that his apparent diffidence masked a confidence and determination so implacable that he himself was made uneasy by it. He flinched from it, tried to disguise it, but it was the unalterable truth.

As long as he was determined to keep her with him, she was happy to live with it.

Life wasn't entirely smooth. On the night after the talent contest there was a dance for the passengers. Wanting to dazzle him, Olivia did herself up to the nines, including wearing one of the dresses she'd bought at the last minute before their departure. It was another *cheongsam*, this time in black satin embroidered with silver, and even more alluring than the last, which made Lang eye her wryly.

'You wouldn't be trying to make me jealous by any chance, would you?' he murmured.

'Think I couldn't?'

'We'll have to see.'

She soon realised her mistake. The events of the night before had given Lang a reputation guaranteed to fascinate everyone there. The girls lined up to dance with him. Their men lined up to prevent them. When they couldn't do that they danced with Olivia instead, hoping to aggravate him.

But they had mistaken their man, as Olivia could have told them. Lang seemed oblivious to everything except the succession of women in his arms, which was obviously the clever way to react, even if she did find it personally aggravating.

Watching him from a slight distance, she could admire his graceful, athletic movements. With her imagination heightened to fever pitch she mentally undressed him, feeling those same movements against her, not dancing but loving her powerfully. Her own dancing became more erotic, something she couldn't have controlled if she'd tried. And she wasn't trying.

Just once he looked directly at her and their gazes locked in the perfect comprehension that so often united them. He was doing the same as she, teasing and enticing until they were ready to haul each other off the floor and into bed. Excitement streamed through her, making every nerve tingle with anticipatory pleasure. If only he would make his move soon.

Meaning to urge him along, she allowed herself a little extra wiggle. The result was all she hoped. Lang bid his partner a hasty goodbye, made it across the floor at top speed and hoisted her into his arms.

'You've gone too far,' he said firmly.

'I hope so. Better too far than not far enough,' she said, reminding him of his own words in the zoo.

By this time they were halfway down the corridor. When they reached the door of their suite, Olivia opened it and Lang kicked it shut behind them. When he tossed her onto the bed she reached up to undo the *cheongsam*.

'No,' he said, removing her hands. 'That's my job.'

'Then get on with it,' she ordered him, edgy with frustration.

He needed no further urging. By the time he'd finished the dress was in tatters on the floor, followed by her underwear. When they were both naked he drew back, breathing heavily, kneeling beside her on the bed. His arousal was hard, almost violent, yet he had the control to stop there, looking down at her with a glint in his eyes that was new.

'You promised to throw me over your shoulder,' she reproached him. 'What happened?'

'I'm a gentleman,' he said in a rasping breath.

'Nah, you're a coward. If you'd kept me waiting any longer, I'd have thrown you over *my* shoulder.'

'That's because you're no lady.' He lay down beside her until his lips were against her ear. 'I watched you dancing all night, and believe me you are *no* lady.'

She gave a sigh of deep contentment. 'I'm glad you realise that.'

His hands were touching her, but differently from before. The movements were fiercer, more purposeful, as though something that had been holding him back had disappeared, releasing him. Now he loved her with a driving urgency, with power, as well as skill, conquering and taking where once he would have waited for her to give.

At the end she was exhausted but triumphant. She'd always suspected that this forceful arrogance was one of the mysteries that lay behind his mild manners, and there was deep satisfaction in having tempted it out at last.

'Are you all right?' he asked quietly. 'I hadn't meant to be quite so—adventurous.'

The other Lang was back, the quiet one with perfect manners. But she'd seen beyond him now, and she liked what she'd discovered.

'Perhaps we should try it that way a few more times,' she said with a contented smile. 'I rather enjoy not being a lady.'

He laughed. 'Were you actually trying to make me jealous tonight?'

'I suppose I was,' she said in a pensive voice. 'But you did quite a bit yourself.'

'You couldn't expect me to ignore your challenge.'

'But it's not fair. I have so much more to be jealous of than you.'

'You think I'm not jealous of Andy?'

'Who? Oh, him. You shouldn't be. You know all

about him, and I know nothing about your love life—unless you expect me to believe you've lived like a monk.'

She thought he paused a little before saying lightly, 'Certainly not. I told you about Becky Renton—perhaps not everything, but—'

'Spare me the details of what happened behind the bicycle sheds at school. I don't even want to know about the girls you took to the Dancing Dragon.'

'I explained.'

'Yes, I remember your explanation—very carefully edited, which was probably wise of you.'

He regarded her wryly. 'Do you want chapter and verse?'

Warning bells went off in her mind. This was straying into dangerous territory.

He was lying on his back with Olivia on her stomach beside him with a clear view of his face and its suddenly withdrawn look. Two instincts warred within her. She was curious about his life yet reluctant to sound like a jealous nag.

Let it go, she thought. She'd just had the clearest demonstration of what she was to him.

'Of course I don't want chapter and verse,' she said firmly. 'I know you must have played the field. It would worry me more if you hadn't.'

She put an arm about his neck and lay over him, her face against his shoulder, feeling him curve his arm to hold her more closely.

'There is one I'd like to tell you about,' he said at last. 'So that there are no secrets between us.'

'All right. Go on.' Now the moment was here she only wanted to back away, but it was too late.

'I was like you for a long time,' he said. 'I never let myself get too far into a relationship. I knew where I was heading and I didn't want anything to get in the way. But a few months before I left England I fell in love with a girl called Natalie.

'Everything seemed perfect. We planned to get married and come to China together. But one day I found her looking through advertisements for houses, hoping to buy one for us to live in. When I reminded her about China, she laughed and said, "Isn't it time to be realistic?"

'I understood then that she'd never really meant to come with me. She'd thought of it as nonsense that I'd get over. When she realised that I was serious, she became angry. She forced me to choose between her and China, and so—' He paused. 'And so we said goodbye.'

Olivia had raised herself so that she could look down at him. He turned his head to look at her, and now she wished she could read what was in his eyes.

'Did you ever regret letting her go?' She had to ask, although she feared the answer.

'She'd been deceiving me all that time, keeping a distance between us when I'd thought we were so close. Our minds would always have been apart.'

'But if you loved her—it's not just minds, is it?'

He glanced at her naked body leaning over him, the beautiful breasts hanging down so that the nipples touched him, and he caressed them gently.

'No,' he said softly, 'it's not just minds. But you and I have everything—minds, as well as hearts and bodies. Have you not felt that?'

'Yes, from the first moment.'

'You would never hide your thoughts from me, or I from you. I didn't tell you about Natalie before because I was afraid you would misunderstand and think it had more importance than it has.'

'And how much does it have?'

'Some, for a while. But now none at all. She married someone else last year, and I'm glad for her. If we'd married it would have been a disaster, because we would each have wanted something the other could never give. There's nothing there to make you jealous. The wisest thing I ever did was to wait for you.'

She lay down against him, reassured and content. It wasn't until the last moment that it occurred to her that there was something ominous in the story, but before she could think of it she was asleep.

Only one person was welcome in their secret world, and that was Norah.

The boat had a computer link-up and Olivia had brought her laptop. Now they both enjoyed going online to her. She and Lang would embark on a chat as though taking up where they'd left off only a few minutes before. Norah liked him as she had never liked Andy, Olivia realised.

He talked about the Yangtze, describing the view from the deck until her eyes shone.

'Oh, that must have been so marvellous!' she exclaimed. 'What a sight!'

'Perhaps you'll see it yourself one day,' he suggested.

'That would be lovely, but I'm old now. I don't think there are any long journeys for me.'

'Who knows what the future holds?' Lang said mysteriously.

Listening to this, Olivia wondered if she was reading too much into a few words, but they seemed to lead in only one direction. If she and Lang were to choose a life together, she would have to move permanently to China. His life here was too settled to allow any doubt.

For just a little longer they could live in this private universe where the real world was set at a distance. But soon the practical decisions would have to be made.

They said goodnight and hung up. Lang was regarding her with a question in his eyes.

'Something troubling you?'

'I was just wondering about Norah. She's very old, and when you talk of her coming here…'

'She's not too old for China. Old people get treated very well here, better than in many other countries.'

'Yes, I know, but that long air-journey.'

'Can be made a lot more comfortable with an upgrade.' He gave her a conspiratorial smile, reminding her that the word had a special significance for them. 'We just buy her a ticket in business class, where she can travel in comfort, stretch out and go to sleep. I think she'd like it here.'

'Lang, what are you saying?'

'I'm just looking ahead, down many different roads, but they all lead to you, my love. Let it happen as it will.'

Yes, she thought, that was the way. Fate, something she'd never believed in before, but which now seemed the only way.

Yet the flight arrangements he'd mentioned showed that he'd been thinking about this in detail, planning for the day.

He partially explained the mystery as they lay together later.

'It comes from belonging to two different cultures,' he said sleepily. 'One side of me believes in fate and destiny, good luck, bad luck, being touched by another world we can't control. The other side makes graphs and looks up flight timetables.'

'Which side of you is which?'

'They're mixed up. Both cultures have both aspects, but they speak with different accents.

Sometimes I tell myself how completely I belong here. I love my Chinese family.'

'And they love you dearly too. Biyu talked of you being "a little bit English" as though that bit doesn't matter at all next to your Chinese quarter. It must be wonderful to be so completely accepted.'

A slight shadow came over Lang's face.

'What is it?' Olivia asked. 'Have I said something wrong?'

'No, it's just that you speak of them accepting me.'

'But they do, that's obvious.'

'I know it looks like that, and I'm probably imagining that the acceptance isn't complete. I simply have this feeling that they're holding back just a little.'

'But why?'

'I don't know. All I can tell you is that I feel they're waiting for me to do something, or say something. But I don't know what it is.'

'I think you're wrong. They're not holding back at all. They're so proud of you, and they're especially proud that you came here and chose them. Biyu did this.' She tapped her breast. 'And she said, "In here, he is one of us".'

'She actually said that?' There was something touchingly boyish in his eagerness.

'She actually said that. So doesn't that prove you're accepted?'

'Maybe, but I don't think even they know that something doesn't fit.'

'Then you have to be patient,' Olivia said. 'It'll happen naturally, and you'll all know by instinct.'

'I didn't think you believed in trusting your instinct.'

'But it's not *my* instinct we're talking about.'

'Perhaps it is. I think that whatever we seem to be talking about we're also finding out about each other—and about ourselves.'

'Yes, it's alarming when you start to discover that you're not the person you thought you were,' she agreed.

'What have you learned about yourself?' he murmured, his mouth close to hers.

'Things that alarm me. Things that I'm not sure I want to learn.'

'Tell me about them.'

'I'm just not the person I thought I was—but, if I'm not, then who am I?'

'Does it matter?'

'Of course it matters. What a question!'

'I'm serious. Why do you have to know who you are? It's enough that you *are*. And, besides, I know you. You're a dragon lady—wild, brave, inventive, everything that's powerful and good.'

'To you, yes. But that would mean putting myself entirely in your hands.'

'Don't you trust me that much?'

'It's not that, it's just—I don't know.'

'Believe me, I know what it's like to put yourself in the hands of the woman you love and to realise that, if she understands you, it doesn't matter whether you understand yourself because she's wiser than you are.'

He might have been talking about Natalie, but the warmth in his eyes told her what he really meant.

'Perhaps you should be careful,' she whispered. 'Who knows if I can really be trusted that much?'

'I do,' he said at once. 'I'd trust you with my life, with my heart, soul and all my future.'

'But we've known each other such a little time.'

'We've known each other for over two-thousand years,' he said. 'Ever since the moment I caught a glimpse of your face and knew that I'd gladly give up everything else in my life in order to be with you.'

'Is that you talking?' she asked in wonder. 'Or Renshu?'

'Ah!' he said with satisfaction. 'I said you understood me. Yes, I'm Renshu, and so is every man who's ever loved as much as I do. And I know one thing—I can't be without you. You must stay with me for ever or my life will be nothing.

'I know you can't abandon Norah, but I don't ask you to. She has been your mother, and from now on she will be mine too. She'll be happy in China, I'll make sure of that. Don't you think I can?'

'I think you can do anything you set your mind to,' she said in wonder.

'Does that mean yes?'

'Yes, yes, *yes*!'

Flinging her arms about him, she hugged him with wild joy and he hugged her back powerfully. When they drew back to behold each other's faces she saw that his was full of mischief.

'I was so afraid you'd refuse me,' he said meekly.

'Liar, liar! You never thought that for a moment,' she cried, thumping him. 'You're the most conceited devil that ever lived.'

'Only because you make me conceited,' he defended himself, laughing. 'If you love me, how can I not have a good opinion of myself? I merely bow to the dragon lady's superior good sense. Ow! That hurt!' He rubbed his thigh where she'd landed a lucky slap.

'I never said I loved you,' she riposted. 'I'm marrying you out of pity. No— Ah, wait!' Her laughter died as something occurred to her. 'You never actually mentioned marriage, did you?'

'I didn't think it needed mentioning. It has to be marriage. Of course, I'd really prefer to keep you as a concubine— No, no, I give in!' He fended off a renewed attack, securing her arms and keeping her close for safety. 'You don't think Tao and Biyu and the others would let me deprive them of a wedding, do you?'

'Shall we go back to Beijing and tell everyone?'

'Not just yet. Let's go off on our own for a while. You once mentioned Shanghai? Let's go there. But, in the meantime, let's dress for dinner. Put on your glad rags because you're going to enjoy tonight.'

CHAPTER TEN

As THEY were having dinner he explained what he'd meant. 'After this we'll go back to the little theatre,' he said.

'Not another talent contest, please!'

'No, they're doing a play with music. It's based on a fable that goes back centuries, and it's known as the Chinese *Romeo and Juliet*.'

'Star-crossed lovers?'

'That's right. He was poor, her family was rich. When they couldn't marry, he died of a broken heart, but she went to his tomb and— Well, wait and see.'

When dinner was over they slipped into place, securing a table near the stage. Gradually the lights went down and plaintive music filled the air. Zhu Yingtai, a beautiful young girl, appeared with her family, pleading with them for the right to study. They were shocked at this unladylike behaviour, but finally let her go to college disguised as a man. She sang of her joy:

'Other women dream of husbands,
But I do not seek a husband.
I choose freedom.'

As the scene changed Lang whispered provocatively to Olivia, 'She's looking forward to a life of learning and independence, with no male complications. I know you'll approve.'

She smiled. It seemed such a long time since she'd been that woman, and the man who'd released her from her cage was sitting so close that she could feel his warmth mingling with another kind of warmth that was part memory, part anticipation.

In the next scene Zhu Yingtai, now dressed as a man, met Liang Shanbo and they became fellow students. They grew close, singing about their deep friendship.

'Our hearts beat together.
All is understood between us.'

'And yet he doesn't suspect that she's a woman?' Olivia mused.

'Perhaps friendship is also part of love,' Lang murmured. 'If they'd been able to marry, the fact that they could confide in each other might have sustained them through the years, making them strong while other couples fell apart.'

His face was very close to hers, his eyes glowing

with a message he knew she could understand without words. She nodded slowly.

At last Zhu Yingtai revealed her true identity and they declared their love, but it was in vain. Liang Shanbo was poor. Her parents betrothed her to a rich man.

He sang a plaintive ballad, full of heartbreak, saying that his life was nothing without his beloved. Then he lay down and quietly died.

The day of Zhu Yingtai's wedding dawned. She too sang, longing for death to reunite her with the man she loved. On the way to the ceremony she stopped beside her lover's tomb, crying out her longing for them to be together.

Olivia held her breath. For some reason what would happen next mattered to her.

The music swelled. The tomb doors opened. Zhu Yingtai threw up her arms in ecstatic gratitude and walked triumphantly inside.

The lights dimmed, except for one brilliant beam over the tomb. From somewhere overhead a hologram was projected into the light, and two large butterflies came into view. They hovered for a moment before flying off together into the darkness.

These were the souls of the lovers, now united for ever. The audience gasped, then applauded ecstatically. The lights came up and Olivia hastily dried her eyes.

All about them people were exclaiming with appreciation. Lang and Olivia quietly slipped away and went up on deck.

'Did I understand the end properly?' she asked as they strolled hand in hand. 'The butterflies were the lovers, and now they'll always be together?'

'That's right.'

She stopped and looked up at the moon. No full moon tonight, but a crescent hanging in the sky. Lang followed her gaze.

'According to Meihui,' he said, 'the two butterflies didn't only signify reunion in death, but eternal fidelity in life also. She said there were so many different stage versions all over China that one or other was always being performed. When I came here, almost the first thing I did was to find a performance, to see if it spoke to me in her voice, and it did. I was so glad it was on here tonight, so that I could show it to you.'

'Butterflies,' she mused. 'Flying away together for eternity. What a lovely thought!'

'Eternity,' he echoed. 'That's what I want with you, if it's what you want.'

'It's all I shall ever want,' she told him passionately.

'Then we have everything. Let's go inside.'

'We can go on travelling for another couple of weeks,' Lang said next morning. 'And then it'll be back to Beijing to plan the wedding.'

'And that's going to take a lot of planning,' Olivia mused.

'Nonsense, we just give Biyu the date and leave everything to her. In fact, why don't we just let her choose the date?'

'Good idea. She'll be better at planning it than I will.'

Biyu thought so too. In a feverish telephone call, she tried to make them return at once and plunge into arrangements. It took all Lang's strength to resist, and when he hung up Olivia had to take drastic steps to restore his energy. That distracted them so long that they got behind with their packing and nearly weren't ready when the boat docked at Yichang.

From there they took a plane to Shangai on the coast. During the flight, they planned out the rest of their trip.

'We could go to Chengdu and see the panda sanctuary,' he said. 'I've got some more relatives up there, and I'd like them to meet you. But let's enjoy Shanghai first.'

It was a revelation, an ultra-modern, bustling city where almost every inch seemed to be neon-lit. On the first night they took a boat down the river, gazing up at the skyscrapers adorned with multi-coloured lights. Then they escaped to their hotel room on the thirty-fifth floor and watched from the window.

'I'm dizzy being up so high,' she murmured, leaning back against him.

'I'm dizzy too,' he whispered against her neck. 'But it's not from the height.'

She chuckled but didn't move, even when he drew his lips across the skin below her ear, although it sent delicious tremors through her.

'Come to bed,' he urged.

'Can't you just let a girl enjoy the view?'

'No,' he said firmly, sweeping her up and carrying her to the huge bed, where she forgot all about skyscrapers and neon lights.

They slept late, rose late and sauntered out, meaning to do some serious educational sightseeing. They ended up in a theatre where motorbike riders diced with death, crossing each other's path within inches at high speed.

'Well, I've learned something,' she remarked as they walked slowly back to the hotel. 'I've learned never to get on a motorbike.'

They had the elevator to themselves and kissed all the way to the thirty-fifth floor, their minds running ahead to the pleasures to come.

But as they reached their room Lang's mobile phone began to buzz. Groaning, he answered, and Olivia saw him grow instantly alert. The next moment he swung away from her, as though she had no part of what was happening, and went to stand by the window.

He was talking too rapidly for her to follow, and his whole body was alive with excitement. When he hung up, he looked as though he was lit from within.

'That's it!' he cried. 'I knew it must happen some time.'

He hurled himself on the bed and lay back with his hands behind his head, the picture of triumph. Then he saw her regarding him, puzzled, and opened his arms to her. She went into them and nearly had the breath squeezed out of her.

'What's happened?' she gasped, laughing.

'That vacancy for a consultant has come up at the hospital!' he cried exultantly. 'It's a brilliant opportunity. Just what I've been waiting for.'

'That's wonderful. Who called you?'

'Another doctor, a friend who knows how badly I want this. He's put my name forward, and he called to tell me when the interviews start.'

'So we have to go back now,' she said, trying not to sound too disappointed.

'No, nothing's going to happen until next week. We can have another couple of days. And then...' He sighed. 'Back to the real world.'

'But the real world is going to be wonderful,' she reminded him. 'You're going to be a great consultant, and in a few years you'll be in charge of the whole hospital.'

'I hope so. If you only knew how much I hope so. I want it so much it scares me.'

That night was different. They made love and slept close as always, but when Olivia awoke in the small hours she saw him standing at the window looking out, so preoccupied that he never once looked back at the bed.

She wondered where he was now, inside his mind, and concluded that wherever it was she wasn't there with him. It was the first shadow on their relationship, only a tiny one, but perceptible.

Next day he seemed preoccupied over breakfast, and she said little, understanding that he would wish to mull over the situation that was opening up to him. They went out on a brief shopping-expedition, but over lunch he suddenly left her alone and was away for nearly an hour. Returning, he apologised profusely, but didn't say where he'd been. Sadly, she realised that part of him was already returning to 'the real world', where she seemed to live on the margins.

Or did she live anywhere at all? Had she, in the end, been nothing but a holiday romance? Lang had spoken of marriage and eternity, but that was before he'd been offered the chance of the thing he admitted he wanted more than anything in the world.

Suddenly she was in darkness, stumbling about an alien universe. She had survived Andy's betrayal. She knew she wouldn't survive Lang's.

But the moment of doubt passed, and that

evening her fears were eased when Lang suggested talking to Norah.

In a moment they were online, and there was Norah's face, beaming at them.

'Hello, darling! And, Lang—is that you I see?'

'Hello, Norah,' he said, seating himself on the bed next to Olivia, before the little camera. 'How are you?'

'Better than ever since my gifts arrived. Look.'

She held up the tiny figurine of a terracotta warrior in one hand, and a book in the other.

'The postman delivered them this morning,' she bubbled. 'It was so kind of you.'

He told her about Biyu and the wedding plans.

'As soon as we've set the date we'll arrange your flight out here,' he told her.

For a moment Olivia thought a faint shadow crossed Norah's face, but it was gone too quickly for her to be sure. It might have been a trick of the camera.

'What kind of a wedding are you going to have?' Norah wanted to know.

Lang talked at length, describing in detail what would probably happen and the part he expected her to play in it. She giggled and called him a cheeky young devil, which seemed to please him.

'Hey, can I get a word in edgeways?' Olivia protested. 'How about saying something about my new dress?'

'It's very pretty, dear.'

'I chose it,' Lang put in.

'Of course you did. Olivia's dress sense was always a little wayward.'

'Oi!' Olivia cried.

'Well, it's true, darling. But Lang has wonderful taste. You should always listen to him.'

'I'll remind her of that,' Lang said gravely.

'Oi!' Olivia said again, nudging him in the ribs with her elbow. He gave an exaggerated wince, which made Norah laugh more than ever.

'I'm so glad you're having a wonderful time,' she said. 'You look ever so much better. I was becoming afraid for you, but not any more.'

'Don't be afraid for her,' Lang said, suddenly serious. He slipped his arm around Olivia in such a way that Norah could see it.

'I never will again,' she said. 'Darling, you be good to him. He's one in a million.'

'I know,' Olivia replied, gazing back at the old woman with love. Norah beamed back, their understanding as perfect as ever.

'Now I've got some marvellous news to tell you,' Lang said.

'More marvellous news? As well as your marriage? Tell, tell.'

'I've had a call from—'

He stopped as a terrible change came over Norah. Her smile faded abruptly and she gave a choking sound. Aghast, they watched as she clutched her throat and heaved in distress.

'Norah!' Olivia cried, reaching out frantically to the screen. But Norah was five thousand miles away. 'Oh, heavens, what's happening to her?'

'I think she's having a heart attack,' Lang said.

'A heart attack?' Olivia echoed in horror. 'Oh, no, it can't be!'

'I'm afraid it is,' he said tersely, not taking his eyes from the screen. 'Norah—can you hear me?'

Norah couldn't speak, but she managed to nod.

'Don't fight it,' Lang told her. 'Try to take deep, slow breaths until the ambulance reaches you.'

Olivia was dialling her mobile phone.

'I'm calling her neighbour in the apartment downstairs,' she said. 'Hello, Jack, it's Olivia. Norah's having a heart attack—can you—? Norah, Jack says he's on his way.'

'Can he get in?' Lang asked.

'Yes, they've each got a key to the other's place so that they can keep an eye on each other. There he is.'

They could see Jack on the screen now, an elderly man but still full of vigour. He reached for Norah's phone, dialling for the ambulance.

'It's on its way,' he said at last to Olivia.

'Thank you,' she wept.

By now Norah was lying back on the pillow, not moving. They saw Jack try to rouse her, but she lay terrifyingly still.

'She's passed out,' Jack said desperately. *'What can I do?'*

'Don't panic,' Lang said firmly. 'I'm a doctor, do as I say. Place two fingers against her throat to check for a pulse.'

Jack did so, but wailed, 'I can't feel anything, and she's stopped breathing. Oh, dear God, she's dead!'

'No!' Olivia screamed.

'Don't panic, either of you,' Lang said sternly. 'She isn't dead, but she's had a cardiac arrest. Jack, we've got to get her heart started again. First raise her legs about eighteen inches, to help blood flow back to the heart.'

They both watched as Jack put a couple of pillows under Norah's feet, then looked back at the screen for further instructions.

'Place the palm of your hand flat on her chest just over the lower part of her breast bone,' Lang continued. 'Then press down in a pumping motion. Use the other hand, as well, to give extra power— that's it! Excellent.'

'But is it working?' Olivia whispered.

'Don't disturb him,' Lang advised.

As they watched, Norah made a slight movement. Jack gave a yell of triumph.

'The medics should be here soon,' he said. 'I left the main door open so that they could— Here they are.'

Two ambulance crew burst in, armed with equipment, confidently taking over. One of them asked Jack what he'd done, then nodded in approval.

'Well done,' he said. 'She was lucky to have you.'

As they moved Norah onto the stretcher, Jack addressed the screen.

'I'm going to the hospital with her,' he said. 'I'll call you when I know something.'

'Give her my love,' Olivia begged. 'Tell her I'll be there soon. And, Jack, thank you for everything.'

'It's not me you should thank, it's him,' he said gruffly, and the screen went dead.

'He's right,' she whispered. 'If she lives, you did it.'

'Of course she will live,' Lang insisted.

'I shouldn't have left her. She's old and frail. I've stayed away too long.'

'But she wanted you to. Every time I've seen her she's been encouraging you, smiling.'

'Yes, because she's sweet and generous. She must have smiled on purpose to make me think she was all right. She was thinking of me, but I should have been thinking of her.'

'Olivia, my darling, stop blaming yourself. You're right, she is generous. She knew that you needed your freedom and she gave it to you. Accept her generosity.'

'I know you're right, but—'

She could say no more. Grief overwhelmed her and she sobbed helplessly. Lang's arms went around her, holding her close, offering her all the comfort in his power.

Many times in the past he'd held her with passion, letting her know that she could bring his body alive, as he could hers. But now there was only strength and tenderness, giving without taking, all the warmth and compassion of his nature offered in her service.

She stopped weeping at last, because the strength had drained out of her. Normally so decisive, she now found herself floundering.

'Start your packing,' he told her gently, 'and I'll call the airport.'

An hour later they were on their way. Lang had found a flight to London for her, and one to Beijing for himself. When she had checked in, they sat in silence, holding hands, trying to come to terms with what had happened. One moment their joyous life had seemed set to last for ever. The next, without warning, it was all over. The speed with which light had turned to darkness left her reeling.

And yet, what had I expected? she asked herself. *We were always fooling ourselves about bringing Norah to China. I have to go to England and his life is here.*

How bitter was the irony! The woman who'd

been so sure she could command her own fate had been swept away by a tide of love whose strength she was only beginning to appreciate now that it was slipping away from her.

'I've got something for you,' Lang said. 'I bought it to give you as a symbol of our coming marriage.'

'Oh, no,' she begged. 'Don't say that. I can't bear it. How can we ever marry?'

'I don't know,' he said sombrely. 'I only know that somehow we must. Don't you feel that too?'

'Yes. Yes, I do. But how can we?'

'I had hoped that we might make our home in China and Norah could come here and live with us. I still hope for that. She will recover in time, and all will be well. We have only to be patient.'

She looked at him with desperate eyes, longing to believe that it could be that easy, but she was full of fear.

'We must never give up hope,' Lang persisted. 'Don't you know that whatever happens some day, somehow, we must be together?'

'I want to think so, but how can we? I don't know how long I'll be gone, perhaps always.'

'However long it is,' he said, taking her hands between his, 'it will happen at last. There will be nobody else for me. So in the end we must find each other again, because otherwise I shall spend all my life alone. Now I've known you, there could never be anyone else.'

'You make it sound so simple,' she said huskily.

'No, I make it sound possible, because it is. That's why I want you to take this.'

He drew out a small box and placed it in her hands. Opening it, Olivia saw a brooch in the shape of a dainty, silver butterfly: the sign of eternal love and lifelong fidelity.

'I bought it yesterday, when I was gone for that time,' he said. 'I've been waiting for the right moment to give it to you, but I never thought it would be like this. Wear it and never forget that we belong together.'

'I will wear it always,' she promised.

Overhead a loudspeaker blared.

'They're calling your flight,' he said. 'Goodbye—for now.'

'For now,' she repeated.

He took her into his arms. 'Remember me,' he begged.

'Always. Just a few more moments...' She kissed him again and again.

'You must go—you must go.' But still he held onto her.

The call came again.

'Oh, God, it's so far away!' she wept. 'When will we see each other again?'

'We will,' he said fiercely. 'Somehow we'll find a way. We must hold onto that thought.'

But even as he said it there were tears on his

cheeks, and now she could see that his despair was as great as her own.

The crowd was moving now, carrying her away from him. In agony she watched him grow smaller, fading, until the distance seemed to swallow him up and only his hand was still visible, faintly waving.

The flight from Shanghai to London was thirteen hours. During the interminable time Olivia drifted in and out of sleep, pursued by uneasy dreams. Norah was there sometimes, laughing and strong as in the old days, then lying still. Lang was there too, his face anguished as he bid her farewell.

She managed to get a little restless sleep, but it was tormented by ghosts. There was Norah, as she'd seen her on-screen only a few hours ago, looking dismayed at the thought of the flight to China. Now Olivia realised that she hadn't imagined it. Norah had known she wasn't well, and she'd hidden it.

From beneath her closed eyes, tears streamed down Olivia's face.

Jack was waiting for her at the airport, his face haggard.

'She's in Intensive Care,' he said. 'She was alive when I left her an hour ago, but she's bad, really bad.'

'Then I'll get there fast.'

'Shall I take your bags home with me?' he offered. 'I expect you'll want to move into Norah's place.'

Until that moment it hadn't dawned on her that she had nowhere to go. She thanked him and hurried to the hospital.

Once there, she ran the last few steps to Intensive Care, her fear mounting. A nurse rose to meet her, smiling reassurance.

'It's all right,' she said kindly. 'She's still alive.'

Alive, but only just. Olivia approached the bed slowly, horrified at the sight of the old woman lying as still as death attached to a multitude of tubes.

'Norah,' Olivia said urgently, hurrying to the side of the bed. 'It's me. Can you hear me?'

The nurse produced a chair for her, saying, 'I'm afraid she's been like that since she was brought in.'

'But she will come round soon, surely?' Olivia pleaded.

'We must hope so,' the nurse said gently.

Olivia leaned close to Norah. It was hard to see her face through the tubes attached to aid her breathing, but the deathly pallor of her skin was frighteningly clear. She seemed thinner than before, more fragile and lined. How could she have gone away from Norah knowing that she was so frail?

But she hadn't known, because Norah had been determined to prevent her knowing. During their talks she'd laughed and chatted, apparently without a care in the world, because to her nothing had mattered but that Olivia should be free to go out and explore.

Now she was dying, perhaps without regaining consciousness, and she might never know that the person she'd loved most had returned to her.

'I'm sorry,' Olivia said huskily. 'I shouldn't have stayed away so long. Oh, darling, you did so much for me and I wasn't there for you.'

Norah's hands were lying still on the sheet. Olivia took hold of one between both of hers, hoping by this means to get through to her, but there was no reaction. Nothing. Norah didn't know she was there, and might never know.

'Please,' Olivia begged. 'Don't die without talking to me. *Please*!'

But Norah lay so still that she might already have been dead, and the only sound was the steady rhythm of the machines

Olivia laid her head down on the bed in an attitude of despair.

CHAPTER ELEVEN

SHE must have lain there for an hour, holding Norah's hand and praying desperately for a miracle.

When it finally came it was the tiniest, most fragile of miracles, just a faint squeeze, but it was enough to make Olivia weep. Somehow, through the dark mists, Norah had sensed her. She *must* believe that. She must—she must.

She awoke to the feeling of someone shaking her shoulder.

'I'm sorry,' she mumbled. 'I didn't mean to go to sleep, but jet lag…'

'I know,' the nurse said sympathetically. 'Do you mind waiting outside while we attend to her?'

Olivia almost sleepwalked into the corridor and sat down, leaning back against the wall, exhausted. Inside her head there was a howling wilderness of grief, desolation and confusion. It felt as though that was all there would ever be again.

She forced herself to think clearly. She should call her mother.

Melisande answered at once. As briefly as possible, Olivia explained what had happened and that she was at the hospital.

'Norah could die at any moment. How long will it take you to get here?'

'Get there? Oh, darling, I don't think— Besides, she's got you. Since you went to China she's talked about nothing else. You're the one she wants. Keep in touch.'

She hung up quickly.

Well, what else did I expect? Olivia asked herself bitterly.

The nurse appeared, signalling for her to come back in.

'She's opened her eyes,' she said. 'She'll be glad to see you.'

Norah's eyes were just half-open, but they lit up at the sight of Olivia.

'You came,' she whispered.

'Of course I came.'

Norah closed her eyes again, seemingly content. Olivia sat there, holding her hand for another hour until the nurse touched her on the shoulder.

'You should go home and get some rest. She's stable now. Give me your number and I'll call you if anything changes.'

Norah's apartment was dark and chilly. Olivia stared at her suitcases which Jack had left there for her. She knew that she should make an effort to unpack, but it was too much.

With all her heart she yearned for Lang, yearned for his voice, his comforting presence, the feel of his body close to hers. He was so far away—not just in miles but in everything that counted. Suddenly it seemed impossible that she would ever see him again.

She began to wander aimlessly around the apartment, trying to understand the depths of her isolation. Less than twenty-four hours ago she'd been the happiest woman on earth. Now the ugly silence sang in her ears, perhaps for ever.

He'd promised love eternal, but what was in his mind now—her or the all-important interview for the job? She was suddenly convinced that he must have forgotten her as soon as they'd parted, drawn back to his 'real' life.

She should call him, but what was he doing at this moment? With her mind fuzzy, she couldn't work out the time difference. He might be talking to somebody vital to his career and resent her interrupting.

She took out her mobile phone and sat staring at it, feeling stupid. After a while she put it away again.

Then it shrilled at her.

'Where have you been?' came Lang's frantic voice. 'I've been waiting and waiting, thinking you'd call me as soon as you had news. When you didn't, I nearly went crazy. I started checking the flights to see if anything had happened to your plane.'

'Oh, heavens!' She wept.

'Darling, what is it? Is she dead? Tell me.'

'No, she's alive and holding on.'

She told him about her journey—her arrival and the moment when Norah had seemed to become aware of her. She hardly knew what she said. She was almost hysterical with relief that he'd reached out to her.

'So it's good news,' Lang said. 'If she's survived the first twenty-four hours, then her chances are fine. She'll be well in no time.'

'What's been happening to you?' she asked.

'I'm back in Beijing.'

'Have you done anything about the job?'

'No, it's still only dawn here. When the day starts properly I'll get to work. Then I'm going to get myself a video link so that we can talk face to face.'

'You can call me on Norah's. I'm living there for the moment.'

'Go and get some sleep now. You must be in need of it. I love you.'

'I love you,' she said wistfully.

She hung up and tumbled into bed, trying to tell herself that Norah would soon be well; Lang had seemed sure. After all, he was a doctor. But she knew in her heart that he was being too optimistic too soon. If Norah made only a partial recovery they would be faced with huge problems and she guessed that he didn't want to think about them just yet.

She went to the hospital early next day. Norah was still unconscious, but after an hour she opened her eyes. Her smile as she beheld Olivia was full of happiness.

'I thought I'd only dreamed that you were here,' she murmured.

'No, I'm here, and I'm staying to look after you until you're all right.'

'What about Lang?'

'He's fine. I've talked to him.'

'What was the marvellous news he was going to tell me?'

'There's a big job coming up and he reckons he's in line for it. He's very ambitious.'

She went on talking softly until Norah's eyes drooped again and she drifted into a normal sleep.

'Is she going to make it?' Olivia asked the nurse softly.

'The doctor thinks so. Despite her age, she's very strong. It's too soon to be certain, but it'll probably work out.'

She went home feeling more cheerful than she'd dared to hope. Norah would recover and their plans could go on as before. She *must* believe that.

The next day Lang hooked up online and she saw his face for the first time since their goodbye. The sight gave her heart a jolt. He was so near, yet so far. She gave him the nurse's words.

'What did I tell you?' he said cheerfully. 'Biyu will be delighted. She'd actually pencilled in a date for our wedding—the twenty-third of next month. When I explained about the delay, she was very put out. So was Hai. He was practically lining the fish up to be caught.'

Olivia laughed shakily.

'Tell them I'm sorry to disappoint them, and I'll be back when I can.'

How hollow those words sounded to her own ears.

'They'll be glad to hear that. Wei's fiancée is writing a new song to sing at the wedding. I've got an interview for the job next week, and someone has dropped me a private hint that my chances are good.'

'Darling, I'm so thrilled for you. It'll be everything you always wanted.'

'You know better than that,' he told her.

'Yes, I do. It's just that things look different now that we're so far apart.'

'But we aren't far apart,' he said at once. 'In here—' he tapped his breast '—you're still with me, and you always will be. Nothing has changed.'

When he talked like that it was easy to believe that things would work out well. But when they had disconnected there came the time, which she dreaded. Then the distance became not merely real but the only reality.

Inch by inch she slipped into a routine. In the morning she was a housekeeper, shopping and cleaning. In the afternoon she visited Norah, now out of Intensive Care.

In the evenings she linked up to wait for Lang to appear on-screen. It occurred to her that she was following much the same timetable Norah had followed while waiting for her to call from China. When the connection finally came it marked the beginning of her day. When it was over, she counted the hours until the next one.

With a heavy heart she realised that this was how it must have felt for Norah years ago, waiting for news of her lover overseas, until finally there was nothing left to hope for.

One day Lang didn't appear at the usual time. When he finally came online he apologised and said he'd been helping out at the hospital.

'There was an emergency and they called in all hands. I've decided to abandon the rest of my vacation and go back to work. It could be useful to be on the spot—just in case.'

'I think that's very wise,' she said cheerfully.

'It means I don't know exactly what time I'll be calling,' he said.

'It doesn't matter. I'll stay hooked up permanently so that I'm always ready.'

Which was exactly what Norah had done for

her, she remembered, and the similarity made her shiver.

On the day of his interview she waited by the computer for hours and knew, as soon as she saw him, that things had gone well.

'I'm through to the next stage,' he said triumphantly. 'I have to meet the whole board next week.'

That meeting too went well, and Lang confided that several board members had spoken in complimentary terms of his work at the hospital over the last three years. He said it without apparent conceit, but she was certain that he knew exactly how good he was.

Then a problem developed. His name was Guo Daiyu, and he was brilliant, Lang told her despondently.

'He didn't hear of the job at first, but someone told him recently and he hurried to apply. He has an excellent reputation, and he's the one person who could take it away from me.'

She comforted him as best she could, but she could see that the thought of losing the prize at the last minute was appalling to him.

It was ironic, she thought as she lay staring into the darkness in the early hours. Lang talked romantically, he spoke of his family's legend of love, but beneath it he was a fiercely ambitious man who knew the value of practical things.

She still believed in his love, but she also knew that

the coming struggle was going to reveal each one of them to the other in a way that might destroy them.

Now she found herself remembering the story of Natalie, the woman he'd loved but had given up because she'd threatened to divert him from his chosen path. That path had included China and his professional ambition, and nothing would be allowed to stand in the way. Nothing. That was the message, clear and simple.

Then something happened. It was stupid, incongruous and even amusing in a faintly hysterical way, and it cast another light on the turn her life was taking.

After some nagging on Olivia's part, her parents visited Norah in hospital. They giggled a lot, said the right things and left as soon as possible.

Her father seemed faintly embarrassed to see her, but that was par for the course. He muttered something about how she must be short of money, pressed a cheque into her hand and departed, confident of having done his fatherly duty.

The cheque was large enough to make Olivia stare, and since she was indeed short of money she accepted it thankfully, if wryly. But she wondered what was going on.

She found out when her mother telephoned that evening.

'Darling, I have the most wonderful news. You'll be so thrilled—but I expect you've guessed already.'

'No, I haven't guessed anything.'

'Daddy and I are going to get married.'

'Married?'

'Isn't it wonderful? After all these years we've discovered that our love never really died. We were always meant to be together, and when that's true nothing can really keep you apart. Don't you agree?'

'I don't know,' Olivia whispered.

Luckily Melisande was too wrapped up in herself to hear this.

'We've both suffered so much, but it was all worth it to find each other again. The wedding is next Friday and I want you to be my bridesmaid.'

She should have been expecting this, but for some reason it came as a shock.

'Melly, I really don't think—'

'Oh, but, darling, it'll be so beautiful. Just think of it—true love rediscovered, and there, as my attendant, is the offspring of that love. Now, come along, don't be a miserable old grumpy. Of course you'll do it.'

'So I said yes,' Olivia told Norah next day. 'At least, she said yes, and I didn't have the energy to argue. Somehow I just can't take it seriously.'

'Oh, it's serious, all right,' Norah said caustically. 'You can't blame your mother. Time's getting on, and it was a very big win.'

'What was?'

'Your father had a win on the lottery some time back.'

'So that's where the cheque came from.'

'I'm glad he had the decency to give you some, even if it was just a way of shutting you up. He's rolling in it at the moment, which explains a lot about "love's young dream". Or, in their case, love's middle-aged dream.'

'Oh, heavens,' Olivia said, beginning to laugh.

She attended the elaborate wedding and endured the sight of her parents acting like skittering young lovers. At the reception almost everyone made speeches about the power of eternal love, and she wanted to cry out at the vulgar exhibition of something that to her was sacred. Afterwards Melisande embraced her dramatically.

'I'm so sorry you're here alone. Wasn't there some nice young man you could have brought? Well, better luck next time. We don't want you to be a miserable old maid, do we?'

'I suppose there are worse things than being alone,' Olivia observed mildly.

'Oh, no, my darling, I promise you there aren't.'

'I'm very happy for you, Mother.'

'You did promise not to call me that.'

Olivia's sense of humour came to her rescue.

'If I can't call my mother "Mother" on the day she marries my father, well, when can I?'

'Pardon?'

'Never mind. Goodbye, Mother. Have a happy marriage.'

Soon it would be the twenty-third of the month, the day on which Biyu had wanted her and Lang to marry. They had laughed at her determination, but now Olivia's heart ached to think of it.

'She's consoling herself with Wei's wedding,' Lang told her. 'He and Suyin were going to wait until autumn, but she ordered them to make it the twenty-third, so they did as they were told.'

Olivia dreaded the arrival of the day but it started with a pleasant surprise. Opening a parcel delivered by the postman, she discovered a butterfly brooch that exactly matched the one Lang had given her. On the card he'd written,

Do you need me to tell you that it's all still true? Call me as soon as this arrives, any time.

It was midnight in Beijing but he was there waiting for her.

'Thank heavens!' he said fervently. 'I've been praying I wouldn't miss your call.'

'You should be getting some rest,' she chided him fondly. 'You look tired.'

'I can't rest until I've talked to you. Tell me that you like it.'

'It was exactly what I needed.'

'Tell me that you still love me.'

'Yes, *sir*,' she said, giving him a mocking salute. 'I obey.'

'I'm sorry.' He grinned. 'I don't change, do I? Still giving orders.'

'Giving direct orders isn't really your way. You're better at pulling strings from behind. I guess you're just practising an autocratic manner for when you get the job. Has anything happened?'

'It'll be any day now. Darling, you still haven't told me that you love me.'

She was feeling lighthearted for the first time in weeks. 'Well,' she teased. 'Let me see…'

She was interrupted by the sound of his phone. He snatched it up, and immediately became angry.

'What, *now*? All right, I'm coming.' He turned back to the screen. 'That was the hospital. I have to go. We'll talk again tomorrow.'

'Lang, I—'

But he had gone.

She sat very still for a while, looking at the blank screen. Then she went to bed.

Next morning the doctor said to her, 'Norah can't be left on her own, but if you're going to live with her then I think we can send her home.'

'Yes, I'll always be there,' Olivia assured him quietly.

Norah was sent home that very afternoon. They hugged each other joyfully and settled down to chat, but almost at once Norah was too tired to continue.

Olivia put her to bed and sat with her for a while, feeling the responsibility settle around her shoulders.

Lang came online early that night. One look at his beaming face told her everything.

'You got it!' she exclaimed.

'Yes, they confirmed it today. I now have a three-year contract at more money than I was earning before. I can afford a really nice home for you.'

Out of this only one thing stood out.

'You've already signed the contract?'

'I took the first chance before they changed their mind. I only wish you could have been there with me to make everything perfect.'

So that was it. He'd committed himself finally and, by a cruel irony, he'd done it on the day Norah's return home had made her frailty even clearer than before. If anything more was needed to confirm that their feet were set on two different paths, this was it.

She smiled and congratulated him, told him of her happiness and then of her love. His look of joy was the same she'd seen before, as though nothing could ever change.

'I love you so much,' he told her. 'I can't wait for our life together to start.'

He parted with the words, 'Give Norah my love. Tell her to get well soon.'

'I will,' she promised.

To her relief, the connection broke. In another moment he would have seen that she was weeping, but he didn't see it, nor the way she reached out to touch the screen as though he were really there, then drew away quickly because he would never be there.

An hour later she looked in on Norah, who'd just awoken and was cheerful.

'Come and sit with me,' she said, patting the bed.

As Olivia sat down the light from the bedside lamp fell on the silver butterfly pinned to her shoulder.

'That's such a pretty brooch. I've noticed that you always wear it, so I guess it must be special.'

'Yes, it's very special,' Olivia said.

'Did *he* give it to you? Don't worry, I won't pry if it's a secret.'

'When have I ever kept secrets from you? Yes, Lang gave it to me at the airport when we said goodbye.'

She removed the butterfly and laid it in Norah's hand. The old woman drew it close and studied it intently.

'It's so beautiful,' she whispered. 'It must have a special meaning.'

'Butterflies are a symbol of eternal love, because of an old Chinese legend.'

She told the story of Liang Shanbo and Zhu

Yingtai, how they had loved each other and been forced apart.

'When she stood before his tomb, it opened and enfolded her. A moment later two butterflies flew up and away into the sunset, together for ever.'

'Together for ever,' Norah whispered. 'Even death couldn't divide them. Oh, yes, that's how it is.'

'How have you endured all these years without him?' Olivia whispered.

'But, my dear, I haven't been without him. In my heart he has been with me always, waiting for me as Shanbo waited for Yingtai. When my time comes I shan't be afraid, because we will take wing together. You're very lucky to have Lang. He's a man of great understanding.'

'But what can come of it? How can I ever marry him? How could I have engaged myself to a man I'd known only a week or two? Of all the people to do such a daft thing, how could I?'

'But you mustn't give up hope. You've got your whole future ahead of you. I couldn't bear it if you sacrificed it for me. Please, my darling, don't spend your life in bitter regrets, as I have, always thinking how different it might have been if I'd only—' She broke off.

'But you couldn't have changed anything,' Olivia protested. 'He died in the army.'

'Yes, but…' Norah was silent a long time, but then she seemed to come to a resolution. 'I've told you so much about my love for Edward, but there's one thing I've never spoken of to you or anyone. Things were different fifty years ago. Couples were expected to wait for marriage before they made love.

'I loved Edward so much, and when he wanted us to make love I wanted it too, but I was afraid that he'd despise me afterwards. So we didn't. I was *sensible*. I could tell he was hurt, afraid I didn't love him enough. I told myself that I'd make it up to him when we were married.

'But in those days we still had National Service, and he had to finish his time before we could marry. He was sent abroad suddenly. It should just have been a short tour of duty but he was killed by a sniper, and the world ended for me. Night after night I wept, but it was too late. He'd died without really knowing how much I loved him. Oh, Edward, Edward, *forgive me*!'

Suddenly it might have happened yesterday, and she sobbed without restraint. Olivia gathered the old woman into her arms and her own tears fell. For years she'd thought she understood Norah's feelings, but now she realised she'd never guessed the yawning chasm of grief that had turned her life into a nightmare of emptiness.

When Norah's sobs had subsided Olivia controlled her own feelings and managed to say, 'But things are different these days. Lang and I have made love.'

'Then you know what you mean to each other, and you mustn't take any risks with that. Don't let me see you wishing every day that you could turn the clock back.'

'I've been thinking. I'm going back to China to clear out my apartment and talk to Mrs Wu. I'll see Lang again, talk to him. Maybe we can come to some arrangement with me dividing my time between China and here. If not, well…'

'Oh, no. You mustn't finish with him.'

'I'm not leaving you alone.'

'I'm not alone. There's the rest of the family.'

'Oh, yes, Mum and Dad prancing around like the world's their stage. The others who send you the occasional Christmas card. I have to be here at least some of the time. He'll understand.'

'Perhaps he'll return to England.'

'No.' Olivia set her jaw stubbornly. 'I'd never ask him. Besides, he's already signed a contract.'

She didn't mention the other reason; the story he'd told her about the woman he'd left rather than change course had carried a hidden warning.

'I fixate on something,' he'd said on another occasion, 'and I stick with it. It doesn't make me a nice person.'

She hadn't seen the warning then, but it was clear enough now.

She clung to the thought that they might still be together, that somehow life could be arranged so that she could divide her time between China and England. It was a wildly impractical idea, but it was all that stood between her and the abyss.

At night she slept with Ming Zhi in her arms, gripping her more tightly, more frantically every time, as though hoping to recover the caution and wisdom by which she'd always lived.

She'd prided herself on those qualities, but in the end they had failed to save her from falling in love so deeply that she belonged to him body and soul, for ever. She could almost have laughed at herself, but the laughter would be terrible and bitter.

She knew that Lang loved her. But he was the man he was, a man made of granite beneath a gentle surface.

His face came into her mind as she'd last seen it in real life, not merely on the screen: the sadness as they'd parted, the yearning look that had seemed to follow her. Then she thought of how he'd beamed when he'd told her he'd got the job. He would survive their parting—if there had to be a parting—because he had something else. And she would survive knowing that all was well with him.

That was as far as she dared to let herself think. But the temptation to see him once more, to lie in his arms one last time, was too great to be resisted. From it she would draw the strength to live a bleak life without him.

She hired an agency nurse, a pleasant young

woman who got on well with Norah from the first moment. She moved into the apartment at once, leaving Olivia's mind at ease.

The only problem now was what to say to Lang when they next talked, but he solved that by texting her to say he would be at the hospital all night.

She texted back, informing him that she was coming to China.

That was how they communicated now.

CHAPTER TWELVE

THE taxi seemed to take for ever to get from Beijing Airport to the apartment, and Olivia had to pinch herself to stay awake. When at last she was in her room, she left a message on Norah's answer machine, saying that she'd arrived safely. Then she lay down, promising herself that it would be just for a moment, and awoke five hours later.

Soon she must text Lang. He would text back, telling her the first moment he could spare from his busy schedule. Somehow they would meet, she would put her plan to him and perhaps they would have a kind of disjointed future. Or perhaps not.

Exhausted from the flight, she could see only the dark side. He would refuse. He had another life now. He didn't need her.

One part of her—the common-sense part— reckoned it would have been wiser not to come here. They could have talked online and decided their future for good or ill.

But common sense—such a reliable ally in the past—failed her now. The yearning to be with him again was intolerable. To part without holding him just once more, without feeling his body against hers, inside hers, loving her as only he could love—this would have been more than she could bear.

She put her hands up over her face and a cry broke from her at the thought.

But she was a dragon lady, strong and resolute, one who faced whatever life threw at her no matter how painful. If love failed her she would have the memory of love to carry her through, and this one final night that she had promised herself.

There was a knock on the door. Throwing on a light robe, she hurried to it and called softly, 'Who's there?'

'It's me, Lang.'

She had the door open in a second. Then he was in the room, holding her fiercely, covering her face with passionate kisses, murmuring her name over and over.

'Olivia, Olivia, it's really you. Hold me—kiss me.'

'Yes, yes, I came because—'

'Hush,' he whispered. 'Don't let's talk, not yet.'

She couldn't reply. His mouth was over hers, silencing everything but sensation. He was right; this wasn't the time for words. She wanted to belong to him again, and it was happening fast. He had the robe off in a moment, and then there was only the flimsy night dress, which suddenly wasn't there any more.

She tried to help him off with his clothes but there was no need. He was already moving faster than she could follow, and when he was naked she could understand why. His desire for her was straining his control. He almost tossed her onto the bed and fell on top of her, loving her with a fierce vigour that would have made her think he was a man staking his claim if she'd been capable of thought.

She'd forgotten how skilled he was with his mouth, his hands, his loins. But he reminded her again and again, demanding without mercy, but giving with no holding back.

Their final moment was explosive, leaving them both too drained to do anything but clasp each other and lie still. Lang's eyes were closed, and he might have fallen asleep. She tightened her arms about him in a passion of tenderness.

'I love you,' she whispered. 'You'll never know how much I love you because I don't think I can find the words. And perhaps you wouldn't believe me, because how can I explain it?'

'No need,' he murmured. 'Don't talk.'

He was right. No words now. She was back in her dream, where only he existed. Nothing else in the world. She slept.

She knew something had gone wrong when she

awoke to find Lang sitting by the window. She'd
dreamed of awakening in his arms, seeing his face
looking down tenderly at hers. After their passionate love-making, he should have found it impossible to tear himself away.

But he sat there, seemingly oblivious to her,
absorbed in a conversation on his mobile phone.

She lay back on the bed, stunned and disillusioned. It had never occurred to her that she was
already on the fringe of his life.

At last he finished the call, turned and looked at
her, smiling when he saw she was awake. He
returned to the bed to take her eagerly into his
arms.

'Thank you,' he said. 'Thank you for coming
back to me. Let me look at you. I still can't believe
you're actually here. Kiss me, kiss me.'

She did so, again and again.

He was the one to break the embrace, laughing
and saying, 'If we don't stop now I'll have to make
love to you again, and then I won't be able to give
you my news.'

'What news?' she whispered.

'I'm coming back to live in England with you.'

'But—you can't. Your new job—'

'That was my boss at the hospital I was just
talking to. I spoke to him yesterday, asking him to
help me get out of the job. I knew it wouldn't be
easy, so soon after signing a contract, but he said

he'd do his best. It was between me and Guo Daiyu, and Guo might still be available.

'He just called me to say it's good news—Guo can start almost at once. I wanted to tell you last night but I didn't dare. There was still a chance that it wouldn't work out and I wanted to be sure first.

'In a couple of weeks I'll be free and we can leave together. We'll stay with Norah and look after her. And when—when she no longer needs us, we'll return to China.'

'But you'll lose the job when it means everything to you!' she cried.

'No, it is you that means everything to me. I'll do anything rather than risk losing you.'

'But you said—when you told me about Natalie—and how you couldn't put her first.'

'Of course I couldn't. Because she wasn't you. I parted from her because there was something I wanted more. But I can't part from you, because there is *nothing* I want more. Nor will there ever be. Do you remember I told you that first a man needs to understand himself? Through you I came to understand myself. I'd believed that no woman could ever mean so much that she could divert me from my path. But then I met you, and found that I was wrong. Only you mattered. We must get married at once. I won't take no for an answer.'

'Get married?' she whispered.

'I can't go on any longer without being married to you. If you don't become my wife, then my life will be empty and meaningless until its last moments. Don't you feel the same?'

'Oh, yes, *yes*! But you never said anything about coming to England before, and—'

'You never asked me,' he said, with a touch of reproach. 'But that's my fault. I talked so much about myself and what I wanted that I left you no space. The fact is that nothing matters to me except being with you. We'll come back one day, and there will be other jobs.'

'Not this one. You'll have to start again among strangers and lose what you've built up.'

He drew her close so that his lips hovered just over hers.

'Shut up!' he said, lowering his mouth.

It was a kiss full of tenderness, not passion. They had all they needed of passion, but for now it was a promise for the future that counted, and the peace that flooded them both.

There was a knock on the door. Lang released her and went to open it. Olivia heard murmuring for several minutes. When he returned, he was holding a paper.

'That was your landlord,' he said. 'I told him you were leaving this apartment today.' He showed her the paper.

'It's my final rent bill,' she said. 'Receipted.'

'I've just paid it. He wants you out fast, because he's got someone else ready to move in.'

'You've arranged all this?'

'Yes, so let's hurry up with your packing so that I can deliver you before I have to go to work.'

'And where exactly are you going to deliver me to?'

'To the family. You'll have my room until we're married in two weeks' time.'

'Now you're giving orders again. None of this new man stuff, respecting my right to make my own decisions?'

Gently he took hold of her shoulders. 'Olivia, darling, that's what I've been doing up until now, and look where it got us. No, this time I'm taking no risks. The family will keep their beady eyes on you and make sure you don't escape. Now, let's hurry so that I can deliver you into the hands of your gaolers and get to work.'

They found the family leaning out of the windows watching for his car, and by the time it drew up they were on the step, opening their arms to her, waving and cheering. Lang had to hurry away at once, pausing merely to tell them, 'Don't let her out of your sight, whatever you do.'

The women promptly formed a guard about Olivia, laughing to indicate that they were all sharing a joke. Yet it wasn't entirely a joke; Olivia knew. Lang had endured the loss of her once, but he couldn't endure it again, and now he was nervous when he was away from her.

'We have so much to do before the day,' Biyu said as they drank tea. 'We must talk about the big plans to be made.'

'Lang told me you'd already have everything planned down to the last detail,' Olivia told her.

'He's a cheeky devil,' Biyu said serenely. 'What does he know about anything important? Now, down to work. This is an album of pictures we took of Suyin's wedding. It was very traditional, very beautiful, and yours will be the same.'

'You think a traditional wedding would be right for me?' Olivia asked.

'Of course. What else?'

Leafing through the album, Olivia had to agree with her. Both bride and groom wore long satin robes of deep red, the symbol of joy. She was suddenly seized by the desire to see how handsome Lang would look in this wedding garb, which had an air of stately magnificence.

'Now, we have lots of shopping to do,' Biyu declared.

'You mean, you're actually going to let me out of the house?' Olivia joked. 'I thought you promised Lang that you wouldn't risk my running away.'

Biyu's eyes twinkled. 'Oh, but four of us will be with you at all times.'

'Why didn't I think of that?'

One of the little girls named Ting, who was about twelve years old, confided, 'If you escape we have to give Uncle Mitch his money back.'

'He's *paid* you to guard me?'

'Of course,' Ting declared. 'Twenty yuan a day. Each.'

'That's about two pounds. You're definitely being underpaid.'

'Also some sweet buns,' Ting admitted. 'If you escape we have to give them back—but we've eaten them, so please don't escape.'

Olivia doubled up with laughter. After her recent misery everything that was happening felt like a happy dream, one from which she prayed never to awaken.

In the end eight of them went out, since nobody was going to pass up a shopping expedition. There were gifts and favours to be bought for all the guests, most of whom would be family members making a special trip in from the country.

'Will there be many?' Olivia asked when they paused for tea.

'About a hundred,' Biyu said casually.

'There were only eighty for me,' Suyin said with a giggle. 'You're *much* more interesting, ever since the day he brought you home.'

'One thing I've always wanted to know,' Olivia said. 'When I was there with him that night, you were all so wonderful to me. I know you were being courteous to a guest—'

'But you sensed something more?' Biyu helped her out. 'It's true. Not every guest would have been shown the temple and told the things that you were. But we knew you were his future bride.'

'He *told* you that?'

'Not exactly. It was the way he spoke of you—with a note in his voice that had never been there before. He'd only known you a few days, but something was very different. He sounded a little shy, tentative—for the first time in his life, I'll swear. I don't think even he knew what he was giving away.

'We honoured you as his future wife so that you would know you were welcome in the family. These last few weeks, we've been holding our breath, hoping that things would come right.'

She became suddenly serious. 'You were able to walk away from him, but he wasn't able to walk away from you. That makes you the strong one.' She added quietly, 'Dragon Lady.'

'He told you about that?'

'Of course. If you only knew how proud of you he is! He is a strong man in every way but one—you are his weakness. Never forget that his need is greater than yours. It gives you power, but we all know you will never misuse that power, and we can give him into your hands with easy hearts and minds.'

'Thank you,' Olivia said softly, so deeply moved that she could hardly speak. 'I promise that I won't betray that trust.'

Biyu smiled. 'You didn't need to tell us that,' she said.

Arriving home, they plunged into a discussion of details. Biyu insisted that everything must be done properly.

'So we must first seek and obtain your parents' consent.'

'At my age?' Olivia said, scandalised. 'Besides, they're on their honeymoon in the Bahamas. They won't be back for ages.'

'But there is your great-aunt Norah, whom Mitchell says is like a mother to you. He tells me that she likes him.'

'She certainly does.'

'Then she'll say yes when we talk tonight. You must show me how to work this video link he talks about.'

Biyu was fascinated by the reality of it later. Norah was up and waiting, and she crowed with delight at the news. Olivia introduced her to the family members who were at home, and Biyu explained about the ceremony of consent that would take place that evening.

'Then I'll catch up on my sleep and be ready,' Norah said.

By eight o'clock that evening they were all

gathered around the screen for her appearance. The first thing she did on seeing Lang was to raise her thumb triumphantly in the air. He responded with the same gesture, which made everyone else do the same.

Lang introduced Grandfather Tao, who greeted her solemnly, and embarked on a formal speech in which he praised the bride and groom—but especially the bride—finishing with, 'Do you give your consent to this marriage?'

Norah smiled and inclined her head, saying, 'I do give my consent, with all my heart. And I want to say how proud I am to be connected with such an honourable family.'

Everyone bowed to her. She was one of them now.

As Lang had said, Olivia was installed in his room. He hadn't thought much further ahead than that, and it came as a shock to him when the young women of the house, determined to protect the bride's virtue, gathered outside her door, barring his entry.

'Very funny,' he said wryly to Olivia, who was doubled up with laughter.

'Well, we must do everything in the proper way,' she reminded him.

'And where am I supposed to sleep until the wedding? I have to move out of my own apartment in two days.'

'We can find you a couch somewhere in the

north house,' Biyu promised him. 'It won't be for long. Now, you may kiss your bride a chaste good-night and leave.'

Conscious of his family's eyes on him, he kissed her and departed hurriedly.

Had they been planning to remain in China, there would have been the ceremony of the bed, when a newly purchased matrimonial bed was installed. This had happened at the wedding of Wei and Suyin a few weeks earlier, and they were making their own bed available for the bridal couple on their wedding night.

The result was a modified version of the ceremony in which the bed was moved a few inches to symbolise installation, after which it was covered with various fruits, and the children of the family, symbols of fertility, scrambled to seize them.

These days Hai was in his element, conjuring fish from all directions, while Biyu took care of the rest of the banquet. Because the words for *eight* and *good luck* were similar it was customary to have eight dishes, not including dessert. Shark's fin soup, crab claws and as many fish as he could find formed the basis of the feast.

On the last night before the wedding Lang came to bid Olivia goodnight, and they strolled in the dark garden.

'When we next see each other it'll be at the wedding,' he said. 'No regrets?'

'Not if you have none.'

'None at all. Are you still worrying about the job?'

'How can I help it? You may have lost the chance of a lifetime.'

'There'll be other jobs,' Lang said.

'As good as the one you've given up?'

He frowned a little, troubled that she couldn't understand what was so simple to him.

'It doesn't matter,' he said. 'I made my choice, and it was the right one. While I have you, I have everything. Without you I have nothing. There was never really a choice at all.'

'That's what *he* said,' came a voice from the darkness.

They hadn't seen Biyu there. Now she came closer.

'He?' Olivia asked.

'Renshu,' Biyu replied. 'Those must have been his very words.'

'"While I have you, I have everything",' Lang repeated slowly. '"Without you, I have nothing". Yes, that's what he said to Jaio when he went to rescue her. And she understood that he meant every word and she could trust him never to have any regrets.'

He was looking at Olivia as he said this, a slight question in his eyes.

'Yes,' she said joyfully. 'She understood. It took her too long, but in the end she really understood.'

Biyu touched Lang's cheek.

'Congratulations,' she said. 'You are truly a son of Renshu.'

She drifted away into the darkness.

'That was it,' Olivia said. 'That's what you were waiting for, the moment of complete acceptance. It came in its own time.'

'As you said it would. You were right, as you are right about everything. I can safely put my fate in your hands, and tomorrow that is what I will do.'

He drew her close, not in a kiss but a hug. Their bodies pressed tightly together so that in the darkness they looked like one person. Looking back at them, Biyu smiled in satisfaction.

Because there were so many guests the wedding could not be held at home, and a hall had been booked two streets away.

Norah was with her as soon as she rose. Suyin made the connection and kept the camera on Olivia as they prepared her in her red-satin gown and dressed her hair in the style of a married woman, as she would soon become.

Norah watched it all in ecstasy. She had rested all day so that she would be fresh enough to stay up overnight, and now she and her nurse sat together, eyes fixed on the screen.

The groom, accompanied by the sound of drums and gongs, arrived in a sedan chair to collect his bride and take her to the place of the marriage. Olivia was pleased to see that he looked as splendidly handsome in traditional attire as she had known he would.

At this point there was a small delay. The groom requested that the bride appear but the bride's attendants, in accordance with tradition, refused to produce her until mollified by gifts. Since the attendants were the children of the house, there was a good deal of horse trading, led by Ting, and the price rose higher and higher.

'How are they doing?' Olivia asked Suyin from behind the window.

'Ting is driving a hard bargain,' Suyin chuckled. 'At this rate, you'll be lucky to be married today.'

At last Biyu intervened, declaring that enough was enough. The children seized their prizes and scampered away, squeaking with satisfaction.

Then it was time for the bride to get into her sedan chair for the journey to where the ceremony was to take place. All around her firecrackers exploded as she began her journey.

As they travelled she couldn't help thinking about Zhu Yingtai going to her wedding in a similar sedan, stopping it beside Liang Shanbo's grave and leaving it to join him for ever. It was in memory of this that Lang had given her the silver butterflies, and now she wore them both on her dress.

The wedding itself was simple. In the hall they

approached the altar and spoke the words of homage to heaven and earth and the ancestors. There followed the declaration of homage to each other, expressed formally, but saying so much more than mere words could ever convey.

One of Lang's young cousins had undertaken to care for the laptop with the camera, and he did his duties so well that Norah saw everything close-up.

When the little ceremony was over the bride and groom bowed to each other. Now it was time for the feast. An elaborate paper dragon bounded into the room and performed a dance to loud applause. Then Suyin sang the song she had written in their honour:

'Now our family is happy
Because you are a part of us.
This you will always be,
Near or far.'

Hidden by the heavy red satin, Olivia reached out her hand for Lang's and felt him seize her in return. They both understood the message: near or far.

There was an extra touch that she hadn't expected but which filled her with happiness: Suyin went to stand before the camera and sang directly to Norah, repeating in English the words she had already sung, welcoming Norah as one of them.

Everyone saluted Norah, and she in turn raised a glass.

At last it was over. The crowds faded, the noise was silenced, darkness fell and they were finally alone.

'Are you happy?' Lang asked as they lay together.

'If this is the only happiness I ever know for the rest of my life,' she replied softly, 'it will be enough. I have everything.'

'And I shall give you everything in my power,' he vowed. 'All I ask is your love and your eternal presence.'

Her lips answered him silently, and after that nothing more was said.

They lingered two more days, paying visits of respect to those who had come in from distant places to be at their wedding. Then it was time to go. Everyone came to see them off at the airport.

Lang was very quiet, but sometimes his eyes rested on Olivia's shoulder where she had pinned the two butterflies, symbols of eternal love and fidelity. He was content.

At last the goodbyes were finished and they were on the aircraft, gliding down the runway, taking off.

Higher they climbed, and higher, with the ground falling away beneath them until they were in the clouds. Then the clouds too disappeared and they were up in the clear, brilliant air, still climbing. Olivia watched through the window, entranced by the beauty. But then...

She blinked and gave herself a little shake. She was dreaming; she must be. Because otherwise she could have sworn she saw two butterflies flying together.

That was impossible. No butterfly could climb this high. When she looked back, the illusion would have disappeared.

But it persisted: two bright, darting creatures fluttering here and there, until at last they turned and winged their way towards the sun, blended with the air and vanished as if they had never been.

Full of wonder, she turned to Lang and found that he too was looking out of the window. Then he smiled at her and nodded.

Norah lived another eighteen months, finally dying peacefully with Olivia and Lang holding her hands.

She was cremated, and when they returned to China they took her ashes and laid them in the little temple with the ashes of Meihui.

Her photograph is there today, with one of Edward close by. They stand opposite the pictures of Meihui and John Mitchell.

Beside them are more pictures, of Lang, Olivia and their baby son.

Above them on the wall are written the words of the faith by which Jaio and Renshu lived two-thousand years ago, and which still survive in their descendants:

Love is the shield that protects us from harm.

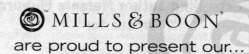

MILLS & BOON

are proud to present our...

Book of the Month

Snowbound: Miracle Marriage
by Sarah Morgan from Mills & Boon® Medical™

Confirmed bachelor Dr Daniel Buchannan is
babysitting his brother's children and needs help!
Stella, his ex-fiancée, reluctantly rescues him and,
snowbound with his makeshift family, Daniel
realises he can never let Stella go again…

Enjoy double the romance in this
great-value 2-in-1!
Snowbound: Miracle Marriage
&
Christmas Eve: Doorstep Delivery
by Sarah Morgan

Mills & Boon® Medical™
Available 4th December 2009

Something to say about our
Book of the Month?
Tell us what you think!
millsandboon.co.uk/community

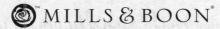

millsandboon.co.uk Community

Join Us!

The Community is the perfect place to meet and chat to kindred spirits who love books and reading as much as you do, but it's also the place to:

- **Get the inside scoop from authors about their latest books**
- **Learn how to write a romance book with advice from our editors**
- **Help us to continue publishing the best in women's fiction**
- **Share your thoughts on the books we publish**
- **Befriend other users**

Forums: Interact with each other as well as authors, editors and a whole host of other users worldwide.

Blogs: Every registered community member has their own blog to tell the world what they're up to and what's on their mind.

Book Challenge: We're aiming to read 5,000 books and have joined forces with The Reading Agency in our inaugural Book Challenge.

Profile Page: Showcase yourself and keep a record of your recent community activity.

Social Networking: We've added buttons at the end of every post to share via digg, Facebook, Google, Yahoo, technorati and de.licio.us.

www.millsandboon.co.uk

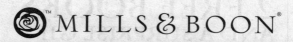

2 FREE BOOKS
AND A SURPRISE GIFT

We would like to take this opportunity to thank you for reading this Mills & Boon® book by offering you the chance to take TWO more specially selected books from the Romance series absolutely FREE! We're also making this offer to introduce you to the benefits of the Mills & Boon® Book Club™—

- **FREE home delivery**
- **FREE gifts and competitions**
- **FREE monthly Newsletter**
- **Exclusive Mills & Boon Book Club offers**
- **Books available before they're in the shops**

Accepting these FREE books and gift places you under no obligation to buy, you may cancel at any time, even after receiving your free shipment. Simply complete your details below and return the entire page to the address below. You don't even need a stamp!

YES Please send me 2 free Romance books and a surprise gift. I understand that unless you hear from me, I will receive 5 superb new stories every month including two 2-in-1 books priced at £4.99 each and a single book priced at £3.19, postage and packing free. I am under no obligation to purchase any books and may cancel my subscription at any time. The free books and gift will be mine to keep in any case.

Ms/Mrs/Miss/Mr_____ Initials _____

_____

Surname _____
Address _____

_____

_____ Postcode _____

Send this whole page to: Mills & Boon Book Club, Free Book Offer, FREEPOST NAT 10298, Richmond, TW9 1BR